THE DOCTOR FROM CORDOVA

THE DOCTOR FROM CORDOVA

A Biographical Novel
About the Great Philosopher Maimonides

Herbert Le Porrier

TRANSLATED FROM THE FRENCH
BY BARBARA WRIGHT

DOUBLEDAY & COMPANY, INC., GARDEN CITY, NEW YORK

Library of Congress Cataloging in Publication Data

Le Porrier, Herbert.
   The doctor from Cordova.

   Translation of Le médecin de Cordoue.
   1. Moses ben Maimon, 1135–1204—Fiction.   I. Title.
PZ4.L5864Do [PQ2623.E563] 843'.9'14
ISBN 0-385-11472-9
Library of Congress Catalog Card Number 77–16930

. . . and Ichabudonosor begat O'Donnell Magnus and O'Donnell Magnus begat Christbaum and Christbaum begat Ben Maimun and Ben Maimun begat Dusty Rhodes.

James Joyce Ulysses

1

I, MOSES the Spaniard, an exile from Jerusalem, the firstborn son of the late Judge Maimon, in the sixty-fifth year of my age, am here revealing my evil thoughts. My good thoughts, as you know, have been recorded in many letters and books which circulate around our great inland sea, from Baghdad to Narbonne, and beyond, as far as Trier and Coblenz on the banks of the Moselle and the Rhine. No matter where your steps may take you, whether toward the Orient or the Occident, some part of me will have preceded you there, and you would only have to mention my name for doors to be opened to you—whether in friendship or in suspicion.

You know me well enough to concede that I take no pride in this. It is far from true that this sort of itinerant reputation has brought me any real satisfaction. At the most accurate reckoning I could count ten sincere detractors for one alleged laudator, and I quickly learned to guard against them, so that neither side has succeeded in affecting my spirits. I have always shared whatever learning I had, not like the rich man distributing alms, but rather like the poor man who divides his coat or his crust of bread into two, without expecting anything in return, unless it is a little more clarity along the paths of the world. My only merit will have been that I stood aside from the way of the foolish, and today, now that I am stricken in years and death encloses me, I see that I am nearer to the shadows than to the light, perplexed among the perplexed, igno-

---

* The year 1200 of our era.

rant among the ignorant, a fool among the foolish, and more than ever solitary.

What use will it have been to me, all the knowledge that I have accumulated, mastered, and sown in the pastures of the world? To make me believe myself wiser than the common run of men, to allow me to rub shoulders with the secret of the universe and to purr in contentment like the cat wrapped around my legs, to delude myself in the appropriate manner without altogether deluding myself, since I am capable of observing my own failure. I thought I was storing up and distributing gold, but it was sand. I wanted to subdue my pride, but I gave it free rein. I was aiming to remake life, but mine is departing. Has the moment finally come for me to taste the depths of bitterness?

You who were my pupil and who have become my master, in your far-off, primitive Provence, I entreat you to conceal in the depths of your heart and in the secrecy of your house the revelations I am about to make. I ask you to remain in this instance my unique confidant. I ask you never to let this document be seen by an unbiased eye. Burn it, rather than let it be exposed to such an affront. There is no word that cannot be compared to that idol which the Latin barbarians named Janus, and that does not lend itself to contradictory interpretations. If my good thoughts have brought me so much hostility, what might I not expect from these, which I have never dared to formulate openly? For a long time now, being the dark side of my nature, they have tormented me. They are elusive, insofar as I have done my utmost to keep them at a distance, and yet importunate, insofar as it seems that I attract them in full force. Now that I am older, I see clearly that without them my philosophy would not be complete. In the Holy Book it is written that we must serve the truth with the best and the worst that is in us, and I have only obeyed in half measure. What would be the value of a certitude if it were not accompanied by a doubt?

Ever since the day when, still a child, I realized that I was different from other people, throughout a thousand vicissitudes which nearly broke me, until this late hour when I am writing to you, my eyes so tired by the candlelight that they are watering, I have been obsessed by one single passion: to seek the truth, not as an obsolete and unknowable object, but as a state which it is vouchsafed to us to attain by dint of the utmost perseverance, patience, and humility. I have always protected myself as best I could against everything that might be of a nature to distract me from that quest. Can I say that I have achieved my aim? Yes and no. I have never cheated, but that does not mean that I have succeeded. The more my mind became filled and diversified without ever succumbing to lassitude, the more uncertain my project seemed to become; it retreated as the horizon over the plain, as the wind over the sea. I should not be a man had I not deluded myself by this exercise, had I not, quite unintentionally, deluded those who were expecting to hear the good word from me. Since I was held to be a scholar, it was understood that I must be in possession of knowledge which it was my duty to pass on. It was in this way that I built my niche, on the scale of the inhabited world, open to all who wished to draw near to me. My visitors were many, but the niche remained empty —infinitely vast for the elderly adolescent who preceded me and who follows me, devoured by his own enthusiasm.

Not altogether empty, however. Could it be because I consider you exceptional that I make an exception for you? When you came to Egypt to study with me, your great curiosity about the natural sciences, the ease with which you plunged into both Hebrew and Arabic writings, the pertinence of your philosophical speculations, immediately gained you a high place in my esteem. In the first days I reproached myself for this too spontaneous predilection, for it was clear that there were grounds for reservations. You were frivolous, lighthearted, unmethodical. You wanted everything immediately, without discrimination. In your behavior and speech there was a permanent, subtle mockery that irritated me. You had not been born into the faith of my forefathers, you were of the race that has never stopped persecuting us and shedding our blood. But the look in your eyes was frank, your voice was confident, your bearing upright and supple. But you read Latin and Greek as no one in my entourage had ever done before, and I had the utmost difficulty in keeping up with you in this domain. But you were open to our law as no stranger had ever been before, and I had to deploy all my vigilance in order not to be overwhelmed by your questions. Before you, I had had many disciples who were all alike, but you were like none of them. When I was not in your presence, I promised myself that I would be circumspect; the moment you appeared, my scruples vanished. It was not easy to assimilate the charm of your person and the excellence of your mind, the freshness of your youth and the earnestness of your concentration, and for a long time I struggled with my reservations. But when, only a few months after your arrival in Fostat, you showed me your first makamats,† I became aware of the great joy you were giving me, a joy that has never weakened. If it had been in my power to mold a son to my own liking, I should have created him in your image, so true is it that elective paternity is a remarkable temptation for every man who has reached maturity. You know that Providence subsequently endowed me with a son of my own seed, but the years pass too slowly over him, and too quickly over me; he is still an adolescent, and I have no means of telling whether he will fulfill my desires.

The three years you spent with me were full of lessons for us both. My slow, methodical mind, and yours, so quick and inspired, achieved a rare quality of understanding. After you had learned geometry and logic, astronomy and physics, we were already some way along the shortest path leading to prophetic initiations and to medicine. I gradually conceived and developed a great project for you which was nourished by a great hope. More than once I found myself weighing your qualities against your defects, but the scales were always equally balanced. Lucidity and pride, enthusiasm and immodesty—in you they were happily matched. You were inclined

† Short narratives in rhymed prose combined with verse, practiced by Arab scholars.

to excess in everything, but what in anyone else would have
alienated me, in you attracted me powerfully, though to me philosophy had always meant the golden mean. The truth is that not all
men are to be measured by the same yardstick. In you, a prodigious
destiny was taking shape. When you returned to your realm, so
lacking in well-educated men, you would accede to the highest
office: I saw you as a bishop at the very least, a Pope perhaps, and it
was of no small concern to the Hebraic communities, whose insecurity was so great on the other side of the Pyrenees, that the Pope
should be a man of heart and feeling like you.

To a certain extent my projects for your future were political,
why deny it? You had told me of the lively expectation in your
country of a culture other than that of arms, of the ever present
memory of an Abelard in whose footsteps you wished to follow
with an ever stronger determination based on experience and, above
all, with less naïveté and ostentation. For my part I maintain that
only knowledge can improve men, and not the blind faith taught by
your scholars, which explains why my people, whose vocation it is
to know, should be without equal in all the world. You acknowledged this, in clear and simple words, when you informed me of
your conviction that the world had failed to take advantage of a
great opportunity when it misunderstood and deformed the Judaic
message. That day I felt the urge to press you close to my heart;
but does one embrace a future Pope? I withdrew, and prayed alone
for your glory. No doubt I prayed badly.

In the same period, considerable events were taking place on our
doorstep. Frankish Syria made a brutal thrust toward the Nile, only
to be ejected by the Caliphate of Baghdad, which came down with
all its weight on Alexandria and Cairo. There were thousands of
dead, an appalling famine, terrifying epidemics, and I had great
difficulty in alleviating so much suffering around me. You were
constantly by my side, braving dangers and contagion; duplicating
my arms, my brain, and my sadness. You were infinitely more vul-
nerable to the horror than I was, not that I had become inured to it,

one never becomes inured to such things, but because I had become strengthened by age, which could not be the case for you. Your natural gaiety became clouded, but I did not imagine that this would be irreparable. We were faced with immense tasks, which had no connection with our strength or our learning.

Deprived of study, of meditation, and of poetry, mutilated, we made our way among the ruins. I knew in my heart that this paroxysm would have an end, at least for a time. Perhaps you did not know this. My mind was too much engrossed to heed the change that was taking place in you. Had I observed it, should I have been able to change its course? Egypt was dying. Enfeebled by centuries of extreme poverty among the people, by the corruption, lechery, and ostentation concentrated among the few, she had been able to play skillfully on the cupidity she aroused, plotting with the Greeks against the Crusaders, with the Crusaders against the Turks, with the Turks against the fanatics of Aleppo, and with the latter against all the others, entering into alliances and betraying them at the very moment they had been concluded. Terrorized from within by the Assassins, and from without by innumerable rivalries, Egypt surrendered, in torpor and in relief, to the conquest of Salah ed-Din Yusuf.‡

I shall have more to tell you of this man who became my protector and friend. For the moment, I am concerned with your departure. One morning you appeared before me, your bag slung over your shoulder, your eyes full of tears, your voice trembling. You had had enough, you said, of this life full of monsters and of despised innocence, of this despair, of this sterile exhaustion, of this fathomless squalor. You wrung my heart, but I asked no questions. My mind was too much distracted by my sorrow to try to hold you back. What could I have said to you that would have been capable of withstanding your reasons? You had not, like me, been taught from father to son to come to terms with adversity; you did not belong to my people, who had never allowed the faint glimmer of

‡ Saladin.

hope to be extinguished, even at the height of the tempest, at the darkest point of the night. For twelve centuries and more, we have had a vital appointment to keep: next year in Jerusalem. But you had only an appointment with yourself. I accepted the fact that you would go out of my sight, but not out of my life. The political policy that I had based on you was nullified by your conversion to solitude, but I have never regretted it. Have you found abiding peace in your mountains, among your sheep and your goats? I am almost convinced of it, and in one sense I envy you.

I wish you well.

I could conclude my book here, though I had anticipated that it would be long. The essential has been said. It remains for me to tell you of my wanderings and my errors, the inevitable advance toward failure and annihilation. This is a secondary matter. "What is the importance of what is only of importance to me?" as the Cordovan poet Al-Mrhô so excellently wrote: And he added this further thought with which I am also in accord: "A life is worth nothing, but nothing is worth a life." You will not do me the injustice of supposing that it is to enhance the value of *my* life that I am undertaking this elucidation. The one I am seeking to reach is in the mirror of which you are the foil, and it is in order to aim high that I have need of your far-off participation. I know what it has cost me to be present in the world. I have always paid in ready money, without demur. Give or take a certain amount of dross, I know the exact price of existence. What I have done proceeds neither from grace nor from chance: it was a deliberate undertaking, begun half a century ago in full lucidity and pursued without intermission in spite of various adversities. I took it upon myself to introduce order into disorder, logic into the welter of events and ideas, and rationality into the perplexities of the Word. Others before me had exerted themselves to this end, others after me will apply themselves to it, it is the work of a househusband similar in every respect to that of a housewife: the moment one's attention is diverted, the dust accumulates and must be removed.

In some ways I have been greatly helped by this chaotic century, which invited a prophet but was rewarded only with philosophers. This is little, I agree. Yet we must be satisfied with it. I was, and I am, one of their number, neither better nor worse than the others. I have read much, I have meditated much and written much—these were my greatest joys. If today my eyes are becoming dim, it is not because they have been blinded by a new truth, but through usage; if my memory is becoming faulty, it is not under the weight of new facts, but from saturation. There remains, and this is becoming urgent, one last enigma for me to resolve: myself, my painful and asthmatic person, the kernel of this life which is worth nothing but which nothing is worth, which is of importance to me but which is not of importance. I shall not seek rest until I have spent my last strength on this elucidation.

A merchant from Marseilles is due to sail from Alexandria with a cargo of silks at the next moon. Whatever pages I have managed to scribble he will take to Ibn Tibbon, who, without reading them, will have them sent to you. Other fragments will reach you by similar channels. Piracy at sea and banditry on the roads of Provence constitute a grave risk that some parts of this book will be lost. My fears of such an accident would be lessened if I were to have a copy made, but the temptation of this risk overrides all other considerations. Why should I worry about lacunae in a work that deals with a lacunary existence? Behind my back, time is running out. No continuity can resist continual usage. The universe itself is a succession of solids and hollows. When it comes to the final reckoning, can any life aspire to anything more? In former days, when I began a book I used to pray earnestly that it would be granted to me to finish it. This one was finished before I even began it, and I have nothing to ask unless it be fidelity to my memory.

You will no doubt have noticed that I have omitted to invoke God. He will have his hour. He has them all.

2

IN the days of my youth a very important conference was held in Fez, to which many scholars from all over the known world traveled. My father took part in it. The subject under discussion was the designation of the land most propitious to the free development of man. The debate was heated and lasted for several tens of days. Each doctor first argued for his own country, and next for Greece, which for long remained the favorite; but Persia, the Kingdom of Damascus, Samaria and the banks of the Jordan, Lower Egypt, Provence, and even the town of Paris, each stood a good chance until the very end. When he returned my father gave the community a florid account of this conference, for we had earned the place of honor: it was Andalusia that had won the final vote. Al-Andalus, my province, consummate harmony between nature and man, whose pearl was Cordova.

I do not claim that such a decision constitutes any sort of proof, and I have reservations as to the utility of this sort of loquacious assembly. Even though they have remained in fashion, I have always refused to associate myself with them. They are a waste of time and breath. Neither am I more favorably disposed toward ecclesiastical or political congresses, which claim to settle the fate of peoples but which have no other power than to ratify already existing situations, when they do not break up in discord or confusion. Present-day reality constantly supplies us with deplorable examples of this. All things considered, I prefer philosophy: it enables scholars from distant lands to get to know each other better and to assess their learning. It was in this way that my father made acquaintances at Fez who were later to save our lives. For the moment, however, I am concerned with extolling Cordova, my town.

It is no longer possible, today, to understand the grace that was inherent in living there at that time. I, who was born in that theater and who can count ten generations of ancestors reclaimed by its humus—was I sufficiently aware of it before I lost it forever? For the child that I was, its grace went without saying, it flourished like the hibiscus flower in our patio, iridescent and ever new, silky as a summer dawn and of so subtle a perfume that one would have to have been a bee to experience its intoxication to the full. Nowhere else have I ever encountered the taste of its air, the savor of its water, or the sweetness of its shade. Forgive me this emphasis. It is exactly suited to the object whose evocation impels me to lyricism. Cordova, my town, I have loved her and hated her in the same breath, I weep for her both for my sake and for her own. Cordova cannot be depicted, cannot be described; you would have to have felt her as I felt her when my senses were quickening; you would have to have steeped yourself in her as I steeped myself in her. No doubt she still contains streets, houses, people who come and go, and this will be so for a long time to come, but Cordova is no longer there, and perhaps she will never again be there, for her grace has been eradicated by fanatics, and grace is not reborn from its own ashes.

Cordova, my town. I had rights over her, just as she had rights over me. It is commonly held that she was founded by the Romans. I have a better suggestion. It was my very remote ancestors of the first Babylonian diaspora who invented her, as they invented Toledo and Granada. It was they who chose her site on a bend of the river; it was they who there perpetuated the first settlement. They were peasants, artisans, merchants, scholars, all intermingled in just a few families living at close quarters on the routes of the ancient world, and once they had allowed themselves a moment's respite to get their breath back, Jerusalem was already being reborn on the northern bank of the Guadalquivir, which is supposed to have been called the Baetis in those days.

I really have no intention of giving you an abbreviated geography and history lesson; I only wish to return in thought to the scene of my childhood in order to clarify and understand my affiliation. There was no clash between the new settlers and the surrounding Iberian villages; at least there was nothing to indicate any such thing. Cordova prospered, became a borough and an open town. The fields south of the river were plowed and harvested, the local handicrafts acquired a renown that attracted the merchants, wool was spun, leather and iron were worked, earthenware jars were filled with olive oil, churns were replete with honey, and when evening came all the men in the community, both young and old, met for study, according to the Law.

. This was not yet Cordova, my town, but its seed was already there. What did it matter that the Romans had turned it into a fortress? Their genius was imperiously stamped on it by the building of a stone bridge over the river, and by an aqueduct which went up to trap the water on the sierra and make it run down to the heart of the town. Did you know that Seneca the orator and Seneca the philosopher came from our Jewry? Destiny was on its way; there was to be no stopping it.

The world in those days was like a sieve shaken by anger. There were empires that lasted a century, and empires that lasted a day. Something was trying to be born, something that nobody yet recognized, and which is only born in order to die: I mean man as an individual human being. Jerusalem had been destroyed, Athens forgotten, Alexandria was in ashes, Isfahan engulfed in her legend, except in the nostalgia of a few, whose insensate dream was to rebuild a city of happiness. Who could forsee that the lot would fall upon Cordova?

There was great confusion at first when the Arabs invaded the peninsula. But hardly were they established in the safety of their alcazars than their ferocity was immediately forgotten, and their traditional preciosity came to the fore. They brought with them that refinement of taste and those subtleties of the enjoyment of both body and mind that contributed so much to the splendors of the Orient and to the envy of Europe. When the day of my birth arrived, Cordova was in its third century of peace and enlightenment. In the whole history of mankind there is no equivalent of such a successful fusion of three cultures, each one of which contributed its best to the common elevation. The inherent genius of a privileged place and the specific genius of three fundamentally different people were quietly awaiting the birth of a work of art. The Hebraic community, the smallest in number but the oldest in date, had deposited in the bottom of the basket everything it had in the way of learning and dialectical skills, and manual dexterity in the art of shaping forms; Islam had contributed the rugged poetry of the limitless spaces, its art of living and the pride of its time-defying architecture; the Latins gave their pragmatism and their endurance, their rhythm and their common sense. It was a marriage both of love and of convenience, which united the soul and the flesh, liberty and respect for others, the currents of the depths and the eddies of the surface; it was the Cordovan miracle.

You know my aversion to the irrational, and the word *miracle*, so frequently used in this connection, shocks me. A grace which is perpetuated over three hundred years derives its powers of maintenance and renewal only from itself. I would accept the word *prodigy*, but would reserve the right to confine it to natural dispositions. The work of art was stirring in the womb. There were indeed quarrels and rivalries, coolnesses and reconciliations, pettinesses and scandalmongering, abuses and crimes. But nothing could deflect the town from her prodigious destiny.

Certainly the Arabs were the masters, and Allah the Unique occupied heaven. Cordova had no choice. She became Arab, in language and in clothing. Morals and souls remained pure. God, after all, was not necessarily in the place tradition assigned to him. Those children playing ball on the towpath, those men crossing the Roman bridge or loitering by the street stalls, those women gliding with tiny steps along the white façades, were they Jews, Christians, or Moslems? No one would have been able to tell. No one cared. They were Cordovans, even if they had only just arrived from Tetuan or Saragossa. Certainly, the town described three concentric semicircles, following the river: on the periphery the Spanish Mozarabs, in the middle the Moslem Arabs, in the center Jewry; but the streets were alike, the houses identical, the people interchangeable, and I never felt as if I were crossing a frontier when I went from one end of the city to the other, nor did I ever feel out of my element when I was away from home. All the inhabitants of Cordova had adopted the dignified carriage of the head imposed by the Arabs, which was why it was sometimes said that the men were proud and the women intractable, though nothing was more superficial than this opinion. Cordova had produced a people who, in any case, had no reason to bow their heads. At the prayer hours all faces were turned toward the East, and it was perhaps a sign of the most profound understanding that all should look together in the same direction. One third of the town abstained from work on Fridays, one third on Saturdays, and one third on Sundays, without anyone having any objection. We even had an agreement with the Castilians never to fight on those three days, and so far as I know this pact was never broken. On the occasions of the great festivals that marked the end of the harvests, all the peoples mingled harmoniously in the town squares to the sound of tambourines and guitars. Diverse yet united, Cordova enjoyed her liberty.

Neither rich nor poor, even though at the extremes there were both rich and poor. Everyone had enough to eat, enough to drink, and found the wherewithal to cover his nudity. The money that was amassed here or there was immediately distributed all over the town. Even the Caliph kept only what was necessary for his maintenance. The palace he had had built six leagues from the town served his prestige more than his needs, and Al Mansur, ashamed of such luxury, had it razed to the ground; its Carthaginian and Numidian porphyries were used to build the municipal library, which became the most opulent in the known world.

In an age when, in your northern capitals, the inhabitants were weltering in the dust or wallowing in the mud, there was not a single street over the length and breadth of our town that was not paved, and not only for the comfort of the feet but also for the pleasure of the eye: bricks, tiles, and lava stones were intermingled in skillful arabesques, in polychromatic checkers, quincunxes, or stars, which were the admiration of our foreign visitors. Not a house but had its own patio where a fountain murmured over its glistening basin, and where palm, myrtle, and bougainvillea flourished.

Being men of the desert, the Arab conquerors worshipped the shimmering waters of the sierra with almost religious fervor; they had diverted part of the rudimentary canalization of the Romans into a system that transformed the whole town into a town in flower. In the surrounding countryside, on the heavy alluvial soil of the river, olive and pomegranate trees flourished, with rice and sugarcane, cotton and spices, whose abundance poured rivers of gold into the city; and I have so far said nothing of the façades of a whiteness that shocked the eye, of the wrought-iron, scrolled balconies, of the beauty of the public buildings; nothing so far of our innumerable schools, of our squares planted with spruce and cypress, of our university, the most renowned in the whole world, into which all year long crowded three thousand students from all over the world. Let us agree with a tranquil heart that the Fez conference had not acquiesced in an error of judgment.

I need only lower my eyelids for a moment in order to be back there. Come—I'll take you with me. This is the Jewry, with its rectilinear streets covered with stone carpets. Mules trot, dogs run, turbaned men walk with a long, supple step, carts pass one another. Almost every porch reverberates with the sound of the loom, the flat-headed hammer that caresses the copper, the bellows of a forge, the rasp of the cooper; here, a blast of scorching air tells you that the glass is melting in the furnace; there a particular odor informs you that the tanner is at work. At this window, his magnifying glass screwed into his eye, the goldsmith is chasing a piece of jewelry; at that window the clothier is assembling the various pieces of a caftan. Can you hear, on the other side of the walls, the shrill voices of the women? They are quarreling, and only they know why. On the square, the peasants behind their stands are displaying pimentos, tomatoes, lettuces, while clusters of figs, dates, and grapes are hanging up to dry.

Somewhere in the distance a mu'adhdhin is calling to prayer, and some people fall to the ground, mumbling, true Moslems or false converts, no one knows, while others remain standing, renegades or members of other sects, no one cares. Neither selling nor buying is halted; worship does not encroach on the fundamental activities of the city. Women bundled up in their clothes pass, chattering.

You, a man of the north—I can see and hear you furtively swatting your cheeks: your skin is too light, it attracts the flies, and they make you swear. You don't know, and you can't know, you lukewarm-blooded traveler, that the fly is also one of God's creatures, and that it has an intimate share in our existence by peopling the sky with birdsong. Are you, as I am, overjoyed by a feeling of fair distribution and balance? Are you, as I am, afraid that such an arrangement of place and persons will prove too fragile to last? No doubt, since we are linked by profound fellow feeling. Throughout my Cordovan childhood and youth, and even during the time I went away to escape an enchantment that had become unbearable, I never went to bed one single evening without thinking of all the calamities that might well descend on my town the next day. These are thoughts which anyone who does not carry persecution in his blood finds it difficult to understand.

Simple reflection taught me the obvious fact that however long this happy state of Cordovan affairs had lasted, it was still only temporary. Did I mention three centuries of peace and light? It was only partially true. My grandfather had to flee his house, driven away by the Berbers, and the community had to scatter over the whole of the peninsula like a flight of swallows. Our places of prayer were razed to the ground. It so happened that the fury of the new masters was of short duration, the Jewry was able to repopulate itself, and my grandfather to return within its walls. The people of Granada, warned too late, had left a thousand dead in the ruins of their pillaged town. The Roman conquerors had established their major rights over Cordova. The Visigoth rulers imposed theirs, in all legitimacy. The Arab invaders established their incontestable supremacy. We, the founders of the town, were no more than tolerated in it. Do you understand the anguish I felt, so deeply committed as an adolescent to such a landscape and a climate?

But here is my father's house. Let us go in. The wrought-iron gate onto the street happens to be open: we are expected. A long, shady passageway engulfs us, its paving made shiny by the friction of the passing years; a faint trace of fried onion floats on the air. The clamor of the outside world has been forbidden entry here. One flagstone has worked loose, the third after the threshold, and surprises one by seesawing under one's foot: each time I walked over it I promised myself to remind my father to tell the mason; hardly was my foot raised than the promise sank into oblivion. Then suddenly there is the sea-green dazzle of the patio, the sea-blue of the basin of the central fountain with its silver thread splashing, and the luxuriant growth of the palm trees and lianas, with the fluttering of hundreds of those extravagant iridescent butterflies that are hibiscus flowers. The flies buzz in the fresh, imprisoning heat, sparrows stir in the branches. A leather curtain flaps: it is Élisée, our hunchbacked servant, bringing you as a sign of welcome the misted pitcher of cool water and the pewter goblet filled with rose-petal jam. She places her knotted finger across her thin lips, and her crooked chin points toward the interior of the house: my father is there, engrossed as usual in important business. Silence must reign.

Do you imagine that this return disturbs me? My old heart has not missed a beat. There have been too many afflictions, too many deaths, too much indifference. Cordova was a soft, downy bed where it was good to sleep and dream of poetry, of science, of fraternity; did half a century need to pass for me to realize that this was a meager dream? After all, the promises contained in the freshness of the dawn were not false. Poetry, science, and fraternity did hover in the sky of my town; it was the astonished young man that I was who was not in his place. I was watching myself grow; in reality, I was asleep. I was preparing myself to grasp the world; in reality, I was dreaming. What was most concrete in the plighting of my troth to Cordova was embedded in the spirit, not in the flesh. We are a people with a memory. The oral tradition takes precedence over the written tradition. An indelible learning traverses our great dismembered body. This is another of those propositions that you Edomites cannot possibly understand: the evil done to one of us flows down a labyrinth from which there is no longer any issue. It is a long time since we reached saturation point; there is no more room for new suffering. As the light makes a covenant with the shade, so our memory makes common cause with oblivion. To forget is not not to know; it is not to think about things. While the Jewry in Cordova was enjoying its ease in a lasting temporary state, the Teutons were massacring us on the Rhine; the Franks on the roads of Byzantium; the Berbers in the plains of the Atlas; in Rome, in Castile, in Provence, spittle rained down on our heads; we were sold as slaves in Babylon and Salonika. The winds that blew over Cordova were heavy with weeping and wailing. Our Jewry knew, but did not think about it. There was never a time when we were not collecting money in order to alleviate the most pressing misfortunes; to ransom a slave, to pay a forfeit to a too pressing monarch. At the same time we were embellishing our town, our houses, the impulses of our hearts and minds, we were producing an abundance of poets, doctors, astronomers, and philosophers, in the fallacious hope that the world would one day realize that it needed us. The world did sometimes realize this, when it was morose or sick, when a comet appeared in the sky or when the dispute on the sex of angels reached stalemate. It deprived us of our revenues, our economies, and our lives when the danger was past, and the cycle could recommence.

Was it important that Cordova stood outside the currents, that people came there from all sides to acquire the richest silks, the softest carpets, the most limpid gems, the most well-founded science? It was important, certainly, but none the less absurd. Replacing myself thus in the golden setting of my childhood, I discover a picture book traversed by a serious, sad young man, proud of the prowess of his town and of the prowess that he is secretly preparing, but frightened at the idea that all this might not be real. No doubt he would have to remake the world, enter into rivalry with the Creator himself, bring to light in himself a fragment of God. This idea had been making its way since time immemorial, it glinted for a moment in the water of our fountain, and then vanished.

3

YOU didn't know my father: He had just died when you arrived in Fostat. It was through him and against him that I matured. In my memory he is situated outside time, both reassuring and terrible, both present before me and present in me, an old man who was somehow eternal. As you no doubt know, he had been the Prince* of the Cordovan Jewry. This office came down to him from his father, who held it through his own father; it reverted by right to the man who was the wisest and most just, and for more than two hundred years these qualities had been unanimously attributed by the community to the Maimons. It was my duty, as the firstborn son, to succeed, one day, to this office. My father judged me unworthy of it. I had no desire for it.

It is only here, in Egypt, in the proximity of the great monoliths which we in Spain could not even imagine, that I have been able to form a more accurate idea of my father. In Cordova, I should have compared him to an olive tree; he had its dense, firm-set trunk and its sparse crown which cast only a meager shadow. By that I mean that however agile and skillful his thoughts and activities, he was less a man than a function; invariable and invariant, endlessly repeating himself and never contradicting himself. My first picture of him is superimposed on the last: a solid, heavy man, rather short in the leg, his belly rounded but not aggressive, holding himself very

---

* An archaism surviving from the Roman occupation. It generally designates the *principalis* (president) of an assembly; in this case, the chief of the community.

straight, his back well arched, his beard bushy and square, his eyebrows shaggy under his skullcap or turban. He never walked in any
other way than with short, measured steps, gliding along in his
babouches; as if to bend the knee, even when on his feet, would not
have been proper to his condition. Beneath his furrowed brow and
his heavy eyelids his penetrating look possessed the intensity of a
sermon. He spoke little and, whether at home or in the Council, said
no more than was necessary. I have no recollection of ever having
seen or heard him manifest impatience, or yield to anger. If something did not meet with his approval he would avoid it, and not return to it unless obliged to by the force of circumstance. Was
he sometimes beset by uncertainties, debates with his conscience,
regrets? This is possible, but there was never any sign of it. He
only delivered finished products, judgments without appeal,
opinions without reservations, definitive predictions, in brief and
muted words, similar to his steps. Was he sometimes weary, did he
ever suffer from toothache, or stomachache; were there nights
when sleep eluded him? I was never aware of anything of the sort.
One morning, in Fostat, he did not leave his room at his accustomed
hour, and I found him dead in his bed. For his departure from the
world he had managed to be as he had been throughout his life—
summary and definitive.

In those days our Jewry counted nearly twenty thousand souls,
all of whom to some extent resided in the soul of my father. There
was not a single event of any importance that could remain unknown to him for long, or which did not require his jurisdiction.
He knew the names of all the families who belonged there; the
strength of the alliances of the ones or the extent of the discord of
the others; the good or the bad business transactions of this one or
that; who was lying and who was telling the truth; the reason for an
arrival, the cause of departure. Both the everyday and the exceptional were directed his way just as the water rushed down onto the
town. Not a day passed without many people coming to ask his advice, without his being requested to settle a dispute or a quarrel,

without someone submitting some question of conscience to him. When he did not have a ready answer, he would shut himself up for an hour or two and search for it in the sacred texts. You know that the people of the Orient are gifted with exceptional mnemonic faculties. My father's memory was prodigious; in itself it was the equivalent of a whole library. He only had to read a manuscript once to know it from start to finish. The hours that anyone else would have used for rest or enjoyment, he devoted to study. In order to keep his mind alert, he observed a complete fast one day a week; it is true that he made up for this on the other days, gulping down quickly and abundantly whatever Élisée, put in his bowl, never lifting his eyes from the book he was reading. He was not a man, he was a function.

He had been brought up so that, by tradition, he should have no private life, nor ever yield to a desire, an outburst of temper or a wave of affection. The only luxury he allowed himself was the cleanliness of his body, the ceremony of the hot bath, the regular visits of the barber who attended to the square cut of his beard, the white linen that he constantly changed under the dusted, brushed, washed caftan, the irreproachable arrangement of his coif, and that only because Élisée saw to it, and because it would not have been right that anyone should be able to find fault with the appearance of the prince. He received passing strangers in his house, bearers of manuscripts, oral questions or messages, and for this, the house had to be well kept, to do honor to the community. As a shepherd, all that interested or concerned my father was his flock. The political, juridical, and moral guidance he exercised so strictly and with such devotion came down to him, he said, in direct line from the Patriarchs, and this may well not have been farfetched, for the origin of the history of the Maimons is lost in the mists of time.

I lived thirty years in the shadow of this man, and I do not remember having had a single private conversation with him. I called him Rabbi, and spoke to him in the third person; he called me son of the butcher's daughter—I will tell you why. Our domestic regime was extremely modest. My father took not the slightest interest in it, just as he had nothing but scorn for material possessions or comforts. In spite of the great responsibilities he assumed, he liked to say that we were poor. This idea is worth developing, for "poor" in Cordova certainly did not have the same meaning as it did in Provence or in Egypt. It meant that my father was not in receipt of any remuneration whatsoever, either from the commune that absorbed him or from the individuals he served, and it was out of the question that he ever should receive any such remuneration, in conformity with the tradition that forbade anyone to use the Torah to cultivate his own garden.

The only tools my father knew how to use belonged to the Scriptures, and this knowledge excluded the very idea of profit. He had never been willing to have anything to do with the profane sciences, which he held to be useless when they reproduced what had already been revealed, and harmful when they propounded theories that were contrary to the Law, for only the Law was just. And after all, his office and his studies would have left him no time to engage in any sort of lucrative activity.

He had no income, neither was he in possession of what might be called worldly goods. The house belonged to him, no doubt, and so did the mule. We owned, within two hours' walking distance south of the river, a vineyard ten thousand feet long interplanted with fruit trees. This land, originally reclaimed by a Maimon and cultivated throughout the centuries by successive Maimons, was recognized as ours by letters patent which my father conserved; it provided us with the wine for the Sabbath and the Passover, with peaches in the spring and grapes in the fall, and with enough to pay Élisée's wages, except when the soil had been too maltreated by the heavens. My uncle Joad made us a small allowance from what remained of my mother's dowry, and Judah Halevi, our near neighbor, who squandered things on an ostentatious scale, diverted into our direction the overflow from his kitchens.

Poverty, certainly, but sustained by a sublime indifference. We did not have to wonder about the source of the oil for our lamps, about the nature of the process by which our table was supplied at mealtimes, how the mule's stable rack was filled, or who provided the firewood. Everything that was necessary for our maintenance arrived quite naturally and satisfied our needs. Can you imagine a more enviable poverty?

To the foreign visitor, our way of life must have seemed opulent, because a river of gifts ran through the house and permanently stagnated in it. No one who was in need of my father's science ever appeared before him with empty hands, and all, and in particular the most dispossessed, set their hearts on offering something that should not appear niggardly. Not a day passed without the appearance of some silver or copper ware, pieces of linen or silk, furs or jewels, and all this was piled up in the chests, adorned the alcoves, littered the corners, hung from the rafters in the most impressive disarray. Every week my father had one or two basketfuls taken to the community's treasury. The foreigners left us, some carrying off a St. Andrew's cross, others a ring. There was never, to my knowledge, any occasion when my father parted with one of these objects for his personal profit, or when he misrepresented the meaning of the offering. The repository of the Law and of an excess of goods, he stood at the crossroads from which radiated justice and wisdom, generosity and the solidarity of our people.

This was the man on whom my first glance alighted, but I didn't see him, because he himself barely looked at me. Here, we are touching on a vast misunderstanding which has weighed heavily on my destiny. I venerated my father, as the Law prescribes; I didn't love him, for he had no love for me. Apart from the fact that there was no place for me in his overstocked mind, he harbored a private resentment against me. I was not his son; I was the son of the butcher's daughter who had been his wife. This must have caused him much unhappiness, but even this he was incapable of showing; all that transpired was a certain kind of sadness—but a sadness that hurt.

When my father had reached the age of forty and the moment had come to provide himself with descendants, he asked for the hand in marriage of the daughter of Menahem, the butcher. In the opinion of all sensible men in the Cordovan Jewry, this marriage was totally unsuitable. No one but the daughter of a scholar or man of science would traditionally have been in her place in my father's house. Why had he, who so respected the customs, allowed his choice to divagate in this way? I refuse to interrogate chance or Providence—both are beyond my scope—yet I maintain that I inherited a special kind of grace from this source of life. This is not a philosophical matter; it depends on the action of very real circumstances.

If my father did not take a wife of appropriate rank, it was because he had not found one with a dowry large enough to allow her to enter into an alliance with a man who was not in a position to earn a salary. The scholars and men of science in Cordova despised material riches, with the exception of a few prodigals like Judah Halevi who combined debauch with celibacy. Another limitation was due to the fact that over the whole length and breadth of Andalusia, Islam had produced a demographic imbalance by its customary polygamy. Eminent Moslems were eagerly in pursuit of our girls, who were more attractive and more passionate than those of their own clans. Had not the prophet himself set the example when he married Rehana and Safiya, captives from Medina?

Our Council of Sages was not in principle opposed to such unions, which sealed alliances that offered some reassurance for the future. A political calculation, certainly. But a system of legitimate defense. Was not a minority that was both closed and open such as ours—enclaved within a swarming mass whose reactions were both unforeseeable and explosive—was not such a minority justified in assuring its security and survival? The prosperity of our masters was already partly derived from the renown of our goldsmiths, our drapers, our merchants, our doctors, our philosophers. Should we forbid our daughters to contribute to the common cause? Particularly as they did not need much persuading; in a well-off Arab house their existence was far more pleasant than it was among us. It followed that the seraglio thinned out the ranks, and there were some gaps. My father had waited for a long time, which meant that he had hesitated for a long time. Perhaps he had also had the idea of renewing the blood of the Maimons, which had become thickened as the result of prolonged and restricted endogamy, for most of the scholars were distant cousins.

I would not assert with any confidence that he had formed a real attachment to the immature being that she was: my mother was not yet fifteen when she stood beneath the canopy. She was not yet twenty when she died. Between these two major events, my father had fulfilled his obligations by begetting two sons: me, the elder, destined for study, and David, the younger, destined for commerce. The maelstrom of progeniture had abated. My father could now forget about it, and he did forget about it. It was out of the question to have any dealings with the Menahems, who were nothing but peasants, in spite of the allowance they made us, which my father accepted as a matter of course. Life was back to normal—except for the fact that this normal life did not want me, and I did not want it.

Whatever I may have seen of my mother, I have forgotten; but her image is in me, and even today I can evoke it whenever I wish. I used to see her brother Joad in secret, and I was always questioning him about her. He delivered my mother to me gradually, in motley bits and pieces which I carefully tucked away in my memory box; a detail here, another there, finally amalgamated into a human personality. Her rebellious hair, her forehead a half-moon beneath it, her jaunty, almond-eyed look, her peals of laughter, and her light step, a happy mixture of the Orient and Andalusia—how proud I was to owe to them half of the man I was becoming! What did it matter that she had never learned to read, much less to write, and that she had to sign with a trembling cross the pact that bound her for the remaining days of her life? Apart from that, she could do everything: run in the fields, bite into an unripe apple, sing at sunset, bleed and cut up a ram, bake bread, lie or tell the truth according to the circumstances, forecast the weather by watching the way the birds were flying. The intuition and common sense that I have been able to apply to my studies came to me from her. My father was mistaken: I wasn't the son of the butcher's daughter, I was the son of that particular butcher's daughter. I was also the nephew of Joad, the peasant, who taught me many essential things.

There are the data. Young Moses can now be born.

4

YOU asked me one day to give you a succinct definition of Judaism, but I couldn't. Tonight, I can: Judaism is that spiritual culture in which the same verb is used for *to know* and *to love*, in which a single verb also suffices for *to eat* and *to learn*. These are not fortuitous ambiguities, or linguistic uncertainties; they are intermingled actions. *To learn, to know*—these are physical incorporations, embraces, carnal relations between being and matter. They are also the pleasure that follows the satisfaction of an expectation, which only needs a little nudge in order to become fully aroused.

The path to wisdom does not lie in the accumulation of knowledge, as some accumulate riches; it lies rather in the recognition of one's own reality in the world, and in one's judgment of it. It lies in the renewal in oneself of the mystery of the Creation. If this were not so, would the child that I was have been able to endure the existence that tradition imposed on him?

Twenty teeth in my mouth, legs which still faltered when they tried to run, still barely able to articulate a properly constructed sentence. Up before dawn, my eyes heavy with sleep, my body contracted by the chill of the night, I have to find my own way to the yeshiva, toward which other equally unsteady boys of the same age are converging. It is a square, roughly lime-washed room with a stale smell which has something to do with rancid oil. Wooden benches are lined up along the walls. The young congregation take their places, under the penetrating look of the master, who is testing his long cane against the skirts of his caftan. Woe betide anyone who yawns: he has immediate reason to be sorry for it. He is equally sorry for it when he scratches his hair under his skullcap, or when he sticks a finger up a nostril. The ideal would be for these children to be made of wax and bran, not of flesh and blood. But this would be a false ideal: the test would lose its meaning. It is precisely flesh and blood that must be incorporated into this apprenticeship. Is the master too severe? An idle question: he is the master. His function is to master, so that mastery shall be set in motion. Letters, figures, words, that an ingenuous look deciphers, that a hesitating fingernail follows. Sounds pass through lips, are rolled between tongue and palate, are released in the throat, the child swallows them, and makes them his forever.

Do you think that in the yeshiva boys learn only to read? They also learn to eat phrases which are at first insipid but which, by dint of being ensalivated, sucked, and masticated, finally produce a delicious taste. Thou shalt love God the Eternal Father with all thy heart, and even thy lower instincts! What is the meaning of this injunction? Is it possible not to love him? How can you know that all your heart is committed, and not just a part of it? Among the synonyms for the word *heart*: thought, intelligence, will, strength, power—which ought we to prefer, and why? What is an instinct, and by what sign can we recognize that it is low? If we reject our lower instincts, doesn't that mean that we are denying God some part of the love that is his due?

The morning passes on these questions, and the whole day. Less and less tired as the hours go by, the child surrenders to the magic of the words, and he is awake and refreshed by the time night falls and he runs home to his father's house, where a single night of dreams will have to suffice him to digest what he has just assimilated.

By the time he is six, unless he was born an idiot, deaf, dumb, or blind, he will have reading and writing at his command, assets that no persecution has ever been able, nor ever will be able to take away from him. Whether the future then molds him into a road mender or a doctor-philosopher, he will have reaffirmed the covenant with the Word, our sacred pact. Rich or poor, powerful or wretched, he has been given the means to pursue, every day of his life, a dialogue with the ineffable being. I suggest as a subject for your meditation this phrase from the Talmud: *The world is suspended in the breath of little schoolchildren.*

I was that little boy. One of a thousand. In every street in the Cordovan Jewry there was a yeshiva in which the breath of the world was suspended. We were not unaware of the fact that the rest of the town breathed to another rhythm. The young Arabs round about drew on their prodigious memories to recite suras and hadiths by heart; those who learned to read and write were far more rare. As for the Spaniards, they had no school, apart from the one that trained their future scholars. The little donkey boys and goatherds read their signs and symbols straight from the great book of nature, and developed their muscles in minor brawls.

I am not claiming that at that age I could have attached any value judgment to our singularity. There was no other way of life for me than to follow in the footsteps trodden by our ancestors. I was entering with tiny steps into the great spiritual adventure of my people, not even guessing how original this approach was, as it was so common among us. Did I ever long for the great open spaces, for a path that led into the undergrowth in the wood, for a living spring? I no longer know. It is possible. In the state of fascination and constraint that weighed on me as a budding scholar, there is no doubt that I would have taken these inclinations for lower instincts, and that this suspicion would have incited me to ward them off with all my strength. Just as I had to eat to live, so I had to study to live. My sky, my woods, my springs, were written on the pages of my books. I did not doubt that one day I would be capable of putting them back in their proper places.

Happy, or unhappy? How can I decide, after so many years, so many events? I had schoolfellows, but I had no friends, no accomplices. The verb *to play* did not enter into my vocabulary, and had no equivalent in it. Do you think I suffered from not setting fire to a heap of rubbish, or tying a tin can to a cat's tail! I knew of the existence, and of the turbulence, of the gangs of boys and girls who were always playing around on the empty lots and down by the river; I pitied them a little, but I envied them more. Our master spoke of them severely, and dismissed them as the opposite of the example we were to follow. They would never attain truth and wisdom. They had been forbidden access to the kingdom of light. They had not been *chosen.* I finally came to envy them less and to think more highly of myself, but without too much conviction.

I admitted that there might be two ways of life: the good and the bad. I thanked Providence for having placed me in the good way, but without enthusiasm. The promise contained in the covenant remained abstract. However inexperienced I might be, I already knew that the price to pay could be excessive. The massacre of our brothers in Worms had severely shaken our Jewry, and I was not unaware of what had taken place. In the Maghreb, intolerance of our people was once more coming to the surface in murderous little waves. One for all and all for one, our master explained to us. Where *was* that corrupted soul who was delivering us up to vengeance? Moreover, the cane left marks on my skin that burned more surely than the fires of Gehenna.

At home, neither mother nor father. A hunchback who was always complaining. And a fat, chubby baby who crawled all over the place, flourishing his bottom. If anyone had asked me in those days whom I loved, I should have answered without hesitation: Élisée. She was admirable in her devotion and her efficiency. Deformed, and as ugly as sin, she had a beautiful, somber look in which there was a permanent gleam of rejected goodness. We understood each other, and this made me feel good. During my free time, though I had so little of it, I liked to be near her, in the patio or in the house, and she would stuff me with jam and with absurd stories. When she couldn't think of any new ones she would repeat herself, and I was always on the qui vive to see that each successive version coincided precisely both in detail and in intonation with the previous ones.

So it was true. She told me how she had been captured during a Turkish raid on Smyrna, where she was living quietly with her parents, who were cloth merchants; and I used to go and bolt the street gate to keep Élisée safe, from then on; how she had been violated and left for dead in an olive grove; and I sometimes saw her in my dreams, her belly laid bare and her thighs covered in blood; how she had been taken in caravan after caravan along the African coast, offered for sale in all the slave markets without anyone wanting to buy her because of her hump and her ugliness; and I decided to become a great doctor to make her walk straight and become beautiful; how she had ended up in Cordova, where my father, hearing that she was a Jewess from Smyrna, had her ransomed by the community, which immediately emancipated her; and I thought that my father was a great prince; how it had suited her, as she had no close relations left in the world, to replace my mother, who had just died; and I decided that if fate had been cruel to Élisée, it had been even more cruel to me.

On Fridays the yeshiva let us out early in the afternoon. The house welcomed me with a festive air, with all the lamps lit, all the flagstones polished with oil, the food for a whole day laid out waiting on the white tablecloth. Before nightfall Élisée gave me my bath. Her knotted fingers then lingered over my skin, exploring its hollows and protrusions, passed and repassed over the sensitive places, and her unlovely face was strained in an intense effort of meditation. Against my will, this manipulation disturbed me, and this I attributed to the lower instincts which were supposed to contribute to the love of God.

I wanted it to be over as soon as possible, yet I hoped it would continue. Was it that my skin remembered my mother's hands? Was it that a curse had descended upon me? I was torn between laughter, tears, and anger; I was irresolute, paralyzed by shame, irritation, and an ineffable languor.

Week after week Élisée progressed, her teasing became more precise and more insistent, and my confusion was equally swollen. What exactly was happening in my body, whose mystery I had not hitherto recognized? In my nudity there was as much strength as weakness; in my mind, as much acceptance as refusal. I rose, and yet stayed where I was, terrified of the inevitable approach of the voice from heaven which, at any moment, might ring out and call me by my name. Was I too destined to go down to dust?

But heaven remianed silent; Élisée, on the other hand, spoke. She explained to me in her own fashion the second chapter of Genesis, and as in this domain too she repeated herself, I knew that she was telling the truth. I had known—all my life, it seemed to me—that I was not innocent. I had observed out of the corner of my eye the cock mounting the hen, the he-goat mounting the she-goat. I didn't understand this mechanism, but I did understand its necessity. It was according to the law of nature. That we were supposed not to look, not to talk about it, and act as if it didn't exist, proceeded from the rites of adults, which I didn't understand either.

I had also had a presentiment, it seemed to me, that there was not such a great distance from the cock to the man as people were at pains to make us believe. When I read that Adam *knew* Eve, my voice became hoarse, my ears buzzed. It suddenly became clear to me that reality was not written with the same signs and symbols as books. This was a remarkable discovery. Once again, the world had been split into two. And yet, in truth, it could only be one, and I already promised myself that I would exert the utmost vigilance in order not to miss it. I was enormously relieved when I read, later, in the Talmud, that *even a voice from heaven does not prevail over what exists*. Others before me had known torment and uncertainty. The author of this commentary had chosen. I too made my choice. It was a man's life that I must lead: humbly, proudly, and above all —with lucidity.

One Friday, when I was about eight or nine, I curtly intimated to Élisée that from then on I would take my bath alone. I no longer needed her hands to explore my body; mine were perfectly adequate. Élisée emitted a sort of hiccup, flung out of the house, and I didn't see her for three whole days. For a long time after that there was a coolness between us.

5

IF I had been a brilliant pupil at school they would probably have told me so. My father's increasingly disapproving attitude toward me constantly reminded me of my mediocrity. I must admit that the son of the butcher's daughter did him very little honor. The association of the Maimons with learning was a firmly established fact of natural selection in the Jewry in Cordova. Their father's seed endowed the firstborn males with an outstanding natural aptitude for biblical science. Though it was not hereditary, this kind of mandarinate was nonetheless congenital. And now this thread, which had stretched down through so many generations, was about to be broken with me. I was not the son my father had been hoping for. He resigned himself to this betrayal. I had to resign myself in my turn and, in order not to despair, to discover my own particularity.

I was still unaware, in those days, that logic had been codified by the Peripatetics, and that the Mutakallimun Arabs used it with virtuosity. The very notion of logic must have been strange to me, and also the notion of the concrete, which no doubt already dwelt in me. For the moment, my only talent was for common sense, which, my father made no mistake, came to me in direct line from the butcher's daughter. I was not unintelligent. I understood without the slightest difficulty the apparent meaning of phrases. I had no trouble in remembering what I had read. I was highly capable of debating it according to the recognized principles, of leavening the various ready-made interpretations, of playing at being strong-minded, taking the master with his cane as my model. Today, I think that I must have felt that this teaching was too simple, too easy, and therefore of little interest.

I was lacking in zeal, and perhaps also in ambition. When I was not being questioned I preserved an obstinate silence. I did not bring myself to the fore, as others did, to try to please, to attract praise. The master often complained to my father that I seemed to be asleep when I was in fact wide awake. The cane had ceased to be a remedy; its tip fell too often and too smartly to conserve its virtues. Have you observed how easily a child will come to terms with coercion and boredom? To escape into fantasy is a sure and time-honored recipe. The flight of images has no duration; it enables you to wait until the unpleasantness has worn itself out and become dissipated.

I was keeping myself in reserve for better times, when studying would become a path to freedom. In the meantime, I nevertheless had to agree to subject myself to too strict rules, and to behave at least honorably, if no more. The happy mean between the duality of presence-evasion required no more than a modicum of practice. It was only half of me that dreamed, but this was enough to make the master permanently antagonistic toward me. No doubt he thought he was acting advisedly in keeping my father regularly informed. I would then be the object of a black look from Judge Maimon. The sideslip into the slaughterhouse had decidedly not produced a good intermixture. My father would have been even more perplexed had he known how much I had begun to love the slaughterhouse, in the person of my uncle Joad. But before that I had scented scandal, and had not considered that its offense was so very rank.

6

JUDAH HALEVI lived on a grand scale and was the subject of a good deal of controversy. He would no doubt have been excommunicated for his morals, as I was later to be for my writings, had he not been illustrious and inspired. His reputation as a skillful doctor extended beyond the limits of Andalusia. It was said that he had several times been summoned to the Court of Castile, and that he had returned with an escort of mules laden with precious objects. The great of Estremadura or of the Levant did not hesitate to cross the lines in secret to have themselves taken to his house. His skill was no less in demand by the Maghrebin and Andalusian dignitaries, and neither was he sparing with his assistance to the poor of our town.

Local gossip attributed the most contradictory traits to him: for some he was greedy, brutal, and ruthless; for others, generous, kind, and charitable; so the truth must have been that he was sometimes this and sometimes that, according to the circumstances and to his mood of the moment. You will approve, I think, of my setting little store by this sort of tittle-tattle. A personality like Judah Halevi cannot be imprisoned in a few epithets. The turpitude that this backbiting attributed to him—or that he attributed to himself through his contempt for the conventions—in no way detracted from the admiration that no one refused him. A much sought-after doctor—yes indeed; but above all an incomparable poet, the most influential in Moslem Spain since the voices of Ibn Nagdela, Ibn Gabirol, and Ibn Ezra the Elder had been stilled. In the Cordovan

Caliphate, poetry was rightly taken to be the one state of supreme beatitude to which a human being is allowed to accede during his lifetime. Many scholars went in for versifying, but there was only one poet like Judah Halevi, and the peoples of Andalusia, though so disparate, all instinctively knew this.

A poet cannot be described, cannot be explained; all we can do is approach him, discover him, and love him.

The adolescent I then was, subject to the full ferment of rising sap, more tormented by the meaning of language than by its possible beauty, did not feel the slightest inclination toward lyrical elation in himself. At its acme, poetry is silence; but it was, on the contrary, the boisterous and excessive side of this personality that excited my curiosity. Judah Halevi lived in a big, several-storied house with many windows, all of them glazed, near our own. I knew—from whom? from Élisée, no doubt—that he lived a dissolute existence there, and that it was only thanks to the protection of his muse that he had not yet been struck down by arrows of lightning from the heavens. Although a member of our Council of Sages, where he never showed his face, he openly flouted the Law, profaned the Sabbath rest, offended his mouth with venison and other forbidden foods, and devoted himself to no other cult than that of his own pleasures. His house harbored a harem in which demoniac creatures permanently languished; barely nubile houris brought at great expense from the Maghreb by slave dealers, and still beardless catamites. All this little community spent the whole day bathing, perfuming themselves, chattering and quarreling under the supervision of two matrons and three blind musicians. After nightfall, strange chants were wafted over the rooftops. Judah Halevi received at his table his friends from Cordova, Granada, or Seville, Arab dignitaries or rich merchants, sometimes Spanish emissaries, and the fete continued far into the night, sometimes into the first light of dawn.

On the way to school I had to pass this long, sleeping façade, and each time I felt my back stiffen, my neck go rigid, so afraid was I of drawing some reflection of this opprobrium upon myself. And yet, no hurricane blew through the air vents, no pestilence oozed out of the joints. Outside the gate dozed a monumental emancipated slave —according to Élisée, an Ottoman—keeping sentry duty over vice. His feet stuck out beyond the porch, so that you had to walk around them or step over them. I occasionally risked a look out of the corner of my eye but I never observed the slightest grimace of a succubus or incubus mixed up in the foliage of the inner garden, one of the best kept and most opulent of the Jewry. Water splashed in the fountain, parakeets fluttered around a perch. Why was I not one of those winged creatures, to be able to witness those bacchanalia that caused so many tongues to wag in Cordova! Was the doctor-poet reality or myth? Were there really, in this apparently affluent and peaceful house, young captives whose modesty had been assassinated—boys of my own age delivered up to sodomy? Élisée claimed that it was at the height of his orgies that Judah Halevi found the most pathetic cadences of his poems to the glory of the land of Zion. A scribe was present, and wrote them down. Copies then circulated among the scholars, who went into raptures over them. Did God know about these frenzies? Did he accord his special indulgence toward these magicians of the sacred Word? Judah Halevi was said to be the master of the purest biblical language that no one had spoken for centuries past; he was equally at home in the most elegant Koranic language—he alternated rhymes and assonances, and varied rhythms, just as he also occasionally composed in Latin hexameters. Later, much later, copies of these poems came to my notice: he really was a great elegist, inspired from on high. In those days I could not have understood this. In those days it was the devil who was tempting me.

I was to meet him once. You must be expecting me to confess my immediate disappointment: he had neither horns nor a cloven hoof, and he didn't give off the slightest odor of sulphur. Reality reduces the imaginary, just as gelidity compresses the fog; this only makes its discovery the more startling. The scene has remained so highly colored in my memory that I can reproduce it without the slightest discontinuity. When I got home from school that evening, my father sent for me. He was in his study with Messulam, his copyist, and with a visitor whose features I could at first barely make out, as he had his back to the lamp. He was a man of my father's age, with receding hair, his head uncovered, very elegantly dressed in an embroidered silk gown. I observed the whiteness of his long, delicate hands, which seemed to lead an independent existence. It is easy today to assert that I immediately knew who this visitor was; his look, penetrating the darkness, told me without the slightest possibility of a doubt.

"Firstborn son of Maimon," he said to me in a high-pitched voice, "peace be on you. May you become just and wise like your father, who is my friend." "Judah Halevi," I replied, without thinking, "I want to be like you, a doctor, a poet, and a libertine."

There were some muffled laughs around the table. I had a vague idea that my remark was inappropriate, but there was no going back on it. My father was combing his beard with his fingers, always a sign of his extreme displeasure.

"Interesting," said the visitor, "very interesting. A poet and a libertine? I don't know. They take talent. But a doctor, you can be. That can be learned." Messulam, the copyist, was rubbing his ribs against the edge of the table, no doubt to control an excess of mirth. The dim light of the oil lamp was flickering, and fantastic shadows were dancing on the wall.

"My son will be a Judge of the Law, like all firstborn Maimons," my father said calmly. "Don't put ideas into his head. He has enough as it is; there's no need to add to them."

"It isn't necessarily a bad idea," replied Judah Halevi. "It hasn't turned out so badly for me." He turned away from me and resumed the conversation my arrival had interrupted. There was a lump in my throat and I was incapable of moving. "I'll be a doctor too," I murmured, more to strengthen my decision than to displease my father. This was the first time I had ever dared confront him openly.

They were discussing the political situation. Judah Halevi was doing most of the talking. Fluttering over my head I heard phrases constituted of word-objects, some of which were unknown to me, though their meaning reached me with unprecedented acuity. My father occasionally contributed a few confused grunts. Messulam was rolling his eyes. In the north of the peninsula the Castilians and the Aragonese were preparing for a large-scale offensive. The defeat of the Spaniards at Zalaca had nevertheless left them Toledo. That being the case, a new attempt at reconquest would not be lacking in attraction, all the more so as Andalusia, divided and parceled out into *taifas*, or principalities, was a prey that was both easier to overcome and more reasonable to covet. "Well, yes—but!" my father put in. "If Cordova becomes Spanish, we shall be Spanish. What's wrong with that?"

Judah Halevi abruptly turned toward me. "Can you read Arabic letters?" Surprised by this question, I needed a moment's reflection before shaking my head. I could just about make out the Kufic, but the cursive—not at all. "I have a very rare copy," he said, "of Ibn Sina's* *Canon on Medicine* in a Hebrew translation which follows the original text line by line; it's from the Sunnite Arabic, which is quite close to our own. I will have it brought to you tomorrow. It will give you some idea of medicine, and also of our great writers." "I shall forbid him to read it," said my father, without raising his voice.

Once again the two men forgot me for a time. "The Spaniards," Judah Halevi went on, "mistrust us. Their idolatrous hate is dormant, but not extinct. They are not sparing of their salaams and sumptuous gifts to me personally, but I am not deceived. We have lived too long with the Arabs. For a Castilian, an Andalusian is either an enemy or a traitor, and when the military undertake to massacre, woe betide anyone who stands in their way. The Arabs have rapid horses and an extensive empire. We have slow legs, and where

* Avicenna.

is our hinterland? But it is not the Spaniards I fear the most for the moment. That will come later—much later."

He paused, and contemplated his long, delicate hands in the faint light of the lamp. My father grunted. Messulam bared his teeth in a fixed grin. Every word that was said pierced me like sharp metal. A fanatical sect, the Almohades, was spreading irresistibly over the plains of the Atlas. Austerity, purity, and cruelty, these were their fundamental messages. "They will be here before the Spaniards," Judah Halevi prophesied. "The Andalusian emirs, the great land-owners, and the merchants will welcome them with open arms. And then—let our Jewry beware. Woe betide us!" "This has happened before, with the Berber Almoravides," said my father. "There were some dead. There were some survivors. The Arabs' civilization is explosive; ours is retractile. In both cases these are reflexes for sur-vival. The Latins are cold, passionless rulers. We are caught be-tween the two. What can we do? Pray. Hope."

My father suddenly seemed to realize that I was still there. "You may go," he told me. I left the study without a word. Why, in fact, had I been summoned? Who had had anything to say to me, if not my own inner voice? I went into the garden to think over what I had heard. Above the rooftops was the spring night, with its stars, its odors, and the rustling of leaves. Swallows swooped down, drank from the fountain without slackening the speed of their flight, then bounced up again into the milky sky. An extraordinary exaltation was making my flesh tingle. There was a place where I was expected; there was a little niche carved out for me in the huge niche of the living; and everything that I possessed, whether tangi-ble or intangible, whether already achieved or to be achieved in the future, had received the order to move in that direction without delay. I had just discovered impatience.

I never saw Judah Halevi again. The next day, as I was passing his house, the emancipated Ottoman slave beckoned to me and handed me a big book, its cover all crinkled and cracked. This book has never left me since you saw it in my house in Fostat. I have let it be known that I wish to have it buried with me. My son, I think, will see that this is done.

What I had not known, and only learned later, was that Judah Halevi had come to bid farewell to my father. He was leaving Andalusia. He was leaving Spain. Accompanied by his last favorite, a sixteen-year-old houri, he was departing for the land of Israel, there to end his days. He made the journey by sea, narrowly escaping storms and pirates, and landed at the port of Ashkelon as the summer was drawing to its close. When he reached Mount Zion, with Jerusalem the Golden lying sun-drenched beneath his feet, he flung himself in ecstasy onto the ground, the tears running down his face. A passing Frankish horseman saw an old Jew in the middle of the road, lying in the dust and stones. Do you think he gently turned his steed aside in order to avoid the obstacle? No: he spurred it on, over the recumbent body. An iron-clad hoof shattered the skull offered up in communion with the nameless. This was, I suppose, a gallant soldier of Christ who was perhaps even in peace with his own soul. *Dieu le veult.* Those brains scattered in the dust were no doubt balm upon the wounds of the crucified Christ, an advance contribution for the salvation of the murderer. Priests had preached it, bishops confirmed it, the Pope vouched for it. Why should this Crusader of Love have hesitated to exterminate such vermin?

Thus ended Judah Halevi, whom some call Juda ha-Levi; scholar, aesthete, and libertine.

7

IT was a cock that was responsible for my friendship with my uncle Joad—a superb cock weighing at least six pounds, all bronzed and palpitating, with a high, triple, turgescent crest, and destined to become our Sabbath soup. I had never, until that day, associated the content of our plates with creatures of flesh and blood. All our food was spontaneously produced in Élisée's pans by a magic operation whose secret was hers alone. I don't know what unexpected obstacle had made it necessary for her to put the cock in my arms. She had tied its feet together with a long, thin cord, whose other end she knotted around my wrist.

I set off, not really understanding and yet understanding only too well, with the bundle of warm feathers pressed close to my chest, gazing fixedly at the round eye of the beautiful bird whose head was swaying to the rhythm of my steps. All the way, I murmured friendly words into its ruffled neck, but they had no effect on my anxiety. It was a hot day; I was perspiring. There were crowds on the riverbank, people and animals going upstream and downstream, women washing clothes, ragged children, merchants vociferating behind their gaping baskets. No one took any notice of me, trailing my shame. Did it occur to me to set the cock free? It's possible. But we were attached to each other. Even if I had managed to untie the knots, the cock would have been recaptured. Its fate was sealed. I was going with it to execution.

Uncle Joad's slaughterhouse was at the end of a blind alley on the outskirts of the Jewry, but it could be more easily reached by an ever open porch giving onto the towpath, which the animals came through. The paved courtyard felt sticky under my feet. Joad was rinsing it down with great gushes of water from a bucket when he caught sight of me. He was a stocky, vigorous fellow, all muscle, with red hair and stubbly cheeks. Older than my mother, he must have been just thirty or a little over. He immediately understood my distress, and reassured me. The whole purpose of the science of ritual slaughter was to minimize the necessary evil, and to operate according to strict rules which had been codified through centuries of usage to numb the sense of suffering.

Joad showed me his knives, whose blades were so sharp that they could cut through a plume in midair. The slightest notch in the steel made the tool unusable. He tested the blade on the back of his hand, made it bleed, and assured me that he had felt nothing. Rapidity, precision, and a perfect knowledge of the vital connections combined to some extent to justify the sacrifice; for while it is necessary to man's survival to feed on the animal he has nurtured, he is forbidden to transgress against it by making it suffer.

All the while talking to me in a calm voice, Joad had relieved me of the cock and was stroking its crop with his fingertips. Suddenly there was a long, heavy fluttering of wings, a flight of feathers, and a few spasmodic tugs against my wrist. A blackish pool was spreading at my feet. A few more convulsive movements in the feet, and it was all over; what was lying on the stone was no more than a piece of flabby meat that Joad picked up by the claws and felt the weight of, like the connoisseur he was. Then he blew into the feathers on its rump, to assess the thickness of the fat. "You see?" he said. "It'll make good soup, this rascal." I had a lump in my throat and couldn't answer. Of the movements that had deprived my beautiful bird of its life, I had seen nothing.

My aunt arrived with two or three little children clinging to her skirts, another in her swollen body. The glass of water and spoonful of jam she gave me did me good. "I've got a ram to do," said Joad. "Would you like to stay?" I didn't want to, and yet in a way I did.

The whole business made me rethink a great many ideas which I had accepted as immutable. A broad smile appeared on Joad's lips. "You'll come back," he said. "You have to know about these things if you're going to become a man."

I did, indeed, go back. I saw Joad implant a sort of banderilla in the throat of a lamb, and this banderilla was in actual fact a jet of blood flowing out of the animal, with its life. On the eve of one feast day, when the housewives had left, each one carrying her bundle of soup for the family, and when twilight was beginning to descend on the courtyard all covered in feathers, in which there stagnated the insipid stench that death invariably trails in its wake, I saw Joad, his arms lacquered up to the elbows and splashed all over with wasted life, standing there alone, as magnificent as Samson surrounded by the Philistines. I saw him once again strike down one of those black-coated bovines that seem to be dancing when they gambol in the pasturelands, and shivering calves who sucked at the air until their dying breath.

Of course it was horrifying, and more than once my stomach turned over, but I stood fast, fascinated by the irrevocable nature of what was taking place. A movement that was a mere nothing was sufficient to demolish the work of creation—which, perhaps, only hung by the thread of this mere nothing. Was Joad the devil, or was he the model of what I was going to become?

I knew from the very beginning that he was a simple, generous man, placid and pious, who loved animals dearly and who taught me to love them. In his naïve way he made me aware of the great natural cycles in which each species occupies its allotted place in order to be in equilibrium with the whole, the *upsurge* of the earth from which emanates and into which is absorbed everything that has matter and form. He said that he too was in his place, innocent of all the blood he shed, and useful to those who had appointed him to this position by virtue of what had been written: that man should have dominion over every living thing that moved upon the earth, for *it was good*.

He explained the parts of the bodies to me, and the parts of the carcasses after he had opened them. Thus I learned to distinguish the blood vessels—some of them firm and gaping, others flaccid and folded over; not to confuse the sheen of a nerve with the sheen of a tendon; to separate an aponeurosis from a muscle, an organ from its surroundings, the container from the contained. And I made the astonishing discovery that a chicken's leg is constructed in the same way as that of an ox or a man, and that despite the diversity of forms, the matter remained identical. At the age I then was—ten or twelve—this discovery was overwhelming.

One day Joad gave me a sheep's heart to dissect. I brought to light oddly contorted cavities, concealed channels, assortments of tangled-up pleats and bands, without the slightest idea of the hidden order of this construction. I found the same system in the heart of a duck as in the heart of a heifer. Joad didn't know how it functioned either. At first it beat, just like mine, in these animals' breasts, but then, once out of the breast, it became an ordinary piece of meat from which movement and sound had fled forever. I had imagined that I was exploring a certain mystery, but as the mystery deepened I began to discover the real depth of my ignorance.

I am not, nor have I ever been, given to sentimentality, and I have no recollection of having stopped, even at the height of my agitation, drinking the soup or eating the mutton stew that Élisée poured into my bowl; for I too saw that *it was good*. Like Joad, whose conscious accomplice I had become, I felt innocent. I saw myself as established in an order, an order itself established for all eternity, in which the earth belonged to the seed-yielding grass, the grass to the beasts of the earth to use for their nourishment, and the beasts to man, for him to kill and eat, and finally the earth belonged to man, that he might glorify God and enjoy him forever. This movement seemed to be laid down once and for all, like that of the spheres in the firmament, like that of the quarters of the moon, and *it was very good* to have eyes to see it and intelligence to recognize it; but this did not and could not be a part of the model of justice that had been given me and which I had made my own.

No doubt it was *very good* for man to eat mutton; was it *as good* for the sheep? Since they have never been able to express their opinion on this point, the problem was radically resolved before it was ever posed. My greatest trouble at that time was caused by the fact that I had no one to share it with. Joad suffered from no doubts as to his way of life. My father would have ridiculed me, and sent me back to the Scriptures. At the yeshiva, questions had to be publicly formulated; the class would have thought me a fool, and my answer would have been the swish of the master's cane. I was alone with my torment; I lost myself in it by day; I dreamed of it by night.

What if, instead of having made me what I was, Providence, of its own inscrutable will, had made me a sheep or a calf? Was it perhaps in order to discover an unexpected response from them that I had undertaken to search their hearts? The scent of murder that clung to the courtyard of the slaughterhouse, that fetid, sickly breath that assailed my nostrils the moment I reached the gate, how could I be certain that the victims didn't smell it too? There was not one who did not make a vague movement as if to try to escape, but what could they do against their fetters, against force, against what had been decided?

I saw the guards push Joad under the gallows, so as to hang him by the neck until he was dead; he too made only an imperceptible backward movement when he saw the scaffold, just a moment before he resigned himself. It may perhaps have been good for the Emir to put Joad to death; the whole of the Cordovan Jewry, including the victim, could well have done without that goodness. And I, a helpless onlooker, still a beardless youth, who loved my uncle like an older brother, I forced my eyelids to leave my eyes open, so as not to lose sight of the slightest spasm, because there may well have been an answer to a question in this death agony.

I hardly dared formulate this answer, but there was no doubt that it already existed in me. Whether the world had been created and molded, as our sages think, or whether it had always existed throughout all eternity, as the philosophers assert—and the major divergence of opinion of our century, and perhaps of all centuries, lies precisely in this dilemma—*it was not good*. The whole of my budding reason rebeled against the introduction of a value judgment. How could I acquiesce in this mark of divine self-satisfaction whose expression is an imposture? The wolf and the lamb will never lie down together, the gazelle can only count on the celerity of its legs to escape the hunger of the lion. The world was what it was, and I had much to learn to see it more clearly and to recognize some of the obscure forces which converge and diverge in torrents with neither beginning nor end.

The look from on high which had judged that it was *very good* —either it had seen nothing, or it wanted to take advantage of us. For I could not take it as *good* that man should have dominion over beast, the great over the small, the strong over the weak, the rich over the poor, one nation over another nation, one faith over another faith—and yet *that was so*, and no mighty wind of wrath ever blew to put an end to this abuse.

If we were to believe what was written, it was we who were responsible for this sin, and it was *not good* that man had been led into this temptation and then punished for succumbing to it. My personal temptation was to know; the origin, our sages said, of all the evil upon the earth. But ignorance could only be ignorant of evil, it could not combat it. For my part, I had convinced myself that it was necessary that evil should be combated. And thus I was very gradually entering into the circle of damnation.

No one around me had any idea of my anguish, with the possible exception of Joad, who guessed at it from the eddies on the surface. He couldn't do enough for me. I was the son of his dead sister, for whom he felt affection, as I was beginning to feel affection for my brother David. I was also the heir of the Maimons, who, as tradition had it, descended in direct line through Rabbi Hanassi from King David in person. In Joad's presence I felt invested with a princely quality, with him acting as my vassal. However pressing his business, he always had time to devote to me. He would take endless trouble to explain whatever I wanted to know, and he never spoke in the tone of haughty amusement that grown men so easily adopt with adolescents. For the first time I had encountered an adult who, in spite of his height, his strength, and his age, was not trying to dominate me and who respected me for what I was.

Even though he bore the name of a famous warrior chief, and daily caused rivers of blood to flow, he lived in a state of profound peace. Every day, after his unspeakable work, he purified himself with floods of water, and sat down in front of the Book, which he read from beginning to end every year. He knew the Torah by heart, and obeyed it to the letter. Unlike many of the working people of Cordova, he had a dazzling set of teeth. "It's the smell of the meat," he used to say, laughing heartily. Even when he had just washed, his powerful body smelled of perspiration, and his red hair of grease. He spoke slowly, pushing the words out with his killer's hands, and in this fashion formulated thoughts that were often profound.

About natural phenomena, with which he was at his ease; about animals, his companions, whose language he said he understood. Apart from the slaughterhouse, where he was born, and which he would leave to his firstborn son when the time came, he owned three hundred head of sheep which grazed on the slopes of the sierra, watched over by shepherds and dogs, and which he housed during the winter in the sheepfold adjoining the courtyard. Joad was comfortably off, and the allowance he made to my father caused him no hardship. No one who asked him for alms was ever sent away empty-handed. He had a penknife with twelve blades brought from Toledo especially for me: I still have it. Every time I visited them his wife made it her business to stuff me with delicacies, and if I occasionally had a little money at my disposal it was because Joad had slipped it into my pocket.

These visits were not made without causing some slight disturbance to my scholastic life; just occasionally I would fail to appear at the yeshiva, and by the same evening my father would have been informed of it. Deprived of liberty as I was, I considered it an insult not to be able to undertake the slightest action without having to justify myself. I waited for the storm; it didn't break. The first time I was simply treated to a more prolonged look; after that it was by deep sighs that my father expressed his displeasure. The slaughterhouse was closing its ranks. Once and for all he had decided that I was the ugly duckling in the swan's nest; my activities only half surprised him. One evening, however, as my absences that week had increased, he spoke to me:

"You keep walking around the house," he said, "but you never go into it. I am afraid that you may stay outside it all your life." I felt unusually calm as I answered him: "The Rabbi," I said, "speaks like the Book, through symbols, and it is through symbols that I shall try to explain myself. It is true that I am walking around something. What is a house? An enclosed space set apart from open space. I must first know and put to the test the objects I want to shut in with me, and they are scattered on all sides, in no sort of order, in the infinite. Shall I take this, or that? How can I be sure that I am not making a mistake? Is it preferable to go in one direction, rather than in another? Open space has no limits; a house is strictly limited; once all the furniture is in place it is almost impossible to change it. It is not through dissipation, Rabbi, that I divagate; it is through diligence. I do no evil and I want no evil. I seek it only to expel it from its haunts."

My father remained silent for a moment. "What you want to know," he finally said, "has already been written. Many eminent men before you have tested what it is right to take, and what it is right to leave. It is enough to follow their example. None of your thoughts can be new. All have been examined, weighed, and formulated, no error can have been perpetuated, such is the teaching, such is the house which is opened to you for your dwelling place, and yet you hesitate?"

His elbows on the table, my brother David kept turning his eyes from one to the other of us. Never had he heard so much talk of this sort during a meal. Élisée had frozen into a strange, expectant posture. "I do not deny," I said, "the profound virtues of our teaching. It is nearly five thousand years old; the world has changed, but it has not. From century to century it calls for thousands of pages of commentary, containing as it does so many obscurities, archaisms, and contradictions, referring as it does to conditions and events that have disappeared from the memory of the people and whose meaning is lost. But it is also our land of Israel that accompanies us everywhere, and everywhere renews our old covenant, and in that respect it is incomparable. We are the seed and the fruit of this teaching, and I make it mine according to the Law. Where is my sin if it assuages only half of my hunger and thirst for knowledge?"

My father was combing his beard with his fingers. Although troubled, he listened attentively. "What are your plans?" he finally said. My answer had had time to mature; it was ready. "My inclination, Rabbi, is toward profane teaching. I would like to learn mathematics, geometry, astronomy, and the natural sciences; logic and metaphysics; medicine and politics. Though my program has a beginning, it has no end." Slowly, my father bent his head. "On condition," he said, "that you do not touch these books on the Sabbath. Tomorrow I will find you someone who will teach you geometry and astronomy according to the rules." "Thank you, Rabbi," I said. "Thank you with all my heart. There is no need to look for anyone. I have already found my master."

I had the feeling that my father knew. No doubt he preferred not to talk about him.

8

W‌HEN I went to visit Uncle Joad I sometimes passed a
strange man on the riverbank. Tall, slender, his body encased from
neck to ankles in a tightly fitting white wool caftan which made
him look even taller, his turbaned head held very straight and his
eyelids half closed, his angular face emerging from a pitch-black,
flat collar beard—from a distance he looked like a walking birch
tree. Passers-by respectfully made way for him; some bowed a
greeting without ever receiving the slightest salutation in return. It
was quite clear that he was lost in his thoughts, this man who
walked with the supple, measured step of someone who knows who
he is and where he is going.

I made inquiries, and soon discovered his name, which in any case
was known to me: Muhammad Ibn Rushd.* Like me, he was a de-
scendant of one of the most ancient Cordovan families, and his father was the exact homologue of my father in the Moslem community: a judge, as his grandfather had been, and mine too. I learned
with amazement that he was barely ten years older than I, and that
he taught Koranic law and natural sciences at the university; at the
same time he was pursuing his medical and philosophical studies.
They said he slept only four hours a night, and that he had already
read all the books.

I leave it to you to imagine the fascination this personality immediately exercised over me. He was the incarnation in broad daylight
of the model I had been seeking in the shadows. I will not dwell on

* Averroës.

the excessive confusion and the self-centered gravity that is the natural concomitant of adolescence. When I saw him coming toward me from a distance my blood raced, my throat became dry, my legs gave way beneath me—all of which were signs of a profound disarray, the prelude to an imminent state of bliss. I leaned against one of the posts on the bank in order to observe him at my leisure, not even having the slightest hope that his veiled glance might one day fall in my direction. Never, it seemed to me, had I seen a nobler face, a prouder bearing, a more serene presence. The flow of his caftan revealed first one foot and then the other, shod in Cordovan thonged sandals, and it was only by this movement that the statue showed any sign of life. His arms remained crossed over his chest. A big diamond glistened on one of his fingers.

In the time it took to watch him go by I had shriveled up in my skin, unhappy to be so negligible, to be nothing, and yet determined to leap into the footsteps of his reputation and to surpass it, if possible, by reading all of the books myself before I was twenty. I leaped in imagination to a future which was fairly close, yet inaccessible. I could already see myself walking with hieratic step through the streets of my town, weighed down with all the secrets of the major initiations, while the pious, bowing low, stepped aside to let me pass. The insensate presumption of youth: stupid fatuity! I was swollen with envy, but did nothing; I saw myself as having arrived at my goal, but I remained where I was. I'll do it tomorrow, I told myself. Tomorrow I'll speak to Ibn Rushd, he'll take me by the hand and lead me. I had observed at which moments he passed by, and each time I went to all possible lengths to make my decision aleatory, dependent on fortuitous circumstances, which always refused me their complicity. The mule didn't lift its tail when I had counted up to ten, the pigeon didn't fly away from the post on which it had perched, the cloud shaped like a bull's head didn't move as I had hoped in front of the sun's disk.

There then followed quite a long period, a month, perhaps, or more, during which this prodigy didn't appear at all. I will draw a veil over my various states of mind which swung between amazement and panic, between all sorts of fears and peaks of hope. I had often thought that I was nothing but a lazy creature who was doing violence to his own nature, and that my father was not absolutely wrong to despise me. I hadn't been brought up to play games; the only ways I usually had of expressing myself were on the one hand my reveries and on the other hand my school work, with nothing in between the two. No doubt I wanted to possess knowledge, but I wanted it to come to me of its own free will; I didn't want to have to take it by force. It was already the fall, the wind was blowing hard along the banks of the river, when at last I recognized his silhouette from afar. I knew at once that this was the day. And it *was* the day.

I suddenly found that I had jumped in front of Ibn Rushd and barred his way. I observed that he smelled of amber, and this disappointed me. He contemplated me for a moment without surprise. "Peace be on thee," said he, having given a little cough in the hollow of his hand. "Peace be with thee," said I, in a strangulated voice. For long minutes we could find nothing to say to each other. According to the custom, it would have been unseemly of me to come to the point without preamble, and discourteous of him to question me about my reasons for disturbing him on his way. One of us was supposed to make a remark about the weather, to observe that the swallows had arrived early this season, so we were probably in for a hard winter. (I rather think this was he.) The answer to this was that Cordova had the advantage over Granada, where six months of winter alternated with six months of hell. (I rather think this was I.) After which we were allowed to smile amiably at each other. "I am the firstborn son of Maimon," I said. Ibn Rushd gave a little cough, covering his lips. "I know your father's name," he said. "He is a great judge." I immediately found the rejoinder. "My father is only a poor ignoramus in comparison with yours. Peace be on them."

Once again there was silence between us for long minutes. I got into a muddle with my words in a digression or Uncle Joad, the sacrificer of our commune, whom I sometimes visited in order to dissect hearts. For the first time since we had been face to face Ibn Rushd seemed interested.

"You dissect hearts? Why?" "To see. To learn. To understand what it's for, and how it works. There's a rapping spirit inside, which disappears when you open it. It seems very complicated." Brief squalls of wind raised swirls of dust and, toward the west, the sky was black with rain: it was coming from the sea. Ibn Rushd gave another little cough into his fingers and observed me in amusement from under his half-closed eyelids. "A rapping spirit?" he said. "What makes you think that? In actual fact it's very simple." "Everything is simple, when you know it. Whoever made hearts must have known. Our master, at school, often says that you can only know what you know how to make. I don't think he's right."

A heavy cart drawn by four oxen came straight at us. Ibn Rushd took me by the shoulder and pulled me out of the way. "How old are you?" he asked. I answered: "In less than a year I shall be admitted to the community of men." "You look older," he said. "Your master is not right. I shouldn't know how to make a heart. But I do know how it is made, what it is for, and how it works. It's written in Galen, and all the authors who came after him. And Galen could well have copied it from other books which have disappeared. Which were perhaps copies of even more ancient texts. The world is already very old, and it starts again every minute. Would you like me to explain it to you?" "I was going to ask you to, if you wouldn't mind." "What is mine," he said, "also belongs to my brother. But it might get you into trouble. Do you know that I am regarded as a *zendik*, a subversive, a freethinker? Some even say that I am ungodly. Your father would certainly not like you to spend much time in my company." "My father lives his own life. I have mine to live. In 'freethinker' there is freedom, and there is thought. Such a program would suit me perfectly." He gave a short laugh. "I like you, son of Maimon. I was the same at your age. And I haven't changed. Even though I am a miscreant, I say with the Prophet: 'Give food to those who hunger; give drink to those who thirst; give knowledge to those who hunger and thirst after knowledge.' I must go now. If you don't change your mind, come to the orange garden tomorrow after the second *çalat*.† I shall be waiting for you by the Palm Gate." "Our sages say the same thing. I shall be there." "Peace be on thee, Ben Maimon." "Peace be with thee, Ibn Rushd."

† The canonical prayer for the afternoon, between the moment when the shadow is as big as the object and the moment when it is twice as big as the object.

9

WHAT started for me that day was without doubt the happiest period of my life. This interim was to be short, for adversity was already gathering momentum, although as yet it was far from Cordova, far from my thoughts. Contrary to all expectations, the winter was mild, the spring early and gentle, the summer magnanimous; but why should I bother about the seasons? I felt like a sponge, stranded in a dried-up backwater, into which water had suddenly started flowing abundantly, and I was soaking it up voluptuously to the limit of my powers of absorption. Unknown forces were arising within me and pushing me out of the niche in which I had for so long been held back by my corporeal density. I went from surprise to surprise, from discovery to discovery, intoxicated with myself and with that part of the substance of the world which I was allowing to flow through me, without bothering about the unseemly things that this same world was producing in a never ending stream.

I think it unlikely that my infatuation would have left me in ignorance of the fact that Andalusia was disintegrating like badly mixed plaster. The plague appeared on the Málaga coast, made its way up to Antequera, jumped onto Cádiz and Seville. The gates of Cordova were closed and guarded, and while the epidemic lasted I, like everyone else, wore a garlic necklace under my shirt. This must have been the right recipe: we were spared. Near Almería the earth quaked, the mountain moved, and engulfed villages and outlying districts. There was a war between Granada and Jaén, with neither victor nor vanquished, only thousands of dead on either side. At Andújar, the Guadalquivir broke its banks and overran the plain over a distance of a three days' walk, carrying with it houses, people, herds and flocks. A hailstorm destroyed all the harvests in the province of Osuna, and famine cut savage swaths through the population. Further to the north, in Spanish territory, discord reigned between the princes, at the same time as they were proclaiming their furious intention of driving the infidel out of the peninsula. Still further away, the combined crusade of the King of France and the King of Germany was being brought to a standstill at Antioch, after having put the road from Byzantium to fire and sword.

But it was to the south that the heaviest clouds were gathering. Having seized the Maghreb, the Almohades, fanaticized by Ibn Tumert, had crossed the Strait in their masses and were camping at Jabal Tariq. Their rallying cry: *One God! One Faith! One Caliph!* was beginning to terrify the southern *taifas*.

But why should I worry about the convulsions of the earth's crust and the folly of the human vermin, about the wrath of the heavens and the treachery of the earth, about the fact that the marabout at the Roman bridge was prophesying that the end of the world was nigh, and sternly stigmatizing the licentiousness of the morals and the lapse from piety of the times? No tempest was moving toward Cordova, my town, which was satiated, calm, and curled up in its well-being, remote from the roads of misfortune. Never had the festivals been more joyous than that winter, never had there been such rare merchandise on display, more delectable fruit in the markets, more mules and horses in the streets, more animals in the stalls and sheepfolds; never had the oil from our olives been more unctuous, the wine from our vineyards more delectable to the gullet, the attire of the affluent more elegant and pleasant to regard. Money flowed as the water flowed down the hills; to some extent it splashed us all, even me, for my uncle Joad was filling my pockets more and more generously.

Why did I bother to listen even with only half an ear to the travelers' tales of the people who were once again being allowed into the town? All of a sudden there was a great stir in our house. People whose very existence I was unaware of, even though they were close relatives of my father, put into harbor there for a few days or a few weeks, en route for other horizons: silent men with nothing to do, peevish women, mischievous children, having salvaged nothing from their various disasters except their skin and some exiguous personal belongings. I remember the Rubens, who had suffered disaster in Almería, and who arrived practically naked. Two of their sons had been carried away in a river of mud; the third, a child of six or seven, when he thought he was alone used to sing a merry refrain celebrating the pleasures of travel. I paid very little attention, but many years later this tune and those words came back to haunt my memory, in which they still re-echo.

I especially remember my uncle Emmanuel, the clepsydra maker from Ceuta, who was fleeing the Almohades' persecution. He was a handsome old man, slow of speech and sparing of gesture, who looked grotesque in the too wide and too short caftan my father had given him to cover his nudity, for he had arrived in rags. But he brought with him one of his water clocks, which comprised all his worldly goods, and he made me a present of it. He would squat on the threshold of our house in the full sunlight, with a vacant look, his hands motionless and flat on his knees. Only the slight trembling of his beard made it apparent that he was muttering under his breath. I imagined Job thus, on his pallet bed, thanking the Lord. A shameful thought came into my mind every time I passed him: how can one be a refugee? What kind of panic is responsible for people allowing themselves to be reduced to this pathetic wandering state which inevitably exposes them to begging and charity, if not to dependence on the uncertain solidarity of the family or clan? Was it cowardice, or heroism? Obstinacy or renunciation? A defeat or a victory? The alternatives were too weighty and almost led me to make the kind of extreme judgments I mistrusted.

Why had Uncle Emmanuel fled the house of his fathers? Without a trace of emotion, he told me. The very morning the warriors of the new Caliph, Abd Al Mumen, seized Ceuta, and while the last defenders of the town were bleeding under the knives of the assailants, the qadi took the Jewish quarter by force and ordered its inhabitants either to become converts to Islam within the hour or to leave forthwith. Many chose the road to the mosque, where the Imam awaited them. Some protested, and were slaughtered on the spot. Emmanuel had neither wife nor child. He had walked out of his house, carrying his latest clepsydra, whose mechanism he was still adjusting. He bowed to the qadi, and left. A Pisan ship took him aboard and put him ashore at Algeciras. It took him more than two months, walking over the mountain paths, to reach Cordova. Once there, he was only waiting to get his strength back before going on further.

What did that mean: further on? I could imagine no concrete place outside Cordova. Emmanuel made a vague gesture with his hand. "Further on. Spain, perhaps. Or Provence? Naked came I out of my mother's womb, and naked shall I return. What happens between these two events is of no importance. I should have liked to have had a son to whom I would have passed on the secret of the clepsydras, which has come down to me from the family." "A son? You, Uncle Emmanuel?" This was how I discovered that he was not yet thirty-five years old. My astonishment wrung a smile from him. "I've only become old in the last three months," he said. "Before that you should have seen me." He stood up in front of me and tried out a dance step, which nearly made him fall flat on his face. With his too big, too short, threadbare caftan flapping against his calves, he looked like a scarecrow being blown about by the wind. I felt like laughing and crying at the same time.

"I don't understand," I said. "So much trouble, a life ruined, just to avoid the simulacrum of a conversion. It's out of all proportion." Panting, his emaciated face hidden in his hands, Emmanuel let himself fall back on his haunches again. After a moment he said: "There's nothing to understand." And, as I was turning away, he called me back. "Do you think I'm mad, boy? Say it right out—you think I'm mad. Your father, who is giving me board and lodging, thinks I'm mad. Since I left my house I sometimes even think I'm mad myself. Maybe I am? There were many who took the road to the mosque, with the Rabbi at their head. I neither blame them nor approve of them. It's their own business. There were some who didn't know what to choose, so the qadi made the choice for them, and this made me feel sick because it was a horrible sight. And then there were others, of whom I was one, who felt uncomfortable, and who preferred to leave everything behind and depart with a *no* of stone in their hearts. I am speaking for myself. I hesitated for a second, and then it was *no*. I'm not claiming that it was God himself who put this *no* in me, or that he owes me anything for this *no*. He has made a big clock; I used to make small ones: it isn't customary for people in the same trade to make presents to each other. The thing is that I am not very assiduous when it comes to piety. You never know where it's going to lead you, so the prudent man takes his precautions. I said my prayers morning and evening, just to be like the rest of my people, and I still say them, and I shall say them until my dying breath, because I, Emmanuel, am bound to this prayer by a pact whose origin is almost forgotten, not by a swindle. I have never been stupid or naïve enough to believe that God observes and weighs every one of us at every one of his instants. He must have more important things to do. I know how much trouble my small clocks gave me. What about the big one, then! A moment's distraction, and everything goes wrong. You can imagine how little difference it would have made to me to say *Allahou akbar* instead of *Adonai elohenou*, especially as the one is the translation of the other, and no one knows by now whether God doesn't understand Arabic better than Hebrew. And yet, I said *no*, and I left without a single backward look. And yet, I liked to laugh, I liked to sing, I liked my work, I was highly thought of in my district and in the whole town, I was short neither of the essentials nor of that part of the superfluous which makes everyday life sometimes good, and I was thinking at that very moment that the time had come for me to find myself a wife who would give me a son to whom I should have taught the secrets of the trade that came down to me from my father. Idle notions. And when I was brutally faced with the alternative of choosing between what I had that was good and what was confused in me, the result was a dreadful feeling of discomfort which elicited that terrible *no*, which I was powerless to resist. Do you think I didn't know that a forced conversion has not the slightest value and does not really commit anyone? God would have forgiven me, he forgives everything, that's his job. But I couldn't do it. To live from one day to the next as if I, Emmanuel, had never existed? To watch my words, my gestures, my whole way of life, and risk giving myself away at every moment? To hide when I wanted to say my prayers, and to be afraid of being discovered, or denounced, or slandered at the whim of an ill-disposed neighbor? To set up my bed among falsehood and mendacity, to realize that I was giving in to blackmail and to pretend to be satisfied with all this? I had to say *no*. As you see, my boy, I *am* mad . . ."

Emmanuel didn't regain his strength. Every day I observed that he was a little grayer, a little more brittle. He died before the end of the winter and was put in his coffin naked, as he had wished. His place didn't remain vacant for long. A refugee family of cousins from Tarifa took it, when it was still almost warm.

10

HAVE I deluded myself about my happiness in those days? I don't think so. Uncle Emmanuel had caused me some emotion, but it was something more like irritation that I felt toward the other outcasts. I considered them a nuisance, feckless, and arrogant under their false humility. No matter what my father did to make their exile bearable, they were always dissatisfied. It was never enough. Inaction gave the men's faces a mask of perpetual reproach. At home they had had this or that, which they suddenly missed terribly. The Tarifa cousins tried to turn their closer degree of relationship to account to give them the advantage over the Almería cousins; the strict equality of their condition revolted them. They counted every minute of their time at the fountain, they observed with an expert eye the content of their plates, they almost argued over the air they breathed, the water they drank. The wives competed in trying to manipulate Élisée, who protested with cries and tears. The brats infiltrated imperiously into every nook and cranny of the house, shamelessly laid our garden to waste, or, in pitched battles in the street, concluded the strife initiated by their parents.

My father acquiesced in all the claims, smoothed down some, consoled others, but he was not often to be seen. He had fixed up a study in the communal house next to the synagogue and only came home to eat, pray, and sleep. He retained this habit even when all the cousins had dispersed and there were no new invasions to be feared for the moment. Would the political situation in Andalusia become stabilized? This was to be hoped, though not really believed; this was to be believed, though not really hoped for. We didn't think about it too much, relying on the superstition that it is fear which opens the floodgates to misfortune. Cordova remained under the protection of the heavens, and under the wise government of her Moslem, Jewish, and Christian officials who had made of her a model city in which the art of living and the works of the spirit could flourish, a fortress against every evil spell. It was not surprising that she aroused covetous glances, waves of cupidity, to converge on her from the surrounding districts.

The Jewry liked the refugees, who confirmed the fact of Cordova's power and stability. It also liked to see them leave, so that its praises would be sung far and wide, and so as to make room for others. The migrants, for their part, paid moderate lip service to it, and secretly resented its need of their testimony. Thus, the situations were as well balanced as possible. It was only the marabout by the Roman bridge who prophesied all day long that the time was nigh.

As for me, I was keeping more elevated company, such as Pythagoras of Samos, Euclid of Alexandria, Ptolemy of Ptolemais, and also Alfarabi, Ghazali, and Saadia. I still put in an appearance at the talmudic school in the mornings, and had profited far more from its teaching since I had only been attending part-time. The new master no longer had cause to complain about me to my father, who had given up taking me to task. The day of my thirteenth birthday I had my bar mitzvah in the presence of the Council of the Sages and its prince, who, for the first time that I could remember, smiled at me and said a few friendly words. The son of the butcher's daughter was being admitted into the ranks of the initiated, and this integration deserved a certain indulgence.

For me, this change of mood came too late: a good-for-nothing I had been; a good-for-nothing I would remain. Throughout the ceremony my thoughts kept echoing Uncle Emmanuel's words: *a pact, not a swindle*. Moreover, if the preparation for this public enthronement had intimidated me, I found the actual performance dull, and after its completion I was disappointed. Nothing definite had been accomplished. The seal of God placed on my forehead left no mark. I felt neither more grown-up nor better; no change in quality or condition informed me that from now on I was a man among men. *They* were boisterously rejoicing at this fact. I was pummeled, congratulated, and kissed, after which everyone returned to his own pursuits, leaving me a little sad, a little at a loss. I knew better than anyone the length and bitterness of the path I still had to tread in order to become a man who would be open to the world, according to the model I had made for myself.

A strange attachment drew me toward Ibn Rushd, my master. He remained cold and distant, sometimes wounding when he indulged his sense of humor at my expense, but always prepared to guide and help me. I loved him. He had introduced me to the library, which immediately became my second, if not my first, home. Nothing on earth can be compared to it, not even the Ptolemaic library in Alexandria which was destroyed by fire. Can you imagine a more sumptuous sanctuary, as big as a whole town, comprising dozens of buildings separated by gardens where orange trees and cypresses grew, and where a labyrinth of ambulatories was scattered with fountains and shady places eminently suitable for meditation. Here the sound and fury of the world was stilled. Here survived all the poetry and science of every inhabited place. They reckoned that there were more than four hundred thousand books in wooden or leather coffers. A whole tribe of copyists, calligraphers, illuminators, translators, students, and readers worked here in silence, each absorbed in his own task, or dreams, or meditations. There was a saying current in those days: If you have a jewel to sell, go to Baghdad; a sword, to Seville; but if you want to part with a book, go to Cordova. For three centuries our city, at great expense and without haggling, had been collecting the most useful and the rarest manuscripts, and was taking the greatest pains to ensure their conservation. There were Egyptian papyri, Aramaic scrolls, texts of every conceivable kind: Sanskrit, Hebrew, Greek, Latin, Persian, Syriac,

Maghrebin, Andalusian, both originals and Arabic transcriptions and translations, in a light sleep and ready to be called back to life at the first appeal of the curious or the erudite. It is said that the Caliph Al Haqim maintained a whole army of emissaries all around the great inland sea to seek and buy the wherewithal to stock the library he had founded with the money bequeathed by one of his concubines, and that for some of his books he had paid as much as a hundred thousand piasters.

All this fortune could be mine; it was enough to want and to desire it, and I wanted and desired nothing else. The moment I was released from school I ran to the sanctuary to resume my reading where I had left off the previous day. Ibn Rushd had guided me in my first choices. He started me with geometry, mathematics, and astronomy, subjects which were fairly easy to fathom. Logic, medicine, and philosophy were to come later, but my impatience was too greedy, I threw myself into everything available, without method, annoyed that the days were so short, the hours so fleeting, the obscurities in the texts so numerous, and my powers so limited.

Twice a week, after the second çalat, I joined my young master in the orange garden of the mosque. The rim of Al Mansur's great fountain served us as both seat and table; in rainy weather we sought the protection of the peristyle. Ibn Rushd answered my questions, and explained what I found difficult or what in his opinion I had not understood properly. Sometimes he made me read poems by Motenabbi or Habib, or brought me elegant madrigals of his own composition. Sometimes other young people would come and form a circle around us; then the discussion turned to Aristotle, the mentor we all revered. Ibn Rushd knew the *Organon* by heart, and quoted whole pages of it without the slightest hesitation. Even though he didn't know enough Greek to study Aristotle in the original, he owned most of the Syriac translations and compared or criticized their merits or defects. He himself was preparing to write a vast commentary on Peripatetic thought. Could I tell you how much bliss I experienced as the disciple of such a master?

I didn't understand half of what was said, but I did understand that it had to be said because it was Truth itself that was speaking. When the conversation turned to philosophy, I could only keep quiet; even to be allowed to listen was an unmerited privilege. Ibn Rushd made a god of Aristotle. I made a god of Ibn Rushd. It took me many years of apprenticeship and thought before I was able, much later, to sort out what was theory and what verbiage. The real doctrine of the Stagirite is far from well-known to us; what we know of it comes from rough and ready transcriptions which themselves come from rough and ready translations, and many subtleties and nuances must have got lost along the way, or changed their meaning according to the whim of the copyist. In spite of so many uncertainties, Alexander's tutor dominated the intellects of our time. Aristotle, Ibn Rushd used to say, is the beginning and end of all knowledge. He laid the foundations of the most noble disciplines of the human spirit, and carried them to absolute perfection. Nothing can be removed from them, or added to them, without detracting from perfection itself. That all this should be combined in one single man was a strange and miraculous thing, and made him the equal of God.

My young master blasphemed, and well he knew it; and we who listened to him knew it too. But thunderbolts did not fall from the sky, the earth did not open to engulf the impertinent, the gentle breeze that wafted the leaves of the orange trees didn't turn into a tornado. For my part, I derived from these acts of effrontery the delicious thrill of a danger victoriously defied. It was possible, then, without any specific risk, to think and to say things of exceptional gravity which were forbidden by the faith of Ibn Rushd as they were by mine, and to place a man, even were he an Aristotle, on an equal footing with God, who has no equal. In some periods of history, such thoughts would have warranted death, for even if God did not kill, his zealots were perfectly capable of doing so in his stead.

Had I made a remark of this sort to him, my father would have banished me from his sight forevermore. And yet my young master dared. In the very shadow of the mosque! Was there not perfection in such an act of freedom? One evening, in bed, I was still thinking about it; it disturbed me so much that I couldn't get to sleep. And what if I too dared? I had no need to do violence to my feelings to believe that I saw Ibn Rushd also as the equal of God. I uttered the phrase several times in a loud and intelligible voice. And it was in the very act of committing the sin of blasphemy that I fell asleep. The next day Élisée stopped me as I went past her on my way to school. With an ironic smile she told me that I had been talking in my sleep and that it was time for me to know woman without delay.

11

ON the left bank of the river at the summit of a hillock overlooking the Roman bridge were three windmills. The largest was used to crush olives; the smallest, to grind corn; the middle-sized one, to press the must recently trodden underfoot. The owner of this industry was an obese Berber, who also hired out saddle and cart horses. As it often happened that the carters resented having to cool their heels at the doors of the mill, and seeing that this waiting period frequently resulted in brawls, the cunning miller-cum-horse dealer had added to his enterprises the operation of a public seraglio at the bottom of the knoll, in which the men could relax while awaiting their turn.

Similar establishments flourished on the outskirts of the town, but this particular one owed its reputation to a concatenation of circumstances. The carters' season lasted only for the time of the harvest. When the sails of the windmills stopped revolving, the golden youth of Cordova were pleased to take their walks in that direction. Whereupon the Berber renewed his staff and employed the services of a doctor who visited each morning and kept a strict watch on matters of hygiene. Vintage wines replaced the crude stuff drunk by the carters; silks and velvets swathed the couches covered with newly carded wool. For eight months of the year the mill seraglio was transformed into an annex of the university. There was not a future doctor but had undergone a probation period there in either an intermittent or a continuous fashion. Ibn Rushd made no secret of the fact that he frequented the place assiduously.

You know that our Scriptures are not sparing of their advice in this domain, and that our Sages point an accusing finger at the unworthy who delight in it. I myself have written much on this base exercise, and, in particular, a complete treatise on the use of sex, at the request of the sultan Alafdal. This book of mine is considered authoritative, and yet I did not put all my knowledge into it. I could say worse: my knowledge is not without confusion. I find myself forced to observe that my opinion is like a weathercock, now facing this way, now that, at the will of the wind. I agree with our doctors that it is degrading to think about this subject, contemptible to talk about it, and abject to surrender to it; at the same time I must accept the obvious fact that so many people, if not most, choose to dream of it, have the art of speaking of it, and find some elevation in indulging in it.

I am not forgetting Ibn Rushd, who agreed with Aristotle in declaring that this sense was our greatest shame, but added that he took infinite pleasure in being a shameful man. The paradox of the freethinker? In those days I was a shameful young man, but without the pleasure. Like new wine in old bottles, my sap was boiling in my shriveled flesh. Burning furuncles pierced my skin. I had nightmares whose subjects still made me shiver when I was wide awake. Élisée had guessed correctly: it was time, but time for what?—salvation or damnation? I read in the writings of our Sages: *If you feel excited toward concupiscence, and you suffer from it, hurry to the house of study, give yourself up to reading and meditation, question yourself and allow yourself to be questioned, and your suffering will undoubtedly disappear.* This I did, but the suffering did not disappear. I read elsewhere: *If you encounter desire, do not flee it; confront it; though it be of iron, it will melt; though of stone, it will shatter.* I confronted it and it neither melted nor shattered.

Was I to suspect that our Sages were lacking in wisdom? Or to accuse myself of applying their recipes badly? Had God or the demon invented this mechanism to put us to the test, or to torture us unendingly? The deeper I plunged into the dilemma, the less clearly I could see. It was not so much the thunderbolts of justice that alarmed me. My whole being rebelled against the ineluctable character of a process which I felt myself incapable of mastering. It was not a question of strengthening my will against whatever was aiming to destroy it; it was a question of becoming an angel—and that was out of the question. The beast had its word to say, and it said it without the slightest remorse. It had the best part, because it had awarded itself the last word.

To succumb to desire—that was not serious. But to succumb to our condition—that was terrifying. This defeat implied the recognition of our kinship with the animals, and threw doubt on everything we had been taught; it led to consequences whose implications went beyond even the most judicious understanding. Either the demon was behind it, in which case the essence of all nature was demonic; or the share allotted to us by the Law proceeded from an impossible wager which was lost in advance. The fly on the fly, the cock on the hen, the ram on the ewe; they, to give only a few examples, had not eaten of the fruit of the tree. A singular genesis, that which brought out of the dust in pairs everything that lives, except for man, who only received his companion to the detriment of his own substance and with the prohibition of appreciating her nudity.

Of the very long line of our theologians, I am the first to have systematically maintained that the word of God was cast in symbols, and that it is only the development of our intelligence that enables us to discover its meanings. This most uncomfortable doctrine has caused me many enmities, which scarcely surprised me. I have spent my life introducing a logical meaning into that which apparently had none. I have confronted allegory, tried to force it to discard its mask, taking it for granted that the Law could only be just and wise, and lead us to the heights. I have often had to recognize the insufficiency of my understanding, and cut short my proofs on the threshold of an impasse. This was my personal drama, of which no one had any knowledge. I fought with the revealed word in an attempt to impose truths which became diaphanous the moment I entertained the illusion of having them at my mercy. These were my good thoughts. What of my evil ones? Today, after a lifetime of reflection, I am profoundly aware of the fact that the theologian I tried to be, and the naturalist I became through force of circumstance, have never managed to coexist in peace.

There is what I believe. There is what I think. There is what I do. There is what I undergo. Yet I have only one envelope to offer to this diversity which inexorably pulls me in different directions. Through what senseless pride did I take it upon myself to teach my fellow men a science which, in myself, was only confusion? If you have read my books carefully you will have noticed how abundantly I employ the expression: *It is clear that* . . . If this phrase flows so frequently from my pen, it is precisely because nothing has ever been *clear*.

Would this be to acknowledge that I have cheated? Not that, either. I intoxicated myself with different lines of argument and these had a sufficiently sobering effect to introduce a certain sense of security into my drunken states. I maintained that the genetic sense is the lowest in the hierarchy of the senses, and physical enjoyment a mortal poison, in order to offer a reward to my obnubilated mind which refused to adapt itself to my body and persisted in taking refuge in a factitious immateriality; but I never doubted that mind and body were of the same essence, my entire work testifies to this. Why this lie, then? So that everyone should be free to find his own truth.

In my commentary on Aboth, in my treatise on the dietary laws, in numerous passages of the Moreh,* you can read many final condemnations of this impulse which inclines man toward woman's nakedness, and the satisfaction he derives from it. I had the honesty to add that this exercise is not too harmful to young people, and that it

* TRANSLATOR'S NOTE: The Moreh Nebuchim: Maimonides' *Guide for the Perplexed*.

was less dangerous to keep habits than to break them. In this way the door remains open to nature, but closed to excess.

Forgive me this digression: It has not led me away from my subject. Today, at more than sixty-five years old, I am free of these emotions, or almost so. I am able to regard the work from a distance, and explain my ideas on it without passion. How could I have discovered this detachment at the age when my voice was breaking? My mind would have been too willing to follow the exigencies of my flesh had not my fear of the irremediable held me back. On occasions I imposed puerile mortifications on myself, as for instance remaining seated all day long without leaning back, or retaining my urine until I could bear it no longer, or even exposing my hand to the flame of the lamp, which rewarded me with a smell of scorched horn. The only benefit I derived from all this was the conviction of my weakness. The Beast was jibbing; and if it allowed itself to be put to sleep, it was only in order to reawaken immediately, more exigent and more imperious. I felt lost, yet not too distressed by my perdition. The Beast was betting on a certainty; to resist it was assuredly a greater folly than to yield to it. The idea that it was possible to make an ally of it had not yet crossed my mind. Day after day my weariness of this hopeless and inglorious combat made headway against my fears. And the day came when I had to acknowledge defeat.

One evening, then, as the discussion in the patio of the orange trees was languishing and coming to an abrupt end, I followed Ibn Rushd and a few others to the mill seraglio. I was expecting to discover Gehenna, but what I found was rather a naïve replica of Eden: a luxuriant garden, filtered scintillations from photophores, clinging perfumes, and velvety quietude. We were served countless glasses of Málaga wine. My young master and some of his pupils, suddenly in great spirits, recited poems of a tumultuous lyricism. Music, song, and dance all merged together in the flow of the hours. It was just gay enough not to be sickening, and just indistinct enough not to be vulgar. Before the night ended a barely nubile young slave, smooth and satiny as a pebble burnished by the river, gently helped me over the threshold. By the time I had become aware of it, it was already in the past.

What could I tell you of all this that you do not already know, so common is this adventure? That I had regained my liberty, perhaps. Peace, and not only that of the body, but also that of the soul, reconquered at the price of the Fall. No more need to hurry to the house of study; I could go there now with a light step, not to stupefy myself, but to gain deeper knowledge. No more need to mortify my flesh; on the contrary, I was grateful to it, rich as it was in the creative force whose ascent rendered vile only what was already vile, but ennobled what was noble. Sin is what troubles the soul; my soul survived the test in a pure, limpid state, washed clean of all its accumulated stains. I felt neither triumphant nor defeated. I felt different, quite new in a renovated envelope, as if I had just, by my own efforts, given birth to myself.

The dawn came, with its concomitants of cold and fatigue. Sleepy and silent we made our way home in some disarray. I clung to Ibn Rushd, so much did I need his warmth and fraternity. On the Roman bridge the marabout suddenly appeared out of his stony hole, a pallid specter in the pallid light of the windy morning. I had never found him so alarming: toothless mouth, half his head and half his jaw shaved down to the bone, limping with one bare foot, the other tied up in a straw casing, his ragged shirt flapping around his emaciated body. "Wretched philosophers!" he exclaimed, pointing an avenging finger up to the sky. "Profligates! Degenerates! When the earth quakes with its earthquakes, and when it rids itself of all that lies heavy upon it, he who has done an atom of good will see it, and he who has done an atom of evil will see it likewise. The day of judgment is at hand! The sword is already poised to cut you off in the midst of your turpitude! Terrible will be the anger of the Lord!" In the ordinary way, a small coin was sufficient to coax him into silence. None of us thought to produce one, and we hurried by. For a long time the shrill voice of the marabout pursued us with imprecations and insults.

When I arrived home, the black look of my father was guarding the threshold, *like the sword of fire that turned this way and that,* as it is written. This was the first time that I hadn't slept in my own bed, and my father had sat up waiting for me. He seemed not so much angry as distressed. "You only came into the world," he said, "for the base things of life. Go away; I no longer recognize you." Whereupon he stepped aside and let me enter. Élisée gave me a hot drink, led me to my bed, and tucked me in. "Go to sleep, young man!" she said gently. "When you are rested the old grumbler will be in a better mood, I can guarantee that." In spite of my fatigue it was a long time before I fell asleep. Surreptitiously, the silence of my room entered into me, and the smell of fresh wax polish and, one after the other, all the familiar surrounding objects, and even the walls moved together to encircle me, but all this magic had no more power against the decision that I had just irrevocably taken: to leave my father's house as soon as I awoke.

12

To leave. Without delay, without compromise, and without return. You know that I have always opposed astrology, that bastard speculation which imposes on the credulity of the simpleminded. But I must admit that those born in the spring have a tendency to act on hasty decisions which may be irresponsible and lead to extremes, and that this impetuosity is my basic characteristic. I had made a decision but without any project in mind; it was purely negative. I had to break my bonds, and if Cordova was included in this rupture, then so be it. Where I should go, what I would do, I had not the slightest idea, but this was of no importance. To go away—that was all that mattered.

It was still dark when I awoke. I realized the need to take certain possessions: an overcoat, because autumn was approaching; a blanket, perhaps; a knife, certainly; my prayer shawl and phylacteries, and the book by Ibn Sina that I had been given by Judah Halevi.

While I was fumbling about trying to squeeze these objects into a bundle, a dim light appeared in the door to my room, and shadows jumped up and down on the wall. With small, muffled footsteps, Élisée came up to me. The wick of her candle was smoking and it looked as if the flame might go out, as the hand which carried it was shaking so. I had stopped tying the little cord. I was afraid the hunchback would start screaming. "Keep quiet!" I entreated her in a whisper, when she was close enough. Sunk down between her shoulders, Élisée's yellow face was twitching all over. "You're going away?" she asked, in a barely audible voice. Reassured by this sign of complicity, I acquiesced. "And where are you going?" A vague gesture, to indicate that the world was a big place. "Will you come back?" I hadn't yet considered this. "I expect so." "When?" "One day: soon, perhaps. Later, certainly." Élisée wedged the candle end into the slot in the table. "Go and kiss your brother," she said. "Don't wake him up. Just look at him. And, if you can, kiss him."

She opened the door without a sound, picked up the candle again, and preceded me. I understood too late that the hunchback was setting a trap for me. The open mouth with its distended lips, the curly head, were caught in the flickering gleam. A lump came into my throat, and tears came into my eyes. Little King David. I had been so entirely concentrating on my own affairs that I had forgotten him. Long, silky eyelashes were shadowed on his cheeks, and sleep gave him a jaunty look that I had never seen on his face. He was sleeping like all children do, sprawled on his back, having thrown off his covers, the slit in his nightshirt widening with the pressure of his regular breathing. A few beads of perspiration had formed at the corners of his nostrils. Six or seven years old? I wasn't exactly sure. He had already been going to school for several years, to the same master whose cane hurt so badly.

Élisée replaced the covers over the naked chest. "Kiss him!" she whispered to me. I couldn't; if I kissed my brother I would not be able to leave. From the next bedroom, whose door was ajar, came bubbling snores like the deep gurgling of a well. Poor David! Between a too old father and an infantile hunchback, who would be able to help the child find his way in life unless it was I, his elder brother, who had been helped by chance? Just as brusquely as I had made my decision to leave immediately, it became obvious to me that I would have to return very soon. I had no right to break this bond, however light the knot that held it together.

"Go on, kiss him," Élisée hissed at me again, accompanying her injunction with a rough push in his direction. I shook my head obstinately. The ruse was too obvious to deceive me. I won't be away for long, I thought; just a few months; a year at the most, and the

person who comes back will not be like the one who is going away
—a branch broken off from the trunk and floating between two
streams; I shall have grown my own roots. I stretched out a hand
and ran two fingers over one of the unruly curls falling over my
brother's forehead. I'll see you soon, David. I'll try to remember
that you may need me. I couldn't stand it any longer, and rushed
out of the room.

Élisée followed me with her hurried little steps. In the patio she
caught me by the arm. "I've put some water on to heat," she said.
"I'll make you some tea; at least you won't leave here with an
empty stomach. And anyway—what's the hurry? At least wait until
dawn." "The base things of life are sticking to my skin," I said, raising my voice. "I don't want anything, thank you." Élisée struck
herself on the forehead as if she had suddenly had an inspiration.
"And what about money—have you any?" My silence was as good
as an answer. "Even so, you'll need a little. Wait, don't move!
Whatever you do, don't move! Promise?" She disappeared but soon
came back, panting, and waving a leather purse which she insisted
on tying around my neck, while I was fixing my bundle on my
shoulder. "You won't find it too much," she said. "And what about
your news? Will you send me news of you? Swear that you'll let
me hear from you!" For me, the most difficult moment was past.
Now all I had to do was take the first step. "How can I send you
news of me, Élisée? You can't read." She clung to me once again,
her arms around my neck. "There are always plenty of people coming and going. If you meet any of them who have to pass through
Cordova, tell them. Do you swear?" "I swear," I said. I had to undo,
one by one, her spider's fingers, to free myself. As I was hurrying
down the darkness in the corridor, my foot stumbled yet again on
the loose tile. This was the second sign my house had made to me to
remind me of my duties. A child, and a stone. That was all I needed
to make me already begin to feel homesick.

You couldn't see two steps in front of you, the night was so dark.
Half a century has passed since then, and so many more memorable

events have occurred, but that young man groping his way through the dark, deserted street—I still seem to feel his heart beating down to the tips of my fingers. Even if you had put him to the torture he would not have admitted to being afraid, and yet the fear in him was as immense as the unknown into which he was voluptuously penetrating. Fear that behind me the house might raise the alarm and recapture me, that the city should suddenly produce waves to make it impossible for me to pass over dry land, that the desert to be crossed should be too wide, the liberty to be conquered too well-defended, that this flight should end in a failure that would contain the failure of my whole existence. Fear without reason and without content, but cold, lucid, stretched to breaking point, and to the point of breaking me with it, between a refusal and an appeal.

No light, no voice, came to my aid. The steps I was taking were no recompense for the step I had just taken. Yes, though, for it was to the memory of my legs that I owed the fact of finding myself on the towpath leading to my uncle's slaughterhouse, and I immediately understood that I could not leave Cordova without having spoken to Joad. And to Ibn Rushd. Without needing to give them any explanation, or to ask their help, I was certain of being understood and helped by them. Thus I allowed myself a respite which might perhaps contain the wherewithal to temper the folly of my escapade.

On my right, the river water was lapping against the hollows in the bank and the wind was blowing low in the bushes. Not a star in the sky. I dragged my feet along the ground so as not to come up against an obstacle that might trip me. In front of me the grass occasionally rustled: a rat or a grass snake disturbed by my approach. This riverbank, so pleasant and full of animation during the day, was sinister now. At one moment I thought I had made a mistake and gone too far, the way seemed so long. It was by smell that I finally recognized the slaughterhouse yard. The gate was barred on the inside but there was a passage through the wall, which I took. Like whiplashes the dogs threw themselves on me; they recognized me before it was too late and escorted me, wagging their tails. I hadn't the slightest idea of the time. The stable door was fastened only by a latch. There was an acrid warmth inside, and things were stirring in the depths. I managed to find a corner with dry straw. My head on my bundle, I fell asleep again.

13

"WELL, yes," said Joad. "You may be right. Or you may not be right. Who can tell? You're the right age, after all, to see something of the world. I too, when I was thirteen or fourteen, went to have a look elsewhere. There are other rivers, other towns, and it's incredible how everywhere else there are people just like you. When you've had enough of traipsing about on the dusty roads you will be quite pleased to come home, I can guarantee that. Your father is a just and good man, but he thinks no little of himself. If he really is of royal blood, as they say, how much of it is left after forty-seven generations in the Diaspora? Barely more than one drop or two. And how can you recognize that a single drop of blood is royal? In any case, blood is putrescence. I, Joad, know what I'm talking about. A scholar, true; royal, maybe; a martinet, certainly. Anyone who can't do anything with his ten fingers makes no more impression on me than a fly. It's with their hands that men make their salvation, not with their heads. Mind you, I'm not saying anything against your father. I'm talking in general terms. I'm sure that his pride will suffer when it is known in the town that the firstborn Maimon son has run away like a thief in the night, and that he has gone to seek his fortune. It will do him good to gnash his teeth a little in shame. He'll be even happier than you when you come home safe and sound, without having fallen. Because you won't do anything dishonest, I have confidence in you. It makes me laugh when I think how he will sweat royal blood. He won't show it, but that's what he'll do, and it will be a good lesson for him. I've been expecting something like this to happen for a long time. Now it has happened, and it's only fair. The fact remains that you aren't only the son of that one drop; you also received a good five liters of blood from my sister, and we are decent folk. No later than this afternoon I shall have a letter of credit drawn up which you will be able to negotiate in any town in Andalusia, and even in the countries of the Spaniards or the Tsarfats,* if it took your fancy to visit them. Right! Don't say anything! You don't like the idea? Take the letter, just the same. In the first place, I'm not giving you alms: it's yours by right. And then—I'm not encouraging you to throw the money down the drain. It's too difficult to earn. And if you manage to get by without touching it, so much the better. An educated boy like you can find employment wherever he goes. If that's what you want to prove to yourself, you can consider that it's already proved. Don't forget that we are a big family, and that you are Ben Maimon of Cordova. With a passport like that anyone can go right around the world without ever getting into trouble. But it's better to have a spare wheel to one's carriage. You never know what may happen. And it looks as if something is going to happen before long. The last news we had was that the Almohades have launched a spearhead against the *taifa* of Ronda. You may say: And what of it? What will come of it is that they will spend the winter there, but when the spring comes they will push on in wedge formation to Osuna and Écija. What they are interested in is Cordova, and maybe also Toledo. Are you thinking that they won't dare? That the Emir of Cordova has a hundred thousand men-at-arms at his disposal? In the first place, they *will* dare, because they have landed more than five hundred thousand horsemen from the Maghreb, all as excited as monkeys in rut and as cunning as hyenas. And in the second place, because the Emir's army is rubbish: one half of it consists of obese mercenaries, the other half of emaciated slaves. When the Almohades reach the river, both obese and emaciated will disintegrate like a herd of donkeys before a lion. And their commanding officers

* TRANSLATOR'S NOTE: The French.

are even worse. There is more than one among them who openly deplores the decline of morals, the ease with which those who already have money can gain more, the decline of faith, and, above all, the corruption brought about by philosophy. What the leaders of these troops long for is a hard, strong hand. The Almohades supply it, under their horses' hoofs. One God. One Faith. One Caliph. Haven't you noticed that these graffiti are spreading in the Arab part of the town? I can imagine only too well what is going to happen. The head of the army will open its arms, the body of the army will open its legs, the Emir will have himself transported to Granada, and then to Almería, whence he will take ship for the Levant, and *we*—we shall be left with the fanatics. Do you think I'm exaggerating? I only wish you were right. What do I know about it? We shall simply have to take what comes. You know that people who suffer from rheumatism can feel a storm brewing. Personally, I am suffering from Judaism; I can feel persecution brewing. We have been here in peace and tranquillity for too long. You may perhaps have a drop of the blood of kings circulating in your veins? Circulating in mine there is assuredly a pint of the blood of the prophets. Nothing is easier than to foresee the future: it's enough to announce catastrophes and calamities—they are smoldering like fire under the earth, and are never far away. You say that such times are past? That the world has entered into an era of intelligence? That Cordova is a city that is far too civilized to return to barbarity? That the men of all the communities have come to know, to accept, and to appreciate each other? There is something in that. If stupidity and savagery are not natural states, Cordova still has a chance. What God, up there, has decided for us, he alone knows. If he is preparing one of those tests for us of which he alone holds the secret, I, Joad, shall do my utmost to suffer it with dignity. I've said enough! Go and brush your hair, it's full of straw. My wife will give you something to eat. As for me, I can't wait to get to town. I have things to do there."

14

IBN RUSHD showed not the slightest surprise when I announced my departure. In spite of the difference in age and status, our relationship had very soon become one of confidence and friendship. Seeing us strolling about together, no one would have suspected our respective roles of master and pupil. The past year had leavened me. I was half a head taller than my father, and I was within an inch of the height of Ibn Rushd, who towered over the average Cordovan. Without boasting, I was aware that I had made such rapid progress in the sciences that it was sometimes my opinion that prevailed in our discussions. He never showed the slightest resentment if I argued against him and turned out to be right; on the contrary, in such a case he expressed a satisfaction which did not stem merely from courtesy; it was more as if I had honored him by having remembered the *Almagest* better than he.

When he praised me to his other students I was never quite sure that I could tell when he was being ironic and when straightforward. Perhaps he didn't mean a word of it? He was a man of sun and sand. An extreme formalist, he seemed unattached to any form, and his language, which was of a rather haughty elegance, might have meant anything either haughty or elegant, but its meaning, after all, remained unimportant. The Word had no more consistency than a sand dune blown about on the riverbank at the mercy of the winds.

In exchange for the help he gave me, he had asked me to teach him the science of the Talmud, in which he was much interested.

Thus the master became the pupil, and the pupil the master, which to a certain extent equalized our relationship, but this may simply have been his way of relieving me of my burden of gratitude. Whatever may have been the reason for his behavior, I was passionately attached to him. Sometimes I would take umbrage when I felt he was neglecting me. I wanted to be as important to him as he was to me; at these moments, by a humorous word or a pat on the shoulder he would put me back in my place—which was that of a young man of fourteen in relation to a man of twenty-three.

He was writing a dissertation on Aristotle's physics, which made his prestige unassailable, but he spoke of his work with humility and discretion, like someone who is not at all sure of himself, and this made him accessible in spite of everything. Whereas my character inclined me toward clear-cut patterns of behavior, his development was all in nuances. It would have been difficult to bring together two more dissimilar beings than we; nevertheless, we did resemble each other. We were, and I can say this although he was a heretical Moslem and I a respectful Jew haunted by doubt, in the same vein. I called him Master; he called me Brother; there really was mastership and fraternity of spirit between us. Some element of deliberation and stiffness made me seem older than my age, while insouciance and a certain affectation made Ibn Rushd seem younger than he was. At a distance we could be taken for twins; close up, we could feel that we were equals. He had already traveled in Spain. How could he be surprised by my project?

"Be sure to go to Toledo," he told me. "I know a pupil of Ibn Ferrizuel's there: he dissects corpses in secret. You'll certainly be interested in that. You might even be useful to him with your skill with the lancet. Galen's treatise on anatomy is chock-full of faults. Everything must be relearned; everything must be rediscovered." And, while he was talking to me, I knew that I would go straight to Toledo, and that I would stay there as long as was necessary. He himself, Ibn Rushd, was thinking of going there toward the middle of the winter. So we should meet in Toledo. "Don't let yourself be distracted by pleasures," he went on. "Intelligence is like clay; it must be kneaded until your strength is exhausted if you want the vase to be a success. Don't forget that the path you have chosen is long and difficult; it is also dangerous. Two powers govern the world: the one that produces strength, and the one that produces the spirit. They will never become allies. It is a fight to the death between them. So you must realize that you are a target, and that you may have to pay dearly for the side you have chosen. When the earth is peopled with scholars, we shall have won; not before. Be prudent, Brother. Neither show your purse, nor your knowledge, to a casual acquaintance. And never stop learning. A man's entire life is barely enough."

We were strolling with measured tread around the fountain. The orange trees were already heavy with fruit. Through the Gate of the Palms, which was wide open, the gradually diminishing light was reflected against the forest of little columns and the tracery of the arcades leading to the infinite depths, which offered to the eye one of the most beautiful assemblages in the world. The night wind had swept the sky clean. The swallows were bouncing up and down like balls. How sweet it was to be alive, that late afternoon, in Cordova, in that serene moment when two friends gave each other the pleasure of halting time! "When are you leaving?" Ibn Rushd asked me. "Tomorrow, at first light," I said. He bowed, his two hands crossed over his lips. "I wish you a good journey, Brother. Peace be on you." "Peace be with you, Master. I hope to see you soon."

15

IT took me nearly a month to reach Toledo, walking over country and mountain paths, through fields and woods. There was no demarcation line between Moslem Spain and Christian Spain, unless it was the profound void of a landscape from which human activity had withdrawn. Several days sometimes went by in the most complete solitude, without a single village appearing on the horizon; there was nothing but ruined and abandoned houses and the heavy silence of cemeteries. Here and there a home still stood among the debris, but the people had barricaded themselves in and let loose their dogs. I had great trouble in finding any food other than in abandoned orchards, which provided a safer shelter than walls without a roof.

Once I passed a caravan of Arab horsemen; one of them gave me a piece of bread and promised to go and see Élisée. Another time a peasant forgot his scruples and took me in for two nights. For four centuries the Orient and the Occident had been disputing this scorched earth, abandoned now to desolation. People still killed each other there in sudden futile fits, without anyone gaining the slightest advantage. On all the distant promontories, in no sort of order, stood watchtowers: when they were square, made of pink bricks, and crenellated at their crown, they were called *ribats*, and were Arab; when they were round, made of bluish stone, and perforated with loopholes, they were called *castillos*, and they were Spanish. Some were only a stone's throw apart, on hillocks separated by a narrow ravine, like two cocks waiting to hurl themselves on each other, Imam against Bishop, Duke against Emir, but the only living things I saw as I approached their battered doors were brambles and flies.

If a single God had made the world, with what rage he was un-making it—and without achieving his end! He was reducing humanity to a state where it could neither quite live nor quite die! How oppressive it was to breathe the air of a dead village, a field overgrown by weeds, the carcass of a horse besieged by vultures, a charred forest! If God knows, is he God? And if he doesn't know, is he God? Ibn Rushd used to speak of imposture, and I used to shiver when I heard him. On the way to Toledo I shivered at what I saw. When my discouragement and sadness would allow me to go no further, I sank to the ground at the foot of a tree away from the path and read Ibn Sina. I knew almost the whole of his *Canon* by heart. If there was anything we could do for ourselves in this world, it was to assume responsibility for some part of human suffering, and combat it. It was the only kind of war that made any sort of sense.

One morning, as I was hastening toward a stream for a drink, I fell and sprained my ankle. I stayed there several hours, unable to walk. Toward evening I heard voices in the undergrowth: two Capuchin friars, looking for mushrooms. They supported me as far as Calatrava, which fortunately was not far. The fortress frequently changed hands; at that time it had been Spanish for a year or two and an order of soldier-monks occupied the alcazaba erected by the Arabs. They wanted to know whether I was a refugee. I proudly declared that I was not. For obvious reasons, everything coming from the south was suspect. To be a refugee would have attenuated the offense. But even as a stratagem, I found it repugnant to claim a status that was not mine.

Among the monks were several converts, one of whom, now calling himself Father Solomon Gaddhafi, was of Andalusian origin. My father's name was known to him and in a sort of way he stood guarantee for me. I was well treated, and stayed several days in the monastery, long enough to recover from my fall. Father Gaddhafi treated my ankle with an embrocation whose secret, he told me, he had been given by a Chinese. The effect on the swelling and the pain was so rapid that I found myself insisting on knowing the composition of the remedy. The Father took a lot of persuading but finally gave in: it was a decoction of flowers and poppy leaves, evaporated over a slow fire, and then mixed with oil of sesame. I owe to this recipe some of my most spectacular successes with sprains.

The Father also gave me a great deal of other information. About conversion, in the first place. He had the profound conviction that the God of Israel no longer loved his people. The covenant had been made in a one-way direction; time and events had emptied it of its substance. How could one persist, against so many proofs of abandonment? To bear the burden was nothing; never to know rest was nothing; to expose one's throat to sacrifice was nothing. There was no longer any place for hope in the world. He, Solomon Gaddhafi, had found that he could no longer continue to nourish himself on parables alone, whose only merit was to hide reality from him. The reality was that God was still hesitating to make his choice between the two great bands of his faithful, but that many signs indicated that his decision was imminent. In the East, as in the West, the cross was triumphing over the crescent. As for the star, it was now no more than a faint glimmer of light on the point of going out.

No one and nothing had put any pressure on him, the Father, to become a convert, unless it was his awareness that a profound change was taking place in history. The King of Castile, Ferdinand, the third of that name, was a generous and tolerant prince. The Jews were made welcome in Toledo. Their craftsmanship and commerce contributed to the wealth of the kingdom. Some occupied high-ranking positions in the army and the administration, and one of the intimates of the King, the Minister of the Treasury, was none other than Judah Ibn Ezra, a nephew of Moses Ibn Ezra, who taught philosophy at Cordova. As for him, Solomon Gaddhafi, he had been ordered to assist in the transfer of refugees to Toledo. The Jewry there counted no less than twelve thousand souls, and it was the monarch's wish that it should be increased. "Good Christian seed," said the Father. "Sooner or later they will all recognize where the truth lies." "Don't you rather mean where their interest lies?" I asked. "Interest? Truth? They're the same thing," Gaddhafi replied dryly. "What matters is to serve God, whether we speak to him in Hebrew, in Arabic, or in Latin. There's no doubt that it's Latin he understands the best. It would be a sin to speak to him in a language he no longer understands. So be it!"

When I was on the point of leaving for the north, the Father made me a present of a flask of his embrocation and gave me a sack full of victuals and several letters of recommendation to eminent personages in Toledo. "Go, my son," said he, embracing me. "The future lies in a Christian Spain. The Moors will go back to the desert, which they should never have left. The Lord will stretch forth his mighty hand and strike them with his righteous judgments. In his name and with his aid, the Christian princes will purge the peninsula of them, and we shall strip them of their riches, and of their lives, to punish them for their obdurate caprices. Cordova too will be Spanish, and Granada, and all Andalusia. Think, my son, of where your place is. Love God, and God will love you."

The Father accompanied me along the path that wound around outside the fortress. He had been very good to me. I owed it to him to tell him what I thought. "My place? It is on the earth, which bears fruits and seeds, among men made like me. I don't know whether the covenant has been broken, as you say, but I do know that I will never agree to replace it by a bargain. If I love God, it is for the sake of loving him, not to trade with his love; and if God loves me, he who is all love, what need has he of my love? You see, Father, and I believe the same applies to almost all of us—no one taught me to love God. I was taught to fear him. My childhood has been a long journey through fear. This started with my father, the

inflexible guardian of our Law, and it continued with the books full
of remonstrances, warnings, and threats. The heavens contained
nothing but thunder and lightning. Try, I entreat you, to remember
the weight of all this on a child's heart. He doesn't die of it, true;
there are many other occasions for him to die. But he comes out of
it either broken or a cheat; either a sheep or a wolf. But fortune has
granted me her favor and protected me on all sides, and I have freed
myself from fear. He who roars and demands vengeance, he who
spreads suffering and injustice, he who forsakes and abandons—he is
not my God. I put him to the test, and he cracked. He cracked
here, in my chest, and I have let the pieces fall by the wayside. And
he who made the spheres, and the moon, and the creatures that take
root or move under the moon, he who in peace and justice could be
my God—him I have not yet learned to love with all my heart. I am
in a sort of halfway house; I have left fear behind me but have not
yet arrived at love. At this moment, I feel free. I am going to
Toledo—but where is my soul going? It has three choices: to
remain free, to fall back into fear, or to escape into love. I don't
know, I really don't know, Father, which choice my soul will make.
If I were to give it some advice, I would recommend it to remain
free. It is only if I am free that I can aspire to any self-respect; unless I am free I shall be nothing but a manipulated object or a
shameful slave. No, Father, I want no other place than that which is
natural to my status, even if it were a thousand times more advantageous; I do not wish to love God in exchange for his love. The covenant between the people of Israel and the creator of all things cannot be broken; since at least one of the contracting parties is eternal,
the engagement is valid for all eternity. As in a mathematical equation, when one of the terms has the value of infinity, the whole
equation takes on the value of infinity. Our star may now be no
more than a faint glimmer flickering under a shower of ashes, but if
the little flame is extinguished in one heart, it is rekindled in another. For how long? Until we have regained our liberty. Even if
liberty and peace fall to our lot for only a brief moment, that will

be our moment of eternity. There, Father—that is what I had to say to you. The cross? The crescent? A friend today, a torturer tomorrow. Empires rise and fall. The pride of the ones, the fury of the others, plague, famine, and earthquakes, Israel in shreds, whipped by the winds of history, our kingdom annihilated and trodden in the dust under the feet of giants, and in the midst of all our torments, our covenant unimpaired, not fragmented between those who bear its burden, but intact, as one atom of gold contains all gold; as one drop of water qualifies all water."

We had arrived at the foot of the hillock. Father Solomon Gaddhafi clasped me in his arms one last time. "I don't know if what you say is true, my son. But what you say is good. May peace go with you."

Many days' walk still separated me from Toledo. The farther I went, the more populated the countryside became. Here and there, clusters of woolly creatures were nibbling at the already close-cropped grass on the hillsides. When a round tower appeared on a little hill, it sometimes bore wings whose slow navigation scraped against the low sky. I was wary of the white villages nestling around a church tower, perched like skullcaps over the crests: it was not unknown for travelers to have been stoned in them, or torn to pieces by the dogs. Isolated shelters became more and more infrequent, the nights became colder, and I walked long hours through the rain as I skirted La Mancha, where, the Father had told me, it never rained.

I was nevertheless making progress, though not alone, as I had both hoped and feared. If I had been less certain of the lucidity of my mind, I would have taken for a prophetic vision the cohort of old men who were gathering in my wake—balls of translucid vapor of ancestors wrapped in gold-and-silver-embroidered shawls, jumping up and down and beating their breasts with nervous little blows, their staccato prayers only just managing to emerge from their lips. They were all there, from Rabbi Hanassi, who carried his thousand years very lightly, to my father, who brought up the rear. How could I doubt the reality of this escort, floating along with me like the centerboard of a ship; it gave me ballast, it gave me meaning. You will realize, I think, that I am in no wise animated by vanity when I consider this genealogy that has been uninterrupted for so many centuries. Nothing in its continuity is merely suppositional— our visceral memory vouches for that. My grandfather possessed a fragment of a scroll written with his own hand by Rabbi Hanassi, who was the Prince of Galilee during the reign of Hadrian; this manuscript was lost at the time of the Berber invasion. And even though the thread of the flesh may have its knots, the link of the spirit has no hiatus.

The young man making his solitary way to Toledo was the entire people of Israel, which, though hampered by the weight of its message, was going back to its land of origin—this was the murmur of the old men disappearing in puffs of mist behind my back. It was no longer even a question of God, it was merely a question of ourselves, and of our interminable anxiety to introduce a just order into the affairs of men; of our fervent desire to believe that, at the end of all our sins, felicity would open wide her arms to welcome us. Our long history and its sufferings could do nothing. The experience of our senses could do nothing. Like the silt at the bottom of a well, the folly of hope had deposited its strata in the depths of our souls, and mine had already received its full quota of sediment. I did not hope in the same way as the old men, but I did hope for the same fulfillment; my faith was not identical to theirs, but it was no less total.

Had I told Father Gaddhafi that I felt free? This was a remark which had no real substance. I belonged to the old men, to Israel, to the Book. I was their emanation; for as long as my existence lasted I was their thought-bearer, their Word-bearer, and, if things went well, their standard-bearer. I could not, and would not, escape the decisions of my flesh, any more than I could escape the decisions of my mind. Through the black looks of my father, the old men took me to task because of my sideslip into what they considered a perversion. I was not going along the straight and narrow path; they were right. But they condemned what they refused to understand, and there they were wrong. The aim was not to strike a balance between matter and form, between body and mind, between the profane and the biblical sciences. The aim was rather to extract what they had that was indisputable, and also common to them both: the interrelationship of men in the real world.

This was the moonstone I picked up on my journey.

𝕰 16

TOLEDO is, of course, a superb city, perched on its bank of granite, and reflected in the green waters of the Tagus. I had not come from so far just to admire its string of churches, its synagogues decorated with arabesques carved in plaster and porphyry, its roofless Moorish baths and its dilapidated alcazar, overgrown with brambles. As soon as I arrived I took lodgings with Ibn Ferreol, who was also known as Avensola, the King's doctor.

He was a lean, short-legged man in his forties, almost corseted in his doublet of embroidered velvet trimmed with lace, his beard cut to a point, in a fashion unknown in Andalusia. He had only two moods: melancholy and anger, and he veered from one to the other with a quickness that was always surprising, and he did this several times a day, according to whether he retained or exuded his black bile. More than once I have seen him in a fury for laughable reasons: a book out of place, a dish served too hot or too cold, a dull patch on one of his boots. In such a case he would strike the culpable maidservant with a birch, or even kick her in her fleshy parts; after which, full of remorse, he would have her brought back, ask her pardon, and gratify her with a piece of silver. Apart from Spanish he spoke Arabic extremely well, and read Latin and Hebrew fluently. We had agreed that I should work as his scrivener in the mornings to repay him for the favors I was receiving. After a month of this regime I realized that it was making me waste too much time. Without further ado, I negotiated Uncle Joad's letter of credit, which enabled me to make my contribution without giving up any more of my freedom.

Avensola occupied the ground floor of a vast stone house on the Puerta Nueva, opposite the Murallas. I slept in a wretched little unheated room at the top of the house. From my attic window I could look down on the ruins of the Roman circus and part of the fairground where the big market was held once a week. Beyond it could be seen the roof of the community hospice; this was an absolute novelty in Spain—the invention of the Bishop of Toledo to provide a shelter where the poor could die.

Although he drew a substantial benefice from it, my master was loath to visit it, though he was nothing loath to send me in his place when a Sister of Mercy was a little too insistent in demanding his intervention. The first time I entered this Gehenna I came very close to fainting. Only the presence of the two women in their nuns' winged cornets calmly attending to their patients held me back when I was on the verge of flight. Until that moment I had imagined medicine as a sort of privileged order capable of developing and opening out the superior faculties of the intelligence, a sort of lofty combination of heart and mind which conferred powers on the errors and faults of nature and mankind, a way of pleading for innocence, of attenuating the wrath of God, however justified it might be. Given that one had been prepared by the appropriate reading, the practice of medicine should not present any major difficulties. At its best it was a conversation in a salon; at its worst it was a battle to be fought against the forces of evil, with a reasonable chance of coming out of it the winner.

Never forget to wash your hands after having touched a sick person. Never fail to implore divine mercy on his behalf. Never ask a fee from the impecunious. Always receive with humility any signs of gratitude from those on whom fortune has smiled. You were with me through war, famine, and plague—you know what I am talking about. But the precocious adolescent whose pride had pushed him to leave his father's house—what did he know of all this? In total innocence, he fell headlong into the worst of maledictions. A vision of horror, the pestilence of the cloaca, the groans of hell.

One of the women in the winged cornets led me to a bed on which three specters were lying, one of whom was screaming dreadfully. I observed him for a moment, myself struggling not to faint, after which I ran to the Puerta Nueva to describe the case to my master. He gave me an unguent, half of which was to be applied immediately and the other half three hours later. By the time I arrived back, panting, at the hospice, the man was dead. That was my introduction to medicine.

For a whole day I could not come down from my garret; I was shaken to the depths of my being by my violent emotions. Toward evening my master sent for me. I had neither eaten nor drunk since the morning. To my great shame I realized that I was hungry, and that I was deriving both benefit and pleasure from satisfying my appetite. The maidservants treated me with that half-mocking, half-sympathetic manner that people usually employ toward the feeble-minded. The situation was entirely beyond me. I no longer knew where I was: grieved to the point of despair, and yet eating with some appetite, and, what was more, exposed to mocking glances. Was I on the wrong track? If so, I could still go back: I would simply have to admit defeat and follow in my father's footsteps.

But the good humor of the serving girls finally elicited Avensola's black bile. He chased them out of the room. "Milksop!" he exclaimed, when we were alone. "One doesn't enter a woman with a flabby member, and one doesn't enter life with a heaving heart. One remains outside, like those wrecks you saw, neither alive nor dead, just good enough to rot slowly. That's not God's work, it's ours. Look at the blacksmith, the carpenter, the agricultural worker—everyone who has to fight with matter to give it shape. Look at their hands, and you'll understand! You must allow calluses to form on your soul, you must grow sinews in your heart and steel in your veins, otherwise you will drift like a straw in the wind. As from tomorrow you will go back to the hospice. You will learn to expel pus, to clean up discharges, to smell excrement, for that too comes from man, and that is how he is made. Yes, my boy! Those who taught you that what flows in us is pure spirit were mocking *your* spirit. Either you dominate evil or evil dominates you—that is the whole secret of life. The riffraff that end up in the lazaretto—either they have had no luck or they haven't known how to use it—often both at the same time—but this is not worth a single tear. In any case, you are not going to help them by your trembling. If you aren't capable of plunging your hands into all this up to the elbows, then go back to your daydreams and don't try to get involved in men's professions. There's nothing to stop you from consoling people with a kind word, that does no harm. But the good you may do lies in your cold determination and the skill of your hands. Go to bed now. Sleep on it. And when you have made your choice, you can tell me whether it is yes or no."

Like many Latins of mixed race, Avensola was composed of an inextricable blend of common sense and double-dealing, against a background of unsatisfied vanity. I should certainly not have awarded him any prizes as a master. The idea of finding another must certainly have occurred to me more than once, but I had no one to advise me, and there was nothing to prove that I would profit by the exchange. The fact that I did not admire Avensola did not detract from his science. I was his only pupil, and this was to my advantage. I had access to his laboratory, in which he boiled up his theriacs and pounded his unguents according to mysterious recipes that he promised to reveal to me when he decided that the time was ripe.

His greatest preoccupation was his search for the philosopher's stone. He used to play with the crucible and the retort, he would manipulate sulphurous vapors and soft ashes, all the while muttering inscrutable cabalistic formulas. "I've almost found it," he confided to me. "Almost. Almost. All I need is the merest nothing, and I shall have it." I asked him what he would do with it when he'd found the formula for transmuting base metals into gold. He looked at me pityingly: "I shall be rich. What a question!" "And when you are rich, Master?" "I shall have the world at my feet. The King, the Bishop, even the Pope will prostrate themselves before me. I shall have power such as no one has ever had before."

He had read in the stars that their conjuncture was eminently favorable to him. While waiting to become rich and powerful, he was never-failingly mean: I even surprised him eating and drinking in secret, supplementing the frugality of our communal meals. But his knowledge of Herophilus, Dioscorides, Galen, Hippocrates, Al Razi, and Ibn Sina was more than reassuring. He possessed no fewer than fifty works by the master of Pergamon, and was only too proud and willing to quote whole passages from him by heart, and to facilitate my reading of him. My memory was entrusted with many Latin texts, the translation of which was often uncertain. Teaching me was really the only activity in which Avensola was not mean. I suspected him of ostentation when I observed such alacrity in him. All things considered, I had nothing to complain about: I had come to Toledo to learn, and I was learning.

Late one evening there was a great to-do. The maidservants had withdrawn, the lights were dimmed. Suddenly the door swung open and four louts came in with a long package wrapped in a greasy piece of cloth. The package was taken down to the cellar, stuck on a marble table, and uncovered by torchlight: it was the corpse of a beardless man with a long wound in his neck. "He's been bled white," Avensola observed with satisfaction. He gave them some money and the louts withdrew. This livid corpse lying on the table made no impression on me whatsoever: it was the faithful replica of a person, made out of some waxy sort of material, heavy to manipulate and cold to the touch: even its nudity was not offensive. "Don't breathe a word of this to anyone!" my master warned me. "Personally I'm not risking much. And in a way, neither are you. But the gravediggers are risking their lives; the law would be ruthless with them."

I promised to keep my mouth shut, even under torture, which gained me a laugh that was amplified by the vaults. With the *Ars parva* within reach of our hands we worked late into the night, exploring the entrails of this wax model. Avensola prepared a great exhibition of the viscera, and I helped him according to his orders. The physical pneuma was sticky and humid; only the smell, which was already strong, differentiated it from that of the sheep or the calf. We observed that the large vessel of the liver was not in the place indicated by the book, that the shape of the gall bladder did not coincide with the description of it, and that the nerve in the diaphragm emerged in quite a different place from where one was advised to look for it.

Avensola decreed that this corpse was an anomaly. It was impossible even to imagine that Galen could have been wrong. "Just think," Avensola confided to me, "that a consultation with him cost the common man up to forty sesterces, and that he was responsible for the health of Marcus Aurelius, Septimius Severus, Caracalla, and all the beautiful ladies in Roman society, without ever having the slightest setback. A doctor like that isn't a man, he is the equal of God." This remark stirred a vague memory in me but I didn't have time to pursue it because we had work to do, and it couldn't wait. We had to separate the organs with cloths, and inject a mixture of water and ink into the vessels with a clyster. After which I was authorized to take a rest.

It was very late the next morning when, with infinite precautions, Avensola introduced some visitors into the cellar; there were about ten of them, wrapped in capes, their hats pulled down over their faces, silent, ceremonious, appearing not to know one another. It seemed to me that at least two of the newcomers were women, but I could have been mistaken: the shutters were closed and there was a minimum of light. Incense was burning in an earthenware brasero on the ground, and the visitors were covering those parts of their faces that were still visible with thick, perfumed handkerchiefs.

For almost two hours Avensola expatiated on the anatomy of the viscera, while no one else spoke a word. My master was in his element, the ease of his words and gestures bore witness to that. Here and there he allowed himself the odd humorous word, at which he no doubt was the only one to smile. The resin torch at the head of the table was smoking, and it also threw flickering gleams of light over the eviscerated corpse and the row of unknown people hugging the wall. The mixture of effluvia was so strong that it quite overpowered one's sense of smell. My temples were in the grip of a violent headache, and at times I found it difficult to breathe. But Avensola showed no signs of weakness. From beginning to end, his lecture remained firm and well constructed.

When he had finished his lesson the visitors left the cellar, and the house, one after the other, still as stiff and silent as when they arrived. No greetings were exchanged. My master didn't move from his place. When I went over to him, I saw that his tears were flowing. I was highly intrigued but didn't dare ask him the reason, and he himself said nothing.

During the next three days we finished stripping the limbs to the bone. This corpse was certainly a bad representative of his category: numerous tendons, muscles, nerves, and vessels were not in the place where the infallible Galen had situated them. "Let us hope," said Avensola, "that the next one will be better formed." It was high time to have the remains removed by the louts; the air was becoming unbreathable. The result of the experiment for me was that I came to have serious doubts about the veracity of books.

I had a strange adventure. I became very fond of a young girl patient in the hospice. She was about my own age, and was dying of consumption. This event caught me off guard: when I became aware of my emotion it had already taken possession of me. I had been called into the women's ward to cleanse the scabs of a paralytic. I was fully concentrating on the job in hand and shaken by the groans emitted by the poor woman while I was removing what was already dead in her, so I must for a long time have remained deaf to the appeal coming from a nearby bed. "Please! Help me! Please!"

My task finished, I was just about to escape when this cry rooted me to the spot. "Help me! Please!" I saw two enormous eyes staring at me and a delicately outlined, very red mouth calling me. "Please! Help me!" There was absolutely nothing I could do. I hadn't even the slightest idea of what *could* be done for such a case. A word of consolation? Why not? She was still a child, and she was sharing a straw mattress with a legless woman who was squatting on her stumps. "Help me! Please!" Though the appeal was so monotonous and tenuous, it pierced me to the depths of my being, because of that burning gaze, because of that blood-red mouth. I went over and touched her cheek. Her skin was taut with fever, and her breath came in short gasps. It must certainly have been an effort for her to speak. "Please! Help me!"

"It's the same all day long," the cripple grumbled. "That's all she can say. She'd do better to die right away. What's the use?" I leaned over the girl: "Where does it hurt?" "Please," she breathed. "Help me!" It wasn't a complaint. It wasn't an entreaty. It was more like a prayer rising up from the depths of her distress, which was probably not even addressed to me. I stayed there, my arms dangling; it was as if I couldn't move; my whole being went out to that gaze, to that voice, which held me captive. "Help me! Please!"

One of the winged-cornet women came and rescued me. No one knew anything about the young consumptive, not even her name. She had been found sheltering in a doorway some eight or ten days before, already at death's door, but she was taking a long time to die. I ran to the Puerta Nueva to fetch Avensola. He was busy with his retorts; everything took second place to his distillation. Even so, he gave me an emollient electuary, with which I immediately returned to the hospice. I had to raise the girl's head to get her to drink it. She had long, greasy black hair. For a moment her gaze held me. When she had finally drunk it she took hold of my hand and kissed it. "Thank you," she whispered. "Thank you."

I was visited by strange phantasms that night. I saw myself carrying the young consumptive in my arms up to God the Eternal Father, to ask him to justify himself. Contrary to what I might have feared, this approach did not provoke his wrath. He was busy with his retorts in which he was distilling the fate of the world. Here, the idea of being human started with the species. How could God the Eternal Father have bothered with that little piece of gossamer that was an individual? Prodigious destinies were at stake on earth. "I, who am the Lord, what does a nameless girl matter to me when my people are threatened with extermination?" "In well-kept houses, Lord, the slightest grain of salt is weighed and put in its place. A nameless girl, just a sick girl. Cure her, Lord. Cure her, and I will be responsible for the rest. I will take care of her. I will purify her. I will give her a name, my name, in exchange, and together we will sing the glory of *your* name. Cure her for me, Lord. I shall no longer be able to live in peace without her." "Who are you—you who were only brought into the world for the base things of life? How dare you present yourself to my face? Have you promoted yourself to the rank of prophet, without my having charged you with that mission? Do you take me for Claudius Galen, who you assert is my equal, and who, for forty sesterces, cured anyone of anything? I am the unimaginable Lord, the Eternal Father of the armies of Israel, which has an army no longer, the Master of the heavens and the earth both intermingled and separate, and I have had a surfeit of your supplications, your sacrifices and your requests, I can no longer stand the boredom of them, and I am shutting my eyes and my ears, for my thoughts are not your thoughts, and my ways are not your ways. But my salvation will soon come. And my justice will soon be revealed. Go back to your own affairs, and take care not to disturb mine!"

I woke up in a sweat, my body weary, my soul uneasy. Was I too going to fall ill? It was a hard winter; I had to break the ice in order to draw water, and force myself out into the limpidity of the early morning to go wherever I was expected. Was it the effect of the electuaries, or of my fervent intercession? The young consumptive seemed to be regaining her strength. She started to take nourishment—just picking at it, it's true, but she was taking nourishment, whereas before she had refused all food. She was cleaned up, had her hair washed and combed, and was given a decent nightgown. The interest I took in her stimulated her, but it stimulated even more the zeal of the women caring for her. Every day I got her to drink the dose of physic freshly prepared by Avensola, and she started breathing more deeply, there seemed to be a slight recession in her fever, and somewhere, in the most secret recesses of the invalid, life was trying to renew itself. And every day, after she had drunk the potion, there would be more energy in the way the girl seized my hand and kissed it, before I even had a chance to try to withdraw it. "Thank you! Oh, thank you!"

Where did I find the name of Mariam, which I still remember? Rather from my imagination than from her lips. She was so far from being able to speak that I thought her deaf, or a native of some far-off country. But she understood Spanish and Arabic perfectly well; it was because of her great fear that her words could find no outlet. So I told her about Cordova and its splendors, the town placed like a huge hand over the countryside through which veins of clear water ran; I told her about the alluvial ribbon of the Guadalquivir, with its ripples caused by the winds from the land and the sea, about my father's house, where I had decided to take her, her, Mariam, when she had been restored to health, where she would live among us as one of the family, and about Élisée, who would teach her the things she needed to know, and about David, my dear brother, who would become a brother to her too. She listened to me with her eyes, whose pupils seemed like bottomless wells.

And then one morning . . . To tell the truth, I was only half surprised. And yet today, more than fifty years later, I still feel a lump in my throat when I remember. I had hoped against hope. I had thought myself worthy of a particular dispensation from Providence and—why not admit it?—of a miracle. One morning I found that she wasn't in her bed. The legless woman told me that Mariam had died, without suffering, during the night.

It is difficult for me to confess the whole of this story. But I must. Two days later Mariam reappeared in the form of a package in Avensola's cellar. Even then, the shock I experienced from this only half surprised me: I ought to have surmised the route that would be taken by a corpse that nobody was going to claim. In my master's organization this corpse stealing was a sort of routine. When the cloths had been pulled back, Avensola expressed his satisfaction that it was a woman. He intended to verify the fact that she really did have two wombs, as Galen had written, one in each ovary, which was in conformity with the logic of nature but which a previous experiment had not confirmed. It was only when he observed the emotional state I was in that he realized the connection between the electuaries and this wax. He showed himself very understanding. "You needn't stay," he said. "I'll work on my own." The whole world seemed to be spinning around me. Absent or present, all I could now do was plead for myself. Innocent or guilty, it was my own destiny that was at stake from now on. Mourning had descended upon me, and it was not a bereavement that gushed forth at first only to diminish almost at once, but on the contrary it was a tiny bereavement that was destined to become magnified with the passage of time until it became my inseparable companion.

From this graceful wax that neither life nor death had corrupted, Mariam was absent: her gaze was no longer there; her swollen lips were no longer there. What good would it do, whom would it help, if I fled? "No, Master," I said, in a loud voice which echoed back from the stones in the vault. "I'll stay with you." I was thinking: with her. I wanted the responsibility for taking the knife to my illusions to be mine, and mine alone. Avensola had the consideration to place a cloth over the dead girl's face. A great feeling of calm gradually took possession of me. After having for so long bowed down before the majesty of science, I was discovering its incompetence. Nature didn't respect its laws. Once again, there was a defect. This wax contained only one womb, which from now on was as useless as if it had been double, and consistent with Galen's observations.

17

IBN RUSHD didn't come to Toledo, as he had planned, or if he did come I didn't hear of it, for our paths were not necessarily bound to cross. However cordial he had been toward me in my presence, he must have been equally forgetful of those he lost sight of. When you got to know him you soon realized that nothing made a deep impression on him. Not that he was superficial; it was that he never gave the whole of himself to anyone. That was no doubt the origin of his unique way of facing the world, which appeared to him as nothing more than a complicated surface. He believed in nothing that he could not see, hear, or touch. Distance and the hard apprenticeship I was undergoing somewhat moderated the spell under which he had held me. I was soon to see him again, to know him better, and to be subjected to the whole array of his charm. But I have first to make a confession, which remains a confused memory.

I was very much alone, that winter, in that beautiful but cold town. Certainly the hospice, Avensola's laboratory, and my books fully occupied my waking hours. I plunged into the study of medicine like the ax into the tree trunk, and the wood was already ringing with the fall of the tree. I observed that the people around me bore the Castilian winter extremely well—but I didn't. Neither my enthusiasm for my work nor the ardor I put into my prayers could manage to warm the frostbite that had infiltrated the depths of my being. It was in this state that I came to know one of Avensola's maidservants.

This would not be worth mentioning had it not given rise to consequences. I have arguments to advance in my defense, but I am not certain that I want to justify myself, or maintain that my only error was to allow myself to be taken by surprise. It began when she brought a few sweetmeats filched from the kitchen to my attic; afterward she became insinuating, provocative, impetuous; and the moment came when I allowed myself to be led astray. A cloud of shame, great snowflakes of remorse, a mountain of resolutions, these there certainly were on my side; but were outweighed, finally, by temptation, contentment, and peace. As soon as I got to the solitude of my glacial garret the question arose: Will she come? Won't she come? I desired both; I feared both. I had no say in the answer to the question. She came, or she didn't come, and in either case I suffered a time of mortification or victory before I could fall asleep.

This became a habit. Then, suddenly, the habit ceased. I questioned myself, both worried and reassured, but I could find no answer. When we met, or when I was served at table, I was often given a long look, both proud and entreating, which left me both ill at ease and puzzled. What exactly was happening? There were too many obstacles to overcome for me to be able to ask for an explanation; at no time did it seem likely that I would be given one. We observed each other from either side of a glass partition which was impossible to traverse.

Then one day—she was no longer there. A different maid was in her place. I could stand it no longer, and dared mention to my master that I was surprised at the change. Avensola certainly knew nothing of the secret of my garret. He informed me, crossly, that the stupid girl had had herself aborted, and that as a result she had a feverish inflammation of the stomach which was endangering her life. In order not to be held responsible, he, Avensola, had promptly sent her back to her family.

Should I tell you the effect this revelation had on me? The more I tried to eradicate my guilt, the more it kept returning in its entirety.

There was a murderer in me, and I hadn't known it. I could do evil, and I hadn't noticed it.

How pleased my enemies would be to get hold of this rod to beat me with! How indignant my friends would be that the image they have been pleased to make of me should be thus tarnished! To the former as to the latter, I would reply: It is written: *Be not just in the extreme, neither play the sage to excess; why shouldst thou destroy thyself?* And also: *For there is no just man on this earth who does good without ever sinning.* And also: *Rejoice, adolescent, in thy youth, and that thy heart should be happy in the days of thine adolescence. Go where thy heart leads, where thine eyes gaze, but know that for all this God will bring thee to judgment.*

The judgment was given. My punishment was the harm I felt at having done harm, not to the Law, which has foreseen everything, even forgiveness by means of the sacrificial lamb, but to a person, even though she was as guilty as I. I imposed a day of complete fasting on myself, and I undertook solemnly to turn aside from the profane sciences, of which I had suddenly grown weary, and from my errors, which led to nothing but trouble, if the servant did not die.

She didn't die. And I was bound by my oath.

꩜ 18

I HAD ALSO grown weary of Toledo. I was homesick for Cordova. Without transition, the spring jumped on the back of the winter and buried it. I too was overtaken by events. That morning, while a very new, very clean sun was making the buds unfold, the bells of the whole town suddenly began to ring at full peal. I had just come back from the hospice. The people in the streets hesitated for a moment, breathing in the mild air, scrutinizing the shining roofs, then hastened their steps homeward. Calamity was in the air: Was it fire, flood, an epidemic? The palette was rich.

At the Puerta Nueva, Avensola had already heard the news. The day before, the armies of the Almohades had stormed Calatrava. The soldier-monks, reinforced by a cavalry detachment, had resisted, and a battle front had been drawn up in the south of Castile. The siege of the monastery looked as if it would last. But Cordova had been taken, her army disbanded, and the Emir had fled. All those who had been suspected of having offered armed resistance had had their throats cut.

I had no other choice than to go home to my family as soon as possible. Nothing good awaited me there, no doubt; I could only hope that it was nothing too bad. Strangely enough, it was the fate of my young brother that weighed most heavily on my mind.

Without my asking, Avensola gave me back what remained of my money. I bought a mule and in three days was in Calatrava, which was still accessible from the north.

There was a great stir in the approaches to the citadel and in its squares. Monks, infantrymen, horsemen, and peasants were jostling each other in obvious confusion around harnessed transports. Here sacks of grain and jars of oil were being unloaded; there stones and barrels of pitch, fascines and poles, were being piled up. Calatrava was preparing to hold out against the siege.

There were many visible signs testifying to the ferocity of the first assault against the ramparts: ladders demolished and burned, blackened hearths and smoking debris, profound wounds in the façades and roofs of the houses. Clouds of cawing crows were wheeling around the battlements, which teams of masons were hastily strengthening. When the wind blew from the south it brought whiffs of decay with it.

Though his features were drawn with fatigue, Father Gaddhafi nevertheless made me welcome. "I was expecting you, my son," he said, pressing me to his iron-clad bosom. "I was worried about you. I worry about everyone who has a hard kernel in the heart of his soul. The harder the kernel, the softer and more fragile the exterior. Peaches in a sack full of nuts. We should be made of stone through and through. And never doubt the wisdom from on high. Events crowd too swiftly upon our carcasses. How difficult it is to be a man!"

I was given a straw bed in the corner of a corridor. How was it possible to rest in this tense, confused murmur? What was happening was extremely serious. If the Almohades managed to invest the town not a single inhabitant would survive, and Toledo would be threatened. On the dry bale of straw that crackled every time I made a movement, I told myself that this war was not our war, but that while we had nothing to gain from it, we had everything to lose in it, caught as we were between the two jaws of a steel vise. I couldn't wait for the morning, to be able to continue my journey. Father Gaddhafi managed to exchange my mule, and put me on a path that wound around the dispositions of the assailants. That same evening I reached the Guadalquivir, and then all I had to do was follow its course.

The nearer I got to Cordova, the more frequently I passed convoys of refugees, some piled into rickety wagons, others riding donkeys, mules, cart horses, or saddle horses, and many people on foot carrying as their only wordly goods a folded mattress on their heads, or a bundle on their backs. These were Spaniards, gravely and silently leaving their homes. They at least knew where to seek refuge and protection.

One of them gave me some news. The town had hardly suffered from the invasion. Taken by surprise, Cordova had fallen in a few hours, almost without fighting. The new masters were settling in. The brief turbulence had been followed by calm. But an edict had already been proclaimed: those who were regarded as infidels by unitarian Islam had three clear days in which to choose either to become converts or to decamp without hope of return. After that period, everyone convicted of apostasy would be put to death after a summary trial. Those who were fleeing did not wish to take the risk of putting on a show which would have exposed them to all sorts of pressures and delivered them up, defenseless, to all sorts of denunciators for whom a new period of glory was at hand. Since it was impossible to live in peace with the Arabs, the best thing was to fight them, and help to drive them out. The man who spoke to me was a blacksmith. He was staggering under the weight of his bellows, the only object he had refused to leave behind.

Here and there, a field trampled underfoot, a gutted house, the remains of a blackened barn. Cordova seemed to be dumbfounded. Deserted alleyways, blocked-up street stalls, huge piles of refuse. My chest was constricted with emotion. Not a single day had passed since I had been away when I had not dreamed of the day when my town and I would be reunited. It was to have been a great fete day for us both; she, the Andalusian fiancée, dressed in all her finery, and I, the prodigal son, bringing her rich offerings amassed in far-off lands. And now the moment had come, and she was a sad orphan girl welcoming home a distraught, perplexed suitor.

My mule's footsteps rang hollow on the paving stones. The

Jewry had gone to earth. Have you ever experienced the anguish of entering a town that has stopped living? A dead person has his place in the order of things. But a dead town, devoid of its sounds, of its dogs, of its birds, of its children, of its women, of its old men? Each time I turned a corner the iron band around my chest became tighter. I was fighting the desire to flee, yet no power on earth could have deflected me from my path.

At last, our house, which seemed to be intact. I tied the mule to the ring. Nothing was stirring in the vicinity. The iron gate was open, which I interpreted as a favorable sign. I had forgotten the loose tile—my foot recognized that it was in its place, and a long shudder went through me, which I felt as a profound caress. Had I been aware, before I went away, of all the love that linked me to these stones, to this smell of fried onions, to this play of light and shade? To these human beings, to whom I was going to offer the surprise of this long-awaited return? But there was no one on the patio. No one in any of the rooms that I crossed more and more quickly, becoming more and more agitated. I called David, Élisée, my father, making the complete tour of the house again, starting from the garden. Still no one. Yes, though—there *was* a voice answering mine, and it came from the depths. I rushed down the stairway to the cellar, where there was a flickering light. Élisée was there, splashed all over with plaster, a trowel in her hand.

"Oh, it's you!" she said. And that was all the welcome I got. "Where is my brother?" I panted. "Where do you expect him to be? He's at school." "And my father?" "At the Council—what else do you expect him to be doing?" "And you, Élisée?" "It was high time you came back," she said. "We'd had no news. We thought you were lost. Dead. As you see, I'm building a wall. A little brick wall in front of the big alcove. We've put the rugs there, and the brasses and silverware, and the furs—everything! No one knows what's going to happen. Your father agrees. I hope you agree too, seeing that you're a man now. Do *you* know what is going to happen to us?"

"Hello, Élisée," I said. "Believe me, I'm really pleased to see you again." "Me too," she said. "I won't kiss you, I'm too dirty. We'll do that later. Go and see your father at the synagogue. They're taking decisions which concern you too. By the time you're back I shall have finished the little wall and I'll make you something to eat. David will be back from school. Everyone will be around the table. That won't have happened for a long time. I'll put a cake in the oven. We'll open a bottle of wine, there's still some left. Go on, I've work to do."

I was already going up the stairs when she called me back. "There's a letter for you," she shouted. "On your bed. It was brought yesterday." With my first glance I recognized the elegant cursive script of Ibn Rushd. The message warmed my heart. "Peace on you, Brother. Events will no doubt have hastened your return. You know that fanaticism and free thought have never got on well together. While we are waiting for the former to get rid of its substance, which is bound to happen sooner or later, the latter is taking the opportunity to go and get a breath of sea air. I own a big house on the sea at Almería. I shall be able to work in peace there on my commentary on Aristotle. The port is a haunt of Spanish pirates, which is the best thing possible for the safety of the inhabitants, and the Emir Motacin long ago established a good library there which King Alfonso has left intact. If it so happened that you might be needing a refuge for yourself and your family, I should like you to know that there is plenty of room for you all there, and that I shall be happy to have you with me. May God protect you."

And suddenly, it was as if I had never gone away, as if the threat was no longer hanging over us, as if the past, the present, and the future were all intermingled in a single instant. Cordova's wide cloak enveloped me, though its material was a little frayed, its folds were somewhat irregular, and it had a slight tear on the reverse side. I found that I was again at ease there in the midst of the things and people I loved, and friendship was there too. I stuck Ibn Rushd's note into my shirt, wrapped myself in my shawl, and went to the synagogue.

Still no one in the streets, except a tabby cat that came and rubbed itself against my legs. In my grandfather's day the Jewry contained many houses of prayer, all of which were burned down or demolished at the time of the first Berber invasion; one alone had been reconstructed, at great expense and with much care. The best ironworkers and goldsmiths in the town had contributed their art. The cabinetwork was made of the wood from the cedars of Mount Hermon. All our foreign visitors praised its beauty. I made an extremely discreet entry into the half-empty room. My father was speaking.

"In a short time," he said, in a neutral voice in which not the slightest emotion was apparent, "when we leave this house of prayer, the Hebraic community in Cordova will have ceased to exist. For how long? The Eternal Father alone knows. For four hundred and thirty years our ancestors groaned under the yoke of servitude, and God heard their sighs, and God remembered his covenant with Abraham, with Isaac, and with Jacob. Does that mean that God had forgotten his people in Egypt? Nothing that exists in the world is beyond God's knowledge. Our ancestors had become ungodly, they worshipped idols, they profaned the Sabbath, they ate unpure food, yet despite their fall from grace God remembered them. And God said unto Moses: 'I have surely seen the affliction of my people, I know their sorrows. I am come to deliver them out of the hand of the Egyptians and to bring them up out of that land unto a good land and a large, unto a land flowing with milk and honey.' And God kept his promise, and the people believed in him because he is the Eternal Father. Today God has thought it right to dissolve our community, the most ancient in the occidental world, by the violence that is being done to us. We have no power over this violence. More than a third of our families have fled to the kingdoms of Granada, Almería, and Toledo. What will be the fate of these uprooted, proscribed, perhaps even persecuted people? We who have decided to submit to this violence, we can only pray for them and for ourselves in the secrecy of our dwellings. However fanatical may be these new masters of Andalusia, I have never so far heard of a Mussulman violating the private life or the conscience of other men. The Arabs are our formal rulers, but at first sight there is nothing to distinguish an empty form from a full one. What are we being asked to do? To say that Allah is great and that Mahomet is his prophet. Well, that has been said. The same will apply to our faith as to thieves in Rome: Everything is permitted, on condition that you are not found out. Among you, doctors and rabbis, there are some who have declared yourselves indignant at such a failure. To them I declare: Everyone is free to choose his own way of salvation. So far as I am concerned, I say: The Almohades have declared war on us. Let the most sagacious of us counter with a stratagem of war. In exchange for our lives, our houses, our fields, and our professions, our masters want nothing from us but words. I say: Let us give them these words. No action perpetrated under duress is considered by the Eternal Father to be a sin. During their exile in Babylon, our ancestors knelt before the statue of Nebuchadnezzar—and God pardoned them. In the days of the prophet Elijah, the Jews kissed the images of Baal—and God pardoned them. It was not to obtain any advantage that they deserted the faith; it was under the pressure of the knife, under the imminent threat of torture. Should we leave? Should we die? Should we use a stratagem? I do not know what will please God. But I do know that he has never despised the affliction of the unfortunate. And we are today suffering under great affliction and great misfortune. This commune, whose fate was confided to me by my father, and my father's father, and down through nine generations of ancestors who spent themselves in the service of our Law, this commune which is the justification of my existence, I am obliged to say that it no longer exists in order to assure the survival of each one of us. This synagogue which is my only fatherland, which I have so dearly cherished, whose high renown I have helped to keep—I have given the order that the entry to this synagogue be walled up, to preserve it from destruction. I will not speak to you of my sorrow, of my distress. I will only speak to you of what my duty commands me to do in order that the people of Israel may survive the calamity that has befallen us. And even if we must continue in anguish, even if in the morning we have to hope that the evening will arrive, and in the evening that the night will grant us the following morning, we must never stop thinking of this prediction: God will be ever mindful of the covenant he swore with your fathers. This is why I implore you, you doctors and rabbis and wise leaders of our people: give our persecutors the small price they ask of us, and let us keep intact the spark of the divine word given to Moses on Mount Horeb. I have spoken."

A long moment of silence followed. Someone coughed into his hand, and then silence fell again. I had never, until now, heard my father pronounce so many words in one single breath. I was overwhelmed. I don't know what inspired me to rise heavily to my feet.

"Rabbi Maimon," I said, "it is not a question of knowing whether God still keeps to his covenant with us, or whether he has broken it in order to chastise us. It is a question of our deciding to remain faithful to this covenant, and to meditate on that other saying of the prophet—that a living dog is better than a dead lion. Our people are unequaled because they have brought God's unique message to the whole world, and it is through and for this message that our people have remained on the earth when so many others have disappeared without leaving any trace in men's consciousness. The destiny of Israel depends, without a doubt, on the will of God, but it depends even more on the will and the vigilance of every one of us."

My father too had risen, his massive back well arched, his beard disheveled. He had not interrupted me. Under his half-closed eyelids he was beginning to scowl. "Who are you?" he called out. "Show your face!" Without haste, I drew back my shawl. There were murmurs. But only murmurs such as are sometimes heard in a gathering of men when opinions are being exchanged in low voices. A sort of legend has grown up about this scene, and in the course of the years it has been much commented on. Some have reported that the doctors among the congregation prostrated themselves to salute in me a budding prophet. This is pure invention, I can testify to that. Others have spread the rumor that I was jeered at for my impious words, and driven in shame from the synagogue. This is equally untrue, I can vouch for that. There were murmurs because the members of the Council had seen me as an impertinent young man who dared to take the floor in their presence without having been questioned, and also because they didn't believe their eyes when they suddenly saw the reappearance of a figure who had been effaced from the community. We were living through a tragic period during which the slightest incident could take on the value of a sign; one of those moments that is as open to a myth as a fecund womb. A pitiless hand was sawing off the branch on which we were perching; once again an absurd plowshare had been pushed into the humus of our ancient culture; violence was destroying our closest ties; we were being forced into a position of free fall, clutching the message of our sacred texts, at the mercy of auguries, whether auspicious or ominous, of the arbitrary, of chance. And in the midst of this great misfortune that had struck at our very existence, I had to expose myself to the ludicrous minor misfortune of facing my father whom I had fled, and I could only do this by asserting that I was different from him, which I really was.

He was the first to understand and to regain his self-control. With small, gliding steps he approached me, never taking his eyes off me for a second. "Your voice has broken," he said. "You talk like a stranger now. Your face is emaciated. You have known suffering. You are much taller. Your forehead is seeking the heavens. I had a son who resembled you. Have you come to take his place?" As he stood there in front of me, stocky and thickset, with his pupils suddenly veiled and blurred while he waited for an answer to his question, for the first time I experienced a feeling of tenderness for this old man who was so weak in his strength. "Rabbi Maimon," I said, "we never bathe twice in the same river. I didn't come back to take *a* place. I came to take *my* place. In the misfortune that has overtaken us, no one has the right to refuse it to me." There were more murmurs. In his energetic way, my father turned to the doctors of the Law who were standing in a circle around us. "This is Moses," he said. "The firstborn of my family. He would have made a perfect prince for the Jewry of Cordova. But the Cordovan Jewry no longer exists. May God protect us."

He took my arm, leaning heavily on me, and we went out of the synagogue. At the bottom of the steps several flat carts full of bricks were standing in a row along the wall. A team of masons was waiting impatiently in the background. Before nightfall, the entrance to our house of prayer had to be walled up. "Don't forget," my father called out in a loud voice, "to whitewash the gilding on the façade." None of the men replied. They were professionals, and pious, and as grieved as we by our common misfortune.

Taking small steps, gliding rather than walking, hanging on to my arm, my father led me to our house. At one moment a sob shook his broad chest. I saw that his eyes were bathed in tears.

𝕰 19

LIKE many Mussulman conquerors, the new governor of Cordova adopted the name of Al Mansur: the Conqueror. In less than a year his horsemen were distributed over half the province and were installed in Cádiz, Cordova, Seville, and outside Calatrava, as the representatives of the Almohade caliphate of Fez. This was the third large-scale Berber invasion on the peninsula. Faced with the painful attempts at coalition on the part of the Spanish princes, Islam was impulsively seeking her unobtainable unity by means of slogans for the sake of slogans, and holy wars for the sake of holy wars. Although each of these invasions had its own kind of originality, the style was always the same. As long as the troops were not overburdened they rode full tilt, but when they had accumulated their fill of booty their momentum came to a sudden halt, for their aim seemed to have been achieved, according to the ancestral ways of nomadic tribes.

This time, too, the extent of the spoils of war soon satiated the desire for conquest. The fortunes of the warriors were assured for some time to come. Like the wise leader he was, Al Mansur took good care not to blow on a flame that was temporarily extinct. He knew that he would be unable to urge his men on any further so long as they had enough for their present needs, although he proclaimed that he himself was pure of all covetousness. He had not mobilized this army of half a million horsemen just for them to take part in the Andalusian carnival and send back the leavings to their master. He professed nothing but disdain and contempt for the riches of the *taifas* that had fallen into his hands. His primary belief was in the bare simplicity and frugality of the desert tribes. Comfort soon led to softness, and he intended to remain the inflexible representative of the Prophet.

His legend was impressive. He took, it was said, only one meager repast a day, and drank nothing but camel's milk. He slept in his scale armor on a goatskin thrown onto the ground, whether he was in a tent or a palace; he had neither wife nor concubine; he was said to boast of being able neither to read nor to write, but of having an unrivaled knowledge of the Koran. Though in the Alcazar in Cordova he disposed of several rooms for bathing and diversions, he used them only for the ritual ablutions, merely causing a few ripples in the mirror-like surface of the basins with the tips of his fingers, in order to be free to give himself up entirely to the canonic prayers at the exactly prescribed hours.

The war he had undertaken was not solely aimed at those kingdoms that he judged corrupt, it was aimed at corruption itself. His sbirri had orders to dash against the rocks whatever they could find in the way of valuable furniture, musical instruments, bottles or jars of wine; the outlets of the town frequently ran red with blood. A store selling silk stuffs was pillaged, so the whole textile trade retreated to the secrecy of their back rooms. Suddenly the jewelers' windows contained nothing but trumpery. Al Mansur's jurisdiction was exercised without viciousness but with method. When he left the palace, riding bareback on his white gelding at the head of his personal guard, headscarfs and manes streaming in the wind, he did not hesitate to turn his horse aside into a vineyard to trample down the vines. Only a person who wished to commit suicide would have lingered in the path of the cavalcade. I only once saw Al Mansur at close quarters. The picture of him that remains with me has been reduced to a scornful mouth which occasionally opened to reveal a set of teeth all the more dazzling in that the beard that surrounded them was of the deepest black.

Such was the man who, one bright spring morning, sent for Ibn

Badia, the dean of the professors at the University of Cordova. Ibn Badia was of my father's generation, famous for having compiled a Greek-Arabic dictionary, which I myself had frequently used. Al Mansur civilly received the professor by the big fountain under the interlaced design of the arcades which let through the light but held back the heat. They sat down unceremoniously on the bare stone. A black slave brought a pitcher of water and a pitcher of milk. According to oriental custom, the conversation began only after the correct silence dedicated to the honor of God.

When he had swallowed a few mouthfuls of milk and dabbed at his lips with a cloth offered him by the black slave, Al Mansur asked after the state of the university. "It is as you wish it to be," replied Ibn Badia prudently. In actual fact it was not doing at all well. Two thirds, if not three quarters, of its students had left Cordova at the time of the invasion. Those who remained were not showing any great enthusiasm for study. The professor thought that the governor, since he was governing, was no doubt aware of this. Even though the temperature was extremely pleasant, Ibn Badia was red in the face, and sweating. He complained of the heat, and drank a big mouthful of cool water.

"What is the use of philosophy?" Al Mansur asked. "Is not all truth contained in the Koran?" Ibn Badia believed that he was in the presence of a man who was quite simply seeking to improve his mind. "No doubt," said he. "The truth has been revealed in the Koran. But the object of philosophy does not lie in the possession of the truth, it lies in the search for truth—on the steep path we must climb in order to attain the pinnacle of thought." Ibn Badia was not too displeased at being able to teach this crude warrior a lesson. "It is like the training for warfare," he said, "which is often more beneficial than the warfare itself." Al Mansur nodded, to show that he had quite understood. "What is more," added Ibn Badia, now more at ease, "philosophy has only ever suggested two antithetical hypotheses to explain the system of the universe: the first is God, immaterial and intemporal, the creator of matter and form: the other is eternal matter, the evolution of the germ and the sudden appearance of form—indeterminate God."

Al Mansur agreed again. "And which of these two hypotheses is taught in Cordova?" he asked, bringing the pitcher of milk up to his lips. "Both, Conqueror of the two continents," Ibn Badia hastened to reply, with the hope of promotion dawning in him. "Both. It is through their confrontation that human intelligence unfolds and becomes strengthened." Al Mansur extended a hand toward the towel. "That is correct," he said. "And what is your opinion about it?" "*My* opinion?" repeated Ibn Badia, perplexed. "My personal opinion?" He reflected for a moment, searching for an expression that would be both precise and elegant. "To be quite frank with you," he said, "the first hypothesis is dear to my heart; the second is dear to my head." Al Mansur belched noisily into the hollow of his hand. All that camel's milk lay heavy on his stomach. "A pity," he said, "a pity that your heart and your head should be at odds. They must be separated." He gave a brief order. The guards forced Ibn Badia flat on his stomach on the ground, and he was decapitated before he had even realized what was happening to him.

Less than an hour later another philosopher, Ibn Ezra, the very man who was later to oppose me and my works so fiercely, was ushered into the presence of Al Mansur. He saw a headless body smeared with molasses at the foot of a pilaster, and a little farther off a bodiless head that no longer looked like anyone. Ibn Ezra was not mistaken in giving credence to his first impression—that this was something of a mise en scène. There was certainly something theatrical about the situation, but there was also a difference: this was no play. It was by way of his knees that terror entered into the person of the philosopher. He fell into a seat, without having been invited to do so, only too well aware of the great violence he was thus doing to the rules of polite society. In the state he was—he recounted the pathetic story to my father—he felt that everything in him was of the consistency of an overripe fig, and that he was prepared to go to any lengths in order to avoid the worst.

Al Mansur had the good taste not to notice anything. He sat down in front of the philosopher. The black slave brought refreshments. The requisite time of silence was dedicated to the honor of God. Butterflies were fluttering over the silver water in the fountain, and a cloud of bluebottles was buzzing around the pilaster. Al Mansur named the deceased. Ibn Ezra didn't react. An icy coldness had penetrated the depths of his soul and had rendered him incapable of the slightest movement. So that thing cut in two was all that remained of Ibn Badia? In itself, the loss could well be considered negligible. An overrated reputation. A dictionary which abounded in errors. A haughty and spineless manner of speaking, and that superior way of always knowing better than anyone else. It is possible to be a philosopher and a scholar and yet at the same time a pompous idiot: the still living professor had never expressed a more subtle opinion on the already dead professor. In the past, the two men had copiously slandered one another. Was Al Mansur aware of this? No doubt. At all events, he refrained from asking any questions of Ibn Ezra, who, in any case, was in no fit state to utter a single intelligible word.

The Conqueror, on the other hand, was in a perfectly fit state to transmit his instructions. The first and most important thing to do was to purge the university and the library of the degenerate material that had accumulated there through the misconduct of some and the failings of others. The only studies to be conserved were those of the Koran. He, Ibn Ezra, was entrusted with the proper execution of this program. To this end he would receive all the help he might request. A great shudder of thanksgiving rose in the professor at the thought that with each passing minute his head was becoming more firmly consolidated on his torso. He had just enough strength to acquiesce. The guards had to help him to stand up and to leave the presence.

Abandoned on the steps of the Alcazar, Ibn Ezra collapsed in the sun, and had to wait a long time for his legs to be strong enough to support him. "I accepted the foul task," he later said to my father, "with death in my soul, in order not to receive it in my flesh. We must be logical: if I had refused I should have lost my head, and someone else would have accepted in my place. Where there is authority, obedience is always to be found. Who knows what terrible brute would have been chosen? I, at least, am not a terrible brute. I shall use all my cunning to minimize the ravages, to save what can be saved. In one sense Cordova is lucky that it fell to me. The future will absolve me and recognize my merits and the risks I ran."

It is not impossible that Ibn Ezra sincerely believed what he said. For my part, I very much doubt it. Men have no real indulgence except toward themselves. There is nothing to be gained by agonizing over the remote past and selecting just one culprit as responsible for such a crime against humanity. At the time I am writing these lines Ibn Ezra has died of old age, and his soul may well be before God. He alone will judge—if he does judge.

This was how, the next day, the systematic destruction of the finest library in the world began. Whole cartloads of books were transported to the riverbank and thrown into a fire fed by branches and faggots. The auto-da-fé was merrily kept up until the end of the summer. It is difficult to imagine how much perseverance and time are needed to transport and transform into smoke the mass of parchment and paper contained in more than three hundred thousand manuscripts. I said "merrily" because it was also a magnificent spectacle for some of the population who daily flocked there to watch it. At a respectful distance and in serried ranks, the people stood around in a circle. You would have listened in vain for a single disillusioned or bitter comment.

On the whole, this act of purification was rather well received. What was being destroyed was the work of the Evil One, the wily spirit that had grown like mildew into the hardness and purity of the faith such as it had been laid down by divine command and the vigilance of the Prophet, and had accelerated the laxity of morals, the shameless cult of increased pleasure. Cordova was finally paying her debts: it was the festival of those who had had no part in previous festivals, the pleasure of those who had more or less been excluded from pleasure. There were even, strange to say, many women among the onlookers, who cheered stridently when the flames reached great heights. The light wind carried the smell of burning over the whole town; no one could be unaware of the Emir's cookhouse on the banks of the river and if, here or there, a criticism or two were formulated, what was expressed was merely bitterness that so much beautiful money had been thrown away in the past—for what did that money represent, if not the sweat of the people's brows?—for the refined pleasures of a handful of privileged people, most of whom didn't even believe in Allah.

On one occasion a rainstorm extinguished the fire and dispersed the crowd: it was nothing but a slight vexation from the heavens. A little pitch and a few faggots sufficed to put things to rights again. Every day, Ibn Ezra came in person to inspect his handiwork. He seemed neither gay nor sad; merely attentive and busy. In general he accompanied the most precious scrolls and manuscripts, Hebrew, Aramaic, and Greek texts more than a thousand years old, embossed leather, inlaid materials—clay or bone—which perpetuated the heritage of Sumer, Persia, Egypt, and the Indian continent, illuminated and calligraphed linens and silks from Byzantium, and the sbirri stirred the ashes with long poles so that not a single scrap should be spared.

In the Jewry, all manifestations of communal life had been dismembered. People entrenched themselves within their families, each turned in on itself. Officially, there was not a single Jew left in Cordova. My father, who had felt the presence of his people around him as acutely as if they had been the new shoots of a plant, suffered more from his isolation than from the loss of his authority. This forced disengagement inclined him to indifference, all the more so as he did not know, and could not know with any accuracy, who had emigrated and who had remained; nor, among the former, who had abandoned the ship and who was still clinging to it in secret. There was a certain risk attached to seeking information on this point. A renegade is easily transformed into a traitor.

At the prayer hour, when all the doors were shut, Élisée stood guard on the patio; she had learned to imitate the cry of the screech owl to alert us. Once a week, on Friday before nightfall, my father convoked a *minian*,* all intimate friends and above suspicion; but who could be sure of himself, or of anyone else? We were never entirely at ease. An oversight, a fit of absentmindedness, would be enough to put us in danger of death. Suspicion hovered over the Jewry, like the smell of scorching over the whole town. Had we not been abandoned by Providence? Was our disgrace without recourse? Of what were we guilty, when innocence was the purest guarantee of faith that remained to us? One for all, and all for one, such was the law of Israel. Even if God was putting us to the test, or punishing us, even if he had forgotten or abandoned us, our major problem remained unchanged. It was not a question of knowing whether we were right to remain faithful to an archaic and sedimentary myth at the peril of our physical existences; it was a question of deciding whether to safeguard or surrender our innermost identity. Why should I, why should my son, no longer be the direct descendants of Rabbi Hanassi, the author of the *Mishnah*, who lived in Galilee at the time of the voyages of Saul (who also is called Paul)? Our tradition was built on a fundamental relationship between man and his destiny, on a primordial idea of justice, on a ritual that distinguished us from the brute beast, and was I to renounce it under duress in order to regain—at the price of a conversion—my peace and tranquillity? With a single word I could rejoin the herd, avoid all ambiguities, free myself from the fear of being discovered and put to death in vile fashion as some have done, as others will do, out of cowardice, or fatigue, or disgust, or despair, or, more simply, out of expediency. I had only a single step to take to become one with the mass of those who held power and abused it. But I didn't say that word, and I didn't take that step, for the

* An assembly of ten believers.

pain of having failed in my duty to myself would have been infinitely worse than that which sanctioned my refusal.

It was a problem of elementary mathematics. No, I was not opposing a fanatical offensive by a fanatical resistance. My dilemma did not lie within the choice between being a proud Jew or an ashamed Jew, within the balance between fidelity or treachery to a fixed idea. My dilemma was whether to be, or to cease to be. There was no doubt that the biblical parable of the living dog and the dead lion still retained all its meaning. I loved life, both in the abstract and in the concrete, and I still love it, now that it is beginning to leave me. I didn't believe, and I still do not believe, that there can be any ideas or theories for which it is worth offering one's existence; but I did believe, and I still do believe, that there are situations which are not worth surviving. I allowed myself the right to pit my wits against my destiny. I refused to allow myself any sort of self-abasement in exchange for the problematical safety of my carcass. My father was right: neither Assyria, nor Babylon, nor Egypt, nor Rome, nor Byzantium had managed to break down our obstinate refusal to cease to belong to our own people. Islam would be no more successful. Cordova under the Almohades was nothing but a bad period to be lived through. The most recent of many.

Cordova under the Almohades was resurfacing, like an overturned anthill, like a gaping burrow. In the Jewry—and I hardly ever left it now—the traders and craftsmen were reopening their stalls. Fruit, vegetables, and poultry reappeared in the market. Whether in the sun or in the shade, both men and women moved around as they do in the rain, keeping close to the walls, alone and hurried, their necks hunched down between their shoulders. No one greeted anyone; no one spoke to anyone; no one knew anyone any more.

Often, in groups of two or three, keeping to the middle of the deserted alleyways, the soldiers of the new Emir made pacific incursions, fingering the materials displayed, observing weavers, curriers, goldsmiths behind their windows, buying armfuls of cherries and spitting out their stones in front of them. "*Allahou akbar*," they said politely to everyone they met. "*Mohammed oüa rassoul ouhou*," people muttered in reply. It would be a mistake to suspect them of exercising any sort of surveillance. They were simply strolling up and down, like overfed idlers, proud of treading a conquered land underfoot, and curious to see at closer quarters those strange, unreasonable creatures who had for so long rejected the true faith of the Prophet. Thanks to them, the correct order had now been installed. As the magnanimous conquerors that they were, they were looking for some form of contact with the natives, but at their approach everything became closed: mouths, hearts, and houses. When they offered crystallized fruits or spun honey to the children, the children fled. The dogs barked raucously as they went by. The Jewry, but lately so alive with people and so welcoming, was acting like a snail withdrawing into its shell.

The breach in the communal links kept every one of us in a state of isolation; the only way of escape was forbidden because it passed through the community. What can be less accessible than a human being locked in a double life? Depopulated, and frustrated to the depths of its soul, our city was like a cemetery. Dozens of soldiers gathered in front of some of the wrought-iron gates which revealed a fountain in a garden, fascinated to see and hear the clear water splashing. Didn't it ever stop? No, it never stopped. For these men, so far removed from their Arab camps, this was an occasion to remember the legend they had heard about how all Jews were to some extent magicians. There is no legend that doesn't contain some basis of truth, and there was the proof, gushing up out of the stone. *Allahou akbar!* It was not at all prudent to rub shoulders too closely with these people, even though they were now good Mussulmans, by the grace of the Emir and of his invincible army.

Between my father and me the events had created a new relationship, with which both of us were able to declare ourselves satisfied. I had demonstrated that from now on I intended to put myself beyond reach of his admonishments, but that I was not renouncing the advice I still needed, and my father was shrewd enough to act as if this situation should obviously be taken for granted. I was distressed to observe that his seclusion was causing him to neglect his appearance. He, usually so upright, was allowing his neck to droop. His square-cut beard had started undulating, and his gliding walk betrayed his fatigue. In spite of Élisée's nagging he refused to change his caftans as frequently as before, and I observed that they were occasionally somewhat stained down the front. Nevertheless, he was still working hard. He was drafting numerous *responsae* on questions of canon law, making a collection of arguments in support of his *Epistle to the Communities*, which was to reach such a wide audience, never-endingly completing his *Hebrew Grammar*, and preparing an *Address* to the Caliph Abd Al Mumen, whom he was thus hoping to convince of the benefits of tolerance and the damage done by intolerance, where faith was concerned. My father spent the whole day in his study, except for the brief meals we took in common. For my part—and since the day after my return—I had gone back to my theological studies. Still without any real idea of where this project would lead me, I devised the plan of a fairly weighty work devoted to the *Repetition of the Law*. You know that this gave rise to fourteen big books, which did not allow me a moment's rest for ten years.

Do you imagine that it is in a boastful spirit that I mention these books? I had my reasons for writing them, and those reasons were to expose folly. Have you measured the extent of folly? Let us try to see things from a distance, I who am writing these lines and you who are reading them. We are in the last Cordovan spring. There will never be another. And already the last summer is stealing up and prevailing over the balance of day and night. The sun ascends high in the sky. The swallows have returned, the buds have burst open and flowers are beginning to appear everywhere. New water comes rushing down from the sierra. Myriads of flies emerge from the dust, the ewes are with lamb, the heifers are with calf, the cherries are reddening, all nature is coming back onto the scene like a canvas whose origin and end interpenetrate in confusion. On the riverbank the fire has been revived. Madmen are throwing whole armfuls of books into the flames. The whole memory of the world is going up in smoke. And three hundred meters away, in the shade of their hundred-year-old house, two other madmen, a father and his firstborn son, are spending all the hours they have to live in writing books that the stake already awaits. But what else is there to do? What does the bee do in the hollow tree, or the trout under the stone, or the seed at the bottom of the furrow? It is assuredly not a natural phenomenon to burn books. Is it natural to write them, when the air is warm and the earth is singing its resurgence?

I allow myself a little more distance, a little more height, and my gaze peers down on the roofs of the Jewry. From twenty thousand souls it has been reduced to ten or twelve thousand; to about three thousand families, that is. Evening descends on Cordova. The trader has shut up shop. The craftsman has put away his tools. The peasant has returned from the fields. The men have hurried over their prayers; hurried, because a threat lies heavy over the shawl and the phylactery, and prayers said in solitude are not true prayers. All have sought, and some have found, a moment of communion with the universal soul. Now comes the moment for the dilection. The wick is turned up, the book opened at the page reached the day before. And then it is the daily Fountain of Youth, the plunge into the warmth of Israel, the return to the Kingdom where milk and honey flow. Is that naïve enough? A waking dream which manages to cause a day lived through with difficulty to end in an apotheosis, which circulates like waves in the ether from one Jewish house to another, over continents and over seas, a fatherland as immaterial as God himself. From this distant height where I now am, I see all those bowed heads, all those gazes becoming veiled in the bliss of rediscovery, and I find the proof of my identity in the book already written, in the book that is still to be written.

On the banks of the Guadalquivir also, the day has reached its end. The auto-da-fé has turned into a pile of ashes smelling of burnt horn which the evening wind carries in long trails along the water in the river. It's a little of my flesh and a little of my blood that is departing, there, and it concerns every man of words and of writing on whom mortal violence is committed. In truth, it was a part of humanity that had been annihilated. I can bear it no longer, and I go down to join my family. My father is in his study, writing a book. In my room, I have started to write a book. Near me, my young brother is reading the Book. Every phrase written or read is both a sign of innocence and a proof of guilt. It would take a mere nothing: that one of those soldiers loitering in the streets in search of the picturesque should inadvertently push open the gate. In any case, my survival is conditional and I am not the master of it, and if any part of immortality has fallen to my lot, it is in the book that it will find its resting place.

20

THE thing happened by a stupid accident. The Emir's usual
butcher had had his shoulder put out by a bull calf, and the cook
needed the meat of three sheep that day for the guards. How to
solve the problem? The steward of the Alcazar, a convert whose
name I have forgotten, knew Joad, and sent a sbirro to fetch him.

It wasn't a palace soldier who appeared at the slaughterhouse, it
was the herald of Destiny. With his natural common sense, Joad understood immediately that his life was going to stop at this point.
He suffered a moment of panic, but very quickly recovered his self-
control. So God was letting him know that the hour had come to
expiate his sins? It was the Sabbath, the Lord's day of rest, and he,
Joad, would not raise his knife. By this refusal he revealed his felony, which was punishable by instant death. *Allahou akbar* as much
as you like, but to profane the holy day—unthinkable. "Impossible!" he said to the soldier. "Go and tell your master that it's impossible."

But the sbirro had been given orders to bring Joad to the palace.
So he would bring him there, come what may. In his thick head the
words were beginning to jostle one another, and his sword was already half out of its scabbard. The more agitated the soldier became, the greater the calm that descended on Joad. The only hope
for his salvation now lay in a sign from heaven. "All right!" he said
to the soldier. "I'll come with you." He didn't even call his wife to
tell her that he was leaving. He simply kissed his last-born, who
started yelling, feeling himself suddenly enveloped in a beard.

Without a backward look Joad left the house and followed the emissary.

As he had to pass through our street, and he caught sight of Élisée behind the gate, he had the idea of sending her to fetch me. Since my return from Toledo, I had paid my uncle only one brief visit. I still loved him as much but he interested me less, and the simple way his mind worked no longer fit with the idea I had of the world. "Come with me," he said. "Perhaps you will be the only one able to give an account of what you have seen." We walked in silence for a moment behind the sbirro. "Don't go, Joad!" I said, "If you love me, if you love your family—don't go! Run—you're swifter than the soldier. Hide wherever you can. Tomorrow we'll get you out of Cordova. Your family will join you. When it has all blown over you can come back to your house." He shook his big red head. "It's the Sabbath," he said. "On that day, Joad doesn't run. Joad walks with the tranquil step that leads to God. Hide? What have I done wrong? What is my crime? Remember Azariah, thrown into the furnace in a time of distress unparalleled in the whole history of the nation. If it pleases the Lord, he will envelop me in the rustle of the dew, and no harm will come to me." Was Joad *so* weary of life? Or was he so stupid as to bring tears to one's eyes? I saw that his face was serene, and that there was a sort of blissful smile on his lips. "It's the Sabbath," he repeated. "God will have pity on me." "God will, certainly, Joad! But the steward? And the Emir?" Joad smiled. "And what about the prophet Daniel?" he said. "He was thrown into the lions' den, and he came out of it without a scratch."

We were already going through the porch into the first enclosure. I shall not dwell on the details. Convicted of apostasy, Joad was tied by the neck to the branch of a fig tree. The steward had slipped a knife into his belt. The verdict was that if Joad cut the rope, he would be free. He had the time of ten heartbeats to make his decision. I begged the steward—in vain—to let *me* cut the rope. "Not you," he said. "Him!" The swine of a renegade refused to be moved from his decision. Joad's quiet determination was worrying his conscience, making his own conversion seem trivial. Perhaps he believed that Joad would weaken at the last moment? For an instant, I too believed it. The rustle of the dew might well be the last resort of life against death. But a single glance at the criminal under sentence was enough to convince the onlooker that all hope was vain. Upright on the stand, Joad's eyes were white. He was no longer with us. His beard was trembling: that was because he was reciting the prayer of Azariah in the furnace: "Blessed art thou, O Lord, God of our fathers, and worthy of praise; may thy name be forever glorified. For thou art just in all that thou hast done to us, all thy works are truthful, strait are thy ways, and all thy judgments truth." There was no moment when Joad's hand went to his belt. Not even the slightest quiver ran through his fingers. It was the Sabbath. Joad did not raise the knife. The steward kicked away the stand. There were a few convulsive movements under the tree. Then it was all over.

My jaws clenched, and, on the verge of hysterics, I walked off along the riverbank, a long way upstream from the area where the books were burning. I threw myself down on my stomach on the prickly grass on the bank, heedless of the sun, which was burning hot, and there, for hours, I was unable to control my sobs. I didn't weep for the death of my mother: I was too young; I didn't weep for the death of my father: he was very old; I didn't weep for the death of my brother: he was too far away. In all my life I have never shed so many tears as I did for Joad: I was weeping for innocence, for perplexity, for imbecility. I was weeping for myself.

🝆 21

NIGHT was falling when I got back to the house. My father was at his prayers. I followed his example, but without finding appeasement. My whole body ached, as if I had been beaten all over. In my distress I had tied the straps of the phylacteries too tightly, and the blood was throbbing in my arm. A cellar-like smell lay heavily in the warm, scorched air. I heard from Élisée that Joad's body had been thrown into the moat outside the first enclosure. It was there that his widow and the mourning women went to recover it. According to the commandment in Deuteronomy the victim must be buried without delay: it is written that the body of a hanged man shall not remain all night upon the tree, for he that is hanged is accursed of God. Dust was already running into that mouth, in which the praise of the Lord had remained suspended. The rustle of the dew had given way to the silence of clay.

Waves of anger rose in a mist from the depths of my distress. I planted myself in front of my father, who was silent, his eyelids half closed. I almost shouted: "Rabbi Maimon! Wake up! We must leave here. We must quit this town that has become a cloaca. Everything just and noble that Cordova has retained throughout the centuries has become putrefied, and it is no longer tolerable. Are we sheep in a pen that we wait passively for the hand of the slaughterer to fall on us? Or simpletons, who hope that the calamity will leave us intact? If we take refuge in silence in the midst of this debacle, does that not mean that we are accepting the role of accomplices? The scorn of God has fallen on the town, and I, Moses, I want to remove myself from that scorn, it is the only way in which we can protect ourselves from it. Are we not men worthy of respect, and, in the first place, worthy of our own self-respect? How can we agree to see the sun rise even once more on this ignominy? It isn't fear that incites me to speak, Rabbi Maimon, it is revolt. We must remove our persons from here while they are still intact, leave this house, this province, which has become rotten to the core, and find a land elsewhere in which we can look each other in the face without shame. Rabbi Maimon, do you hear me?"

I was very near to seizing him by the collar and shaking him. But my father slowly raised his eyelids. There was infinite sadness in his gaze, and yet a sort of wild gleam behind his pupils. "I agree with you, my son," he said. "We will leave tonight, as soon as the moon begins to wane."

With his fingers spread out like a fan he was combing his beard, and a sort of tired smile stretched his lips. "The world is great and wide," he said, "and God is everywhere. It is written in the great Book: 'Happy are they who voyage!' Even the Prophet of Allah said: 'He who can go far will enter Paradise more easily.'"

I don't know what made me burst out laughing. Nervous tension, no doubt. I had been so afraid that my father would raise objections just to temporize, or else confront me with an obstinate refusal. For our salvation we had to stay united. The fact that he was capable of humor in such a moment overwhelmed me with gratitude. With his elbows on the table, David was observing us, his mouth and eyes open wide. He had never heard so much talk in this room. He suddenly stood up and started hopping from one foot to the other, chanting to a tune he had made up for the occasion: "Alleluia! We're going into exile! Alleluia! We're going away!" The scene could well have appeared grotesque: in David's outburst there was a measure of real joy which was stronger than the misfortune that had befallen us: it was because we had turned our backs on despair, and were in possession of a ball of thread which, as it unwound, would lead us toward a new hope. There was a sudden cry, near the door. Élisée was lamenting. "Be quiet," my father ordered her, without raising his voice. "Go and prepare some baskets and boxes. We must pack our bags. When the moment has come I shall go and harness the mules. And don't make such a fuss. It's quite bad enough without your tears."

We spent the evening, and part of the night, in sorting out what we were going to take with us—books, manuscripts, linen and clothes, kitchen utensils—it soon added up to more than the mules could carry. We had to lighten the heaviest bags, forgo this in order to keep that, each time with a pang. Did any one of us really believe we would one day come back to this house? I think that none of us doubted it in his heart of hearts. The most constant factor in our inheritance had always been the habit of impermanence. Exile was to be no exception. There was in Andalusia a town named Cordova, founded and built by our ancestors; and in this town a district as compact as a clenched fist and as open as a full-blown flower; and in this district a place to live in, made by and for ourselves, which had been there for centuries. If a sewer discharged its pestilence into the town, then we had to take to the fields until the sewer had run dry. Six months? A year? Ten years? Time was of no account. We were leaving a temporary state which had lasted for some time, for a temporary state which couldn't last. Such, if my memory serves, was my state of mind.

I had already left once, but had not broken any of my links with my origins. If anyone had told me, that night, that I should never again see the house where I was born, and where I ought to have died, I should have laughed aloud. It must have been the weight of years that made my father more circumspect. At his age, he had learned to beware of certainties. Far better than I, he knew himself to be at the mercy of an accident. But it was only simple justice that he should return to his nest, and he believed in nothing so much as in justice. Excited by the smell of adventure, my young brother was hopping up and down and humming, until Élisée, exasperated, silenced him with a smack. She was the only one who was sad to be

leaving, yet this house was only hers by pure chance. She was thinking of all the dust that would accumulate in her absence, and of
how thirsty our hibiscuses would be when there was no one to
water them. One after the other she took us down to the cellar to
hear what we thought about the little wall she had built to camou-
flage our treasures, whose safety she seemed to have at heart more
than we had. Covered with a thick layer of dirty, dried mud, nobody would guess what was behind the wall, but Élisée's mind was
far from being at peace. She was thinking about the rats, who would
have all the time in the world to nibble at our rugs and furs, about
the verdigris that would eat into our copperware, the tarnish that
would soon ruin our silverware. She climbed up onto the roof to
straighten a tile that might possibly let the water in, tidied up the
chaos in drawers and coffers, put away the last of her crockery,
perfectly dried and polished. Even when the mules were laden and
waiting outside the gate she was still ferreting about in the house,
making sure that not a single firebrand was left under the ashes, not
a single crease in the bedspreads. Her nightmare was that the house
might be occupied by strangers and, what was more, that they
might have some criticism of the way she had looked after it.

She couldn't stop saying goodbye to this enclosed space that had
given her back her individuality and her dignity. I had to go and
fetch her and, for the last time, my foot stepped on the loose flagstone in the corridor. Torch in hand, Élisée was removing the
suckers from the big rose tree. It would have been useless to try to
hurry her. So I went back to wait with my father. He had put David
onto the mule I had brought from Calatrava; slumped over the
animal's neck, my brother was half asleep. The night was warm and
fragrant, the sky white with stars. Tense, and with his head to one
side, my father seemed to be aware of something that I couldn't even
imagine. "Listen!" he said. I could hear nothing. But he, no doubt,
heard: that same night, dozens of families, like us, were preparing
for flight. When it became known, the next day, that the Maimons
had left, the Jewry would be emptied like a basket with holes in it.

Finally Élisée made up her mind, after she had pushed the gate shut and turned the key in the lock. It was over; we were outside. We were leaving behind us a decaying sepulcher, still warm with grief. Reeling like a sleepwalker, Élisée hoisted herself onto the second mule. But the cavalcade still didn't start. Up to this moment all we had been thinking of was our departure, and now suddenly, ineluctably, the question had arisen: where, and toward what, were we going? There was no place for us anywhere in the world. I still remembered Ibn Rushd's letter. Almería. My father had nothing against it. Almería looked as if it might be a temporarily acceptable temporary solution. And it was thus that we turned our mules' heads toward the south.

There was still one obstacle to overcome before we left the town: the Roman bridge with its human screech owl, the marabout. My father had prepared a large coin to keep him quiet, for his cries would have alerted the watch. Awoken by our approach, the madman stretched himself out of his hole like a lemur, all set to launch into one of his prophetic imprecations. The obol, held out at arm's length, softened him. He carried the coin up to his gums, gave a great belch, and produced a hideous grin. "Poor old man!" he said, in a kind of retching voice, "going off to die far away from your house!" Prudence demanded that we made no reply. My father pulled on the halter to get the mule to go on. But the marabout still didn't let us pass. He planted himself in front of me and stuck his half-hirsute, half-hairless face right up against mine. I instinctively recoiled, because his breath stank. Suddenly he put his hand on his heart and bowed low. "By merciful Allah!" he exclaimed. "I can see you, haloed in glory among the living and the dead. Centuries will pass, and Cordova will remember your learning. One far-off day, your effigy in bronze will enter into the middle of this city which you are now fleeing like a thief in the night, and I shall be there to welcome you on your return." His fluting voice carried a long way over the flow of the river. My father pressed another coin between his fingers. With stumbling little steps the marabout finally moved out of the way, swaying from the hips like a puppet. "It's vanity that makes the world go round," he bawled. "Blessed be the donkeys! And may the plague go with you!"

The way was finally clear. We could disappear into the night.

✿ 22

DAY had already dawned when we arrived at our métairie, about which we had had no news since the invasion. The landscape was barely recognizable. The main buildings were no more than a row of blackened stumps. In the adjoining barn, spared by the fire, in a tangle of straw and branches we found some human bones that had been stripped of their flesh by predators and rodents. The rats we had disturbed were still scratching about in the corners, and a flock of buzzards watched us brazenly from the top of an exposed rooftree. Élisée rushed out and vomited against a tree trunk. Not a single plant had been left intact in the vineyard; the furrows must have been churned up by hundreds of horses. Despite this desolation my father decided that we would spend the day in the shade of the fig tree. We all needed rest, and it would be safer if we waited till nightfall to continue on our way. By chance, the well had been spared, and David discovered a battered bucket under the debris. None of us had the heart to eat anything. The moment I lay down in the shade I fell fast asleep.

But that evening, Élisée couldn't get up. I thought at first that she was prostrated with emotion. I soon realized, however, that our hunchback was suffering from something more serious: her breath was coming in short gasps, her skin was hot and sticky, and she was shivering. "I'll be all right," she panted. "I'll be all right in a moment." When my father had reloaded the mules Élisée made a real effort to stand up; she couldn't manage it, and from then on it was obvious that she wouldn't be able to keep her seat on the mule, and that we wouldn't be able to leave. In a broken voice, she begged us to go on without her. There was only one thing to do: stay there for the night.

We carried Élisée onto a straw bed inside the ruined building, where she would be sheltered from the wind, and my father took the mules back into the meadow. Then we held a council under the tree. The situation was strange: I was supposed to know about medicine, since I had studied it in so many books, but I was totally at a loss to know what to do in the present case. Nor could I confess my ignorance, and thus throw doubt on what I had learned. In my opinion Élisée was suffering from an overheating of the body which was at the same time dry and humid, and which caused peccant humors to rise from the liver and stomach. The result was a thickening of the blood sufficient to affect the brain and the tonicity of the limbs. If Galen, Ibn Sina, Alfasi, and Al Talmid were to be believed, she was in a bad way.

"What she needs," I said, "are the good remedies recommended by these authors: oxymel, cabbage seeds pounded in rose water, horseradish syrup, and a ball of camphor." But we had none of that with us, and only the healing principle of nature had any power over the outcome of the conflict that was taking place in the person of our servant. David wanted to know whether Élisée might be going to die. I didn't feel qualified to answer that question with any certainty. God would decide. There was very little we could try; we could give her hot drinks, preferably decoctions of wild spinach, which would work at the same time on the excess of dryness and the excess of humidity; we could impose total rest on the patient, protect her from the heat of the day and the chill of the night, and wait until God made his will known. This last point worried my father. He would have liked some clarification of the length of time we would have to wait, for our situation was precarious. How could I answer such a question? I could do no better than to refer to Hippocrates: two antagonistic principles were opposing one another in Élisée's body: if the principles were of equal strength, the struggle might be long.

By now night had fallen: there was no way we could go and look for wild spinach before morning. I took Élisée a bowl of hot water. She merely dipped her lips into it and refused, with disgust, to drink any more, even though she kept complaining that she was thirsty. She wanted cold water, which was contrary to the teaching of Galen. Avensola had many times turned my attention to the whims of the sick, and to the perverseness of the fact that their wishes were often opposed to medical opinion. I remained firm: hot water or nothing! More obstinate than I, Élisée roughly pushed the bowl away, and its contents spilled onto the straw.

I realize today that it was inexperience and no little stupidity that made me value my uncertain, random knowledge more highly than a natural impulse, however unreliable, and I still reproach myself for having been so blind. I, a future doctor, subjected our faithful Élisée to torture, instead of alleviating her suffering. Irritably, I went and gulped down the maize gruel that my father had mixed over a fire made of brushwood. Before I stretched out next to my brother under the tree I was determined to go and see how our invalid was getting on. She was asleep, with her mouth open; she was breathing with less difficulty than earlier in the evening, which I took for a good sign. By the light of the candle I inspected at length her yellow, unlovely face, which had been capable of such transfiguration as to give first me, and then David, the reassuring illusion of a maternal image. Had we ever noticed how ugly she was? I'm not sure that she knew it herself, for she could only see herself from within, and within she was magnificent. She must have believed herself the victim of some evil spell that had fallen on her after her rape, and which sooner or later would change into a charm. She had told me that her father adored her, and how he never stopped telling her that she was the most beautiful little girl in all Smyrna, and that she had believed him because it could only be the truth. In those days she used to wear linen or silk dresses during the week, and a big red bow that looked as if a butterfly had settled on her hair. In spite of her hump, which was barely visible, she could dance, run, and climb trees, and she knew many stories of miraculous loves in which young gods arrived in the nick of time to propose marriage to well-behaved young maidens destined for happiness. When the janissaries had cut her parents' throats under her eyes, and then six of them had thrown themselves on her and raped her one after the other—that was when she made herself ugly, in order to withdraw from this too cruel world. The very fact of the rape proved that her father was right, because you don't rape an ugly duckling, especially not if you are one of six superb young specimens made like Greek gods, do you? The argument was just worth the price of an illusion. But I—what was I to think? The candle was shaking in my hand, I was so touched by that waxy face and deformed mouth now emitting those quick, raucous breaths, I was so beset by memories, I had so much trouble fighting off the erosion of doubt. Whence came all the evil in the world? Whence came it that I was as impotent to suppress it as I was to suffer it?

The night was warm and milky, full of stealthy movements on the ground and in the sky. A huge, indifferent moon was casting its silver light over the countryside, and scooping out great hollows of shade. The same questions danced endlessly to the same sarabande, and came up against the same answers, which were no answers at all. Somewhere an owl hooted, but there was no echo.

Day was beginning to dawn when I awoke with a start. My father, rolled up in his blanket, was snoring. But there was no one in the place by my side. I thought that David must have gone off to obey the call of nature. But when he didn't come back I went to look for him. I walked all around the buildings, all around the vineyard, I called into the thickets, and the more time passed, the more anxious I became. As I went along I came across a patch of wild spinach and picked an armful.

I was still hoping that my brother would have returned to the tree during my absence. Panic-stricken, I shook my father. "Rabbi Maimon! David has disappeared!" My father rubbed his eyes and grunted. "Disappeared? What do you mean, disappeared?" The sun had penetrated the veil of mist. You could see a long way off into the countryside, over which flocks of crows were wheeling. We searched the place once more, calling until we were hoarse. The morning breeze was playing with the grass in the meadow where the mules were grazing. What had happened to the boy? He wasn't yet nine years old; he had never given any signs of being in conflict with us, or of having independent ideas. And yet our perplexity was stronger than our despondency. It wasn't in David's character to take advantage of our distress to decamp. He couldn't be far away. From one moment to the next he would reappear, and we would all laugh about it together. In any case, there was absolutely nothing we could do.

On the other hand, I had to think about Élisée, and about her fever which was frustrating our plans. She caught me in her somber gaze as soon as I was near enough. "The cheese is on the proper shelf," she said, and I realized that she was delirious. Fine drops of sweat appeared between her pinched nostrils. No, she had no pain anywhere; just the occasional headache, as if someone were sawing through her skull when she moved; but when she didn't move she felt very much at her ease in her mother-of-pearl cradle. "The sea is so calm," she said. "Just tiny little ripples to keep the boat on its course. I must remember to water the flowers."

She swallowed without protest a whole bowlful of the decoction I fed her with a spoon, and she found it good. "Don't hide!" she said to me. "You're little Moses, I recognize you. Go and tell your people that I shall chastise Pharaoh." As I lingered to make the straw more comfortable for her, Élisée suddenly adopted an angry look. "Go away, with your brother Aaron! You will be punished for doubting me." She was getting more and more excited; it was better to leave her alone.

So I went back to my father, who, leaning against the trunk of the fig tree, was reading the Book of Numbers. Engrossed in his reading he didn't even raise his eyelids when I sat down by his side in the shade, for the sun was already extremely hot. I too picked up a book, but I couldn't manage to concentrate on it. After a moment I observed that my father was not turning the pages either. We were certainly both thinking about the same distressing subject. There was no point in talking about it because there was nothing to say. Misfortune, our old acquaintance, that had dogged the heels of our people since time immemorial, had caught up with us, just when we thought we had eluded it by our patience, guile, and wisdom.

I had pitied the fate of the refugees who passed through our house, and here we were, thrown out onto the roads of a scorched earth, our feet hobbled and our heads covered with ashes, Élisée sick unto death, David missing, and what more? This was enough—and yet it was nothing. Even if the ground were to open up and swallow us, or the skies fall on us and engulf us, there would be no room for one more word, for one more tear. A fatalist? No—that I certainly was not, nor was my father, who was no doubt turning over in his mind, with equal detachment, the same bitter thoughts. One day, in the not too distant future, the trampled vinestocks will grow again from their roots, the sap is already preparing itself, and there will again be vines in the vineyard, and men's hands to care for the young shoots and caress the bunches of fruit, there will be grapes, and new wine, and what does it matter if it isn't for us! No, I wasn't a smug optimist either; I didn't believe that I was the object of any particular solicitude, I wasn't thinking in terms of a benevolent Providence that would hold ill fortune back at the last moment. I was not far from being as delirious as Élisée: our little ship had broken away from its moorings, it was drifting along on a slight swell that could turn into either heavy seas or a flat calm, and all I could do, all I could hope for, was to cling to the rudder to keep it navigating in some sort of positive direction, to continue in a straight line without any idea of where we would end up. The guideline was in our hands, knotted, twisted, inextricable, but we still held it, and we would go on holding it so long as we had any strength left in our fingers.

I started, when I heard my father's voice. "I must speak to you," he said. "Anything may happen to any one of us. Élisée will live, or she will not live. David will come back, or he will not come back. In any case, we shall have to take to the road again, you and I, for so long as it pleases God to keep us together. "Rabbi Maimon," I said, "let us leave God out of this. If he is keeping an eye on us, it is not his good eye; and if he is looking elsewhere, what's the use of disturbing him?" My father kept his eyelids turned down onto the book he wasn't reading. "You are impious, my son," he said. "I took it upon myself to accept you just as you came to me. It may well be the times we are living through that make such people. When God decides to speak to you he will see that you understand him. What I have to say to you is more urgent. You must know, then, that we are not unprovided for. You know that I wear, tied around my waist, a leather purse full of silver coins. If we have to pay toll to anyone to let us pass, if we come across any food that is for sale, if a beggar importunes us, the money is there; and if highway robbers come out of hiding in a thicket, the experience of other travelers proves that this will satisfy them. This purse is our first line of defense. We must take care that it is always full. Do you understand what I have been saying?" "Perfectly, Rabbi Maimon. But how does the purse get refilled?" We were sitting shoulder to shoulder, not looking at each other. Uncertain vapors were gathering over the plain, caused by the increasing heat. "How impatient you are!" said my father. "Listen! I also wear, tied in front of my armpits, two other leather purses full of gold coins. A single one of these coins, changed in any town, will suffice to refill the silver purse. If I were to disappear, or if my movements were restricted, I want you to take these purses and wear them the way I am wearing them, and to show them to no one—to no one, I say—for they are bound to arouse envy. Have you followed what I have been saying?" "Still perfectly, Rabbi Maimon. Then we are rich?" My father ran his outspread fingers through his thick beard. I realized that he was finding it an effort to continue. "Rich? You're using a word that has no meaning. It's a question of the sediment of ten generations of

Maimons in Cordova. On the other hand, the word *poor* has a terrible meaning. A poor Jew is a dead Jew. Say that we are not poor, and you will have told the truth. But that isn't all. I am also wearing, tied in front of my groin, two silk purses full of precious stones. They are of different sizes, but all of the best quality and the highest luster. A single one of these stones would suffice for our living expenses for a whole year, and there are more than a hundred. This is what I have decided. When David is of the right age and in the right condition, you are to give him these stones to trade with, on condition that he supports you so that you can go on studying and writing for so long as God grants you your existence. This is my wish."

I was astounded by this revelation. "Rabbi Maimon," I said, "you were right to take me into your confidence. I am your firstborn son, and I am entitled to your confidence. You know that I will not betray it. But you are forgetting that David has disappeared." "If he doesn't come back," my father said, "the stones will be for you alone, and you will extract from them whatever you consider right and proper. Now everything has been said on this subject, and it is a good thing that it has been said. The sun is at its zenith; it is time to think about Élisée's broth and our gruel. Go and draw some fresh water from the well, while I stir up the fire."

It was at this moment that we heard the sound of an alleluia being chanted on the other side of the vineyard. In the scintillation of the midday heat, David was suddenly back among us, dripping with sweat like a child who has finally fallen asleep after a turbulent day, radiating happiness and with his arms laden. He had gone back to Cordova to bring the remedies for Élisée. Everything I had mentioned was there: the oxymel, the cabbage seeds pounded in rose water, the horseradish syrup, and the ball of camphor. The child had told the Greek apothecary, Si-Panake, that Judge Maimon would call and pay for it all later in the day. This touch amused us at first. None of us had any idea that this debt would never be paid.

As for me, I felt fortified: at last I had at my disposal the where-withal to care for Élisée according to the rules. She died the next night, without having come out of her delirium. We built her a vault out of quarry stones taken from the ruins.

23

THE most permanent lesson I learned from Ibn Rushd was to
strive to observe and judge myself with an objective eye. This game
of mirrors lent itself to diversity, but on a basis of consistency.
Thus, I complemented the wooden rigidity of my father with the
suppleness of the reed. He deployed himself in certainty; I struggled with nuances and approximations. His vision of the world had
not swerved by a hairsbreadth from the model laid down in the sacred texts and the commentaries of our sages; mine had been
formed from the realities of our century which were fashioned out
of a multitude of discordant messages, none of which was to be
rejected on principle or without minute examination. My father
said: "God is good," and everything had been said, I thought: "Unless he is not God, he cannot be evil," which is very different. My
father wanted David to be punished for his escapade to Cordova; I
thought it more appropriate to congratulate him, for it had shown
that he had a heart, a mind, and determination—all things to be
revered in a human being.

We spoke of this in quiet, cryptic words while we were making
our way in the moonlight toward the unknown, and while David
was fast asleep, slumped over the neck of one of the mules. What I
thought about God's attributes, or rather what I did not think about
them, put my father in an irascible mood, whereas I understood perfectly well why his opinion should be different from mine. The
immense Andalusian sky, milky and scintillating, invited one's
thoughts to divagate in such a way, but it was also important to
keep ourselves awake and alert: our security and our survival

depended on it. Sometimes my blood ran cold when I heard an unusual sound in a thicket, and until we were certain that it was only a fleeing animal and not a hidden danger, the time seemed interminable. The low flight of the night predators who rushed at us and brushed past us was less terrifying than the invisible stirrings on the ground: it was as if all hostility was concentrated on the level at which we breathed. Apart from these fears, the countryside was simply a void; not even a dog howling in the distance to alert us to a village that was still alive. All we had to offer this desolation was the addition of our own—the fact that we were fugitives whose ultimate hope was to become refugees.

My father maintained that it was impiety that had brought about this punishment. He didn't openly accuse me of being involved in the cause of his misfortune; he, whose words usually expressed only rigid concepts, was now speaking very vaguely. I defended myself against the charge of impiety. I was simply trying to establish a rational order for God that owed nothing to blind faith. You know as well as I do the place people allot him in the affairs of the world. They put him to every conceivable kind of use. I could only imagine him as *not* being put to any use: as insipid, indiscernible, escaping all possible qualification, not even ether—*nothing*. It was only by being nothing that he could be everything. My father called me an arrogant, visionary madman. I answered that if I had been given my reasoning powers by God, it was to use them in a reasonable way, and not to water them down with beliefs that were not supported by any sort of logic.

Thus passed the nights of our journey. At the first glimmering of the dawn we looked for shelter in a thicket or an abandoned hut. When we had water my father did the laundry and we performed our ablutions, after which we let our clothes and our bodies dry in the morning sun. As soon as we had crossed the border into the kingdom of Granada our situation became less precarious.

We were lucky enough to meet a caravan of mules which was headed precisely toward Almería; it was led by a trader from Marseilles. For a reasonable emolument he allowed us to join his *arrieros*, some of whom were armed with short swords and rapiers and looked as if they were eminently capable of using them. The transport was confined to jars of sweet wine and olive oil, there was little to fear from *bandoleros*, and nothing from solitary *rateros*. But the path through the escarpments was exhausting. The Marseillais cursed our slow progress in his barbaric tongue, and complained that beasts and men alike, everyone was trying to ruin him. His whole fortune rested on the backs of the caravan, and every hour wasted on the way was likely to add more days of waiting at the port. It was strange to hear him, for at the height of his lamentations his moon-shaped face got stuck in a sort of hilarious grimace which gave the impression that he himself was amused by it. One evening, at the *venta* where the caravan was resting, the Marseillais came prowling around the three of us, reading our books. "Are you sorcerers?" he asked, in the Spanish of a Frankish she-camel. "We are scholars," my father replied. "That's the same thing," the merchant decreed. "Just arrange for there not to be a storm tomorrow, and for this accursed mountain not to block our path. What about a *bota* of my wine—will that do as payment?" We could not possibly get this obstinate man to listen to reason. His credulity was of no avail: a storm immobilized us for a good part of the next day between two torrents, and the Marseillais took advantage of this to declare that all learning was not worth a tinker's curse. As this seemed to make him laugh, we felt obliged to laugh too, and the result was that he started shouting even more loudly than before.

Finally, after a week of climbing up into the rocks, from defiles to precipices and from gorges to landslides, a vast plain suddenly opened out before us between the trees: the sea, which I was seeing for the first time. In close-set zigzags the path plunged down to the monochromatic surface, scintillating as far as the eye could see. The *arrieros* were singing love songs. The Marseillais was exultant. Our journey was coming to an end, but my heart was heavy with sorrow, for I knew that we were arriving nowhere.

24

IBN RUSHD didn't seem at all surprised to see me at his door. He welcomed me in the most simple fashion, as if we had parted only the day before. He was reverential to my father and pleasant to my brother, giving to each exactly what he estimated to be his due, with his own consummate art. His house seemed a little dilapidated, but spacious. He allocated us three rooms in a wing in which our independence was assured. Despite the exiguity of the furniture, this refuge appeared to us the height of undeserved luxury, after the days we had just gone through. My limbs were weary, I could hardly breathe, but my heart was light.

What a joy it was to feel myself caught up again by the charm of this incomparable friend, who appraised with such a sure instinct the distances between people, things, and events, who calculated so naturally and so precisely the distinction of his manners and the elegance of his words. His presence would have alleviated a stay in hell. Even though the mutterings of time reminded me at every moment that we were outcasts, I can imagine no more pleasant exile than that which we underwent with Ibn Rushd. He had the talent of forgetting us, and then remembering us again, according to the circumstances and tastes of each one of us; he was always there when he should be, and never there when he shouldn't be, so that each of us had his share of peace and his share of freedom; his share of solitude and his share of solicitude.

Necessity and privation develop courage, no doubt, and we had need of it, but nothing strengthens it more surely than friendship of such quality. It was like the flight of the dragonfly, the touch of thistledown, the hint of perfume. It was so light that one might even have feared that it was not there at all, and yet it was: one gesture, one word from Ibn Rushd, sufficed to put every feeling in its true perspective.

Before I had had time to turn around a year had gone by, and the second one was already taking over. All these accumulated days in reality formed only a single one which was constantly starting all over again, like a harsh, nostalgic Andalusian song. There was no place even for a semblance of sadness. What I have been able to observe in others, and what I am certain applies to me, is that although the threat of exile is overwhelming, the actual state of exile is not far from being conducive to a certain kind of euphoria. There is no more than a present to be known, and a future to be presumed; all previous experiences are dismissed, amputated like a gangrenous limb which you remember, certainly, but which no longer restrains and constrains you. So exile opened out for me a sudden liberty full of promise and hope. I was endued with new ardors, exposed to insatiable appetites, urged on to stupendous projects. A temptation toward prophecy? Why not? One only needed to dare, to make oneself worthy. The world was swarming with false prophets! Was not the Truth in need of a mouth to express it? The Word was germinating in me, but so far it was no more than an indistinct murmur. Would it become strong enough to deliver its message clearly? The decision did not rest with me: the illumination would choose me in its own time, if it ever did choose me. I did feel, on the other hand, that I must prepare myself by a greater love—not of God, who had forgotten Israel, but of Israel, which had not forgotten God. To love it more, because its sufferings were continually increasing, because it was faced with the threat of disappearing from the face of the earth, being too tightly squeezed between its own distress and the cruelty of its assassins. It is the same fundamental instinct that incites plants, animals, men, and peoples to perpetuate and maintain themselves. Would Israel be the exception to the rule?

Scattered as it is in the four corners of the world, it is nonetheless subject to the common law. Exile was its euphoria, wandering its strength, obstinacy its guarantee of survival. It not so much needed a fatherland as it yearned to be together, and to evoke, in a language that no one now speaks, naïve old legends full of sound and fury, of withered glory and unkept promises which were a part of its innermost poetry; to hope together, to learn together, to quarrel together, to die together. And, above all, to speak together. The people had lost the power of speech under the pressure of events. Only a very few of the literate remained accessible to the rich diversity of the teaching. If we couldn't reform the people, then it was our teaching that we had to reform, to bring it within everyone's reach.

I shook the dust off my robe and I plunged, head first, into this task which exile assigned to me. No sooner was I installed in Ibn Rushd's house than I was assailed by a passion for work which was not to leave me for ten years or more. I was driven to express in clear, concise language what had become no more than obscurity and confusion under the ashes of the centuries. There was a certain presumptuousness in my enterprise, but from the moment I picked up my pen I knew that I should succeed, and that my goal would be achieved.

My father was no less in the grip of the demon of exile. He couldn't even wait for the swellings on his feet to subside before he set out in search of what remained of the Hebrew community of Almería. Here, not ostracism, but a hiccup of the earth had brought about the ruin of the commune. A complete hill had changed its place, annihilating the commune under an avalanche of mud. The dead had been counted; the survivors had fled in their shirts; only about thirty families remained in a decrepit alley at the foot of the cliff.

My father made a most impressive entry into the synagogue with its sparse ranks. The great Rabbi Maimon, former prince of Cordova? This was too much honor for a handful of wretched people clinging to their despair. They had reached a threshold where, if numbers fell below it, a community would die from the sickness of the void. The impoverished old men with their trembling hands felt the delivery date too close for them even to show the slightest reaction. The persecution whose menace was rising on the horizon would have to be content with very little, or even with nothing at all. There remained just enough room in the cemetery before the Day of Atonement. My father refused everything: honors and offers of service. A fallen prince, he was becoming once again a mere citizen of the world. All he wanted was to be able to pray among the moist heat of bodies united shoulder to shoulder. Even so, he did agree to give a morning lecture at the yeshiva and, if necessary, to give legal advice if the Sages of Almería were at a loss.

For the rest, he had too much to do, and this was not a fallacious excuse. He soon had David apprenticed to an Armenian lapidary, the only one willing to be responsible for my brother's professional training. I myself took on the responsibility for his moral and intellectual education.

After he had performed his various duties my father threw himself into his own work. Within the space of a few days he had drafted and revised his *Epistle to the Communities*, of which David and I made many copies. The next morning I searched the port looking for outward-bound ships to carry this message along the whole length of the African coast, and also to Syria, Greece, Italy, and Provence.

This was a political act of great importance. My father was issuing a call to resistance against oppression. The idea was not new, but it was couched in a new fashion: direct, incisive, prophetic. This document still exists, and will continue to exist for a long time in many libraries, so I shall here deal more with its spirit than with its letter. It began with a perfect balance between two antithetical propositions which mutually reinforced each other: *Israel has lost its land; Israel has not lost hope*. In putting his faith in the future, my father was acting rashly. Israel's hope was moribund, like the Almería community. When misfortune circulates around the world

a cohort of preachers always follows in its wake, and each of its illuminati proclaims himself the chosen one because of his method,
which he maintains has been inspired in him by God himself. In
those days two currents came to a violent head-on clash in the tumult of men's consciousnesses. The first led to holocaust and martyrdom: God only believes in his witnesses who get themselves
killed. There must be no compromise with appearances! Even the
most innocuous compromise is treachery. Bare your throats! The
glaive that causes your blood to flow will make you one of the
blessed. The second current preached total renunciation: There
must be no persistence in idiotic obstinacy! The days of glory are
over and done with. Even though his seat is in the heavens, God is
nonetheless the supreme monarch, and monarchs have the right to
change their ministers for no better reason than that they wish to do
so, and without having to justify themselves. Moses is in irremediable disgrace. The Crucified Christ and Mohammed the cameleer are
henceforth the only securities. Join this side, or join that side; fly to
the rescue of victory and emerge, at last, from your lethargy, which
gives rise only to illusions!

Point by point, my father annihilated both these heresies. He admitted that Israel's position was most precarious. Between the two
great powers its field was becoming dangerously narrowed. The
possibility of choice would disappear through martyrdom or renunciation: the constant factor was disappearance. This dilemma was
manifestly against nature. "What is a people?" my father asked himself. "It is many men who draw on the same reservoir of language
and culture, who effortlessly submit to a complex of identical tradi-
tions, who quote as their authority a common history and a conver-
gent future. In spite of its dispersal, Israel remains a people; in spite
of its misfortunes, its vitality has not been weakened; in spite of the
hostility it arouses, its right to exist remains sacred. Is it necessary
for a people to declare itself privileged and superior to others in
order to prove that this is the case? Such an argument is valid only
in the mouths of demagogues. So long as a people finds its motives

for survival in itself it has no need to plead for this survival, it is sufficient to claim it. Once again the parable of the living dog and the dead lion illustrates the essence of the question. The whole world is inhabited by species that have to fight to remain in it, each according to its own particular method of defense. We are profoundly attached to peace in this world dominated by violence, but for all that we are not without weapons. What does the skate do in the depths of the water to remain a skate? It adopts the color of the sand. To men, God has given intelligence and a prodigious capacity to adapt themselves to circumstances. It would be an offense against all nature were we to disregard the fact that we are special beings, the issue of a special people, whose destiny continues, with no reference to any value judgments, neither better nor worse, but different. It would be a sin against the natural order were we to allow ourselves to be dispossessed of our identity without reacting. In the present situation, our salvation lies in pretense. The choices imposed on us are not of our own making. Those who are biting us today will have no teeth tomorrow. Let us cover ourselves in advance with the balsam that makes us unappetizing. He who extinguishes the lamp that shines on the street protects the light that he harbors in his house. It is not courage that I wish you, it is a foolish virtue; I wish you to practice dissimulation, perspicacity, and guile, which, in the circumstances, are noble virtues. Thus, Israel will live on."

The slowness of communication kept us for a long time uncertain of the effect this message had. My father's tranquil self-assurance occasionally got on my nerves. He asked himself no questions; he had done what he believed to be his duty; for the rest, he relied on Providence. David and I made copy after copy; this required a great deal of diligence and a great deal of time, and the fear that it was all in vain never left me. We were blowing soap bubbles which would either burst or fall to earth out of our sight. I personally had more important work to do. David arrived home exhausted from his day's work with the lapidary; his eyes were rheumy with sleep but he still had to wield his pen for several hours. With small, gliding steps, his stomach well-rounded under his caftan, his neck rigid, my father kept prowling around us like a lynx around its prey. He would tolerate neither correction nor erasure. The page had to be perfect, irreproachably aligned and squared, an enticement to the eye as well as a stimulation for the mind.

Weeks and months passed. How many times had we recommenced the same phrases of a text which did not add up to more than thirty sheets in all? It was also my job to infiltrate the crews, to persuade or pay the sailor who agreed to make himself responsible for its transmission. Then, suddenly, we had the first sign in return, and very soon after many others, from Ceuta, from the Algarve, from Cyrene, Alexandria, Syracuse, Antioch, Marseilles, and Bedras—they came from all around the periphery of the great inland sea, and from further still—from Barbary and the European continent. Rabbi Maimon's *Epistle* had become transformed into a rallying flame, into a creed for resistance. The only one of us who didn't seem excited was my father. "I knew it," he said. "It couldn't have been otherwise. The truth is, I wrote that letter to myself. It was the answer to my anguish. It has given me back my serenity."

It would be folly to claim that my father saved the Hebraic communities from their imminent disappearance. The germ of resistance was certainly latent in most people's hearts. All that was needed was a few drops of dew to help the germs to sprout, and these were the tears that my father's message had caused to flow. That a man existed in the world who could feel so acutely the identity of his shattered people and who was able to find the words to revive the hope that had been overwhelmed by disgust, fear, and lassitude—this seemed to be some sort of a miracle, and yet it was only a very simple reality. Because there were ears to hear, a voice had been raised to speak. There was perfect understanding, right away, between the word that was offered and the word that was received. My father took no undue pride in this; he was satisfied, that was all. He had many replies to make to the replies that were flooding in. Several

old men in the Almería community offered their services as gratui-
tous copyists. He accepted two of them and they came and worked
with him every day. In less than a year his barely furnished, uncomfortable room had become the nerve center of a vast network of
correspondence. If we had stayed in Almería my father would have
recovered, and extended on a worldwide scale, the position he had
occupied in Cordova. But he had other plans, which he told me
only once he had made his decision.

Now that I was freed from my duties as a scribe I could spend
much more of my time on my studies and on my recasting of the
*Mishnah.** In the late afternoons I would frequently go and join Ibn
Rushd in his study. He was tirelessly continuing with his *Commentary on Aristotle* and would read me passages from it, which we
would then discuss. When the weather permitted we took long
walks along the beaches and the cliffs overhanging the sea. We no
longer said: "After the second *çalat*," for by now Ibn Rushd had
quite given up the ritual of prayer. He was caught up in the impossible contradiction between Peripateticism and Koranic dogma,
principally on the concept of the creation.

That God had brought forth the world out of nothingness was
inconceivable to a human mind, for nothing can come into existence
out of *nothing*, as no quantity can be contained in *zero*, unless the
essential meaning of the notions of *nothing* and *zero* are totally distorted. If God created the world out of his own substance, that
would necessarily imply that the substance was anterior to the
desire to create, which would raise the question of the previous existence of a God-creator. Before any sort of theological or philosophical position could be adopted this problem had to be resolved,
and it was insoluble. Or, more precisely, the only possible solution
lay in heresy.

The most attractive logical theory was that of Aristotle, who
postulated the eternity of matter and movement, these being provided with a mediator, the creator of forms—forms which appeared

* A compilation of the oral tradition of the Jewish Law.

as transitory accidents, engendered and corruptible, in immutable eternity, which was non-engendered and incorruptible. But there were other possible hypotheses: the Greek genius had formulated many, as for example that of an evolutionary continuum in which God would no longer have either any place or any reason for existence, and from the moment that an opinion is *possible*, it cannot be rejected as being beyond the reality of thought. The only certainty that he, Ibn Rushd, had acquired had to do with what was *impossible* in the propositions formulated in the dogmas. In the three great religions, he said, which all stem from the same primitive monotheism, revelation opens out onto an *impossible* datum—which deprives them of all credibility.

I objected, for I already disagreed with him, that there was no reason to take the revealed word literally, but that there was every reason to accept it as pure allegory. "Could it be wrong to speak the metaphysical truth? Of course not. The Prophet had the wisdom not to formulate it just any way for just anyone, but anticipated the need for initiation to be approached by gradual steps. I compared this to someone who might feed a baby on wheaten bread and meat, and give it wine to drink. He would indubitably kill it, not because these aliments were harmful in themselves or contrary to man's nature, but because the person consuming them would not be capable of digesting them and benefiting from them. In the same way, revelations could only be set forth in this allegorical and disguised manner, not in the language of adults who have reached a high degree of knowledge and wisdom, but in the language that is used to teach children at a very early stage in their education. That is why the Word was disguised, so as not to blind the less intelligent, and so that the mature man who was capable of penetrating its meaning could discover it in all its clarity."

Ibn Rushd seemed vexed by my argument. "That," he said, "is to take children and simple people for imbeciles. By Allah, that they are not. The truth has no need to make itself so complicated. It is enough that it is true. I have no time for a lying trap that aims only at taking advantage of the credulity of the ignorant. Either there is revelation or there is not. I rely solely on the innate power of the intelligence to climb these gradual steps toward initiation."

Between Ibn Rushd and me a debate never led to a rupture; our divergence did not alienate us. On the contrary, it brought us closer together.

He told me the reason for his precipitate flight from Cordova. A malicious lampoon was being passed from hand to hand at the university. Its title was *The Three Impostures*, and it consisted of a harsh attack on the three established religions. The House of Judah was described as an almshouse for dyspeptic old men, the House of Christ as a repository for bloodthirsty lunatics, and the House of Mohammed as a pigsty. The commentary was particularly hostile to the followers of the Crucified Christ, who eat the body of their Lord, after which, perforce, they defecate it, which is disgusting, and contrary to common sense. Their madness went so far as to claim that God had a wife who, what was worse, was a virgin already promised to an innocent workman, and that he had had a son by her, God who, not having been engendered, could not possibly engender, and that he had allowed this *impossible* son to die ignominiously, allegedly for the redemption of all the sufferings of the world, as if sufferings were a commodity to be sold or bought. But Judaism came in for its share in all this, for its obsolete and ridiculous mannerisms, its obstinate intransigence, and its peevish austerity; and Islam, for favoring licentious living, the cult of the trivial, and uncontrolled cruelty. The lampoon ended with this question: Since the three impostures have been exercising their ravages over the world, has the sun been warmer, the moon brighter, or bread less bitter? Has injustice been reduced by the weight of a single atom? Has virtue increased by the width of a single hair? Has God's compassion been intensified by the sigh of a blue tit? How many human beings, on the other hand, have been sacrificed on the altar of these impostures? Who will ever be able to describe all the horror diffused by these impostors?

Now it happened that a malicious rumor had begun to circulate in the gardens and corridors that it might be he, Ibn Rushd, who was the author of this scurrilous text, which people sought to read rather than to repudiate. Some insinuated that they had recognized it as his style, and this at a moment when no one in Cordova doubted the imminent explosion of Almohade repression. The most elementary prudence demanded flight. He had stayed just long enough to send a few letters, and then leaped into the saddle. "How ignominious!" I exclaimed. "Such scandalmongers should have their necks wrung." Ibn Rushd gave me a sideways look. "That's right, isn't it?" he said. "All the more so as I really am the author of that pamphlet. I had had a little too much to drink, I agree, but like the Prophet himself, the wine only made me more lucid. A good bottle —and I would do it again. I don't repudiate a single word of this indictment. But you see, my brother, the trouble is that its readers find it amusing, while those who concede that there is some truth in it make haste to forget it immediately. Yes, the past was horrible, the present is often horrible, but the future promises to be magnificent! What do people need, then, to be cured of this purulence?" "True faith," I said. Once again he gave me an oblique look. "You may be right," he said. "True faith. But who has it?"

One evening he informed me that he had to leave for Saragossa, and then go on to Seville, where he was to marry. He foresaw a long absence; six months, perhaps even a year. Naturally he was leaving us the use of his house until it was possible for us to return to Cordova.

I was up and about before dawn to wish him a good journey. Sitting light and straight on his mount, he covered his lips with his long, delicate fingers. "Peace be on you, my brother!" This is the last impression I have of him, for I never saw him again. A few months ago I heard that he had died, in his seventy-second year, in Marrakesh, where he was living in disgrace and under house arrest. His remains were taken to Cordova, where they have since reposed. But I am surrounded by all his books, his medical treatises, his philosophical works, his great commentary, and I have only to open the first that comes to hand in order to hear his calm, and ever so slightly haughty voice: Peace be with you, Brother! Peace be on you, Ibn Rushd.

25

SHOULD we leave? Should we stay? Not a day passed without a discussion of this dilemma among us; not an hour passed without its insinuating itself into the mind in one way or another. Against all common sense, I felt that if we were to uproot ourselves from Almería we could incur even more menaces than we had when we fled from Cordova. Not that we had any real belief in the illusion of security that this resting place had offered us. One step had been taken, and beyond that there was no conceivable limit. The world was wide open, avid and uncertain—it was enough to make one's head swim. I was not expecting it to provide me with anything that might interest me; all I hoped for was some quiet corner where I could devote myself to my studies. Such a choice committed no one but myself. The contact with things and people was not exempt from sterility and dissipation. What might have been tempting in human relationships was lost in the tumult from which they were inseparable. How much more reassuring were books; how much more docile were pen and paper!

With Ibn Rushd gone, Almería had no doubt lost all its charm. The mediocrity of the town and the narrow-mindedness of its inhabitants, who were almost all oriented toward the material things of life, offered no incentive to keep me there. But what would it be like elsewhere? Quietude was nowhere on the program of the path of exile. Should we stay? Should we leave? You didn't have to be a particularly subtle strategist to foresee that the next Almohade thrust would be along the coastline, and that we risked being caught again. A conqueror only exists through his victories, and Al Mansur would first work his way through those that would cost him the least. In the north, the Castilians were barring the way to Spain with fierce determination. The kingdom of Granada, powerful and well defended, enjoined respect rather than adventure. The little province of Almería was offering itself more or less gratuitously to the appetite of the new masters of Andalusia. Al Mansur would have had to be a rotten warrior and a simpleton not to take advantage of it, and there were no signs that he was either. Which was the more reasonable attitude: to benefit from the respite or to make the first move? I was personally in the throes of an irritating perplexity, all the more so as reflection could neither evade nor resolve the problem, and its vapors disturbed me in my work.

David, on the other hand, who was insisting more and more on having his opinions heard, was excited at the idea of more travel. He had daydreams about playing leapfrog over the oceans and the continents. However distant the horizon, he was never alarmed. Whenever his apprenticeship allowed him any free time he would loiter in the alleys down by the port, and mix with the sailors who had nothing to do until their ships sailed. Leaning against a bollard on the quay, or a tavern wall, an old mutilated ex-seafarer would tell of extraordinary voyages with an inspired air, and my young brother would sometimes stay and listen to him for hours, unable to tell the true from the false. If a little bald-headed monkey or a bird with gaudy plumage were present, the tales thereby gained in authenticity, and David's feverish nostalgia grew in proportion. The Armenian lapidary was also a treasure house of stories about the annals of the Orient and the splendor of the Indies, where diamonds and spices sprang forth out of the dust when they did not fall as the gentle rain from heaven. The boy swallowed all these fables with such obvious credulity that I was obliged to put him on his guard against this excessive silvering on impressionable clay. This didn't stop him from believing what he wanted to believe, and he began to suspect me of trying to spoil his pleasure. The world was full of magnificent far-off places, and prodigious enchantments. Should we leave? He, David, was ready to do so at any moment. He became somewhat disgruntled because we were taking so long to make up our minds. I felt it prudent to extract a solemn oath from him that he would not leave on his own.

Yes, one day soon we should be obliged to leave Almería. The hope of being able to return to Cordova was becoming more and more slender. They were still beheading people there, and hanging or impaling those who were recalcitrant to the new order. Joad's widow had remarried; her new husband was a sincere convert. She wore the veil and her little boys were everlastingly mumbling passages from the Koran. What was the use of clinging to our illusions? The day was long past when, in spite of everything, it was still possible just to be happy to be alive. Even the memory of such days was receding. The Bab-el-yaoud had taken the place of our Jewry, which would never be revived. "We must abandon the country against which God has unleashed his anger," said my father. By that he meant that Andalusia had definitely rejected us as some sort of waste product. Such a condemnation was too unjust to be suffered without contesting the fundamental merits of the case and without an appeal to history, but our only recourse at the moment was clandestine maneuvering. No authority in the whole world was in favor of our survival, and if God was still inspiring us, it was more than anything else with evanescent grace. Our only resource was to be found in each one of us individually, but how tired we were becoming!

"When are we going to leave here?" David kept asking, impatient as he was to chase his moonbeams. This question was one of those that could do without an answer. I too dreamed of our dead university, of our library reduced to ashes, of our confidence taken by surprise and flouted. What had been annihilated by brute force was irreparable—and yet, how many secret impulses were stirring in the dust of what had ceased to be. The cult of unreality was decidedly a blemish common to our family; it was as strong in me as it was in

David. And just supposing that Cordova, recognizing that she had been in the wrong and announcing her repentance, wished to recall her faithful, and we were too far away to hear her appeal? No one was indispensable, no doubt, but ought we to agree in advance to the failure of our good will? All things considered, my brother was less confused than I, for we carry our eyes in the front of our heads, not in the back. Whether the power of the fanatics continued or did not continue, whether or not Cordova threw up new shoots from her roots like a trampled-down vinestock, it was no more possible for us to have any opening in that direction than it was for time to flow backward, or for rivers to run back up to their sources. A moat filled with amazement and rancor was forming around my hollow dreams.

The only one of the three of us who was protected from the aberrations of dreams was my father. His daily task kept him on the right lines and able to look events in the face. In a sort of way he was the incarnation of the spirit of resistance that he had sent out, perhaps without real foreknowledge, to the oppressed Hebraic communities. Through the testimony of the letters he received in answer to his, which were concentrated on him like the heat of the sun filtering through cut glass, he felt himself multiplied and reinforced, and every day more sure of his determination, for he had a plan. Should we stay? Should we leave? In his mind, this dilemma was not the opposition of abstract velleities; it simply expressed the strict choice between the possibilities open to us. To do nothing, so long as the time was not yet ripe; to act quickly, when it had become ripe. He managed not to say a word about his intentions, now grunting, now sighing, taking refuge in the indeterminate as if he were caught between indifference and indecision, but we were not deceived: he was weakening neither within nor without—he was becoming more than ever like the trunk of an olive tree—closely knotted up in his own sap.

It was hardly a surprise for me when, one winter's evening, as we ate the bean soup that was our staple diet, Rabbi Maimon suddenly held his hand suspended in the air and announced that he had something to say to us. His tone was such that both my brother and I stopped eating. What my father had to tell us was both simple and aberrant. We were to prepare to leave Almería, and the peninsula, as soon as possible and, no doubt, forever. No, we were not on our way to some miraculous refuge, toward any greater security, toward an easier life. We were going to throw ourselves into the lion's mouth, in Fez in-the-Maghreb, the source of all our present woes, the fief of the holy war for Mussulman expansion. My father was expected there. He had been promised that he would be received by the Caliph of the Almohades and be allowed to plead the cause of the Jewish communities under the jurisdiction of the potentate in Africa and Spain.

Unlike his generals, the Caliph Abd Al Mumen had the reputation of having dabbled in literature and of possessing a mind open to reason. The possibility of some sort of dialogue between us came to seem much less utopian now that the Caliph had expressed his interest in it. Such was the information my father had. He, for his part, could speak with the words of thousands of men, transmitted by dozens of letters. He was not going to implore the mercy of God; he did not claim to be able to divert the whims of men's justice; but he did propose to assert the right of the people of Israel to live according to their Law in any land whatsoever, while waiting to be able to do so in the land of their ancestors. And now the moment had come. We would embark the moment the coasting vessel that was to take us to Ceuta was in a position to weigh anchor; that was to say, the following month.

Do you remember the conference I mentioned at the beginning of this narrative? On that occasion my father had formed a real friendship with a very lively young philosopher, Ibn Tufail, with whom he later carried on a regular correspondence. This fellow feeling was all the more surprising in that my father usually forbade himself to entertain such relationships—not on principle, but more from lack of inclination and time. Apart from his proficiency in Hebraic theology, speculation was not his strong point and, apart from his own particular domain, the movements of the heart were not his weakness. What did the two men have in common, if it was not one of those attachments wrought by destiny and which could be explained in no other way?

In the course of the years Ibn Tufail had acquired fame and importance and, with the arrival to power of the Almohades, had attained the very highest office as confidant and private physician to the new Caliph. Asked by my father to act as mediator, he had agreed with good grace, and not without success, as was shown by his latest message. Even so, he advised us to dissimulate ourselves behind Arabic patronymics. This subterfuge displeased my father, but he nevertheless had to submit. From the moment we set foot on the coasting vessel our name became Abd Allah, each of us provided with the Moslem version of his first name: Amram, Musa, and Da'ud—people from Andalusia. "Alleluia!" cried David, his mouth still full of bean soup. "We're leaving! Alleluia!" And he started dancing around the table to express his joy.

My father told me to sell our mules, and this became a little personal drama for me, for no horse dealer wanted anything to do with them. The animals were too worn-out, too badly cared for to interest a new buyer. In despair, I abandoned them on a piece of poor pastureland in the mountains a good half day's walk from the town. The next day they were back outside our front door. I had to make up my mind to dispose of them to the Spanish butcher. Almería would eat sausages made from our mules, in remembrance of us.

Three years earlier the Maimons had arrived, fleeing from Cordova, with two baskets and four saddlebags. One cold winter's morning, the Abd Allahs embarked on the coasting vessel with nine crates full of books and manuscripts. We watched the coast recede. Until we got to the straits, the ship, laden with a cargo of Toledo blades, sailed within sight of the country that had for centuries been our second fatherland. Did I weep? I have forgotten. One chapter of our history was ending. Another was beginning.

ℰ 26

A CAULDRON in which the most unusual stew of the dregs of humanity was boiling and bubbling—that is how Fez, the sacred city, appeared to me within its strong, defensive ocher walls, in a succession of building sites and lines of baroque decay, swarming in its hieratic ferments, turned inside out like a fabulous beast wearing its entrails where its fur ought to be. The cauldron is, at all events, the most constant emblem here—cauldrons piled up in heaps, hanging in clusters, or scattered pell-mell on the ground, being offered in a loud voice to the potential customer at a derisory price which itself is intended to be reduced to half by bargaining, or in the process of being fashioned under the hammer of the coppersmiths, who can be seen elbow to elbow in serried ranks all along the alleyways, in an uninterrupted clamor of metal, sparks, and din which has neither beginning nor end. This concert of copper and iron is the very heartbeat of the town, against a background of steady or spasmodic sound.

This strange people seems to exist only through the noise it produces and consumes, perhaps to protect itself against the windy silence of the desert, whose confines come right up to its outlying districts. The traveler coming from the coast, his eyes, ears, and nostrils lacerated by the sand, must first pass through the gate of the Andalusians before he hears and sees that he has arrived. In the narrow, multicolored passageway under its roof of rushes stands the *guerrab*, the water seller, with his goatskin bottle, his jingling goblets, and his shrill little bell. With great fluid caresses, the traveler drinks in Fez the sacred city, without the slightest suspicion that he is going to be swallowed up by her. One step further and he disappears and merges into the crowd, melts into the collective body, is absorbed into the collective soul. I have said that the desert stops at her gates. This isn't quite true. It rises high up into the sky, visible from all sides on the pink stone of the sacred mountain that extends its shadow over everything that moves here at nightfall.

It was at this hour that we made our entrance with the caravan of the coasting vessel. We spent the first night in the *fonduk* of the scrap merchants—each trade guild possessed its own special courtyard—in the midst of the incessant comings and goings of beasts of burden and human porters, of guttural chants and fierce disputes, while the poultry, perched on the various bundles and prevented from sleeping, cackled their rhythmic despair. The smell of sweat, of grease, and of dung was so incredibly strong that in the end it had a beneficially soporific effect.

At dawn, my father went off on his own to reconnoiter. He didn't come back until the day was dying, bringing in his wake two brutish Mauritanian men and a Chleuh woman, all three of them slaves that Ibn Tufail was offering us as a sign of welcome. We had a house on the heights of Fas-el-Bali, built of good stone and separated from the surrounding mud huts, with a high, wide façade, backing onto the cemetery and facing the souks.

My father was pleased. He always bore in mind the fact that he was to a certain extent an ambassador, even though it was he who had nominated himself to this post. A not insignificant part of his mission depended very closely on the apparent ostentation of our way of life. It would have been a great blunder if we had lived at Fez the almost biblical existence that had been ours in Cordova; it would have been seen as provocation were we to live in the same state of destitution as we had in Almería. What was important here was appearances. Far too big for our needs, with the twelve windows, all glazed, of its façade, the house was just big enough to contain my father's ambitions.

"You must realize," he told me, "that you will be jostled in the street, even sometimes trodden on, if your shirt is soiled, but that the crowd will stand aside in respect if you are wearing a costly burnous. Let us not speak about men's behavior—that would be to generalize—let us rather speak about philosophy, which spreads its light over every man's consciousness. This people is the most generous on earth—on condition that you are not in want. They will only offer you things which you are perfectly capable of procuring for yourself. Be unlimited, and you will be infinitely estimated. If you are poor and weak, you will be stripped to the bone. If you are a beggar, you will be dismissed and despised. Choose your rank, and then impose it on people by your appearance, language, style, and even force, if need be, and know how to die as they know how to die, with courage and disdain. The house we are going to live in used to be the dwelling place of Rabbi Judah Ben Sossan, who was impaled in the marketplace less than a year ago for the crime of apostasy. A servant had surprised him dressed in his prayer shawl, and you can earn thirty piasters if you denounce an apostate. Trust no one, lock up your secrets, exhibit what you don't possess and hide what is yours, for your best friend may succumb to the temptation to sell you to please both the judge and himself. Be distant and courteous toward those who serve you—they would despise you if you were otherwise; be modest with your equals, and aggressive and exigent toward those who are beneath you. Be shameless in seizing what is your due, or what you consider your due—all this is simply part of the moral order. Never renounce an advantage once you have gained it; if you did you would be lost, for he who is caught in the act of retreating is pushed from retreat to retreat until he falls. If you are afraid, or if you are faced with something that is beyond you, do violence to yourself and, if need be, violence to others: this is your only way of salvation. To return to the subject of our house: No leading citizen of Fez wanted to live in it because people say that it is haunted by the ghost of the tortured man. The rent was extremely moderate. I doubled it, even though I would have had no difficulty in halving it. Word of this will very soon spread in the neighborhood. We shall be considered irrational. Irrationality worries people. And anything that worries them is worthy of respect. They will also keep us at a distance, because of the ghost, for they will suspect us of having an alliance with the occult powers, and of being initiated into the secrets of the unnameable, which is an excellent shield to protect our private life. No one will take it into his head to poke his nose into our affairs. Isn't that what we are hoping for? For my part I should be highly honored if the soul of Rabbi Ben Sossan were to come and visit us at night. He was a great scholar and a wise man, and I knew him well."

Served as we were by two men and a woman, it took us very little time to settle in. My father had not accustomed me to being prodigal, but that was what he became, just as naturally as he had previously been detached. He traded one of the finest emeralds to buy furniture and dress us in some splendor. At this juncture David became an apprentice to the jeweler who had bought the stone, and to whom my father had insinuated that he possessed others which were equally fine. He was a Syrian, obsequious and opulent, who was always to be seen in the souks, dealing with everyone around the periphery of the great inland sea, as well-known in Moslem countries as in Christian countries. He swore that the Comneni of Byzantium were his clients, as was the Pope in Rome. On my father's insistence, David received a more than reasonable wage, which was almost sufficient to pay for our food. One word was of the greatest importance in people's conversations, and that was *diffa:* the ceremonial meal, or, more simply, the ceremony of the meal. For those who were well endowed, there was much to be said for the pleasures of the table in the sacred city of Fez. The food was abundant, varied, and moderately priced, and it was appetizingly prepared. If only because of our servants, there was no way in which we could escape the prevailing mode without risk. People judge a house by the contents of the baskets the maidservant carries. We very soon had to get into the habit of physical exercise, and to make a strict rule of going for long walks in the mountains to guard against a plethora of humors. My father was the first to grow heavier, then it was my turn, and even David, who was becoming a man, started to fill out. This point gave us no cause for alarm, however: without the slightest doubt there were lean years waiting for us again just around the corner.

My friend, the tip of my pen tells me that you are beginning to feel a little nervous. Are you thinking that I am doing my best to drown the fish instead of hauling it out of the water to see whether it's a pike or a snake? You must believe me when I tell you that I am not deviating from the essentials, for what are the essentials of a new situation if not the little details of everyday life? My father's self-styled ambassadorship? His visit to the palace? The political consequences of this step? Patience! We had plenty of it, through the force of circumstances. In Moslem countries simplicity is obligatory, but simplicity isn't simple. I suggest that you follow with your finger the line of an arabesque along a wall; then you will understand the torture a straight line can undergo. It could have seemed like folly on the part of a man like my father to plunge head first into the fief of our persecutors with no other guarantee against annihilation than a utopian project and a vague promise. And yet, how much wisdom there sometimes is in folly! How much reason in unreason! Even had he been the only one to believe it and to say it, my father was nonetheless the envoy of the spirit of resistance and maintenance, in whatever place he happened to find himself, and he was supported in this role by having appointed himself the representative of his people.

As for the audience—the principle had been established, word given and received, all of which carried a great deal of weight in a world in which the word ruled. For the rest, Allah alone had the power to decide whether it was, or was not, to be, and Allah seemed not to be in any hurry to intervene. In which case, who would have been so ill-advised as to try to direct the normal course of destiny? When we arrived in the sacred city of Fez, the Caliph had just had himself transported to Marrakesh, whose climate suited him better during the winter months. Long live Abd Al Mumen!—his successor, Abu Yakub, was languishing like a shadow in the background, thirsting for power, and had promised nothing! The Caliph only came back in time to see the first flowering of the roses. No sooner had he once again set foot in his capital than Providence sent him a series of attacks of flatulence which caused his physician much anxiety, and which only came to an end with the first flowering of the convolvulus. Delayed in his seventh calligraphic rendering of the Koran by his borborygms, the Caliph retired for a time into his writings, and it would have been sacrilege to distract him from them. At the first signs of the harvest he was suffering agonies from a hollow tooth; then it was a transient pain in the joints which went the rounds of his august personage; then a period of poetic melancholy, heavy with a hymn to beauty, which saw the light at the cost of a great deal of suffering; then it was a certain sloth in the arousal of the genitals—which mobilized a whole regiment of emissaries to seek out new concubines; and by then the grapes were already ripe. Al Mansur invested and took Almería, and the Court ordered public rejoicing; after which the Caliph was constipated for a long time, and the deciduous trees began to lose their leaves.

Long live the Caliph! While fate was plaguing him in different ways, what other possibility was there for us than to occupy to best advantage the days of waiting granted us? We often met Ibn Tufail. He would come dashing up on his graceful, pearl-gray mare, bringing the latest news of the health of his illustrious patient, unshakable in his conviction that Allah in his great indulgence would soon allow my father to be received. The visitor made a great impression on me because of the extent of his knowledge, his lucid reasoning, and, above all, a quality rare among the men of the Maghreb—his subtle sense of humor. The disdainful curl of the lip so often seen in the expression of the notables was with him transformed into one of continual amusement, so that you could never tell whether he was speaking seriously or not. He sometimes made himself laugh by a witticism whose comic content was too subtle for me to perceive, or he would start playing with contrasts or manipulating paradoxes with such virtuosity that I could only gape. Howbeit, he left me with the impression that if I seemed a fool it was only because I lacked polish and had a lot to learn—which, of course, was very obvious.

Now that my father was associating me more and more with his undertakings, I was present at most of these talks, generally conducted in haste, as Ibn Tufail dispersed his energies in so many different activities that he could never stay long. Apart from the Caliph's emunctories and his concubines' receptacles, he was in charge of the urbanization of the town, which was bristling with building sites, and of the finishing touches being put to the mosque of Qarueen, which was to be the seat of the future university. He was hoping that Fez, the sacred city, would shortly acquire the intellectual luster that the terror had destroyed in Cordova, the Pearl of Cities, and this for the glory and by the benevolence of the master he served.

Was this transfer intentional? Yes and no. It could only be by the will of Allah that the cradle of his most zealous servants should come to hold the place of honor above all the other cities in the world. There was no doubt that one could find fault with the regrettable excesses committed by the military on Andalusian territory: the religious and scientific persecution, the pillage and auto-da-fé of the library, the vigilance of the government and the summary executions, but from where we now stood it was not displeasing to see that proud province being brought to heel. From now on it was a question of rescuing what was rescuable, mainly those who had scholarly brains, which was what he, Ibn Tufail, was engaged in doing. A college where geometry, astronomy, and Koranic law was taught already existed. Architects from Granada were putting the finishing touches to the plans for the first *medersa*, or students' house: sixty rooms on three floors around a patio garden with an ambulatory in Algeciras marble, whose construction was about to begin. Other similar centers were being planned and would be built as the renown of the university spread over two continents.

Thanks to the excellence of his armies and to the politics of austerity imposed on the conquered or reconquered countries, the Caliph had more or less limitless funds at his disposal. It had been demonstrated that riches constituted the best fertilizer for the flowering of the arts and sciences. Ibn Tufail had already made a list of possible teachers, and I had the extreme surprise of reading my name on it—mine, not my father's. I appeared under the heading of medicine, in company with Ibn Rushd. Our visitor revealed to me that he had already seen me at work: he had been one of those present, in disguise, at an anatomy lesson in a Toledo cellar. Avensola had said that I would one day be the king of doctors, and also the doctor to a king. Fate willed that Ibn Rushd would come to the sacred city of Fez only after we had fled.

27

OFFICIALLY, there was no longer a single soul faithful to the God of Israel in the whole of the Maghreb. What, then, had happened to the spirit of resistance raised by my father's epistle? From time to time a stranger would appear at nightfall, bringing either a sibylline message or an allusive word. At the risk of disappointing the visitor and of missing a meeting of kindred spirits, were we not right to be too prudent, and to suspect him? The memory of an impaled man was still vivid in our house. At such a time of despotism, people soon discover they have a vocation as an informer. "Rabbi Maimon? Yes, oh yes! My father knew him very well in Andalusia. A most pious man of great repute and probity. A pity we didn't know what had become of him. Was he still alive? If people say he is in Almería, then that may well be where he is, may it not? An epistle? What epistle? My father was not aware that Rabbi Maimon had written an epistle. If he had done so, he must have had his reasons. Resistance? The first we'd heard of it. Resistance against what? Against intolerance, summary sentences, hasty executions? Let's not exaggerate: people have such a tendency toward overstatement and gossip. Anyone who flouts the law knows what he is risking, and if he is punished, has he not only received his due? Long live the Caliph, Abd Al Mumen, Emir of the believers in the glory of Allah, and supreme judge over the two continents. His will be done, on earth as it is in heaven!

The stranger never failed to echo our praise of the prince. He too was on his guard, no longer knowing whose presence he was in. Be-

ore he had time to turn around, he might find himself sitting on a
stake sharpened to a point. Every month a few uncouth fellows
were obliged to take part in these festivities in front of Bab Mabruk,
the Heretics' Gate; their heads were later put up to dry on the
battlements, where they participated in the feasts of the buzzards
and kites.

One day my father hired two horses and took me for a ride to the
Habuna oasis, half a day's journey to the south. The entire town
consisted of a thousand-year-old Hebrew community practicing the
Babylonian rite, something like a thousand families, who survived
with difficulty as in biblical times from the produce of their trees
and the soil, and from a small trade in polychromatic basketwork
well known to the maidservants of the sacred city of Fez. Now, my
father had received, in Almería, a collective letter from this community in which the call to resistance had struck a sympathetic
chord.

The oasis was perched on a plateau between high cliffs, watered
by a sandy wadi in which some half-starved bovines and hairless
camels were standing, while on the banks flocks of young asses were
allowing themselves to be eaten up by flies without even moving
their ears or tails, in the shade of a row of dusty palm trees. As soon
as we were within sight of Habuna, rabid dogs came running up
from all sides and threw themselves between the legs of our horses.
Broods of hens dispersed, clucking. In the ghetto, clusters of mud
huts built haphazard and exposed to the four winds ran along bits of
alleys gray with filth. Not a man, not a woman, not a child out
of doors, nothing but the raucous dogs escorting us, and the
terrified fowls, fleeing from the horses' hoofs.

We let our mounts continue past the closed doors, past barbicans
hidden behind leather thongs. No sign of human life, and yet I had
a feeling that dozens of pairs of eyes were spying on us from all
around. The heat was terrible; myriads of flies buzzed around our
horses' nostrils. Toward the center of the town we came across a
few stone-built houses, one of which had two floors—no doubt the

dwelling place of a leading citizen. Behind a glazed window, a baby was crying. My father got off his horse and went and knocked on the door. "Shalom!" he cried. "I bring the peace and comfort of a friend who has come from afar." Suddenly my horse reared: a piece of quarry stone thrown from a flat roof had caught it on the rump. "Hear ye, O Israel!" cried my father. "He who inspires me is our one and only God. It is in his name that I am making myself known." A volley of stones was the only response. I was hit on the shoulder, my father on the thigh. He still wasn't discouraged, and started again outside another house; and then another; and the more he persisted, the thicker and faster they came: pieces of plaster, bits of pottery, marl. My horse began to bleed at the nose, bolted, and charged the pack of dogs. I had great difficulty in clinging to its mane so as not to be thrown, and I was able to regain control of it only when we reached the *jebel* path, far from that place of nightmare.

It was a long time later when my father joined me, covered with dust and rubbing his thigh, with a defeated air. This must certainly have been a bitter blow for him. Writing encouraging words in the calm of your study and out of reach of immediate danger, that was one thing; but to brave the complexities of a hopeless situation, and the mass reflexes of a constrained and fearful community—that was another. What was rising from the depths carried up with it the silt from the mists of time, the first imagery of which man had been capable, the first chill of fear of the original couple, half naked in the pale morning of their Fall, outside the gate from now on forbidden to them forever.

𝕰 28

ANYONE other than my father would certainly have lost heart. But only someone who did not know him would have believed him capable of such a thing. He appeared the next day, well dressed, spruce, limping a little but impassive. Habuna had wounded him in part of one limb, but not in his soul. It was only one commune out of a hundred, one shipwreck out of a thousand, one question without an answer. The alternative was not between life and death; the alternative was between being and nothingness, which was quite different. The situation offered no real choice which would be preferable to an opposite choice. Only the depths of consciousness still had a chance to pronounce the final word, in the permanence of a renewal which had perhaps neither beginning nor end. We should have had to be very foolish to suppose that the world was created for our use. We were in it in order to submit to its injunctions and its metamorphoses. Some fled in a forward or a backward direction, others into the clouds or into themselves. The main thing was to find a refuge somewhere to give ourselves the feeling of remaining intact.

Our existence continued on its way, in the expectation of the improbable event that would give us back our liberty. Silence and meditation reigned over the house. My father studied and wrote. I studied and wrote. But what were we looking for in those books and those letters? Does the woodworm ask itself why it burrows? That is its way of existence in this life and in this world. Our personal excavations were aimed at nothing less than perfection. There was a mystery in the density of creation, and virtue lay in penetrating it. Both my father and I were strongly inclined, though in differing degrees, to consider that the greatest good could be attained only through knowledge, which alone enables one to approach, if not to reach, the truth. This was our way of existence in life and in the world. We were drawn along in the wake of models of high lineage who invited us, across the centuries, to imitate them, or even to surpass them. Somewhere at the end of the line was absolute light, imperturbable felicity, and eternal rest. It would be a lie if I were to say that our conduct was free from pride or calculation. Our greatest certainty was that virtue must necessarily be rewarded, and that there was no greater virtue than to be continuously perfecting oneself. I will admit, in the secrecy of this confession, that this was only one point of view, and that it was permissible to yield to other temptations, none of which was exempt from the charge of hiding behind some sort of prejudice.

In the evenings, David introduced his turbulence into our peace. He lived by other realities than ours, even though I found him a docile pupil who absorbed, though he was secretly yawning, the elementary ideas I tried to inculcate into him. He made friends of his own age—donkey boys, water carriers, a tightrope-walking snake charmer. He was on first-name terms with all the fritter sellers in the souks, and could distinguish the different storytellers of Bab Gissa by their style. Metaphysics touched him no more than would a flight of wild ducks, it was just a vague stirring of the air in the heights, but he dreamed more and more of blue spaces and changing climates. He also indulged in little personal transactions with his friends which it was better not to examine too closely; he would trade a copper ring here, or an amber necklace there, and he kept his savings in a hiding place known only to himself. His ambition was to increase his store of money until he could buy back the emerald surrendered to his employer. There was no doubt that he would manage this—it was a problem of simple arithmetic that had many possible solutions.

For my part, I was devoting myself in those days to an arithmetic that was more abstract and less profitable. I had imagined a series of receptacles filled with water up to different levels which would capture the reflection of the celestial spheres. This method would enable me to make a very close estimation of the dimensions and distances of the corporal beings that gravitate in the ether according to the law of God. I thus could demonstrate that the distance between the center of the earth and the highest point of Saturn is a path of some eight thousand seven hundred years, each containing three hundred sixty-five days, counting for each day a distance of eighty thousand steps, each measuring one cubit. I have several times verified these measurements, and I can certify that they are accurate. I imparted this information to the philosopher Ibn Moishe, who was a fellow student of mine at the College of Astronomy and who accused me of exaggerating. He was a Koranic judge and, according to him, such distances were beyond our understanding, for no being of human appearance was in a position to walk in a straight line for eight thousand seven hundred years. Consequently, God could not have willed it, since it was impossible. I invited him to go over the calculations with me. The figure remained the same. Ibn Moishe was still skeptical, but he began to respect me—a fact which before long was to save the lives of all three of us, although at a later date would put me in great danger of losing my own.

It is not without reason that I have taken this detour by way of the stars. Just think, my friend, of the immensity of the heavens, peopled at vertiginous distances with innumerable spherical bodies; think of the smallness of the sublunary world, and of the insignificance of the human species in comparison with the whole of Creation! Who, then, could be mad enough to imagine that all this exists *for* him, and *because* of him, and that it is intended to serve him as an instrument of Providence? Madness! Madness? And yet
. . .

29

IT was not long before he left for his winter quarters in Marrakesh that the Caliph let it be known that he would receive my father. It was agreed that I should be present at the interview. When we entered the audience courtyard Ibn Tufail was near the sovereign. We were invited to sit on velvet cushions, a mark of esteem reserved for visitors of quality. Abd Al Mumen was almost invisible in a great pile of raw silk, supported by a bed of damask-silk cushions. He was a man who seemed ageless, whose skin was very light, who had hardly any beard, and who spoke in a high, fluting voice. He had his back to the octagonal fountain into which a thin trickle of bluish water was lapping. Not a word was pronounced while the servants were placing around us the cups of mint tea and the trays of sweetmeats. From a far-off dais hidden by a porphyry-stucco trellis came the muted, monotonous sounds of several strings and a tambourine. I was pleased to observe that there were no flies.

When we had sufficiently moistened our lips, Ibn Tufail made the introductions. He recalled the antiquity of our family, whose genealogy could be traced back to King David of Judah, our long common history with Andalusia, and the eminent position my father had occupied in Cordova; he added, out of his kindness toward me, some eulogies that I was far from deserving regarding the extent of my learning in medicine and philosophy, as well as in all the other creations of the human spirit.

With a nonchalant finger the Caliph raised one of his eyelids and gave me a colorless look. He asked me my name, and I gave him the one I had adopted on our departure from Almería. Then there was a question about my age. Abd Al Mumen expressed astonishment that it was possible, so young, to know so many books. "He has read them all," insisted Ibn Tufail, rubbing his hands. The audience was taking exactly the turn that he had foreseen. I had been warned that I should have a sort of examination to pass. The Caliph set great store on his own culture, and never missed an opportunity to show it off. He bit into a crystallized plum and his indolent features took on a cunning air.

Was I aware of a very ancient and extremely rare work entitled *Nabataean Agriculture?* Courtesy demanded that I appear embarrassed. I admitted that Providence had placed this book under my eyes, and that I had studied its contents with great care, for it narrates the customs of the Sabean astrolaters who practiced the first known religion into which Abraham was born—Abraham the patriarch of the Hebrews and the Mussulmans. Abd Al Mumen acquiesced, satisfied. "And what do you think of the opinion of Al Razi that Evil is infinitely more widespread than Good?" "I think, Emir of the Believers, that Al Razi is a great doctor but a poor philosopher, and that his opinion should be rejected. Evil is only conceivable in connection with living beings endowed with consciousness, and more particularly the human species. Now, men are a negligible quantity in the magnitude of Creation, which is Good. Therefore, Evil is a negligible quantity, compared with Good, which is universal."

The Caliph nodded his head several times, all the time nibbling his crystallized plum. With an impenetrable expression, my father was combing his beard with his fingers. I read on Ibn Tufail's face that my answers were appropriate, and appreciated as such. The Caliph had still not finished with me. This was the trick question, which I had been expecting. Did I belong to the sect of the Qadarites, who believed in free will, or to that of the Jabarites, who were partisans of predestination?

I took my time to work out my exposition down to the very last detail. "There are," I said, "five possible arguments on this subject, all of which are very old, and founded on reason. The first assumes that there is no such thing as Providence, and that everything that happens in the world is the result of chance and of material necessity. That was the opinion of the Greeks Democritus and Epicurus. The second is that of the Greek Aristotle, who rejects the idea of the Creation having been the result of chance, for the ax would never be able to cut into the bark of a tree if it were not manipulated by the hand of the woodman. Everything that governs the spheres and the moon is regulated by intelligences that admit of neither faults nor exceptions. That is why such things do not occur in the heavens. Under the moon, on the other hand, and in human affairs, certain effects can be attributed to chance, as for instance a building whose foundations have given way and which collapses, causing the death of the people who happen to be inside it, or a ship caught in a storm and sunk, taking with it both the just and the ignorant who were on the voyage. The third opinion is that of the Jabarites. On earth, chance does not exist. Everything that happens has been determined from the very beginning. If the house collapses, if the ship capsizes, their destiny has been rigorously determined in advance. If I am at this moment before you, Emir of the Believers, it is because Providence knew that it had to be, and acted in a way such as to bring it about. The fourth theory belongs to the Qadarites, who teach that man's will is free, in the sense that virtue is consistent with divine Providence, and vice is inconsistent with it. A good man is never punished, unless he is punished for his eminence and his goodness; so the cripple thanks Providence for having made him a cripple, because of all possible ways of existence this was the one most suited to him. The fifth and last opinion is that of the doctors of the Hebraic faith, which allows human beings freedom of choice in all things in the face of God's justice. All these five theories cannot be true. Nor can they all be false. It is incumbent on the man who is trying to make his way toward wisdom and virtue to choose from among all these opinions the one in which he recognizes the most enlightenment and which contains the most truth. So far as I am concerned, Emir of the Believers, I feel that I am still far removed from the stage when things have become clear and obvious. I can only hope that I shall one day reach that stage."

Abd Al Mumen turned to Ibn Tufail. First he drank from his cup of mint tea, and delicately patted his lips with the loose end of his sleeve. "This young scholar pleases me," he said. "When the fruit leaves the tree, it never falls far from the root. There is room for this essence in Allah's orchard."

Even though he was sitting cross-legged, his stomach stretched like a full goatskin, my father managed to bow from the waist. "It is the diversity of the earth which is the cause of the diversity of trees and of men," he said. "And it is the diversity of trees and of men that constitutes the richness of the earth. Such was the will of the Creator."

As he had previously done for me, the Caliph raised one of his eyelids and took his time considering my father. Ibn Tufail was fidgeting on his cushion. He knew that the preliminaries were over and that the conversation was about to become serious. He was on tenterhooks lest some unguarded word should disrupt it. Well-disposed as he was, the Caliph was subject to frequently changing moods, and his displeasure could be incurred by the shadow of even the most innocent word. For my part, I was not worried. I knew my father's skill in the handling of thoughts and of men. "All trees," he went on, "and all human beings, have received their essence from the hand of God. It would be a breach of faith to oblige them to change, for that would not have been the will of the Creator."

Abd Al Mumen smiled subtly. "Your son has shown that you are a Sage. But you are ill-informed about the cultivation of trees and of men. My gardener is very successful with his grafts. So is my government." The Caliph's voice had become more emphatic; even so, he paused. "Emir of the Believers," said my father, "in pure theology, and according to the revealed Law of Israel, every change in nature is a sin. In pure theology, as I said." Abd Al Mumen was still smiling. "And that is why," said he, "and in pure theology, the law of the Koran is superior to the law you have mentioned. It is our duty to improve trees and men, and to perfect nature, which has been given us only in embryonic form. Who protects you from the heat of the sun if it is not yourself, and your inventiveness? However diverse the earth and the essences of beings may be, up there, above the spheres, Allah is One, and everything that is born, and then later transformed and corrupted, fulfills his glory. As it is written in the sura: the worldly goods that you have received are nothing but temporary enjoyment. The fact that the time is short does not alter our right to enjoy it. We elevate what it pleases us to elevate. We abase what abases itself, and the first step toward abasement is to fail to recognize the unity of God."

With long, loose glissades, my father was combing his beard. "Emir of the Believers, God is One, as you have said, and I say it with you. He revealed himself on the mountain in all his magnificence and severity to his people who had come out of Egypt. He revealed himself in the desert in all his splendor and justice to the idolatrous people of Arabia. Here, as there, he chose a prophet to transmit his will, which is One, as he is One. What are we talking about, Emir of the Believers? About praising the Lord and his works. About being submissive and faithful to the Law which he has spread over the world. Are we serving God if we paint cherries green, or apples red? If we stick wings on fish, or fins on birds? If we sew a lion's skin onto a lamb, or hollow out camels' backs in order to bring forth mares? Every living being testifies to God according to its nature and to whatever apprenticeship it has had. I am not merely pleading my own cause, Emir of the Believers. I am pleading that of a people of acknowledged antiquity, a people which, through a thousand vicissitudes, has been capable of conserving its own truth and its own *raison d'être*. How can it be called God's justice if force is used to take away what is its own, since it received it from on high?"

The Caliph allowed my father to speak without showing the slightest sign of impatience. "You put the question well," he said. "I shall try to answer you equally well. At the beginning of its history

the Berber people, to which I belong, was subjected to the Hebrews, and to the Law and rites of Israel, for there was no other
prophet than Moses to transmit the word of God. I am ignoring the
Nazarene here, and his idolatrous followers who bow down before
statues of wood or stone, and who have the effrontery to cut One
into three. From the depths of Arabia to the point where the world
ends, people have always greatly hungered and thirsted after a truth
that would ensure the peace of the soul. Our prophet came, and
brought it to us. From that time on there has been no place for any
revelation other than his. Those who had erred and strayed, those
who were perplexed, came to follow his inspiration and his Law,
and no Mussulman has ever objected to the return of a lost sheep.
Allah is One, and everyone born into the world belongs to the faith
he has spread among us. Those who have been prevented from
doing so are not sinful in their aberration. If they were free, it
would be their duty to join the ranks of the true believers, and woe
to him who later becomes an apostate. I have a revelation to make
to you. I had a similar conversation with Judah Ben Sossan, who
was a remarkable man. Why did he become an apostate? I was extremely distressed. But justice had to take its course."

My father gave a little cough into the hollow of his hand. He was
too subtle a politician not to have heard the door being slammed. If
the Caliph was giving him a warning, it could not have been clearer.
An emergency exit became apparent in the direction of Cordova.
My father ran toward it by a detour of several centuries, empha-
sizing how fruitful had been the peaceful coexistence of the two
communities, which had not merged but had each retained its own
specific character, and how much the town had thereby gained in
renown, and in the quality and standard of its life. This prosperity,
which had been the envy of two empires, had been ended, perhaps
forever, by oppression. "We must praise and respect the work of
God," said my father. "But is not the work of man also worthy
of praise and respect? Did not the prophet Mohammed say: 'Help
your brother when you see him oppressed, and as for the oppressor—
prevent him from doing evil'?"

Ibn Tufail started fidgeting again, to attract my father's gaze. Abd Al Mumen seemed neither less distant nor less attentive than at the beginning of the audience. "I am grateful to you," he said gently, "for taking to heart the salvation of my soul. I often think of it, and I am doing my best to bring it about. The Prophet also said: 'The life of this world is no more than a game.' Fame? Prosperity? They are but vanity. A game, which is perhaps cruel, and certainly absurd. The world waxes and wanes, empires clash, great eddies are caused by the slightest excess of heat or cold and throw whole peoples against each other, like winds against sand dunes, like waves against rocks. This produces dust, reefs, hollows, and protuberances, and also weeping and gnashing of teeth. You speak as the head of a family, and you are not wrong. I speak as the head of a state, and I am not sure that I am right. A merciless struggle has been engaged between the continents, with some men thrusting toward the east, others toward the west; I need all my people around me, in unity and cohesion, to ward off the blows and to return them. Family histories will have to wait. Cordova has been destroyed? We will remake it in Fez. Freedom of worship? A time will come for that. I too like cherries to be red, apples a soft green, birds to have wings and fish to have fins. I have heard the lament of the people of Israel from your mouth and I shall reflect upon it. This people is present on the two continents, and I do not disregard the possibility that it may well act as mediator. For one day we shall have to make peace, in accordance with the will of Allah."

On a discreet sign from the Caliph the servants removed the trays. The audience was at an end. In the main courtyard the steward gave us Abd Al Mumen's presents. He was treating us in princely fashion. Two bay mares, saddled and harnessed, a magnificent prayer mat made of fine silk, two sand fox fur coats, and a purse containing a considerable sum in pieces of gold. "I would have forgone all that in exchange for a promise," said my father. Ibn Tufail joined us. He informed me that I had been put in charge of the anatomy classes in the new Qarueen University.

🔣 30

IF I try, to recall the years spent in Fez, I dimly see a sort of downy cloud spreading out over a great space, which could nevertheless be completely contained in the hollow of my hand. And yet my memory has never failed me and I have never known the idleness which engulfs so many men. It seems to me that I had only one eye open, and that with the other I was fast asleep. What does the baker do? First he kneads his dough and makes it rise—and I conscientiously kneaded mine and allowed it to rise; next he puts his bread into the oven—and my baking time took place in the sort of cotton wool I felt caught up in. I was deploying myself in a vast, flabby duration which was becoming more and more compressed into a dry, concentrated experience. The points of reference that remain are my books, and their weight testifies to the fact that I was sleeping with only one eye. An introduction to formal logic. Mathematical and logical studies for the recasting of the calendar. Twelve out of the fourteen volumes on the teaching of the Law. Copies of these writings were beginning to circulate in Aragon, in Castile, in Languedoc, and in Provence; I was receiving questions on points of detail, and I made it a rule to send considered answers to each one. My letter to the scholars of Marseilles is a book in itself. In the main I received criticism, and I had to make an effort to harden my heart not to let myself be deflected by the ignorant immured in their prejudices, whose number is great, as you know.

My choice was made: to suit some people, and not all. The baking of ideas requires more subtlety than does that of bread; it is not a question of satiating but, on the contrary, of generating hunger. If there is mystery in what cannot be seen, there is no less mystery in what is visible and within reach of our senses, and which some people claim to know, though they do not. People who make the effort to think for themselves, and to substantiate the validity of their acquired knowledge, are rare indeed. In most cases it is only warmed-over provender that they offer to satisfy our appetite; and what is more, it has been so hastily warmed over that it crumbles under the slightest breath of air.

This diversion is to delay the admission that I was not happy in Fez. Though I was not unhappy either. Let me call it detached, so as not to say indifferent, which would be too strong. My father must have felt much the same, though we never spoke of it. David was the only one of the three of us who gave the appearance of light-heartedness and ease. What a strange taste bread must have when its crust and its crumb are not made from the same flour! The ambiguity of the situation was not in itself too weighty. I had an exterior and an interior which did not agree, even though there was no real disagreement between them. In the beginning I had found a certain pleasure in wearing a mask. The better disguised I was, the freer I felt. Every day there was a pretense to be achieved, in order not to renounce anything real, and this *chassé-croisé* was not without its piquancy. That the security it gave rise to was problematical and constantly threatened did not unduly disturb me. I kept my own balance: an unstable balance, true, but the feeling of standing straight and walking unbowed was nevertheless present and reassuring.

The trouble was that my secret isolated me. I could not open my heart to anyone. In the long run it became wearying to have to pretend. My doubts displeased my father; my certainties would have displeased the people with whom I had to come into contact. The slightest exchange of words involved the risk of repudiation, if not worse. I was always on my guard, and this permanent tension did nothing to contribute to my serenity. By chance a political event occurred, and alleviated my solitude.

A *coup d'état* took place in the town of Ceuta, the Almohade governor and his henchmen were massacred and the old order was re-established. The Caliph's armies did not react to this affront. Most of the commerce in the Maghreb passed through this seaport, whose prosperity was due to the incessant arrivals and departures of ships and to the local manufacture of wood and paper, and there was more profit to be gained from a return to free trade than from too much rigidity, it being a verified fact that even the most intransigent doctrines weaken before the imperatives of commerce.

Once Ceuta was freed from the rule of the fanatics, a Hebraic community was very soon re-established there. Its prince was Rabbi Judah, whose oldest son was later to become one of my most gifted pupils. The coast was only three days' ride away, and our mares were swift-footed. My father bought a third mount so that each of us should have his own, and our visits to Ceuta became frequent, particularly at the times of our ritual feast days. We gradually transported part of our property there, and the moment they were finished I entrusted my manuscripts to Rabbi Judah, who had them copied and distributed. We camped in Fez, where my university duties required my presence, but we breathed in Ceuta, where the air was less restricted.

This was no doubt only a temporary solution but it had its potentialities, and it suited us. Elsewhere it was no better, and it might be worse. How stupid are those who hold our errors against us! I do not seek any sort of victory over them; I make it a point of honor not to cross swords with them, for no one has ever convinced a fool of his foolishness. My existence could well have come to its end in this way, straddled between two towns, to neither of which I really belonged and in which it was impossible to find peace. In moving thus between one and the other I maintained the illusion of having dealt with adversity by putting it off the scent. It is a strange sort of mathematics that reduces the bitterness of exile by multiplying the places of refuge. But like me, adversity was sleeping with only one eye, and it awoke again just when I had almost stopped believing in it.

It was Yom Kippur. I no longer remember what had prevented us from going to Ceuta. Since the day before we had been shut up in my father's room observing the strictest fast and in a state of profound contrition. At the very moment when my father was about to begin the prayer for the dead the door was broken down and six guards threw themselves on us. Neither their shouts nor their blows could hold back in our throats the lament that was oppressing us, for from henceforth it was also our own, as we were already among the dead. Our procession through the town was a veritable disgrace, and we were covered with spittle and dung when we arrived at the door of the mosque where the tribunal was sitting. According to the custom, I sank to my knees and kissed the robe of the judge. It was only when I raised my head that I recognized Ibn Moishe. His perplexity at seeing me in front of him, on my knees, covered with filth and already destined to suffer the extreme penalty, gave me a sudden inspiration, like a stroke of folly. "Qadi," I said, "there has been a misunderstanding. There has probably been a mistake. I beg you to hear me out before doing us an injustice. Do not be deceived by our accouterment and by the word of the guards. We were caught in the act—but of what misdeed? What have we done other than honor our dead? Is that a crime? Are we guilty because they lived and died according to the Law of Moses? Surely not? And how could we pray for the repose of their souls other than by the rite that was theirs? How could we call on God's indulgence, and be heard by them, other than in the words they used? This is my father, this is my brother, and you know me. We all respect the Law you represent, but we also respect our ancestors, to whom the true light was not revealed. I appeal to your impartiality, Qadi. I declare that we are innocent of apostasy, in spite of appearances."

Ibn Moishe exchanged a few words in a low voice with his assessors. "You are free," he said. The crowd stood aside to let us pass. The next evening, before the gates were shut, one after the other, in order not to be seen together, we left the sacred city of Fez forever.

31

IT WAS a four-masted Byzantine galley, sailing to Akko* with a load of timber and a band of pilgrims, mostly Edomites but some making the pilgrimage to Mecca. There were almost five hundred people, passengers and crew, on board. The galley had been built to take twice that number. We found room for our horses in the stalls underneath the poop deck, and for us and our row of chests in the stern, at the foot of the catapult designed to inspire pirates with respect. The crossing was supposed to take thirty-six days; it could have been made in half that time if the galley had not cast anchor every evening, either at the entrance to a bay or in the shallows near the coast. There were many things to be bought at the Levantine trader's shop: materials, food for men and beasts, and even straw for litters.

Spring had come, the days were clear and hot, the nights not too cold—this could have been a mere parenthesis in the broken line of our wanderings, but it was in fact a brutal wound, alive with bitterness and anguish. The regular breath of the westerly winds caused my pain too to swell. Just as it was, the world of the extreme west, with all its harshness and ingratitude—I had loved it, and I still loved it, it was responsible for the shaping of my soul and the arrangement of my thoughts, it was responsible for my approach to the world and for the ordering of my memories. I was carrying with me a rich harvest of profound friendships and remarkable joys,

* Acre.

of mortifications and rancors, and that taste for living, swollen with pride and humility, that gives life all its value.

Leaning over the bulwarks in the stern, I watched the wake of the galley for hours on end, and each eddy, each gleam of a wave, made me homesick for Cordova, which I was now sure I would never see again. Years had gone by since that night when with hurried steps we crossed the Roman bridge for the last time, and it was only as a passenger on this undulating vessel among the monotonous lapping sound of the waves that I became aware of the brutal nature of the rupture. The alarming unknown began right in front of the prow. More than ten centuries separated me from that other frightened voyager who was already carrying me in his seed while traveling the opposite direction. I told myself stupidly that after such a long absence we could no longer recognize anybody or anything. Part of me must have been unchanged, as the landscape and the sky must have remained unchanged. Would we be capable of inventing a new way to plight our troth, and together to engage in a peaceful venture on an earth where war was raging? I envied my imperturbable father, who spent unclouded hours rereading the Book of Job. I envied David, who was playing at being a squirrel in the yards of the mizzenmast and the topmast, a game he was much too old for, and who made boisterous friends with the members of the crew. Each, in his own way, was following the path of his own existence: I was not. I tried to force myself to work, but my thoughts were elsewhere. The past held me in its grip, and the future as yet wanted nothing to do with me.

Toward the tenth day, suddenly, at midday, a terrible storm arose. By the time we had reached the coast and found shelter behind a spit, two masts had been broken and many pilgrims washed overboard. Crouching down in the hollow of a coiled rope, clinging to it with all my might, I was violently sick, I lost all interest in both life and myself, I was as wretched as I had ever been and as I had never imagined anyone could be. My father was lying not far from me, and he too was in a bad way. Between two convulsions, with great, uncoordinated gestures, he implored the mercy of the heavens. David had gone down to see to the horses; taking no notice of the violent pitching of the ship, he was trying to calm them and see to it that they were still properly attached. The storm continued throughout the day and part of the night. In the morning we had to put into port for repairs. I left the ship and set foot on land, looking for a fountain. As I leaned over the clear water a strange reflection came up to meet me: the face of a man of uncertain age, with strong features penetrated by a hard, distant look. With the flat of my hand I shattered the image. Too late: it had revealed to me that that day was my thirtieth birthday.

32

MY friend—if you are not Jewish, you cannot understand, and if you are, what need have I to explain it to you? The state of mind of the outlaw who, with his own eyes, as the sun is setting, sees the hills of Galilee come into sight. An emotional state? Certainly; but of what sort, and to what degree? Enough to make you howl with laughter, or choke with tears, if your glottis did not suddenly find itself in an icy grip, if your pupils were not suddenly turned into marble. Enough to make you faint with joy and fear, if the springs of your flesh were not stretched to breaking point, if your heels were not pinned down onto glowing embers, if your head were not covered in ashes. Bliss and sorrow flowing over you in the same torrent—enough to turn your brain, to make your soul overflow, to transform your living flesh into a pillar of salt. And yet neither pitch nor sulphur fell from on high, but the rosy hue of a very ordinary spring evening. And yet, it was only foothills such as you can see anywhere that rose on the horizon, a strip of limpid mist marrying the earth and the sky, a few dark groves and solitary cypresses interspersed between russet hillocks. And yet—what could be more banal than a vessel approaching a coastal inlet which opens out to receive it? Whoever you were, whether scholar or ignoramus, civilized man or barbarian, the approach to Akko as the sun is setting is one of those events that remain forever in a man's memory. Those rust-colored stone fortifications rising sheer out of a sea sparkling with all the colors of the rainbow, in which hundreds of polychromatic boats are riding at anchor, their broad beams rubbing against each other in the opaline luster of the surf. That rain of masts, that spread of sails, of ropes, of nets, that melee of bodies on the bridges and around the shops, those flocks of squalling birds searching for leftovers—all this ferment and fever was aimed just as much at attracting the onlooker as at disturbing him.

Akko is first of all a combination of colors, then a rising tide of uproars, and finally a display of various frenzies. As you know, all Frankish Syria's traffic passes through this port. To travelers of all sorts the kingdom here exhibits its force and opulence—and these are all the more ostentatious in that they are factitious, and insufficiently secured by a tottering empire. But whoever lands there is caught up in the vortex, captivated and subdued, even if he is on his guard against being duped. Our galley was able to come alongside only by forcing its way through a mass of flotsam and jetsam. Night had fallen while this maneuver was taking place. By order of the port authorities, no one was allowed to go ashore until the next day.

Once again I find it destressing to continue my story: it is not that my memory is failing me, but because of the bitterness so intimately linked with these recollections. That we were neither expected nor even accepted in the land of our ancestors—that particular source of bitterness had been bound up with the history of our people for too many centuries for it still to constitute a really acute pain. What hurt was newer and more subtle, and barely conscious during that long night of waiting, when the stones of the jetty were almost, but not quite, within reach of our hands. Judging by what reached us of the movements in the port and the town, the effluvia of the tide intermingled with the odor of incense, the gusts of wind and the distant tinkling of bells, the sudden fervor of the Edomites singing hymns at the top of their voices in an organized choir, and the cantankerous silence of the few pilgrims on their way to Mecca who were walking up and down on the bridge in close formation, I felt as if I were one of the crowd the day before a fair in which buyers and sellers would come face to face the moment dawn broke. We were at the gates of an immense bazaar in which God had been chopped into little pieces to be retailed, according to the law of supply and demand, to the consumers of the Holy Land, provided they had the wherewithal to pay. On this ground we need not be excluded—it was merely a question of the purse hanging from my father's belt.

Under cover of piety, the exercise of which remained purely formal, the petty barons of Toulouse, Poitou, Aquitaine, Anjou, and Lorraine had made periodic incursions into these lands, and set an example of rapacity and double-dealing imitated successively by all the occupying forces, and which became recognized throughout the country as the new spirit from the west. Contrary to the Arab conquerors, who were satisfied with their first booty, gained at little cost, the Crusaders cultivated an insatiable appetite, and would willingly have developed it to infinity had their political insecurity not imposed limits on them. It became a question of first come first served—unless the latecomers plundered their predecessors—it was a question of who had the longest fingers and the speediest hand, who was the most ambiguous and shifty in both word and deed.

The effect of this morality, almost nothing of which remained secret, was that human beings were transformed into merchandise whose value was determined by the amount of wealth they could produce or introduce into the already existing circuits. Our galley was not merely laden with timber and pilgrims, it was also laden with profit, which was at that time for the benefit of King Amalric, who was so obese, it was said, that no horse could carry him longer than an hour. All around the periphery of the great inland sea he was described as the personification of cupidity, fleecing everyone and everything that it was possible to fleece, including his own institutions and orders, which were able to survive only by imitating him. "A poor Jew is a dead Jew, my father had said. Insofar as we were solvent, we perhaps had a chance to survive in the Kingdom of Jerusalem.

It caused me great distress that we would no doubt have to follow the path of baseness and corruption, feign poverty in order not to allow ourselves to be despoiled too quickly, exchange one disguise for another, when my only wish was to recover my own identity. Neither my father nor I could sleep that night. Our gazes searched the darkness in the east for a sign that would enable us to recognize the land of Galilee, which was formerly ours, such as it had been perpetuated in the memory of many generations, a land where milk and honey flowed only because of the will of men, and which had produced that strong line of descendants whose will still existed in the form of a refusal to perish. How much longer could this continue? The walls were closing in on us everywhere in the world. This return to our origins also contained an admission of failure. Even though the promise had been made in our Scriptures as a prelude to the advent of better days, human beings have no more talent than rivers for running backward. We were returning as strangers to a country fashioned by other hands and other heads than ours. Our extinct kingdoms had been commandeered by barbarians. I was too saddened by what I knew and by what I foresaw to yield to the temptation to believe that an act of grace was still possible. During that long night my father appeared so withdrawn into himself, and yet attracted toward the shore, that it seemed he still believed in a revival. Belief was his force—as doubt was mine. David was the only one of the three of us who slept, lying peacefully between the legs of the horses in the shelter of the stall. For him this was only the end of one journey, which was already bringing him near to the next.

Even before dawn broke the quay was crowded with people. In the approaches to Akko, as in the town, and, farther on, on the roads to Galilee, Samaria, and Judea, there were three sorts of inevitable and superabundant nuisances for which we had constantly to be on the alert: the beggar, the seller of holy relics, and the toll collector. Woe betide anyone who tried to escape their clutches; he would be declaring himself either an infidel or a rebel, and would suffer for it before the hour was out by exposing himself to insult or molestation, if not worse, and he would owe his safety only to the speed of his legs. To show signs of haste was to surrender one's dignity: the better course was to submit. Perhaps the one who was the least of a cheat was the seller of holy relics, for he gave something in exchange for the coin he extorted: a splinter from the true cross, a scrap of the genuine shroud, a thorn from the authentic crown, or else—and this was the least costly—a letter of indulgence for a thousand years in purgatory. Who does not need God's forgiveness? There was nothing, on the other hand, to distinguish the beggar operating on his own behalf from the one genuinely devoted to his own saint, or the toll collector enriching himself according to his own sweet will from the one levying taxes on behalf of his government. We, who neither wore the cross nor carried the staff or gourd of the ordinary pilgrim, were taxed, according to our looks, at three or five times the normal rate. Even our horses were declared to be Jewish horses, and my father had to pay accordingly. Hardly had the first toll collector disappeared into the crowd than a second appeared at our heels, claiming to be the only one qualified to levy the tithe from the infidel. My father had the effrontery to ask him for a receipt and he gave us a bit of paper on which he had hastily scribbled something in Latin characters, which turned out to be false when offered to the third toll collector posted at the town gate.

Whereupon an argument arose about the price agreed with the porters of our cases, and once again we had to come to terms, for trouble was already brewing. Like a skiff thrown up onto a sandbank, we landed at the foot of the outer wall, distressed at the novelty of this welcome. Some little way away from the chaos of the crowd and the unloading there was a moment of respite. David had noticed a watering trough and led the horses to it; a toll collector was waiting for him there, in the shadow of the fountain. The only thing that had so far not been subject to any sort of tax was the air we were breathing, and it was clear, fresh air, brought down by a light breeze from the green hills in the vicinity, which were of a strong, rich green such as I had never seen in the world I came from. My nostrils avidly breathed in this fragrance in which the sweet smells of brackens and mosses dominated the sour smells of the tide and the dust. After a thousand years of exile, my lungs recognized that particular fragrance. If I had been struck down by lightning, or if a fanatic had slit my throat, I think I should have died happy.

My father decided to go off alone to reconnoiter, and this was no doubt the best thing to do. He was not away for very long. He came back with a shabby, restless old man whose name was Rabbi Japheth and who held the position of *gaon** in the synagogue. Both men were pushing a flat cart intended for our cases. Our host knew the passages deserted by the beggars, the merchants, and the tax men, and led us without mishap to his house on the banks of the river Quadoumin. On the way, Japheth gave us some information. A puny Hebrew community still existed there, not by the grace of God but by a royal edict proclaimed at the beginning of the century by Baldwin I, who limited the number of Jews authorized to live in Akko to two hundred heads of families, on condition that they were grouped outside the walls and all obliged to follow the dyer's trade. This favor owed nothing to Christian charity but suited the King very well. Because of a very ancient invention that dated back to the Phoenicians, the purple and carmine extracted from the shells in the bay had the reputation, rightly or wrongly, of being inimitable, and had contributed to the fame and fortune of the town since the period when it had been called Ptolemaïs. It had been no less established that only Jewish hands possessed the necessary science to manipulate these colors to perfection. By whole caravans and shiploads, bales of raw wool from all sources and woven goods of all origins received their brilliance and glow here on the riverbank, so sought after throughout the world, from the Indies to the Latin countries, were the purple and carmine of Akko.

* The oriental equivalent of the function of a prince.

The dyer's trade, however, was extremely unhealthy and killed off its workers at about the age of thirty. Japheth was the only old man in the whole commune, because he was the only one who had white hands. His rank as master of justice dispensed him from the work and enabled him to spend all his time studying the Law. On the other hand, he had almost no opportunity to apply it, unless it were to himself. The school was deserted: no boy over five years old was available to be taught—they were all put to work in the dyeing trade. Apart from the Sabbath and the great feast days, the synagogue too was deserted: the men found it too difficult to survive and to pay the tax that allowed them the freedom of the city. The sanitation was deplorable. There was no other doctor than he, Japheth, whose competence was restricted to the traditional rules of hygiene. It so happened that a high birth rate filled the gaps, and the community kept up its permitted numbers, like a shoal of fish among sharks. Japheth's wife was already his fourth, the first three having been killed by the dyeing work, and he had had seventeen children, three quarters of whom had not survived early childhood. Nevertheless, there was no reason for recrimination or complaint. Akko was abounding in wealth, the leavings of which would have satisfied the needs of any other city of the same size; the Queen Mother Theodora, married at thirteen and a widow at eighteen, lived there in a golden solitude worthy of the pomp and ceremony of her uncle, the Emperor of Orient. The amount of trade passing through the port was incomparable; the traffic in goods and pilgrims was incessant. There were enough temptations, distractions, and satisfactions to enable the corporation of dyers to be more or less forgotten.

"Forget all the theories," Japheth advised. A successful felony on the part of Byzantium, he said, an intrigue by the Frankish barons against the Crown, a thrust by the Atabegs of Aleppo, and the magnificent but quite arbitrary equilibrium of the city would shatter like a glass pane under a hail of stones. There was everything to be feared from an unleashing of the passions that had temporarily been quietened under the great tide of good fortune. Here, the word *peace* didn't mean the absence of war; it meant that war was being prepared, being fomented, being unleashed sufficiently far away not to disturb the smooth running of business. But even in these conditions of relative tranquillity it was always salutary for a Christian to kill a Jew, and thus make sure of his place in Paradise. This sort of crime not only went unpunished but was highly recommended to anyone who wished his stay in the Holy Land to bear fruit. The fact that there had been relatively few ritual murders since the last wave of Crusaders did not prove that the taste for massacre had been lost; there were too few people left to be put to death for the gesture to be worth the thought and effort.

But death, Japheth told us, takes no account of suffering, and this was measureless. The Hebraic community was now like nothing more than a form emptied of its content. The respect for life was being lost, because life was worth nothing. The only fraternity that still existed between men was forced on them, there was no more love of one's neighbor, there were no more acts of grace addressed toward the divine. Israel was breaking up in distress, as in Egyptian times, as in Babylonian times. Everyone muttered his prayer, when he said it, for himself, so great was his need to console himself for what was inconsolable. In extreme cases the words uttered lost all meaning, after they had first lost all power of evocation. When a dyer had a few hours of liberty, what was more natural than that he should throw himself into sleep rather than into study or prayer? He was consumed with fatigue; he allowed himself no other hope than a short rest, while waiting for eternal rest. All that remained living was the faith in the permanence of Israel. But life itself did not present the consolation of death. As for going into exile—who had the means, or even the idea, in the midst of all this affliction?

We spent our first evening in the land of Galilee in the low room where Japheth lived. His young wife had laid a smooth white cloth on the table and lit as many candles as the candlestick could hold. There was white bread to break, and Carmel wine in our honor.

However poor he was, Japheth intended to give our arrival something of the air of a festival.

Later on, several dyers joined us, for the legendary name of the Maimons had spread as far as here, and people wanted to see and touch us. We had to describe down to the last detail Spain, the Maghreb, and our long journey. While my father was talking of the events that touched us most closely, I remembered some of the stories told us by the refugees who had passed through our house in Cordova, trivial memories which finally seemed so similar one to the other that it became tiring to repeat them. We each carried our double bag of memories with us, our most precious baggage. Now our own story was laid on top of other stories already heard thousands of times, but it was nevertheless distinct and novel for us who had to live it.

What was more unreasonable than to look for a tranquil place in a world that was not tranquil! In the Occident we had adopted a linear conception of destiny. If this were to break, our entire existence would seem compromised. With the air of Galilee, the oriental notion of a cyclical destiny entered into me. A rupture meant nothing, since everything was accomplished in great revolving circles. We were already completing a loop which was bringing us back to our point of departure. That the distance covered should have been longer than a man's lifetime did not change its meaning.

The dyers listened politely to a conversation they could not understand. I observed these red men, encrusted with dye down to the very marrow of their bones, who probably even wept red tears and whose destiny went around in circles. They were no more responsible for their fate than we were for ours, even though our share of free will made us all accomplices. We were hoping for a revelation from these immobile Jews; they were expecting a message from us. We were both mistaken. There was neither revelation nor message. There were lives to be lived, and that was all there was to it.

When the men had left, weary and no doubt disappointed, Japheth became pensive. "You are very welcome," he said. "But to be perfectly frank I cannot see that your place is here. What could we do with two scholars and an expert in precious stones? And I am not only speaking for our community of Akko, one of the largest in the kingdom. The situation is worse in the rest of Galilee and in Samaria, and it is no better in Judea. There are no more than a few hundred of us left, scattered in isolation, and I should add that the word *we* must be expunged from our vocabulary—it separates us more than it unites us. Over the whole extent of our former territories the Jew has become an outlaw, and anyone may strike him down. This is not the most serious factor: tenacity, chance, and luck go in whatever way is pleasing to God. As I have already said, death takes no account of suffering. The worst thing is that the spirit disappears. No scholar has come out of our ranks for fifty years or more. The sovereign race which governs us has razed our sanctuaries to the ground, but not without profiting from them, and the golden calf has been stood up on its legs again. Our masters leave us our ruined wall and two or three places of prayer in the kingdom because they bring in a good income for them, but are of very little help to us; they allow us to lead our joyless lives, which disintegrate without any outside pressure. Our mainspring is broken. No sudden awakening, no revolt is possible any more; we have no embryonic prophet. There is nothing but a vague hope which, very slowly, is falling asleep. Israel used to be a people who read and wrote, who studied and meditated, in direct touch with grace and thought. Except in the tabernacles we have no more books, no more study centers, no more time, or strength, for meditation. That these might still exist elsewhere in the world does not console us for the desert that has been created here. Thought is like the soil: if it is not worked it becomes parched; if it is not fertilized it becomes sterile. What sort of an existence would you have in the midst of our dyers, almost half of whom can neither read nor write, and none of whom has any conception of abstract reasoning? Judging by my own experience, every year that passes makes me more insignificant. Your presence would certainly do me good, but it would certainly do you harm, and it is not I, Japheth, who must be saved, it is the spirit of Israel, which is still in you. As for your stones? None of us would have the means even to buy the tiniest fragment of one, and no Jew is permitted to sell one outside our community. Ah, if only you were dyers! We should all have moved up to make a little room for you. But scholars? And a dealer in precious stones! When the kingdom belongs to the Franks, and may tomorrow belong to the Greeks or the Turks, unless the Egyptians wake up . . . unless God grants us a miracle . . . That is what I had to say to you. Go away from here! Quickly! And having said that, I repeat: You are very welcome in my house. So long as I have a roof, bread, and wine to share, I will share them with you."

For quite a time I had been observing my father, who was combing his beard with his fingers. I knew that he carried Cordova within himself like an incurable malady, and that he had no plans. The failure of his *Epistle to the Communities* had affected him more profoundly than he had allowed to show, and the circumstances of our flight from the Maghreb had broken his will. We had embarked on the galley going to Akko because it had been the first to leave Ceuta, and it was going far. If the voyage had taken years, even a whole lifetime, none of the three of us would have complained. All we had to do was rely on the winds and the waves and have confidence in the crew. From the moment we had started our journey, leaving could have been an end in itself. My father had never meant us to go back to live in the land of Israel, whose interminable lament he had never stopped hearing. He didn't reply to Japheth, because he had nothing to reply. Yes, though: he wanted to go to Jerusalem, and to Hebron. And after that? In any case, we would not stay in Galilee. Alexandria, perhaps? The Fatimids of Egypt still tolerated the Hebraic communities. So it was still around the same routes that our destiny revolved.

Japheth's face had become drawn. He had a clear, washed-out, almost white look, which penetrated through his snowy, shaggy eyebrows. "Jerusalem!" he sighed. "Ah Jerusalem! If I weren't so old

and tired, how I would have liked to go there with you! I haven't
been back since . . . Since . . ." Japheth was born in the Beth-el district, near the so-called Dung Gate, which leads down to the
Kidron Valley in a steeply sloping alleyway that caught the morning wind. He was nine years old when the Crusaders besieged the
Citadel. "Nine years old," he repeated, covering his eyes with the
flat of his hand. "I have seen everything. Everything! How is it possible to emphasize sufficiently what the soldiers of the Crucified
Christ did in Jerusalem, so that the world shall remember it forever?
Was it not a message of peace, of justice, and of love that had been
left them by him whose earthly traces, they claimed, they had come
to deliver. To deliver from what? To deliver from whom? A Greek
and an Armenian colony were keeping a permanent watch over
their holy places, which nobody had ever thought of disturbing. No
pilgrim from the occidental world was prevented from climbing the
Via Dolorosa and going up to Golgotha, and they never stopped
coming, at Easter time, or for the Nativity. Mussulmans also came
to the Dome of the Rock, and Jews came to the Wall. And there
was no tax man collecting his dues."

He, Japheth, had grown up among his own people. From time
immemorial, perhaps since the destruction of Herod's temple, his
family had hardly ever moved away from its houses, rebuilding
what time destroyed, and putting a roof over the ground outside
the walls when they became short of space. How many were they?
"Many," Japheth declared. "Several thousand families. What need
had we to count? We all knew each other's faces, their names and
their father's names, their habits, their trades. There were dozens of
schools, dozens of synagogues, hundreds of houses, and all around
lived families of Arabs, of Druses, of Syriacs, of Egyptians, each
one self-contained like drops of oil on the surface of an expanse of
water, whose edges touch but do not intermingle. Who could have
told the difference between a donkey belonging to a Jew and a donkey belonging to a Moslem or a Christian?" When they were not
carrying their loads they all grazed the same grass together on the

slopes of Mount Zion or the Mount of Olives. Seen from one of the surrounding heights the town of Jerusalem might appear small, and in fact it was not big. In a single hour a man could walk around it. But it was full. The number of its inhabitants was estimated at more than sixty thousand. "Personally," said Japheth, "figures mean nothing to me. Sixty thousand people, men, women, and children, how many is that? In height? In width? In thickness? What I do know is that in the form of corpses this number covers all the streets up to your calves, and some up to your knees. I was there, I, Japheth, and I saw. I was nine years old, and I remember. They pitched their camps on the Jaffa road, on the Damascus road, on Mount Scopus, men from Normandy, from Burgundy, from Provence, from Flanders, with their women, their children, their livestock, and their priests. How many knights? How many troops? Their line, with four men abreast, could have been a thousand paces long. When they had settled down they advanced one morning in procession toward the Citadel. Seven times they marched around it, singing hymns. This took them the whole day. After which the priests erected their altars and ordered the walls to fall. All Jerusalem was up on the towers and parapet walks, laughing. And with good reason! It was enough to look at those plumed masks, some of which were nearly bursting their cheeks blowing into horns; others were imploring the heavens, and still others were cursing the stones. Naturally we spat on them a little from the top of the ramparts. Naturally we threw flaming bundles of straw down on them, boiling oil, whole buckets of excrement and great armfuls of filth. There was nothing for them to worry about because they were out of reach, at least a hundred cubits from the wall, which hadn't budged an inch. It was already summer, it had been a hot day and it was only just beginning to get cool on the hills. The Jaffa Gate was still in the sun while the Lions' Gate was in moonlight. Was the spectacle going to continue all night? When they had finally realized that the wall was absolutely refusing to obey, they looked very angry, some of them started quarreling and making grotesque gestures, and they finally turned around and went back to their camps. For a whole week we heard them sawing wood and hammering. I, Japheth, didn't understand very well what was being prepared, but I could see by people's faces that it wasn't going to be a simple business.

"The captain in charge of the defense of Jerusalem was an Egyptian named Iftikhar, a proud cavalier with huge mustaches who spoke loudly and shouted even more loudly, but who had only a few men under his orders capable of withstanding an assault. Bedouins. Sudanese. Rapid on horseback, with the javelin and the yataghan—precisely those skills which were useless for the defense of a citadel. The inhabitants had accumulated piles of stones and dipped the bundles of straw in pitch. With the fortified walls it had, Jerusalem ought to be able to hold out. As a matter of pure precaution the Greeks and Armenians, about a thousand families, painted great carmine crosses on the doors of their houses and went to earth in their cellars. A few Jews did the same. With some exceptions, these were spared. Subtle strategist that he was, Iftikhar was expecting the assault to come from the Zion Gate and his catapults were prepared between the crenellations. As it happened, they attacked from the Herod's Gate side, with mangonels, ladders, and wheeled towers as high as the wall, and in less than an hour they had breached it. They were able to begin their *delivery*. When you come to think about it, it's a veritable malady of the occidentals, *delivering*. They are always prepared to sow death and destruction to deliver someone or something. I, Japheth, I managed to climb into an empty night-soil jar; it stank so terribly that no cleric, knight, or foot soldier had the courage to go near it, and that was what saved my life. Even so, I saw it all. They went about things methodically, with knife and scimitar, without any great hurry, as if they had the whole of eternity before them, and in one sense they had, because that was what they had been promised for this ignoble slaughter. The Jews, men, women, and children, were herded into the synagogues and yeshivas and burned alive. Al-Aqsa was also ablaze, full to bursting point with living flesh. I saw their archers dragging little children along by their feet, kicking their skulls in and throwing them, still breathing, into the fires. In the alleyways many women were stripped naked and violated before being hacked to pieces. In the middle of the night, when everything had become calm again because the whole town had been 'delivered,' I, Japheth, I climbed out of the jar. No! No, I shan't spare you any of the details. Every street in Jerusalem was covered with a thick layer of disemboweled trunks, of scattered entrails, of glutinous brains steeped in a sort of red-currant jelly that was beginning to stink.

"A huge full moon was making its rounds above the ramparts. Later—much later—I made some sort of calculations. Admitting that among the soldiers of Christ there were some just men, some who were scrupulous, some who were disgusted, we can attribute to every one of the rest of them at least twenty murders in that one day. Seen in isolation there is nothing excessive about the figure. It is very likely that it can be exceeded. In Jerusalem it was a question of piecework, which necessarily takes longer and is more difficult. You have to get your victim to come out of his hiding place, then catch him, then hold him. He struggles, he screams, he beseeches; sometimes he has the effrontery to defend himself, or even to counterattack. Then you have to stab him and your sword is sticky, it isn't very firm in your hand, it may well be deflected, it can sideslip, or get stuck in a bone. Then you have to start all over again a second, or third, or a fourth time, you have to make sure that the openings are wide and deep enough for life to flow out of them and 'deliverance' to enter, not to mention that it is a hot day, that sweat and thirst slow down even the best-regulated action, and that one has to allow oneself a moment's respite every so often in order to drink from one's gourd . . . No, really, twenty murders a day for each cleric or laic—that was no cause for criticism. There were three to four thousand let loose on the town; there were fifty thousand dead: those are the figures. I, Japheth, managed to escape to the country. A family took me in in Tiberias; then another, in Safed, and I ended up here, among the dyers. The Bishop of Antioch and the Bishop of Tyre organized great festivities and gave thanks to the heavens that Christ's shame had finally been avenged. He who had spoken only of love and forgiveness—they felt obliged to associate him with their thirst for vengeance! I don't know whether the Pope and the other occidental bishops also arranged for public rejoicing. In all objectivity, they had good reason to be pleased and proud. Fifty thousand dead in Jerusalem, that was a splendid sacrifice to offer up to God, and God himself should have been satisfied. I, Japheth, I never had the heart to go back to Jerusalem. I will come with you. I will take you by the safe roads that I know. But we shall have to wait a little while, until the summer is over and the pilgrims have gone. We will go there for the feast days: I, Japheth, I give you my word."

The dawn was turning the windows white. The street was already coming to life as the dyers passed by on their way to work. "Yes," said my father. "We will go and pray in Jerusalem. And then we shall leave this unhappy land."

ॐ 33

IT WAS to be supposed that what Japheth had said was true: that our place was not among the survivors in the Kingdom of Jerusalem. I took it to be no less true that no one has any place reserved for his personal use in any country whatsoever. There were alternatives to be chosen from, situations to accept or reject. Man had been created upright, endowed with various kinds of equipment: legs to walk with, arms to grasp things with, both under the command of the head. If the spirit was dying in the Akko community, should we pretend not to notice, or should we try to revive it? If its state of hygiene was deplorable, was it sufficient just to observe that fact, or was there something to be done to improve it? Anyone who has acquired a certain amount of knowledge but who only uses it for his personal satisfaction is like a miser sitting on his hoard: an object of reprobation and anathema.

Without attacking him directly, I managed to make my father pull himself together and to persuade him to accompany me. One after the other we visited the dye works, and what we saw was total desolation. I don't know whether hell has any substance, or whether people do any cooking there; I don't know whether it is convincing to associate such a crude reality with a doubtful image. I had already seen slaves chained to their forced labor; stonecutters paving their lungs with silica; dockhands broken under their loads; galley slaves ringing the knell of their own existence on the waves. But though the slave is coerced by the whip, he is also to some extent protected by his market value; his life is worth his age, his strength, and his purchase price, which is less than that of a plowing ox but a little more than that of a pack mule, and it is not the custom to work one's livestock to death.

But the life of the Akko dyers apparently had no value, and every one of them carried within himself the whip of violence. So many pieceworkers, so many slaves, so many slave drivers: three divisions that actually all came to the same thing—a trade which hollowed out the gaze and the cheeks, stripped the hands of skin, and made the feet swell with dropsy. What was called the workshop was made of disjointed wooden planks, rotting because of the humidity, and the air that crept in here and there could not hold its own against the sickly vapor exuded by the scouring and mordanting tubs, against the boiling steam that came out of the vats where the coloring matter was concocted. The women's legs were steeped in a river of reddish mud as they worked at the rinsing bowls in which their arms were plunged up to the shoulders; the children were bringing up clear water from the river. Who owned this industry? Everyone and no one. The King, no doubt, just as he owned the Quadoumin, the street, the houses, the people; the only choice the dyers had was to be killed or kill themselves, and this was what still gave them the appearance of being free men, since they cost nothing and produced much.

I started dreaming of medical aid, of preventive medicine, of prophylaxis, of methods that could be invented to protect the workingman against premature corrosion. Realizing that it would take me some time to study this matter in depth, I provided myself for the time being with lint and local remedies to bandage open wounds, with emollient julep, and with an emetic electuary against the catarrh that caused havoc in chests permanently submerged in such vapors. I went from one to the other with my portable dispensary, for no one was yet prepared to come to see me.

The dyers' indifference to their state caused me as much uneasiness as the evils inflicted on them. "What's the use of changing what has been in force since the trade has existed?" they asked me.

"What we need is to earn a little more, to pay less taxes, to have a little time to rest. Dressings and drafts are for the rich. *We* have lived without treatment ever since it pleased God to call us into the world, and during the years he has decided to leave us in it, and he certainly sees how we are afflicted. If he does not remedy our evils, that is because they have no remedy. Why make such a fuss?" I had to argue, to persuade. In the end, reason prevailed and the dyers allowed me to treat them. I was counting on the beneficial effect of the balms and drugs to establish my authority in this matter.

My father too was not unresourceful: he had the idea of getting the children together during the quarter of an hour when they had a break for something to eat, and teaching them the letters of the alphabet, of which they were ignorant. This was going against both their natural tendencies and the advice of their parents. For all the good it would do them to be able to read! In former times our fathers and grandfathers had learned. Where had it led them? To get themselves massacred and burned with their books. It's quite enough for Japheth to tell us what has been written, stories so beautiful that they wring your heart, though there isn't a word of truth in them. And yet God must know about the dyeing trade, he who put so many colors in the sky and on the earth. Here too he had to argue and persuade. In the end it was less difficult than it had seemed at first. In a domain where Japheth would not have been listened to, my father and I were heard because we were strangers who had come from afar, because it was possible that destiny had sent us. Arguing with us was a kind of recognition that we had something to offer them. Even though neither man nor woman, neither adult nor child, deferred to us in any way, they didn't interfere with us. It didn't even occur to them that we were giving our services free, or to think of what these services cost my father.

By pure chance, and once again, David got us out of our difficulties. No sooner had we set foot in Akko than he had entered into partnership with a Greek who had a stall on the port, opposite the wharfs. The object of this trade was a novelty on the shores of

Galilee—the *souvenir from the Holy Land*, which every pilgrim set his heart on taking back for those of his family who could not leave their country. Rings, pendants, trinkets, medals, well made and inlaid with silver thread after the Cordovan manner, so modestly priced that no purchaser could remain indifferent to them. Soon the two goldsmiths employed by the Greek and taught by my brother were not enough, and more had to be trained. Chance played its part. As a caravan was being unloaded David discovered that it contained some saddlebags full of copper stones from King Solomon's mines. This crystal, a pretty greenish blue, either plain or veined, and easy to split, cut, and polish, could rightly be compared with the corundum which came from the Indies, and David got hold of part of the cargo for a song. He had it made into jewels which looked so noble that the Greek never had enough of them to sell. My brother kept in the background, regardless of the risk he was running; his associate, though avid, remained honest, and never tried to go back on their verbal agreement. Their trade prospered and each week David gave my father a larger sum of money, part of which was turned into medicines and the rest used for our keep.

Were we going to prove Japheth wrong and earn our place in the city of Akko? He was right on one point: the life of the mind had no place there. Whenever my medical duties allowed me time, I began to dream of a vast philosophical work which would be an attempt at a synthesis between revealed truths and deduced truths, or, to be more precise, between the teaching of the Scriptures and the teaching of Aristotle. When I compared their essence I discovered more convergences than divergences, and I felt that a close analysis would be sure to reduce or even remove certain apparently fundamental discrepancies. All this work implied a subtle, rigorous dialectic which I felt I was now capable of sustaining. I simply could not conceive of the Hebrew genius and the Greek genius as being so far apart that the gap between them would be insuperable. On both sides human intelligence was in touch with perfection, and in the realm of thought perfection ought to tend toward unity. To flit back and forth from one realm to the other—that was my ambition. I dreamed of this book, and yet I didn't even write the first line; my heart was not in it. For whom should I have written it since, just as surely in her ancient lands as in the far-off world, Israel was forgetting how to read? In actual fact I was too much in the thrall of medicine, and kept delaying my project. Before approaching the things of the spirit I had to put the things of the body in order. I was a little overexalted in this practice, as if the art of healing had been invented for my own personal satisfaction.

I had successes, certainly, and I was proud of them. Idiot that I was! I didn't notice that the dyers' faces, at first indifferent and passive, were gradually becoming more and more unwelcoming when they saw me. I took their heavy silences for approbation, their averted eyes for encouragement, and their gestures of refusal for thanks. Then there was an incident to which I paid no particular attention because I was far from imagining that it was going to bring my practice to an end. One morning I discovered that the expectoration of a man working at the mordanting vat was red. I submitted him almost by force to a medical examination: he was in an advanced state of phthisis. Confident of my authority, I ordered him to stop work at once and go home to bed, where I would visit him. He answered, panting, that it wasn't blood he was spitting, but carmine, and that he would be better before the day was out, with no help from anyone. As his wife was in the rinsing department in the next shed, I called her over, to help me get her husband to see reason. She hesitated for just a moment when I told her how seriously ill he was, but finally eluded me and went back to her work. In order not to lose face with this obstinate man, I gave him a hemostatic potion, thinking that if he became a little weaker he would be more docile. To my stupefaction, he flung the bottle to the ground and went back to his steeping, still spitting red matter into the hollow of his hand.

I urgently wanted to tell Japheth about this. But it was he who spoke of it first. He had received a delegation from the dyers who

invited me politely but firmly, through him, to stop meddling in
their affairs. In this way I learned that the dressings I applied were
often removed as soon as I had turned my back, that the emollients
and emetics I gave them to drink were only drunk by the gutters,
because my lint made their movements heavier and slower, and my
drafts were far too bitter. There was something even more serious:
a young boy who was beginning to recognize the letters of the alphabet had spoken disrespectfully to his father, an offense that constituted a threat to the social order and for which the entire corporation held us responsible. It had therefore been decided that the
Maimons would no longer be allowed into the workshops, and that
if they tried to ignore this ban they would run the risk of being
thrown out.

My father took the affront placidly, as was his wont. But not I.
My eyes were filled with tears of rage and sadness, which old age
has not dried, and I felt a need of air and space. I went and saddled
my horse and galloped off against the wind into the dunes. As I advanced along the shore my horse's joy at feeling the sand under its
hoofs gave me a kind of peace. I didn't meet a living soul on the
beaches, and the solitude also did me good. In the distance, through
the rifts in the mist, appeared the village of Caiphas,* topped by
Mount Carmel, which seemed to be walking on the sea.

In the days after the death of Solomon, Ahab, the son of Omri,
reigned over Israel, and he was an impious king who did evil. His
first wife was Jezebel the bloodthirsty, who had sworn to put to
death all the prophets of Jehovah, for she worshipped Baal, and incited Ahab to rear up an altar to him. But the governor of his house,
who was named Obadiah, hid the prophets of the Lord fifty by
fifty in a cave in Samaria and fed them with bread and water so that
they should survive the drought and famine that the Lord had
spread over the kingdom to punish it. For three whole years the
heavens did not rain down a single drop of water, not a blade of
grass was left, the beasts died of thirst, and many men died of star-

* Now Haifa.

vation and weakness. And the hundred prophets were preserved in the freshness of the cave, while waiting for Ahab and Jezebel to acknowledge their error and expiate their sin. When three years had passed thus, the Lord sent Elijah to see the king, and Elijah gathered together the people of Israel in this very place, at the summit of Mount Carmel, between the sky and the sea, to work a miracle against the four hundred and fifty prophets of Baal. And the miracle occurred. And the people of Israel returned to the Lord their God. And Elijah had the four hundred and fifty prophets taken down to the brook Kishon, and he slew them there.

As I was approaching the summit of Mount Carmel, I noticed a steeple rising out of a clearing. It was a chapel kept by two monks and a toll collector who suggested that I might like to visit the altar built by Elijah. I declined the offer, for I knew from the Scriptures that the place of the miracle was not between the trees where the chapel stood, but on a promontory at the southeast corner of the mountain, overhanging the sea. Following the paths, against the advice of the toll collector, I came to a spur that could well have been the one described. It was a crescent-shaped area which opened out onto the sea, and its center sounded hard under the horse's hoofs. I scratched the moss and uncovered four flagstones arranged as a quadrilateral figure of eight square cubits. There was no doubt that this was the work of men. Even though the stones were nearly worn away by the weather and the vegetation, and there were only four of them and not twelve, as had been written, around their edges you could still distinguish the trench dug to contain the water poured by the servants. But night was already falling over the sea. I put my horse out to graze and arranged the mosses to my liking. I needed to reflect on myself and on my people—which were one and the same thing.

The night was exceptionally clear, the sky studded with stars, the sea sparkling like a silver mantle. Occasionally a light gust of wind would cause a stir in the tops of the pine trees, and it was like a murmur from the night of time, come to make me shiver. Without making too hasty a judgment about the rest of the time I had to live, I could consider that I had reached the middle of my existence. The best I could hope for was that the second half would fulfill the promises made in the first half, without adding anything new. In other words—that it would prolong and broaden the dialogue begun with myself, whose aim was my own awakening. I do not mind repeating the confession that my ambitions were always considerable and that they have never stopped growing, and exceeding my capacities. I therefore filled my granaries with all the corn and hay that my knowledge of the world suggested to me, accepting the obligation to separate the wheat from the chaff and to use only the purest of wheaten flour to make my bread. And this will be a second confession, which I find more awkward: at first I wanted to surfeit myself with that particular bread. But my approach merely led me back to myself. As I saw it, humanity contained only two kinds of individuals: the ignorant, doomed to misfortune, and the knowledgeable, destined to felicity. I may even have thought it true that the sins of the former were diminished by the good deeds of the latter, but this transference did not seem to me to be essential. Whether consciously or not, my aim was to determine my own place and secure my own salvation. Selfishly, I admit. Since I had been offered the choice between certain misfortune and possible happiness, how could I have hesitated? I wanted to become exemplary, and I believe I did everything possible to become so. In the depths of my being, however, there was the still, small voice of prudence, continually murmuring to me that my equations were badly set out, and my calculations wrong. The experience of life I was later to acquire told me this even more clearly. Certain misfortune and possible happiness are not antithetical states, but one and the same state. Humanity is not divided into two clans, the brute beasts on the one hand and the refined people on the other; it is all one and the same humanity, caught between nature and nurture, doing what it can to survive. If I still needed proof of this, the sky of Galilee gave it to me. Immense, milky, impenetrable, with a magnificent display of shooting stars, a silent murmur, it taught me my insignificance and my rejection, like the dyers, a few hours earlier. My granaries were full but I had nothing to give, neither to God nor to men. Because giving is a whole science in itself, a whole art in itself, which I had neither studied nor practiced. I had hoped, naïvely, that this would happen of its own accord, by some sort of outpouring, by some sort of overflow. I was waiting for the hour to sound. I had put myself into a position where I could be called upon, because sooner or later God makes his wishes known to the blessed. In actual fact, and ever since my earliest childhood, I had been nothing but a listening ear. To be someone to whom God spoke—a visionary, a prophet. To be an Elijah, or nothing. To be a voice people listen to. Part of man's condition is that he forms words in his throat; most men expel nothing but noise, though some produce words. If the dyers had rejected me it was because I didn't know how to speak to them. Elijah might perhaps have slain them, but he would have made himself heard. When I come to think of it, such as he has been described to us he was nothing but a bloodthirsty brute, except for the fact that he was obeying orders and slaying for the right reason. In my heart of hearts I was not at all sure that there were good or bad reasons for killing men: their destiny took care of this without need of a helping hand, and the dyers were closer to this elementary truth than I was. But all the prophets of Israel were not necessarily murderers. The tradition consists in announcing the worst, which is relatively easy, for it nearly always happens—even though this isn't quite certain. No other people had got through so many miracles and visionaries, thus the worst was always still to come. It was not said how many prophets Jezebel had had killed, but it was said that Obadiah saved a hundred, fifty by fifty, and that four hundred and fifty had gone over to Baal. This made quite a lot of people who were in conversation with the heavens, so the situation was no doubt not without its advantage. While the people were dying of starvation in the drought sent by God simply to punish the royal couple, the hundred prophets were provided with bread and water in their hiding places. This meant that Providence set more store on their survival than on that of the peasants. Inscrutable are the ways of this justice, which no one may understand but which everyone must praise. And there had to be three whole years of this marasmus before Elijah put an end to it, in the very place where I now was, by a miracle and a massacre. Woe! Woe to the peoples who need miracles and prophets! This is an observation, not a curse. So long as Israel and Judah were poor and unfortunate, all they needed was an occasional prophet for the bad days. The plethora had resulted from the abundance, which itself multiplied the worst. And the worst had happened. The nation destroyed, its people dispersed, persecuted in the flesh and in the spirit. And on all this—total silence from the heavens, which were formerly so talkative! I understood only too well why there was such a sudden lack of prophets. There was no further calamity to announce; no more punishment to promise; no more example to impose. What was needed was a new race of prophets, and it was slow in arising; a new teaching, and it was slow in appearing. Men must be helped to live as well as they could, in the conditions in which they found themselves, and within the bounds of the hope they were still allowed. I had harnessed myself to this new teaching and I had brought it to fruition: fourteen laboriously written books in ten years. This was not yet a revolution but it was certainly an evolution, which was new enough to be misunderstood, and rejected with acrimony just as I had been by the dyers. But I repeat: I am not looking for victory for myself. I am still awaiting a sign from on high. Had I made my plans too hastily? I considered it just that from now on the Word should come from those who know, and not from those who invent fables. If there is truth in poetry, there is no less poetry in truth. In the days when the world was swarming with prophets God preferred to choose his messengers from among the simple, dressed in animal skins or in rags—shepherds, goatherds, camel drivers, as harbingers of his wrath, forerunners of his judgment, bearers of his lightning. You would look in vain for a just man in this crowd of justicers; for a wise man among these miracle workers; for a literate man in the midst of these heralds. Anyone who proclaimed himself a prophet thereby became one. A prophet conversed with God in parables and demanded to be believed and obeyed. Just, wise, and literate men try to converse with men, and want to understand and be understood, so that clarity may emerge from confusion as the real world emerged from chaos. The Word is like a sealed book, but the time has come for us to unseal the books, to open the dead letter and dissect its entrails, to turn metaphors into formulas. Go! my prophetic inner voice told me. Go back to your studies, to your meditations, to your writings! Go among your fellow men and, as a sign of your covenant with them, give them what you can without asking anything in return, neither docility nor gratitude. Don't ask them where they come from or who they are, but what they are suffering from, and if they reject you a hundred times approach them yet again, without thinking yourself a hero, but obstinately and humbly, until they understand you and accept you for better and for worse, and thus you will become someone who is welcome in time of sorrow.

The birds were beginning to stir in the branches. It could not be long until dawn. A little more patience and there would be light outside, as there was now light inside me. The man who had gone up Mount Carmel was already old. It was a new man who would go down with the daybreak.

34

THE summer was drawing to its close, and with it the tide of pilgrims was receding. The activity in the port didn't slacken but there were now more baggage-bearers than cross-bearers to be seen, and the beggars and sellers of holy relics were thinning out. David carried off a masterstroke by selling his share in the partnership to an Armenian eager to make his fortune. As my various efforts to make myself useful to the dyers had failed, there was nothing to keep us on the shores of Akko.

It was not without apprehension that we set out for Jerusalem. Japheth was our guide. In spite of his great age he still had a good seat on a horse, but our progress went at a biblical pace, like an old legend, and we were also anxious not to tire our horses. We passed through the marshy lands of lower Galilee, skirting the valley of Jezreel, between the hills that had seen the passage of the herds of the patriarchs of Ur of the Chaldees, on our way to the promised land of Canaan. *Get thee out of thy father's house, unto a land that I will shew thee, and I will make of thee a great nation.* Never in all history had a migration of shepherds caused such a ferment. And Abram, before he was Abraham, the father of the multitudes, took Sarai his wife, and Lot his brother's son, and he passed through the land unto the place of Sichem, unto the plain of Moreh, and the Canaanite was then in the land. For the grass was green there, that same grass trodden underfoot by our cattle, far from the routes where now dwelt the Edomites. *To thy seed I will give this land.* It was not impossible that the old shepherd and his sterile wife had scented the warm odor of this cypress grove, this balsam forest. We continued on our way, lost in our thoughts, in a storm of images, on a carpet of memories, and the light wind blew indistinct murmurs into my ears, and the echo of unkept promises. Now and then Japheth would raise his arm and point to something in the distance; a steeple, or a pile of gray stones, and only pronounce a mysterious word, like en Nasirah, and it was Nazareth, Ein Ganim, and it was Djinin, Sichem, and it was Nablus, Beth-el and it was Beitin. I had the feeling of being disembodied both physically and symbolically, so much did the legend come alive in the reality, so much did the reality swell with the density of the legend. It was no longer Japheth who was guiding us, it was Abram in person, and Salem where we were going—incomparable peace.

We were in Jerusalem on the fifth day. I wanted to know nothing of this profaned city, delivered up to monks, soldiers, and toll collectors. In the mythology of our vigils there is a second Jerusalem, the real one, placed up in the highest heavens, vertically above the terrestrial city, intact and opulent and eternally renascent as in the time of King Solomon, and kept in reserve to take over when God has so decided. *Yes, I have built thee a house to live in, an abode wherein thou shallst dwell forevermore, made of good stone cut from the quarries so that no sound of any iron instrument should be heard on the sacred hill where the covenant was sealed, and I have adorned this house, both inside and out, with cedar sculpted in the form of colocynths and garlands of flowers, and I have covered the cedarwood on all sides with fine gold, and I have put therein ten basins of polished bronze, and the altar, and the table, and the lamps and snuffers, and the cups and incense burners in fine gold. One part of the wall remained and there grew hyssop and hart's tongue . . .* For three days and three nights we stayed in the dust and debris of the wall, fasting and praying, our souls high up in the house in the heavens, but forced down to earth whenever a toll collector passed. It cost the price of a horse for the four of us to remain stubbornly in front of what no longer existed, from the rising to the setting of the sun. On the stairway into the Temple the Franks had installed their military quarters in the Mosque of Oman, and their stewards in the ruined Al Aqsa mosque. In this place of peace where the sound of an iron instrument was never to have been heard, the clash of spurs, swords, and armor rang out without respite.

We were only a few short days' journey away from Hebron, and from the cave of Machpelah which Abraham acquired for four hundred shekels of silver, current money, which is a burying place for our fathers. The Arabs had built a mosque over our sanctuary; the Edomites had turned it back into a church. It cost the price of the entire grotto to buy a moment's meditation in front of the cat-afalques piled up at the back of a hole in the rock. As we wended our way, Japheth showed us from afar the town of Beth-lehem, *the house of bread*, called Bethlehem by the Edomites, the birthplace of David, first king of the united houses of Judah and Israel, and it was at Beth-lehem that he was anointed with the holy oil, as it has been written, and a star appeared in the heavens on this occasion, a star that has thenceforth never been extinguished over the city.

I suddenly felt heavy; weary of this pilgrimage into the kingdom of chimeras. The rainy season had already begun. Japheth was suffering from a fever and a bad cough. We had to expedite our return, no longer worrying about the dangers we might incur on the way back. Less than a week later, with our host just restored to health by my treatment but weeping over our departure, we embarked on one of those coasting vessels named *Alex* which provided the regular service between Akko and Alexandria.

35

THE war caught up with us in Egypt. Someone once said that history is congealed politics, but it could equally be said that politics is only liquid history; you could easily drown in it, caught between the surface waves and the ground swell, and it is calm bubbles that are often the most deceptive. Yet this is the way of life of peoples whose destinies float on invisible currents.

We arrived in Alexandria at a bad moment, for the town had a clandestine rendezvous with history. Had we been more perspicacious, or better informed, we should have guessed or foreseen it, but men's destinies can only be judged after they have been accomplished, and we had been blinded and fatigued by our storm-tossed voyage in search of a place to cast anchor. Adversity had made us modest. We only aspired to a few square meters, just room enough for us to recline, and pile up our books; and to a few like-minded people as neighbors, with whom we could exchange words and thoughts. Alexandria was tempting.

Alexandria was born from the sea, not from the land; it had a broad forehead, an open gaze, and it breathed deeply. It traded in all sorts of merchandise, and all sorts of ideas. So great a diversity of people mingled there that uniformity could never become a menace. There were schools, a university, and the memory of the fabulous burned-down library that book lovers had patiently been trying to reconstitute for centuries. There was also a Hebraic community of three thousand souls. True, they belonged to the Karaite sect, but they were very close-knit and well-disposed toward discussion, as was proved by the correspondence my father had carried on from Cordova and Fez with the nagid Zebulon, the chief of the community. Alexandria, finally, was a transparent city, traversed by roads so rectilinear that from one gate to the other the eye fell on the green of the countryside or the blue of the sea. The air circulated freely there, and men did the same.

Even though he showed no marked interest in us, as there were divergencies of doctrine between us, Zebulon invited us to stay in his house until we found shelter in that overpopulated town where there was a permanent housing shortage. By the time we had once again accustomed ourselves to the temporary, and had started looking for somewhere to live, war was upon us. To give you some understanding of these events I must try to put things in perspective, from every point of view. As you know, Egypt is governed by the Fatimid dynasty, a schismatic faction of the dynasty of the Sunnites of Baghdad, who claimed to be the only custodians of the true faith and who periodically had recourse to a holy war against their Islamic brothers. In fact, the Caliphs of Baghdad, known as the Syriacs, and the Atabegs of Aleppo, known as the Turks, had a great craving to extend their authority over the fertile valley of the Nile and its so unevenly distributed wealth. Since the beginning of the century a third force had established itself in the crescent of milk and honey of our ancient lands of Israel: the kingdom of the Franks of Jerusalem, who had an equal craving to absorb Egypt. Three great mouths—that was almost too many. None of them could open without starting the others up yelping, but it was in this sustained rivalry that Egypt found its respite.

The year before our arrival, however, there had been a palace revolution in Fostat Al Qahira, that you in the Occident name Cairo. The Caliph Al Zafir was assassinated and a usurper, Dirgham, who was said to be a colonel in the regular army, seized power. The city now insecure within and threatened from without, this soldier thought it politic to form an alliance with the Turks to protect himself against the Franks, and while he was about it to form an alliance with the Franks to protect himself against the Turks. This maneuver was far from stupid, and might well have succeeded. Unfortunately for Colonel Dirgham, his allies took their commitments too seriously. Neither of them knowing anything of the other, a Turkish army and a Frankish army set out to protect Egypt, in other words, to seize it, perhaps without encountering any resistance. The two armies found themselves face to face outside Alexandria, itself taken by surprise. The population of merchants, transport agents, artisans, and scholars had nothing to gain and everything to lose by the clash of arms it was suddenly being offered. The Turks, under the command of Salah ed-Din, were the first to knock on the gates of the city. Courteously, they were invited to enter. The Franks, under the command of King Amalric, took up a siege position all around. From morning to night they attacked each other with catapults, arrows, and firebrands. All the orchards were burned, all the meadows and fields trampled down, many houses set on fire, and many of the poor died of hunger. After three months of this cretinous amusement, as there was still no solution in sight Salah ed-Din and Amalric met in a tent and had a discussion. They agreed that each would go his own way with his army, and leave Egypt alone. At Fostat Al Qahira, Colonel Dirgham breathed a sigh of relief and paid a prolonged visit to his harem. But Alexandria had been destroyed.

During the ninety days of the siege we lived in Zebulon's cellar, perpetually arguing with him. In case you did not know it, and to a certain extent this is only secondary to my thesis, the Karaite sect recognizes the Law of Moses and the teaching of the Scriptures, but repudiates the oral tradition codified in the Talmud. In itself this aberration would have been of no consequence, had not Zebulon turned out to be an aggressive proselytizer: he demanded approval, and was trying to make converts. My father opposed him with the full rigor of the tradition. My judgment was more flexible. I was prepared to recognize that Zebulon's opinions and options were worth consideration, as for that matter were any options and opinions founded on reason, but only on condition that he became less vehement in his desire to convince, especially in a moment when Judaism was disintegrating all over the world. This was sufficient to bring our discussions to a close, for there were more urgent problems to be resolved, as for instance the staggering increase in the price of food and water, the scarcity of candles, the threat of epidemics, and the nerve-shattering effect of all the weapons falling around us. Thanks to David's ingenuity we were not short of necessities; he was capable of picking fruit from a stripped tree and finding flour on a bare stone; he could have made water flow from the cellar walls, he was so quick at adapting himself to new situations. The most annoying thing was that Zebulon and the catapults kept me from concentrating on my work. Well before the siege was lifted my father and I had agreed that we would leave Alexandria as soon as possible.

And at the same time as Salah ed-Din, keeping to his word, was withdrawing his horsemen from inside the city walls and sending them back to Aleppo, King Amalric suffered a serious loss of memory on his way back: he quite simply forgot the treaty he had just concluded, turned his army around, and entered Alexandria, which he immediately proclaimed a Frankish city attached to the crown of Jerusalem. This was certainly not the first time that a monarch had committed such a felony, and history is accustomed to more serious shortcomings, but this was the first time that treachery had impinged on the young Emir of the Turkish mountains, who had his own opinion on honor in general and the honor of kings in particular, which opinion might well have been called naïve, as it was so old-fashioned. Salah ed-Din told me later that it had made him sick with shame. On this occasion he took a solemn oath that he would allow himself no respite until he had thrown the treacherous dog out of the fertile crescent. You know how he kept his word. Like the Egyptian Caliphate, the Frankish Kingdom of Jerusalem had just temporarily abrogated itself. In the meantime, however, Amalric imposed a tribute of a hundred thousand pieces of gold on

Colonel Dirgham and sent a high-class toll collector in bishop's clothes, Hugh of Caesarea, to the capital, to take possession of this tax.

Chance threw us together in the same caravan. I don't know how the bishop found out that I was a doctor. He walked his horse beside mine and questioned me about my origins and my studies. Born in Caesarea, he spoke very good Arabic. Despite his youth—he was twenty-five at the most—he had a very affected manner. But he was extremely handsome, and he looked you in the eye. When we had got through the preliminaries, and paid homage to the renown of Cordova, he asked me if I was an expert in strange maladies. I replied, amused, that every malady was strange, because abnormal, it being normal to be in good health. Every malady, I said, was a stranger to the body and to the mind, coming we knew not how, going we knew not where, always in its own time and as it pleased God. "But something even stranger?" said the bishop. "A malady so strange that to this day no doctor has been able to give it a name." There was a great deal to be gained by clearing up the mystery and curing this malady. I replied dryly that I was not at all interested in gain, but that I would not refuse my opinion if the case was submitted to me. The bishop made me promise to keep secret what he was about to reveal to me. "But," he said, "does a Jew have a word to keep?" "A more reliable one than a Frankish king," I said irritably. I spurred my horse on to put an end to the conversation. When I brought it back to a walk the bishop was again by my side. "Forgive me," he said. "I didn't mean to offend you." "But you have done so," I said. There was silence between us for at least a league. We were going along the great arm of the Nile, between tiny kitchen gardens. The loose soil made a soft sound under our hoofs. The bishop said: "I am going to redeem myself by a mark of confidence. The sick man is the heir to the throne of Jerusalem." I had still not recovered from my anger. "In Jerusalem," I said, "there is only one throne, and it is that of the Eternal Lord who made a covenant with the Hebrew people." The bishop ignored my retort.

He told me that young Baldwin, the only son of King Amalric, was suffering from listlessness and lividity, combined with unheard-of phenomena such as the absence of eyelashes and eyebrows, his nails becoming detached without his feeling the slightest pain, his hair coming out in handfuls like the leaves of a tree in the fall, but apart from that he had a good appetite, good stools, his urine was clear, he functioned normally, as if nothing were wrong, and the king—there was no secret about this—would make the fortune of any doctor who could extricate the prince from this state. The prince was at the moment with the king in Alexandria. Would I agree to return there immediately to be consulted? I did not agree. However, if they wanted to bring the sick boy to Fostat, where I was going, I would willingly see him. The bishop asked me whether I already had an idea. "I already have an idea," I said. "A fairly clear idea. I will make my diagnosis when I have been able to examine the child."

Less than a week after our arrival in Fostat I was summoned with the greatest secrecy to the Caliph's palace. I was taken into the presence of a boy about eight or nine years old, whom I was able to examine at my leisure. "It is what I thought," I said to Bishop Hugh when we were alone. "All the symptoms are present. It is leprosy. The future king of the Franks in Jerusalem will be a leper king." "You must certainly be mistaken," said the bishop. "God cannot wish that." "God can do everything," I said. "For my part, I do not make mistakes." I was dismissed without even a word of thanks.

I will say nothing of Fostat, which you know through having lived there with me. Except perhaps something of its origins, which belong to the poetry of the desert. In the year eighteen of the Hegira, General Amr undertook to conquer Egypt on behalf of the Caliph Omar, the Prophet's successor. When he reached the right bank of the Nile, opposite the ruins of Roman Memphis, he pitched camp for a halt. In the morning he observed that a couple of doves had nested under his tent. Amr abandoned his shelter, which became the first dwelling place in Fostat. A peaceful city was established there, surrounded by a brick wall. Later, a second city grew up by the side of the first. This was Al Qahira, and it boasted a new mosque, the Caliph's palace, and many extremely noble houses. When Salah ed-Din had become master of Egypt, as a consequence of the war that you experienced and hated in my company, he had the two cities joined by a brick wall. Such is the capital at the moment when I am writing. But when we arrived there—my father, David, and I—Fostat, within its brick wall, was still a shady, flowered town, beneath a sky full of swallows. The moment I set foot there a kind of grace descended on me, as if I had rediscovered Cordova.

Though neither the most ancient nor the strongest, the Hebrew community there was one of the most prosperous in the world. In fact, there were two separate communities, one following the Babylonian rite and the other the Israeli rite, each with its own synagogue and schools, but without schismatic rivalry. There were about two thousand families in all, united under the authority of the nagid Nathanael, a highly virtuous judge and doctor, who was also the treasurer to the last caliphs. By a singular division, the Babylonians were almost all very rich and the Israelis almost all very poor. The former were transit agents, merchants, architects, and bankers; the latter artisans, masons, water carriers, and dyers. However, their zeal in the study of the Law equalized them and unified them in piety and devotion. I never heard it said in either of the towns that anyone doubted the probity of the ones or the honesty of the others. Rich and poor alike were highly regarded. Do you remember Karma, the water carrier? No scholar in the capital, not even Nathanael, knew as much as he about canon law. It often happened that people would come and consult him in the street. Then Karma would put his load down on the ground and say to the questioner: "Carry the water for me, so that my family shall not suffer, while I consider your problem"; for he would never accept payment for a pious service. I mention this so that you may understand that the differences of position in the community did not create any real inequality: if the nagid rode a thoroughbred mare on a leather saddle inlaid with silver, and if the water carrier had no other means of locomotion than his own legs, their heads, as men, were on the same level; they could look each other in the face, and talk to each other as equals. Moreover, there were as many rich Babylonians as poor Israelis in the Council of the communes. A person's value was determined by the extent of his knowledge, not by the extent of his possessions. Those who lived on little had more time to devote to study; those who earned a great deal embellished the synagogues, supported the hospital and the schools, filled the library with books, and ransomed Jewish slaves to give them back their liberty. The fact that rich people existed was not a source of scandal, just as there was no offense attached to the existence of the poor, for no one was destitute. On the alluvial soil of the river, life was easy for everyone. Vegetables and fruit grew in abundance on the clay soil, and you only had to plunge a line into the Nile for a fish to come and hook itself. Salah ed-Din had an obelisk erected on the island of Gezira; on this monolith the exact height of the floods is measured, which enables one to know in advance the volume of the harvest. The time is past when this fertile valley was smitten with the seven plagues. Did that mean that its men now found more favor in the sight of God?

My father had to buy a house. He chose one outside the walls, facing north, and spacious, for he was considering remarrying, and he also foresaw that I too might be founding a family before long. Nathanael opened a credit account for him against his own privy purse, an arrangement which left our reserve of precious stones intact. During the whole of this winter Judge Maimon spent his time and energies as if he were a foreman, giving orders to masons and plasterers. He had a fountain dug and water put in it; he had beds and tables made out of wood; he had hibiscus and bougainvillea planted, and he went in search of a maidservant. Proposed by the nagid, he was given a place on the Council of the communes. Patiently, moving quickly with his small, gliding steps, all of a piece, in his own fashion, without a doubting thought and without a moment's weakness, after fifteen years of hazardous peregrinations swarming with perils, fatigue, and sadness, he was rebuilding on the banks of the Nile our portion of the shore of the Guadalquivir. There was no mistaking it—we were like those bumblebees that carry on their cilia the pollen of long-withered flowers.

One evening my father seemed particularly pleased. The last workman had just left our house, the furniture and usual objects were in their place, the water was lapping in the fountain. Tamar, the servant, was going about her business. As we rose from the table, and before going to shut himself into his study and start work, he came gliding over to me—to me because I was the elder—and said, in a voice quite softened with emotion: "You see, my son? We have managed it, after all."

The next day, he was dead.

36

IT became known, I don't know how, that I had diagnosed a case
of leprosy. This did me considerable harm, which it took me a very
long time to overcome. To think about *that illness* implied a sin
which you had to hasten to expiate; to call it by its name sullied
your mouth irremediably. More than any other, it was pure evil, a
scourge from God and an infernal exhalation. How could I have
recognized it in its initial stages without being in connivance with
it? I could have argued in my defense that the symptoms of leprosy
are extremely well described in Hippocrates and Galen, as in all the
good authors of the *çalâm*, but such a defense would not have
helped my reputation, which was suddenly gravely compromised.
Had I not, in uttering the evil word, called down the scourge on the
head of the poor child? His father, the king, was Egypt's protector;
quite apart from my supposed relations with Gehenna, I had been
guilty of *lèse-protecteur*. And even if it had turned out that I was
innocent of witchcraft, I had touched the leper with my own
hands, and my hands from now on represented contagion. What
man in his right mind would agree to entrust himself to them?

I had let it be known in Fostat that I was at the disposal of anyone who wanted to call on my science, and I was forced to recognize that no one did: my consulting room saw neither sick nor
wounded, and remained desperately deserted. In former days this
would not have worried me. The less time I was obliged to devote
to other people, the more freely I could please myself with my
studies and writings. The main divisions of the *Guide for the Per-*

plexed had been decided: there was to be an unprecedented number, nourished by the best milk of knowledgeable reflection. I did not have to innovate. The truth had been said. My task consisted solely in releasing it from the matrix which prevented access to it. It was a work of purification, of molding; of gold washing, in a way. I had been conscientiously preparing myself for a long time. I had explored all the terrains, all the seams, the beds of all the rivers. I knew where the metal was, and where the sand and mud. The time for the sifting had arrived, but it came at a bad moment. The death of my father left me in a situation which disarmed me. I inherited his debts, while the present-day assets representing the fortune of the Maimons went to my brother, together with the responsibility for supporting me.

Now, David was bored in Fostat. He was not happy there. The jewelry trade was in the hands of a few Babylonian families, none of whom seemed disposed to move over a little to make the least bit of room for the newcomer. The numerous attempts my brother made to infiltrate here or there failed, one after the other. A transaction which he had started on his own initiative was stolen from under his nose just before its conclusion. In no way discouraged, David invented a detour: the Nidians, who were well off, also had a daughter of marriageable age in stock. This oblique approach was perhaps worth a little trouble, all the more so as my brother held a major trump card: he was a handsome youth, tall, slim, all black curls, whereas the young lady was already beginning to run to fat. So David began a series of approach moves and obtained enough encouragement for him to persist, until he fell, one evening, into a punitive expedition organized by the Nidian brothers, from which he emerged with a black eye.

The jewelry clan stood fast. To launch a frontal attack would have been madness with so slender a capital as a bag of emeralds, at least a quarter of which would have to be used to pay our debt to Nathanael. Overwhelmed by this impasse, David conceived a bold plan: he would go to the Indies, where he was sure of selling his

stones for a very good price; with the sum thus released he would
buy rough corundrum from the best vein, aquamarine, rubies, sap-
phire, topaz, which he would later have cut and polished in the
workshop he would set up in Fostat. By means of this operation—
and he went endlessly over and over his calculations, and always
with the same result—he reckoned on increasing his capital tenfold,
thus establishing himself as a serious competitor to the Babylonians,
with the firm intention of driving them out of their fief.

Even though this project was wildly audacious it won my approval, especially as I had every reason to have confidence in my
brother's talents. There remained the uncertainty of the voyage, but
there was no reason to suppose that there were more risks in a journey from Fostat to the Indies than from Cordova to Fostat, and they
had been bearable. David hastened his preparations, and the day
came when he threw himself into my arms, with more joy than sorrow. Guided by a Bedouin named Selim, he was to go by way of
the route of the Hebrews to Ras Abu Mussa, where he intended to
embark on the Sea of Rushes.* He was to be away for six months at
the most. He had made sure in advance that on his return he could
count on the services of the best polisher and the best setter now
working for the Nidians, and he was already laughing at the idea of
playing this trick on them in retaliation for his black eye. I went
with him to the town gate. When I saw him, so young and graceful
in the saddle, *a comely person, of a beautiful countenance,* as it was
said of David the Beth-lehemite who was King of Israel, my heart
became heavy with sorrow, for I was suddenly aware that I was
being left alone. For a long time, as his horse bore him away, he
waved his hand to me.

Considered separately, the death of my father and the departure
of my brother were foreseeable accidents in the order of things.
About my solitude, on the other hand, there was nothing accidental.
Since my earliest youth I had taken pleasure in it, I had sought it,
cultivated it, organized my tendency toward it, not as a means that

* The Red Sea.

isolates one but as a mediator that brings people closer together. To my solitude I owe the best of my education and my deepest satisfactions. I was never alone in it; anyone I chose entered it with me, and my choices were many and varied. And now, without warning, I felt it tightening so closely around me that it hurt. This was because its quality had abruptly changed, and assumed an air of abandonment.

My father had abandoned me—there was no other word to describe his desertion. In his lifetime, his way of not being there rendered him singularly heavy and present; his way of remaining silent was the equivalent of whole speeches. I had always been aware of the fact that he was someone inevitable. Since his death, I saw him and heard him only a little less—that is to say, not at all. Just that little difference was enough for the extent of his abandonment to become apparent. As I came and went from one room to another in the great, silent house, looking for I knew not what, I found myself gliding along the ground with short steps, and it sounded to my ear exactly as if my father had passed that way. So I had started sliding myself into a memory, while waiting to become wholly a memory myself. And the more time passed, the more dense and colorful became the projected image of the dead man. The Fostat commune had decreed that there should be a day of mourning on the occasion of his funeral, and this had seemed to me to be appropriate from all points of view, both for the dead and for the survivors. My father had proudly borne one of the great names of Israel, and never relaxed his efforts to strengthen its symbolic meaning; it was a name to honor any cemetery. I was greatly surprised to learn, as the weeks went by, that when the news reached them other communes did likewise and observed a day of mourning. People wrote to me that I had suffered a great loss—and I hadn't realized it; others wrote that this loss affected all the people of Israel—and this I was beginning to realize. I had instinctively kept my distance from the rectilinear furrow that my father had imperturbably plowed in the thickness of the tradition. In that line, no one could do better; to do as well would already have been a great exploit; and it was heartbreaking to think that so much self-mastery risked remaining sterile, apart from the blossom produced by a day of mourning here and there. The mutation that was taking place in this century was expressly aimed at the death of symbols, and I was profoundly convinced that this was only a beginning. That symbols died hard was not new. What I discovered with dismay was that even when they were dead, they kept their appeal. Stiff, and rotting under his flagstone, my father was still drawing me toward him. How much vigilance would I have to develop in order for this loss not to mean my own loss?

I still had a son—my brother—whom I had educated and affranchised, whom I had allowed to go free. There was little he troubled about, and little that troubled him. I had sown in him a seed of justice that had not fallen from the bush of suffering. If my father had received a blow in the eye, he would have murmured that such was God's will, and liberated himself from it by a prayer. If I had received a blow in the eye, I would have asked myself what sin I could have committed, so as to behave better in the future. The blow in the eye that David had received did not incline him to tuck his head into his shoulders or ask himself questions; he was preparing to return it, in his own way and in his own time, as God himself returns punishment for offense. Five centuries of marinating in Islam caused the preserving salt to enter into flesh that was too tender. David was already one of the new kind of Jew who, sooner or later, would emerge from the crucible of humiliation and become a fresh link in the chain of ancient history. This was not a program of vengeance, it was a program of affirmation. It was not the pettiness of an eye for an eye, it was the greatness of a blow for a blow. How easy it seemed for the man comfortably installed among the majority to hand out humiliation to the other man who is already saturated in it. Bishop Hugh meant no harm, perhaps, when he expressed the doubt that a Jew could have a word—a word of honor, that is. I have a confession to make to you, my friend: I was not displeased with my diagnosis of leprosy. There was a trace of satisfaction in me at the indignation of that Edomite. If a Jew is able not to have a word, why should not a proud prince be a leper? It is not by chance that the emblem of justice is a pair of scales. For my part, I, Moses of Cordova, adhered to the program of cutting the claws of humiliation by the excellence of my conduct, the extent of my faultless knowledge, the correctness of my reasoning, and my style. This program was a good tool and a good carapace, as I know from experience, but it was possible that in some cases it might not be enough. David was on a better path—and how I loved him! Day after day my thoughts navigated with him between the reefs of the Sea of Rushes toward the gaping spaces of the Indian Ocean. I transported myself into the gaiety of his spirit and the flow of his muscles, into his *beautiful countenance* and his *comely person*. I was already thinking about his return, and I thought only of this: how he would bring the proud to heel, and I was already looking forward to laughing with him, who knew so well how to laugh.

A few days after their departure Selim had brought back my brother's horse. He had embarked without difficulty on a sturdy Somali ship. David sent me a scribbled note, just to let me know their route, which was via Hulam in the land of Cush, which is also called Zeilan, or Ceylon, where something like a hundred black-skinned Jews lived, who spoke the purest Aramaic from the valley of Jehoshaphat. From there he would go north, along the coast. He had every hope of settling his business to the greatest advantage and very quickly, and of coming home sooner than expected.

I saw Selim a second time, after a month had gone by. The moment he saw me he threw himself down with his face to the ground, and cried out: "Do not curse the bearer of bad news. Your brother's ship sank in the gulf—lost with all hands."

🌀 37

WHAT had always been my most faithful ally, my body, suddenly betrayed me. Instead of the sick coming to me when I was expecting them, it was a sickness that I was not expecting that came, insidiously, brutally, tenaciously. Where did it come from, that pale whore—from my tired entrails or from my bruised soul? Here was yet another occasion to philosophize and to produce a theory about the identity of body and mind—the same theory that caused me so much vexation. It was a question of air, of which space is so infinitely full and yet which from one day to the next I found I lacked. It was water that I was breathing. All the weight of the gulf was lying heavy on my chest. Clutching the wooden part of my bed, my eyes staring and my lips gaping, I tried to catch a fugitive breath. My heart was beating wildly and my vision was blurred. I remained in this state all night long. I felt some relief in the morning, but only enough to realize that this was merely a truce before my symptoms once again became aggravated. I drank an infusion of gentian, which did me a little good. But before the middle of the day the attack had become acute again and lasted for interminable hours. What critical thought the feeling of suffocation permitted me led me to the obvious fact that my lungs were affected.

All sick people ask silly questions, and I was just like the rest of them. Why me? Why just at the moment when I needed all my strength and all my wits? Galen recommends that people breathe only air that is free of all bad smells; I would willingly have breathed in the stinking effluvia of a sewer if only I could have breathed freely. My ribs were in the grip of a vise. The air came whistling in through the opening in the glottis and went out with a sinister gurgling sound, filling my mouth with bubbles. I was drowning on dry land, as David, my brother, my son, my cherubim, had drowned in the waves, and they had killed him, but I was not dying. The crisis approached from the depths of my being by leaps and bounds like a wild animal, prowled around me for a time in ever decreasing circles, and at the very moment when it seemed inevitable that it would flatten me it let go its hold and disintegrated. I imagine that the Asian torture of putting people to the question is like that. In the long run, no doubt, nobody can withstand it; and yet I was withstanding it. Every day I almost died, and I came to wish that it all really would end, so indifferent to my fate had my suffering made me; but then my desire for air brought back my desire for life, and I took pleasure in practically being born again.

This alternation went on for months, for more than a whole year. I dosed myself with many well-tried remedies: with eupneics, with stomachics, with purgatives, all of which had no other effect than to exhaust both my medicines and my knowledge. I did what I could, but the illness did what it wanted. We observed each other with beady eyes, each kept on the alert by the other, ready to spring or retreat in turn according to the circumstances and the strategy of the moment, condemned to be together, each for himself, like God and his creatures, like day and night.

This war nevertheless left me with some moments of respite, which were sometimes long enough to give the desire to work its chance too. I picked up my pen again, but it remained suspended in the air. How is it possible to find the concentration needed to philosophize when the house is empty, when the servant hasn't been paid, when there is nothing to eat but clear soup and mashed grass, when the roof and the bed are debts, when the future is a black hole. The commune, no doubt, would have given me charity, but I was born and bred in Spain. It was enough that Tamar stayed with me out of charity. She called me her *poor master*, and I used to call her *my kind fatty*, for she was so obese that she brushed against both sides of the door, and it was by this exchange of compliments that we sealed our understanding. She warmed up my herb teas when I couldn't breathe, brought whole apronfuls of bruised fruit that had fallen from the trees, or dried dung for her brazier, and her eyes swam with tears when she talked about David. Such a handsome young man! With such a ready laugh! So ingenious in his ways! So full of promise. I ordered her to be quiet. She obeyed me only until the following day.

When my distress was at its greatest I received an unexpected visit: from Bishop Hugh. The Court doctors had finally come around to my opinion, and now confirmed that it was leprosy. The child's lack of sensitivity to pain, and the outbreak of chronic nasal catarrh, left no more room for doubt. Even though the rumor had spread everywhere, this still remained a state secret. There could be no question of relegating the prince to the necessary isolation, or of putting him in a hood and giving him a rattle to warn people to keep their distance. He was destined to be king of Jerusalem one day, and king of Jersusalem he would be when the time came for him to succeed to the throne; moreover, he was of lively intelligence, vigorous of body, strong of character, and his father adored him. With this in mind Amalric had remembered my existence, and the bishop handed me a bulging embroidered purse.

This was the first time I had received an honorarium, but the moment could not have been better chosen. I felt very awkward and embarrassed, but Hugh had the courtesy not to notice this. He asked me on Amalric's behalf whether I knew a remedy which, even if it could not cure it, would at least be able to attentuate the progress of the disease. I told him that such a remedy had been mentioned by several Arab authors, notably by Ibn Sina: it was an oil extracted from a fruit called *Coba*, or *Encoba*, which is gathered from a bush that grows wild in the heart of Africa, toward the region of the great lakes. This oil, called *chaulmoogra*, was sovereign against the illness. Hugh asked me to describe both the bush and the fruit. I personally had never seen either. On the other hand, the natives in the tropics would mistake neither the bush nor the fruit. Let King Amalric send a rapid caravan; without a doubt it would bring back what was needed, and I offered to extract the oil and prepare the remedy myself.

It was so decided, and the bishop withdrew. I saw him again several times before he was killed within the walls of Jerusalem at the fall of the kingdom. Though he had formerly humiliated me, this man later never stopped doing me good. With each of his visits Amalric's purse grew fatter, and this was certainly not unconnected with Hugh. It was through him that you, his first cousin, from Beaucaire and Oppède, came into my solitude, because he had recommended me to you as a teacher. It was also he who prevailed upon Richard, nicknamed "the Lion Heart," to travel from Ashkelon to Fostat to ask me for a cure for the pain in his joints. What a strange man he was, that Richard! When he found that my treatment relieved him he was absolutely determined to buy me from my owner and take me back with him to his island of England, and he was quite astonished when he learned that I was no more for sale than I was disposed to follow him of my own free will. In his perplexity he left me all the gold he carried on him, and this was no little. I only mention these liberalities because I had, at the time, the most pressing need of them. The purest gold that Hugh was instrumental in bringing me was your friendship, which was what my heart hungered and thirsted after the most.

I had another visit at this time: that of an old woman whom Tamar brought me, and whose name I never knew. I was in a period of respite between two acute attacks, my breathing had just become calmer, when this old woman suddenly appeared before me. She had only one incisor left in her mouth, which the tip of her tongue kept hitting, so that her words didn't come out clearly. Nevertheless, I finally understood her. She knew a young man, Abulmale, a steward at the Caliph's palace, orphaned of both father and mother but a serious lad, I could always make inquiries, belonging to the Babylonian sect and of a very honorable though impoverished family, which was why he had had to take that post, in which he was well thought of and had been assured that he would be promoted to chief steward as soon as the position became vacant, which could not but be soon, in view of the age of its present holder. Now, Abulmale had a younger sister, Bathsheba, whom he cherished as the apple of his eye and whom he wished to make happy. A real treasure, this girl; gentle, hard-working, economical, respectable—you could search all Fostat, and Al Qahira, and even Alexandria, and you wouldn't find her like. One single defect: she was already twenty-five. Not that she had not received advantageous proposals, but she was extremely difficult to please and wanted only an educated husband, as she herself could read and write. In a word, and to cut a long story short, she, the old woman, in order to oblige her friend Tamar, and me too of course, at the same time, for Tamar was so devoted to me, she had said to herself that it was sad to think of me being all alone and unhappy, and the girl in question being a virgin for such a long time and also unhappy, she had said to herself, then, that here was a case when there were two things to be combined, and that was the reason she had come to see me, she was entirely disinterested, except for the customary present if the affair came to something, which would be more or less a foregone conclusion when I had seen this treasure who, moreover, was being given a dowry by her brother, a complete trousseau, a leather chest inlaid with mother-of-pearl, and a purse of a hundred gold piasters, cash on the nail, wait a minute, let me finish! In his capacity as second steward, Abulmale had the disposal of a benefice of two hundred piasters a year which he was reserving for his future brother-in-law, in this case it would be the post of doctor to the palace stables, that was to say, to the servants, whether freed men or slaves, and this post could be taken up on the day after the marriage, which could be solemnized during the coming month on condition, it went without saying, that the future spouses had previously met and declared themselves mutually satisfied. In the meantime, the old woman merely asked for one piaster for her trouble.

This visit had a strange effect on me: it divided me into two. Half of me said *no*, the other half said *yes*, and the debate was lively and went on for days, without either half managing to get the upper hand. Each side advanced extremely pertinent arguments which canceled each other out. When the *yes* sent me to sleep, the *no* woke me up, and the next day the roles were reversed. I was caught in the most difficult philosophical problem that had ever been brought to me to judge, for I knew no text to which I could refer. The solution had to be invented, and I found myself at a loss.

In my confusion I went and asked Nathanael for his advice. "Bathsheba *is* a respectable girl," he said. "You have not been misled. But she has a mind of her own: she's touchy, hard to please, her brother often complains about her. But what can you expect? Shouting, jibbing, it's second nature to them, there's something of the she-goat about them all. If Abulmale is to be believed she has a little more than some others, that's why he's paying such a price. She's not bad-looking, she stands up straight, she has a slender waist, and above all she's healthy. She'll wear well. For my taste her eyes are perhaps a bit small, her nose a bit big, her lips a bit thin, her chin a bit pointed. But all these are mere trifles! You can get used to worse. The most serious thing is that in ten years' time she'll have caught up to you in age, and that it doesn't really suit she-goats to be old. I have my own, I know what I'm talking about. But the benefice of stable doctor isn't to be despised, when one is in need and has debts to pay. Mind you, I'm not pressing you. We have plenty of time. These things have to be taken into consideration, that's all I wanted to say. If your brother hadn't gone off with all your stones you would certainly not be in this situation. Never put all your eggs in one basket, that's well-known. Studying, writing books? There's nothing wrong with that, except that man does not live by philosophy alone. It can't be eaten, it doesn't clothe you, it doesn't warm you: these things are necessities. In my opinion the matchmaker came knocking on the right door at the right moment. Have you any other solution ready, or waiting? Medicine, when you have the skill, isn't a bad way of life. It's all very fine to diagnose leprosy in a prince. But what does it lead to? There aren't many princes, and they're always changing. Whereas a clientele gets built up like a house, stone by stone, one on top of the other, and the building will remain standing when it's put up by a mason who knows his trade. Take me, for example—I have the best practice in the capital, but it took me twenty years to get where I am. Once you've got going there's nothing to worry about: it is you who cure your patient, and it is Providence that kills him—get that into your head. But when you're only just starting then it's the opposite: it's Providence that cures, and you who kill. Before these propositions are reversed in your favor you will have a thousand opportunities to despair, and a hundred to die of starvation. Mind you: the commune does have its poor, and it looks after them. But a scholar like you doesn't dip his spoon into other people's plates, he makes his own soup. Abulmale is offering you the stirrup? Then put your foot into it. He knows what he's doing? Then you know it too. Bathsheba comes as an extra. Take her, though. And then wait and see. Some women improve with marriage—I know several cases. There are some who shout too loudly and then die young—I know several cases of that too. And don't forget: a married man is more impressive, he carries weight, he inspires more confidence. In medicine, it's of prime importance. A doctor who has a wife to discuss his patients with doesn't discuss them with outsiders, so their secrets are more or less safe. If the wife gossips, it isn't the doctor's fault. And then—well! The flesh has its demands, and the satisfaction of the senses is well worth a few sacrifices. You have a big house. You should fill it with children. They bring worries, I agree. But who ever told you that man doesn't need worries? The more he has, the healthier he is, that's the law of the patriarchs. You asked for my advice? I've given it to you. There are pros and cons. It is up to you to see things clearly."

I could see nothing clearly. As I did whenever I found myself in great difficulties, and in spite of the fact that I might suddenly have an attack, I saddled my horse and went off to spend a night under the stars. Of all the countries I have been through, Egypt is certainly the one nearest to the heavens. It was not by chance that the Lord was so fond of appearing there. Inscrutable, though direct, are the ways of the Lord. Stretched out in the dunes on the edge of the desert, I recommended elevation to my soul, and it too had no great way to go to be in touch with eternity. Up there was the mystery that contained my mystery. My real debate was not the one Nathanael had described to me. I was seeking neither an insurance against poverty nor an insurance against failure. To take the woman, the dowry, and the benefice, or not to take them—this alternative was concerned with only minor questions. The real question was to know what I was going to make of my life: behave like a good bourgeois or pursue my solitary way into the unknown; ensure my comfort or ensure my salvation? In this very spot, this very night, the two paths intersected, but I had a profound feeling that from now on they would diverge. In short, I was only an old adolescent who had put off coming to any decision. I had let myself be carried along on the back of a certain sort of laziness as if it were an old donkey that almost dies of thirst in between two wells. Was there perhaps a logical chain connecting our flight across the world, my father's death, David's drowning, and my attacks of suffocation? A guideline? The finger of God? It was impossible to decide—and yet I had to come to a decision; it was time. This way? Or that way? Of all the ordeals I had had to suffer, the death of my brother was certainly the most unbearable; it wounded my reason, it flayed my soul, it tormented my flesh. I didn't risk asking God the reason for it; I knew in advance the form and content of the reply. Who would not fear such a silence? I, who had been made man only by the Word and for the Word, I was linked to words, not to their absence. Above me thousands of lights were scintillating, I could have touched them if I had stretched out my hand, and a light breeze was making ripples in the sand. I was nothing, yet I was everything, because I was there, warm and quivering in all this immensity. Since the night I spent on Mount Carmel the answer was within me: I had a man's existence to live, and I had only that. My salvation too was only that. How presumptuous I had been to believe I had the power to escape from my condition! A wife, an income, children, and a stone with my name engraved on it. The most enviable of destinies. The best of hopes. The highest of truths. And thus, my decision had been made. Now I could go home and sleep. On my way back at first light I was surprised to realize that the whole night had passed without a sign of my usual attack.

The meeting took place in a private room in the Al Azhar patisserie. I had spent several hours at my toilet that morning, soaking myself in water that was too hot, shaping my nails, trimming my beard, oiling my hair, smiling all the time at the thought that at least two people in Fostat were doing the same thing at the same time. I was taken there by the old woman, who was swollen with finery like an onion in winter. Abulmale brought his sister and unveiled her in front of me. For a long moment we remained face to face, drinking mint tea and chewing sticky sweetmeats, without finding anything to say to each other. Whenever I happened to look in Bathsheba's direction she just happened to be looking away from me. It was true that her eyes were a bit small, her nose a bit big, her lips a bit thin, and her chin a bit pointed; but pah! You can get used to worse. And what about me? How did she see me? When all the tea had been drunk, and all the sticky sweetmeats swallowed, the old woman signaled to us that it was time to leave. "Yes," I said, as I stood up. "Yes," replied Bathsheba, as her brother re-veiled her. The following week, Nathanael married us in the great synagogue of the Babylonians. I didn't yet know that I was taking back to my house the best of wives. What does that mean: *the best of wives?* A simple testimonial of good conduct and loyal services? I would resent it if I found myself thinking and writing such platitudes. In all simplicity, Bathsheba made it possible for me to have access to both ways—both of them uncertain. If it ever happened that I spoke with God, it was through my wife's heart that the words passed.

38

STAND UP, Moses the Spaniard! Stand four paces away, facing me! What are you doing? Where are you going? What have you to say in your defense?" "Here I am: I am available, with all my attachments. I plead guilty, even though I know I am innocent. This is difficult to understand for anyone who is not pure intelligence. Is this already the last judgment?" "How stupid you are! There is neither first nor last judgment in immutable eternity in which the end and the beginning meet. You were a seed before you existed, and you will be a seed after you have existed, and at each moment of your passage you are judged by the judgment that is in you. To the best of your knowledge and belief, are you innocent or guilty?"

"Both. Or neither. How simple it would be, if only I were certain of knowing the rules of the game. The rules that appear in the reference book are out of date these days, and require only suppleness; and the precepts of the Law have given way to the precepts of the commentaries. What is just, and what is not just, is now no more than the opinion of the interpreters. Is it just that I should be paid by well-washed people, who smell good, to care for dirty people, who stink? At first sight this would seem to satisfy morality. One needs only a little complacency to be able to praise this current of charity flowing in the right direction. Those who *have* are sacrificing to those who *have not*. This could well be in the order of things. I am placed at a crossroads where an injustice is becoming alleviated. What is more, it could not suit me better. The benefice, scrupulously paid, secures me from the need to beg my bread, and

gives me back some of the freedom and dignity that I was beginning to lack. As I keep honestly to the terms of my engagement, I
consider that the money is honestly earned. I can declare myself
satisfied, and therefore innocent."

So be it! In order to arrive at this point I had to enter into a combination of light and shade in which I also pledged some of my
freedom and dignity. Certain mischief makers even said that I sold
myself for a dowry. This was not an entire fabrication. But against
it I could object that the affectations of courtly love, such as you
sometimes cultivate them in Edom, would in our climates be inconceivable, if not risible. Nevertheless, in my case the transaction was
indeed marked by a minimum of feeling. At first sight, once again,
morality would *not* seem to be satisfied. More especially because I
had cheated, by dissimulating the attacks of suffocation which left
me practically infirm. The merchandise I was putting up for auction
was defective. I was not responsible for this but it made me
feel ashamed, and therefore guilty. The least I could fear was
that Abulmale would go back on some of his promises when
he discovered he had traded his sister for a man whose powers
were waning. But the opportunity did not arise. Bathsheba arrived
with her complete trousseau, her leather chest inlaid with mother-
of-pearl, and her purse, from which not a single piaster was missing,
and which I took to Nathanael as an installment on his loan, and I
was given my post as doctor of the palace stables without having to
mention it again, for from the day after my marriage my attacks of
suffocation showed such a marked recession that I felt I could consider myself cured. My body had suffered from a malady of the
soul. The change in my status obtained through the culpability of
an act of cowardice and a lie restored me to myself and justified my
existence.

It took me some little time, on the other hand, to detect the trick-
ery of my position at the palace. The only service expected of me
by those washed and perfumed people who paid my salary was to
protect them against dirt and stench. I was not only an alibi, I was

also an insulator. It was my business to make sure that suffering and pus never had a chance to overflow beyond the limits of the places reserved for labor and service. It was my business to expose my eyes, my ears, and my nostrils. This was still part of the order of things: it was for this function that I was in receipt of my benefice. But I also had to point out to my brother-in-law those of the wounded and sick who were incapable of work, and these disappeared without trace. From being uncomfortable, my position became odious to me, as my innocence quickly became guilt. However indulgent Abulmale was toward me, he himself was only a cog in the administrative wheels, and he was risking his own security just as much as I was mine. The ideal would have been if I could have made the wretched people less wretched. But my powers did not go far, and my science, had it been ten times as great, would still not have sufficed. And yet I had conscientiously gorged myself on the fruits of the tree of knowledge, and I had taken whatever there was from wherever there was something to take: from the Empirical school, who knew nothing and understood nothing; from Hippocrates, who knew that he knew nothing but who understood everything; from Galen, who thought he knew everything but who understood nothing; from the Torah and the Talmud, which, from many points of view, are books of the medicine of the visceral memory; from the philosophers and the astronomers, the theologians and the geometricians, and even from the poets; and out of all this material I had built my theory and my method, which are so well founded in knowledge and in virtue and yet so hollow and useless when it comes to the calamities that crush the poor.

"Because you have a theory and a method?" "Certainly: as the peasant has his plow and his seeder; the blacksmith his hammer and his anvil. No one starts without well-tried tools. I believe it to be fundamentally true that man is in the universe and the universe is in man; that the soul is in the body and the body is in the soul, by a symmetrical effect which has a natural tendency toward equilibrium but which can never keep to it. I see the world as a pair of scales, whose pans are forever rising and falling—it's only a question of an atom more or less—in an alternation linked to the movement itself. But with each oscillation the arm passes through a momentary state of equilibrium, and this state is health, which is good. If a lasting surfeit or scarcity occurs on either of the pans, then there is sickness, which is evil. Such is my theory of the happy medium. Is it foolish?"

"Your question is blunt. I don't say that your theory is foolish. I don't say that it is not. If I have taken so much trouble to hide the truth, it was not so as to allow it to be caught unawares. Carry on—you interest me. Why is it that there are surfeits and scarcities in the world?" "That question does not find me unprepared, and the answer is contained in my theory, which I have long since perfected. Since at this moment I am sitting for my great medical examination, I might as well not limit my ambitions. Therefore, I can see three reasons. The first is in the surfeits and scarcities that Providence scatters around out of ignorance, or absentmindedness, or malice, or vengeance—and these it alone can understand; the second is in the surfeits and scarcities that men inflict on each other; and the third is in our own surfeits and scarcities for which each one of us is personally responsible. Have I passed?"

"Not yet! And what is your method?" "It is very simple, and follows naturally from my theory: it consists in keeping human beings in, or transferring them into, a balanced situation in a peaceable environment; in protecting them against the misdeeds of Providence and the malpractices of other men; in putting them on their guard against all sorts of disorders; seeing that they breathe only the purest air, drink only uncontaminated water, eat only fresh and nourishing food of the greatest possible variety; protecting them against inclement weather and the heat of the sun; making them reasonable and educated; and preserving them from vexation and worry. At this price, and apart from exceptions or accidents, my method produces good health and well-being."

Unhappily for my theory, it is of no use to the fellah consumed by a tertian, quartan, quintan, yellow, or phthisical fever, to the Nubian slave petrified by the sickness that comes from the banks of the Nile,* to the quarryman whose bronchi are paved with silex or the mason more or less crushed under a lintel. Nor is it of use to women swollen with cellulitis or undermined by pregnancies, or to underlings like carters, stablemen, dockhands, and fishermen whose attacks of dysentery, whose inflammations, tumors, and intoxications defeat my vigilance and suffer from my helplessness.

I have not invented a method against poverty, and poverty becomes more attractive to me with every day that passes. I am the doctor of the poor; this is a qualification which should deserve a place in Paradise; but I am paid by the rich so that no scandal should arise to spoil their appetite, and this situation renders me liable to damnation. Innocent? Or guilty? The judgment that I bear within me refuses to declare for either of these alternatives. I submit to circumstances and have no influence over them. I do not know what is contained within the notion of sin, but on the other hand I do know what offenses are, and experience has taught me that they are rarely committed in the places in which they are rife. It is true that the poor are detestable: ugly, dirty, stinking, brutalized, lazy, and swindling. And yet I love them, for I am one of them, a poor man who had the good fortune to be born of a cultured father, in an intelligent town paved with flowers and book learning, a poor man who has known no other hunger than that for knowledge; a happy poor man, whereas they are unhappy poor men. What could I call it, if not love, that stirring of the soul which comes to me from them when I am in close touch with them; that distress I feel when their suffering is greater than my knowledge; that fury when I have to decide on the relegation of a useless slave; that unequaled joy when I have been able to console, comfort, cure. I love them, and they very soon realized this, and they pay me back in confidence what I spend in tenderness. This makes them handsome, clean, cou-

* Probably bilharzia.

rageous, loyal, and a few drops of extract of myrrh do the rest. In every one of them a prince lies dormant, and if they are, and remain, wretched, it is certainly not out of perversity

Some of them can now find their way to my house and are waiting there for me when I come home exhausted from the palace stables. They arrive—and whether they are Jews, Arabs, Bedouins, or Edomites they are all alike. Whether freemen or runaway slaves, whether it is candor, fear, or pain that brings them to me, they take away with them a little hope, and leave behind them a handful of beans, a basket of fruit or eggs, at the very most a scraggly chicken, and I feel honored. No, I am not sublime. No, I am not indulging in false modesty. No, I am not being obstinate. I would not refuse a haughty patient, preceded by emissaries and servants and followed by a purse of gold. One came, surrounded by a great display, a Bedouin sheikh, with a cheek on fire from an inflammation of a molar; he expected to take precedence over all the poor patients and be seen at once. I made him wait. He went to get help elsewhere, and I had no recompense for my tactlessness.

"But just look!" Bathsheba said to me—and this was one of the rare occasions when she disappointed me. "Just look how Nathanael goes about things. He doesn't encumber himself with principles. He has neither theory nor method. But this doesn't stop him from looking after his own interests." What my wife said was true—except that she should neither have said it nor even thought it. Nathanael was the Court doctor. He sometimes visited the Caliph, that Colonel Dirgham who entrenched himself in his palace for fear of an attempt on his life, and who had all his food and medicines tasted by slaves, for he trusted no one, not even his doctor. Nathanael controlled the finances of the kingdom and levied the tribute to be paid to the Franks. Nathanael was responsible for the health of the rich Babylonians, for the organization of the two communities, and for the two synagogues. He was the least available and the least tired man in the whole capital, and also one of the wealthiest and most powerful; he spent most of his time in his garden listening to the musicians and stroking his cats. I would willingly have filched a few patients from him, but he kept a tight hand on them. Rich and poor are like oil and vinegar—they do not mix.

At the end of every month I took Nathanael whatever piasters I had to spare and he pensively wrote down the sum in his book. "They speak well of you," he said. "What is your remedy for hylic swellings of the pneuma?" I gave him the formula, as well as my savings, and he wrote it down in another book. I was not in the least envious of his success, nor did I suffer from my penury. My only enemies in those days were lack of time, and fatigue; and my only real regret was that I could neither study nor write as much as I wished. My *Guide* was progressing slowly, line by line, through the density of the Egyptian night, under my heavy eyelids, in front of my weary limbs. By chance you were there, during the last years of that reign, you who contributed a little leaven to my pain, and who learned from me only one very simple lesson which should be known everywhere: that medicine is the science of weighing up errors and the art of choosing between risks and ills.

39

THEN suddenly there was the great tumult of war, with its cortege of calamities which disgusted you and put you to flight, and Salah ed-Din woke up to find himself the master of Egypt. If this was in some respects a veritable awakening, the suddenness of it remained questionable, for the siege of Alexandria and the treachery of the King of the Franks were bound to lead to it sooner or later. Colonel Dirgham was taken for a walk outside the palace, he who had so feared to leave it, and had his head severed—by the conqueror in person, it was said. The fire of battle was still smoldering in Fostat. Later, Yusuf described all the vicissitudes of this campaign to me in the minutest detail. He had not wanted to undertake it. But as a soldier, he owed obedience to his Caliph in Aleppo. "I set off like a man going to certain death," he said. When he had Egypt at his feet he felt giddy, and had himself proclaimed Sultan. Never had he dreamed of any such promotion. His appetite grew with what it fed on.

Contrary to what had been said about him, he was neither Turkish, nor Syriac, nor a prince. Salah ed-Din was born a Kurd, and a shepherd. He was not yet eighteen years old when a drought robbed him of his flock. With his only remaining belongings, his horse, his tunic, his turban, and his saber, which he wore slung over his shoulder like the Prophet, he went down from his mountain to join the Caliph's army. When he died, at the head of an empire which extended from the sources of the Nile to the sources of the Jordan, all that was found in his privy purse was forty-seven silver dirhams and one single piece of gold. He left neither possessions, nor houses, nor palaces, nor cultivated fields, nor any sort of property, nothing but an empire which, when it fell from his hands, shattered like a piece of porcelain.

How can one capture such a person with words? He was noble, there was no doubt about that, with that greatness of heart and spirit that some people receive through supreme grace. Courteous to the point of affectation, and cruel to the point of blindness; both generous and possessive; both disinterested and covetous. Whatever anyone might say about him, the contrary was also true. He had fashioned himself in the image of the high treetops and the deep valleys, of rainless storms and naked granite, of blazing days and freezing nights; he was not only a mountain dweller, he was also the mountain, and endowed, furthermore, with a noble soul. He loved everything, except wealth, which loved him. Immense fortunes sought him out, but he allowed them to continue on their way. He did evil in making war; he did good in killing villainy. By guerrilla warfare, making surprise attacks at nightfall and disappearing before dawn, a strategy which was always successful, he recaptured more than fifty fortified places, both citadels and fortresses, from the allied Crusaders; he appropriated the lands of Edom, Judea, Samaria, and Galilee as far as the Euphrates and the Tigris; he drove what remained of the Frankish, German, and English armies into Akko, whose defenses he demolished after a murderous siege, though he allowed the women and children to set sail without harming them; he granted safe conduct to King Richard to come and be treated by me in Fostat, but he himself killed Reynald of Châtillon, who fell into his hands in Hattin. Unpredictable? Certainly not. Impulsive? Without a doubt. For he followed certain lightning impulses whose only source was what men agree to call a sense of honor. I personally only know of one act he undertook that was not successful: his pilgrimage to Mecca. When he had pacified all the lands of the fertile crescent and made order in his kingdoms, he began to consider his own salvation and decided to go and purify his conscience in front of the black stone. I tried my utmost to dissuade him from this project in view of his undermined health. Yusuf ignored my advice. On the third day of his journey he fell off his horse, dead.

To me he was of a generosity which consisted in equal parts of indulgence and pride. "Ask!" he would say to me. "Whatever you want is yours." He was irritated by my silences, which he considered provocative, for he detested it when anyone stood up to him. So it sometimes happened that I would ask mercy for a condemned man, a pension for a widow, liberty for a slave. Yusuf would give an order, and I would be given satisfaction. But that same evening he would send me some valuable object, or a purse. Inexorably, my house became filled with silken rugs, rare furs, gold vases, silver plate, and even if I had grown more arms I would not have had enough fingers for all my rings. But my thoughts turned to Cordova, and there was already a niche in my cellar which could be walled up to serve as a tomb for all this treasure. I feasted my eyes on it, and that was the whole of my pleasure. Should my contempt for material possessions be less than that of a Kurdish shepherd? To anyone whose eye lit up in envy I would say: "Help yourself!" and he would not need to be told twice. But good fortune only stayed with me for a short while: such was its wont, and such was my destiny. Though I was certainly reassured by this opulence. My house had been paid for. My servants, who were thin when they arrived, were fat when they left me. My wife no longer set anyone up as an example to me; my own was quite enough for her. A plate of broth at noon and a plate of broth in the evening—that remained my usual fare. I could find neither the taste nor the time for more extensive feasting.

In the beginning of the reign of Salah ed-Din there was a severe purge in all the towns in Egypt. People who had entertained friendly or business relations with the Franks were tracked down and punished in various ways. Nathanael had to resign all his offices and pay a heavy fine. This disgrace brought on a stroke, and he sent for me to attend him. Confined to his garden, he could now hear the music with only a single ear, and stroke his cats with only a single hand. Even though he complained bitterly he was not so much to be pitied: the half of himself that remained intact seemed without a doubt to be his better half.

Now that the Hebraic communities were without a nagid, a vile peculator named Zuta got himself nominated to the position. This colorless and stupid person was the cause of unpleasantness to many people, including me, whom he accused of having collaborated with the occupying Edomites. I was summoned to an emergency court, where I appeared without any great fear. Yes, I had received Bishop Hugh at my house—several times, even; yes, I had had some contact with the young prince of Jerusalem; yes, I had prepared a remedy for him; yes, I had accepted an honorarium in behalf of the king: all these things were in accordance with the customs and morality of the medical profession. Had the devil himself come to visit me I should have treated him in the same way, for such is the law of those of us who are at war with suffering. I was acquitted on the spot, and kept my position in the palace stables.

A few hours later a delegation from the communities came to see me. Zuta had been dismissed. The Councils were unanimously offering to make me their nagid. I thought of my father, who would have been pleased, and I accepted. Thus the shattered destiny of the Maimons was renewing itself, thousands of leagues away from Cordova, and centuries after the defeat of the kingdoms. Certainly there was a difference in numbers, and also in quality. The Babylonians in Fostat were too obsessed by money; the Israelis too incapacitated by their poverty and lack of culture. But to both of them, God was making a sign that he remembered. Would it fall to me, Moses, to bring them together in order to lead them, not out of Egypt, but out of their perplexity, along the path of justice? There was material for prophecy; there was reason for hope. Since the dawn of time Israel had forever been dying and being reborn, like all nature, and was it not perhaps in these cycles that the deepest meaning of the covenant was hidden? I told my visitors that as I was so occupied with medicine and with my work I should have only the Sabbath day to devote to administrative matters. They asked no more. I suggested a program to them: to send for some scholars to teach, some just men to re-establish justice, some philosophers to found a school, and some books to endow our libraries. They wanted no less. I ask you to believe, my friend, that in the hour this interview lasted my head could have begun to feel that my hat was too tight.

One very ordinary morning, while I was busy in the stables, I was asked to go to the apartments without a moment's delay. On a low bed covered with furs I saw a half-clad man who was watching me as I came in. "Jew," he said, "you have the reputation of being a skillful surgeon. Can you relieve me of this ailment that I have, without increasing my suffering?" He showed me a voluminous inflammation deforming his fundament. The tumor was violaceous, soft, and ready for the lancet. This was the first time I had seen Salah ed-Din, that legendary figure, and I took my time examining him. The prospect he was offering me was not of the most advantageous. His body was both muscular and fleshy. Standing, he must have been of middle height. A forked beard and curly hair shining with oil framed his face. "What are you waiting for?" he grunted. "Hurry up! My horse is longing for my saddle."

Two Nubians with naked torsos flanked his bed. Some way apart, a favorite, veiled up to the eyes, was plucking the strings of a plaintive *aoud*. With no great haste, I opened my bag. The idea of cutting into the flesh of a potentate gave me matter for thought. I did not doubt the sureness of my hand, but I did fear the reactions of the patient. Was I perhaps risking my life here? Moreover, Salah ed-Din thought he was putting me at my ease by putting me on my guard: if I hurt him, he would have my arm cut off. I knew from experience that pain makes men of war irascible. "Sultan," I said, indicating the favorite, "can you take that woman's virginity without her being aware of it?" As he looked at me without understanding,

I added: "In the same way, I cannot lance your abscess without your feeling it." A laugh, an enormous laugh was his first answer, and I knew that I had gained the advantage. "Don't worry, Jew!" he said. "That woman is not a virgin. And I will try to control myself."

I used a subterfuge that Avensola had taught me: with the flat of my hand I administered a violent slap to the naked flesh, at the precise moment when the point of the lancet entered the inflammation; the surprise of the first sensation was intended to absorb a large part of the second. Salah ed-Din raised himself up on his elbow. "So you'd hit me, would you, dog? Let's get it over!" "It *is* over, Sultan," I said calmly. "The humor is running out, thick and yellow. Send someone to tell your horse that he can have you in the saddle tomorrow."

That same evening, Salah ed-Din sent me a gold ring set with a stone the size of a hazelnut. For him, as for me, this present was only of symbolic value. "I took it; I'm giving it to you," he said when I went to change his dressing. Thus he expressed in the most concise manner the double, and opposite, movement in which thought was accomplished on the scales of life and death. Between the alternatives of giving and taking, there was God.

Yusuf kept me longer that morning. He questioned me about myself and my family, and told me in confidence as much about himself as I told him about myself. From the very beginning, in equal measure, it was a meeting of two human beings who would not be searching for themselves if they had not already found themselves. Both of us—he through action, and I through study—were profoundly committed to converging paths. As a child, and then as an adolescent, he, like me, had perceived the great murmur of the infinite. We were more or less the same age. The gaze of the little prisoner in the Cordovan yeshiva and that of the little shepherd in the Kurdish mountains must have met in the immensity of space. Like me, Yusuf was searching for the truth, not its changing and evanescent reflection, but in its material density, like a ripe fruit into which one can bite. We wanted it in all its splendor, full of itself, and intact. What should we have spoken about, if not that?

Even when we could no longer use the pretext of changing his dressings, we continued to meet daily whenever he was in his palace. He had given orders: I was to have the run of his apartments as if I were in my own home. Often, the room was full of nonchalant servants and officious counselors. Yusuf would turn his back on them, take me by the arm and lead me into his private room. He made me smell his breath, look at his urine, and inspect his feces—not that he was worried about his health, but in order to justify his generosity to me. Most often it was he who lavished advice on me: I worked too hard; I was short of breath because my heart was strained; I must allow myself a rest in his palace in Alexandria, where the sea air would certainly do me good.

After which we would chat for a moment about what was dearest to our hearts: immanence and transcendence. Yusuf was not educated, and this was one of the reasons for his attachment to me; he was inspired, and this was one of the reasons for my attachment to him. He was said to be a fanatic, but nothing was less true: he had the gift of abstraction to a supreme degree, and his thoughts soared naturally up to the heights. His inborn inclination toward philosophy reproduced the upward thrust of the mountains. For him, the world was frozen in pure verticality. Though he wasn't even aware of it he had become a follower of the doctrine of the Motzalès, for whom religion was the source of all knowledge. The idea that an event could be the immediate or mediate cause of another event was incomprehensible to him. You could find no trace of intelligence in events, he used to say, which could order the things that had to be accomplished. God, in creating the world, had imprinted immutable habits on it that none other than he could change. Clouds and rain habitually went together. Stones moved out of habit. The Nile overflowed its banks twice a year out of habit. The poetry and truth that lie behind the sacred texts are only in fact the movements of poetry and truth that are engendered in the spirit of the practicing believer. Yusuf's spirit was richer in poetry and truth than the Koran that he knew by heart. He was fond of reciting it, but it was his eloquence that brought the verses to life. He didn't for a moment doubt that he was on the path of elevation, that he was on the direct way to the lap of the Prophet. War was also a habit, because God's envoy had said: *Salvation lies in flashing sabers, and Paradise in the shadow of swords; he who fights for my Word to be above everything—he is on my path.*

With the prudence of a snake catcher, I tried to introduce the beginnings of a more rational line of thought into our discussions. I ventured into the intricacies of the system of the Mutakallimun, which I myself opposed, but into which reason could enter; I borrowed from the Peripatetics, the Pythagoreans, and even the materialists, to furbish my examples. It wasn't that Yusuf didn't want to understand; he couldn't understand. I was speaking a different language from him, and it was a miracle that the rapport between us was so complete. I sometimes read him passages from my great book, which was progressing. He would listen attentively, reflect at length, and then opine: "It's very well said. But what does it mean?"

One morning I saw that he was worried. It took him a long time to tell me the reason. He had just received a letter about me, denouncing me as an apostate. As luck would have it, Ibn Moishe, my ex-colleague, the judge from Fez, had passed through Fostat and heard people talking about me. "I swear by Allah," he wrote, "that that dog was a good Moslem under the protection of Abd Al Mumen, the Emir of the Believers, and now he has become a Jew and a rabbi and found favor in your sight. In the name of the true faith, I demand that this traitor shall be put to death." Several times Yusuf passed the flat of his hand over this crumpled bit of paper, as if he were trying to efface its content. His predicament was real, and mine was no less real. Islamic law admitted of no exceptions; no pardon was possible for the crime of apostasy, and he, Yusuf, was the custodian of the law. For several long minutes we remained facing each other, saying not a word, both equally upset. Was Salah ed-Din going to call his guards and hand me over to the judge and the executioner? The silence became unbearable. I was the first to break it. "Sultan," I said, "you must decide as you think best. This letter contains the truth, except on one point: I was not a good Moslem; I was a forced Moslem. You who know the Koran by heart, consider this verse by the Prophet: 'I do not worship what you worship. You do not worship what I worship. You keep to your religion, and I will keep to mine.' This was said and written in the third year before the Hegira in the town of Mecca and in the sight of God." A laugh, Yusuf's enormous laugh, was my answer. Very deliberately, he tore the letter into little pieces. "The Prophet has the answer to everything," he said. "If this informer returns to the charge I shall know how to silence him, by God who is my witness."

We also had much discussion about that Illuminee named Ahab who went all over Upper Egypt proclaiming himself the precursor of the Messiah. He called on the Jews and Arabs to come together under his banner in view of the last judgment, which was now imminent. Several hundred ragged men followed him, with upraised eyes. The procession thus reached the walls of Sanaa, and Ahab ordered the Emir of Yemen to come out of the town and submit to his message. The Emir had a tent erected, and went out. "How am I to know," he asked, "if your message is genuine?" Ahab recounted all the miracles he had performed, to which his followers could testify: walking on the water, changing water to wine, curing lepers, bringing the dead back to life. "Give me some proof," said the Emir, "and I will submit." "So be it!" said Ahab. "But off my head, and that same instant it will grow again on my shoulders." No doubt he imagined that the Emir would not dare; or that God would turn aside the blade; or that a lamb would be substituted for him. But the Emir did dare. The blade was not turned aside. No lamb appeared. This could have been the end of Ahab, but it was not. The ragged men put his remains in a stone tomb and mourned him for a long time. Now Ahab had a family, and they came from a distance to take his corpse home. When they opened the tomb, it was empty. The family spread the news that Ahab had risen from the dead and the procession went back to Egypt, joined by ever increasing numbers of Jews and Arabs in a state of ecstasy. Yusuf had to send a battalion of soldiers to disperse these Illuminati, otherwise a new sect would have come into being. In a world already saturated with sects, this would really not have been the best thing that could happen.

When the flag was furled it was a sign that the Sultan was himself taking part in a campaign. From one day to the next Al Qahira sounded hollow, the geometry of the streets and squares became apparent again now that it was not distorted by the crowds. The sudden disappearance of the garrison restored the town to normal, but after the tumult came the deathly silence of the necropolis. No more soldiers at the gates and in the courtyards, no more slaves in the corridors, no more grooms in the stables: for me it was a time of vacation—which meant a time of more intensive work on my great book. This was growing and taking shape: more than a hundred chapters had been finished and were already circulating in far-off countries. Praise, criticism, and obloquy were piling up on my table. If my correspondents had only realized how little their opinions, whether good or bad, affected me, I think it very likely that they would not have bothered to inform me of them. There was no pride in my indifference. I felt, in advance, infinitely grateful to anyone who would read me. I was offering him the best of my thought. Why was it not possible to tell him by word of mouth that a too hasty judgment one way or the other would be to his detriment, though it would not harm me?

Yusuf used to stay away for six months or a year, and sometimes even longer. He would come back in an impressive cloud of dust, in his *habitual* glory, trailing in his wake glorious names: Gaza, the Kerak of Moab, Bosra, Damascus, Jaffa, Akko, and we would resume our daily conversations each morning at the point where the war had interrupted them. These renewed meetings gave us both equal pleasure. While the people were carousing, and cartfuls of booty were being piled up within the precincts of the castle, Yusuf would indulge himself in a meditation on the senses. For himself, he wanted no other virtue than that of fidelity; no other merit than that of obedience. And what of his victories? A great deal of tenacity and fatigue, a certain way of commanding his troops, and reliable military intelligence; the mistakes of the enemy and the will of God accounted for the rest. He was absolutely sincere when he asserted that the counter-crusade had one single aim: to re-establish permanent peace. He felt hate toward no one, and scorn only for cowardice and deceit. How would it be possible to disseminate the knowledge he had gained about the world: that men had better things to do than to kill each other?

That particular year was more magnificent than the others; there was more rejoicing than ever before. Yusuf brought in his cortege his victory over Jerusalem. But this only seemed to torment him the more, and to make him more eager for purification. And yet he had not perpetrated any massacres, which would have compensated for the ignoble butchery committed by the crusaders. He wanted to demonstrate, he said, the superiority of the civilized captain over the barbarous captains. No inhabitant had been molested. They were all authorized to leave the town with all their belongings, against a poll tax of ten bezants for each man, five for each woman, and one for each child. The religious orders—the Templars, the Hospitalers, and the Mendicants—and the rich, were the first to leave. About three thousand insolvent people remained, whose freedom the Sultan and the Patriarch minutely haggled over, man by man, bezant by bezant. Yusuf brought back sixteen thousand slaves for whom the treasures of the churches either would not or could not pay.

"Jerusalem," he said thoughtfully. "Yeru-Salem, the city of peace. Al Quds, the Holy." From the Tower of David, where he had his quarters, Yusuf had watched the departure of the last inhabitants. It was no more than a piece of wasteland between the wounded walls.

"Yeru-Salem," he said again, holding his arms over his chest. "I took it . . ." He held his arms out toward me and looked me straight in the face. "I will give it to you . . ." As I remained silent, daring neither to understand nor not to understand, Yusuf suddenly became animated. "I am giving you that town," he said solemnly. "I am giving you the lands of Judea, from the Jordan to the sea. I give them to you for them to be yours, and for you to give them back to your dispersed people. Send letters to all the inhabited regions of the world, and announce the news that Salah ed-Din has given you Jerusalem and Judea. Get your brothers to return in great numbers, for there are walls to rebuild, trees to plant, earth to make fruitful, a kingdom to reconstruct."

I threw myself down with my face to the ground and kissed Yusuf's robe. "I will give you my answer tomorrow" was all I managed to utter. I left the palace like a sleepwalker. Instead of making for Fostat, I urged my horse on toward the east. The rest of the day, and the whole of that night, burned by the sun and perished by the cold, I pleaded within myself both the cause of dreams and the cause of reason. They must have been worried by my absence; they must have been looking for me in a panic. I was torn between the demands of my flesh and the demands of my spirit; lost and at the same time at peace; wretched and at the same time triumphant. Thus, God had spoken to me, and I had to give my answer to God.

Came the hour when I was able to appear before Yusuf. He was as tense in his anticipation as I was firm in my resolution. "My answer is no," I said. "What you are giving me, Sultan, is something that your sons will want to take back from me. There are many of them. Seventeen, if I am not mistaken." He interrupted me roughly. "My sons are all totally incompetent—they're all wet rags. They think of nothing but their personal pleasures." "All the more reason," I said. "When they see the rebuilt walls, the new forests, the orchards in blossom, their covetousness will be so great that not one will have the strength to resist it. We shall have to fight to defend our possessions, arms in hand, and my people are no longer taught such activities. Your gift, which is only justice, would be poisoned by all this. It comes both too early and too late: too early in the centuries, and too late for me: I am already an old man. My pen is already falling from my hand. What would happen if it were a saber? The day will come, Yusuf. The promise will be kept, because it has been renewed from father to son for a thousand years and more. It will choose its time, and it will choose its men. It is not for now, and it is not for me."

The next year Salah ed-Din died, as I have said.

40

MY FRIEND, it is not I who am finishing this book, it is the book that is finishing me. My time is now so short that the days feel like centuries, and the years like moments. Only yesterday I was still able to ask myself what I was going to do with my life, but today the time has already come for me to decide what I have done with it. The reckoning too has not much farther to go: I have accumulated a great deal of fatigue. Its weight will soon be too heavy to bear.

As he had foreseen, Salah ed-Din was flouted by his sons. They have torn the empire into shreds and are closing their teeth on its bleeding morsels. One was killed by a dagger, another by poison, and a third was drowned in a well. The survivors make war against each other when they have nothing better to do. Jerusalem has not been rebuilt. Philistines from Gaza are camping on the bare slopes of Mount Zion. Judea has not been replanted, and the desert is spreading.

One of his heirs, Alafdal, the one who took Egypt, is a bibulous young man who divides his time equally between bed and board. When he is not indulging in debauch with his women he is fostering his attacks of flatulence, and in either case he claims that he cannot do without me. I had to write him a treatise on proper diet and the care of the intestines, and a practical guide to coitus. He knows my books by heart but his character is such that he cannot accept restraint. Debauch will kill him, if one of his brothers does not do so first. Alafdal demands my presence every morning. Bathed, perfumed, limp, he will not let me go until I have made the entire rounds of his person and answered a hundred questions about his state of health that particular day.

When my horse goes up the hill in Fostat it is not his heart that beats more quickly, it is mine. Sometimes I have so much difficulty in breathing that my sight becomes blurred and my ears hum. My ankles are so swollen with edema that it feels as if they are enclosed in a pair of iron collars. I am suffering from an eversion of the eyelids which causes my eyes to water incessantly, and it frequently happens that I am not in control of my bladder. Shall I one day find time to consult a great doctor? My courtyard and my antechamber are full of people of all sorts—some of whom have come from very far away, and who have been there since yesterday—waiting for me to be able to see them. I feel a little bitter at the thought that most of my patients are less ill than I. And yet the fact that I can still be of use reassures me. I swallow a cup of broth, and until late into the night I hand out remedies and consolation. My method is no doubt not without value, since so many people come crowding in to receive some part of it.

Only when I am at last alone, when silence has fallen, can I again take up my pen. Am I once more deluding myself about the significance of my writings? I am bitterly disputed, which proves that I am alive. But when I reread myself, I have to admit that I am caught between two systems which have lent themselves to a mixture but not to a combination. To try to introduce God into reason, and reason into God, is a foolish enterprise. I have been ambitious, yet timorous, so that I did not go far enough into my folly. No, the lion and the lamb do not lie down together. I have invented nothing new, but how would that have been possible? Long before I was even in the seed, the world was complete, science was complete, medicine was complete, and philosophy was complete. What there was to be known, is known. Nothing more will emerge from the human spirit. My only originality—and it is as old as the destiny of Israel—the only contribution I have made in the course of my tormented life, has been that of having preserved and transmitted, against all odds, my innermost identity.

And perhaps that is not so bad.

I wish you well.

PRAYER

O Lord, fill my soul with the love of art and of all creatures. Preserve me from the temptation of allowing myself to be influenced in the exercise of my profession by the thirst for gain or the pursuit of glory. Strengthen my heart so that it may be ever ready to serve both poor and rich, both friend and foe, both just and unjust.

Help me to see only the man in the sufferer. Keep my mind clear in all circumstances, for great and sublime is the science that aims at preserving the health and life of all creatures.

Give my patients confidence in me and in my art, and help them to follow my advice and my prescriptions. Keep all charlatans away from their beds, and the army of their relations proffering never-ending advice, and their nurses who always know everything: these are a dangerous breed who through vanity cause the best intentions to come to naught.

O Lord, make me indulgent and tolerant toward obstinate or ignorant patients.

Make me moderate in all things, but insatiable in my love of science. Preserve me from the idea that I can do everything. Give me the strength, the will power and the opportunity ever to increase my knowledge, that I may thereby benefit those who suffer.

Amen.

Moses ben Maimon, the Spaniard.

POSTFACE

Moses ben Maimon, or Abu Imran Musa ibn Maimun ibn Abdallah, also known as Maimonides, or RaMBaM, nicknamed "the Eagle of the Synagogue" by the Christian Scholastics, born in Cordova in 1135, died in Cairo in 1204, has survived through his writings for many centuries and is still active in many people's minds, even if his medicine, his theology, and his philosophy have been superseded. New editions of *The Guide for the Perplexed* are continually being brought out, and other works are still being published. An exhaustive edition of his works is in preparation in Jerusalem. More and more monographs are being written about him at regular intervals. He has had a decisive influence on the thought of the last eight centuries; among others who gratefully acknowledged their indebtedness to him are Thomas Aquinas, Bacon, Descartes, Leibniz, Spinoza, and Kant. It was he who was responsible for Greek science and philosophy gradually gaining a foothold in Europe: it was not until the Renaissance that men thought of returning to the originals.

A person of some eminence, it will be agreed. But does this therefore mean that he is sacrosanct? Insofar as he still makes his presence felt today, has he not become part of our common heritage? What has once existed can do so again, it is enough to give it a new existence. We are not among those who preach that history repeats itself, and that there are lessons to be learned from it. We think, rather, that history is built according to a limited number of patterns—of structures, in the contemporary jargon—which are linked to humanity's permanent lines of force, lines which can sometimes be disentangled and which it is not unimportant to try to redraw, the better to understand who we are. Renan—who was very much at home in the Judeo-Arab middle ages—wrote that to have recourse to history is "to reproduce at will, and in oneself, the different types of the life of the past." This opens wide the doors to the unconscious, to the imaginary, and to temerity.

And then, present-day realities are catching up; analogies are appearing where one least expected them. It has been shown that light can be thrown on any situation by means of any other situation, and that is what has once again been attempted here. It was not a question of leaving events, dates, and places where an evanescent documentation, an uncertain chronology, and an approximate topography had placed them. What was necessary was, on the contrary, to rearrange them at will in order to give them a new coherence. In general, however, wherever the facts were ascertainable they have been respected.

The more one has to do with them, however, the less one can take historiographers—not to be confused with historians— seriously: either they faithfully copy one another or they contradict one another with acrimony. We are obliged to come back to Renan, and to extract the truth from itself. This will no doubt displease exegetists, philosophers, theologians, the erudite, and all sorts of other specialists. But this is their problem, not ours. Here, the supposed truth of history gives way to the intangible truth of this particular story.

—HERBERT LE PORRIER

NOTES

The lampoon *The Three Impostures* (or *Impostors*, according to the transcriptions) perturbed the world of the Scholastics for more than three centuries. Many times condemned to the stake—and its readers to the gallows—this work was generally attributed to Averroës, "that mad dog who, urged on by an execrable fury, never stopped barking at Christ and at the Catholic faith" (Petrarch).

The text of Rabbi Maimon's *Epistle to the Communities* has been conserved in its entirety. It nevertheless seemed to be more relevant to reinvent it, being faithful more to its spirit than to its letter, rather than to reproduce it, even fragmentarily, so true is it that the same ideas are expressed differently from one historical period to another.

The occasional quotations from *The Guide for the Perplexed* have been incorporated in the text indiscriminately, and always according to the spirit rather than to the letter.

It is more or less certain that Saladin intended to restore the Kingdom of Jerusalem and to get great numbers of the Israelites of the Diaspora to return to it, not only because he believed in the specific dynamism of the Hebrew people but because he would have favored the creation of an autonomous political entity—a buffer state, in today's terms—between the Syriacs and the Egyptians, whose incessant rivalries were a permanent threat to peace in a Palestine liberated from the Crusaders.

In 1935, on the 800th anniversary of his birth, a bronze statue of Maimonides, to which people from all nations had contributed, was erected in a little square in the Jewry in Cordova. Naturally the effigy was not taken from any known document, but is simply the product of the sculptor's imagination.